A Very Wicked Arrangement

Scarlett Avery

Edited by John Hudspith

Proofread by Chrissy Becker, Jamie Betts, Melody Fuhrman, Angela Tyler, Lisa Fearday, and Jacqueline (Jacks) Larson.

ISBN 978-1-77498-121-4

No part of this book used automated software or AI in its creation. The content was written by a human (Scarlett Avery, the author). The cover was professionally designed and the interior was professionally formatted.

Dedication

For my readers who are unapologetic about their addiction to smut, but also need all the feels.

Get the A VERY WICKED ARRANGEMENT Secret Chapter

Join my mailing list and grab the Exclusive Secret Chapter or Storyboard for this romance.

Great extra goodies. Hot deals. Zero spam.
www.MyRomanceAddiction.com

Chapter 1

Angelica

Leaning against the kitchen counter, I shove a spoonful of ice cream into my mouth, cursing the universe.

The second the creaminess and ice-coldness of my dessert concoction hit my tongue, I can pretend to forget all about my shitty morning.

Without ice cream, there would only be darkness and chaos.

I can't remember who the wise soul is behind that quote, but I wholeheartedly agree.

I'm about to dig in for another spoonful when I hear keys at the door.

The sound of my sister's heels clicking against the wooden floor of the entrance resonate throughout the apartment, announcing her return.

"Ange!"

I don't bother answering my sister. The apartment we've lived in since we were five years old isn't very big. She'll find me soon enough.

Arya appears in the doorway, barefoot.

She squints her green eyes at me. "Ice cream at eleven-thirty in the morning on a Thursday?"

"Not just ice cream, but *boozy* ice cream." I scoop up said boozy ice cream and lift it at eye level. "Haagen-Dazs vanilla ice cream with a generous dose of Baileys."

"You splurged?!"

"The Irish cream liqueur is a Christmas gift from a client who appreciates my contribution to her writing. As for the ice cream, it was on sale. With the coupon I downloaded online, the pint came to only three bucks."

"Delicious and frugal. What a winning combo."

It's the only way we can afford dessert these days. Turbulent times and all. "Booze. Fat. Sugar. The ultimate soothing trio."

"In other words, you pulled out the heavy artillery."

"I had to. Since it's cocktail hour somewhere on the globe, boozy ice cream is perfectly acceptable."

"Rough morning?"

"A shitty morning that tops an even shittier week."

She approaches me and places a hand on my shoulder. "What happened?"

"I had a heated conversation with a client—"

"Don't tell me, the author who would rather die than cut back page after page of incessant internal dialogue?"

"Yes, that one."

"You fired her as a client?"

I shake my head. "*She* fired me as an editor. Apparently, I was dwarfing her creative genius by suggesting she cuts back on her characters' inner reflection, curtails her overuse of adverbs and unnecessary italicized words, and uses pussy instead of moist vaginal walls."

My sister rolls her eyes. "You don't need that kind of negativity in your life."

"Perhaps, but I need the money. Just in case you forgot, we're up to our eyeballs in debt."

"How can I forget? You keep reminding me."

I bite off a bitchy reply.

One fight per day is my quota.

I change the topic. "You were cagey as to why you had to get out of here so early this morning you aren't exactly a morning person."

My sister sighs.

"Is something wrong?"

"Well, the nighttime medical service called me last night to let me know my doctor had a cancellation. So, I set up three alarms to pull my ass out of bed to make it to his office for an eight o'clock appointment."

"You're sick?"

She shakes her head.

I expect her to elaborate, but she just looks at me in a way I can't quite decipher.

The delightful pleasure I was deriving from the boozy ice cream concoction is long gone, replaced by worry. I drop the bowl on the countertop.

"What's wrong?"

She averts her gaze.

I place a hand on her arm. "Talk to me, Arya."

Her green eyes meet my own.

"My va-jay-jay is sick." Her lips pull down in a frown. "I have bacterial vaginosis."

I take a step back, my eyebrows dipping low.

"It isn't contagious, Ange." She lets out a self-deprecating laugh. "It's an extreme form of yeast infection and it's annoying as hell."

"That's why you were complaining about your lady parts itching?"

"Yes. That, and the unpleasant fishy smell coming from down there." She screws up her nose and points at said sick va-jay-jay. "Despite the use of feminine spray. I figured it was time for a doctor's appointment."

I cringe.

"At least we know what the issue is now. It's not like you contracted gonorrhea. Even an extreme case of yeast infection is curable."

"So pragmatic."

"It's my job as the big sister."

"You beat me into this world by fifteen lousy minutes. You'd think that after twenty-two years, you'd stop reminding me," my identical twin says.

"Keep dreaming, Ary." I'm unlikely to stop reminding her of that any time soon. "I assume the doctor gave you some kind of prescription cream?"

"Yes."

"Shit. More expenses."

"I know. I'm sorry. It's not like I planned for this to happen."

I cross my arms over my chest in frustration.

She lets out a sigh. "Even when I try to make things right, the universe conspires against me."

"What are you talking about?"

"I was trying to find a better paying job than waitressing."

I'm swept away by a momentary wave of excitement at the idea of making a dent in our colossal debt. Even though three months ago she upgraded from being a barista at a coffee shop to waitressing in a trendy sports bar in SoHo, she still makes minimum wage. The super sexy outfit guarantees generous tips, but living in New York doesn't come cheap, even when you live in one of the boroughs. "Did you find one?"

"I did." Thank you, God! "But I might not be able to make

it. The doctor told me that, given the severity of my condition, it might be seven days before the infection clears up. In the meantime, he cautioned me to be careful. That's a problem with my new job. A big problem."

"Your condition should have no bearing on your new job. I'm sure whatever cream your doctor prescribed will help with the smell, if not eliminate it all together."

"It doesn't work like that in this type of job..."

Well, that was cryptic.

"What kind of job is it?"

She presses her lips in a thin line.

"You're not going to tell me?"

"You have to promise to keep an open mind."

"Wasn't that what you said when you introduced me to your ex... the one who sold us tickets to board the Titanic?"

"The Titanic sank and everyone dies, except for Rose. She lives on to tell the story."

I cock an eyebrow. "The last time I checked our bank account, we were doing slightly better than the people who drowned on that ship, simply because we're still breathing. Not because we have their wealth."

"See"—she points an accusatory finger at me—"this is why I'm hesitant to tell you about my new job."

"Just spit it out, Arya."

She takes a breath. "On my last day at the coffee shop, after pulling the evening shift, I bumped into one of my regular clients. She doesn't look much older than us, but there's something about her... she always looked like she had her shit together. I usually see her dressed down, but on that day, she looked like she had stepped off the catwalk during New York fashion week. That's when I found out she wasn't a trust fund baby, she wasn't married to a billionaire, she didn't have a sugar daddy, and she wasn't a creator of a wildly successful app—"

"And what happens when you have to actually fuck for money?" I ask.

"That won't be for another three months, but I'll make a heck of a lot more money than simply being arm candy."

Of course, she can't see the forest for the trees.

"But Arya... that's wrong."

"Desperate times call for desperate measures, sis."

"There must be other jobs in New York that pay more than waitressing and don't involve you selling your body."

"First"—she lifts a finger in the air—"unlike you, I don't have a college degree. Two"—she lifts another finger—"I'm not being pressured into this. Three" —a third digit goes up—"Todd vets his clients with CIA-like diligence. He meets all of them in person. Most of his clients are referrals from other satisfied clients. You know how it is. Rich guys know other rich guys."

"No, I don't know how it is. And neither do you."

She tuts. "Stop worrying your pretty little head, Angelica. I'm going in with my eyes wide open—"

"Are you really?"

"I totally am!"

I pinch the bridge of my nose and exhale a loud breath laced with annoyance. "Have you even taken into consideration the risks?"

"The rewards trump the risks." Her retort is as quick as a whip. Consequences don't apply to Arya McQuinley. Typical. "When I have sex with random guys, I may or may not come—most times I don't. Of course, to avoid bruising the guy's ego, I'll fake it. The reality is, you don't always know what you're getting in bed. Sometimes it's toe-curling. Sometimes it's wham! Bam! Thank you, ma'am! Sometimes, you get an unpleasant parting gift..."—she points to her lady parts— "like an infection. With Todd's high-end clients, even if I have to fake it, I get a prize, aka lots of dollars. Not the case with a random dude."

This is exactly the kind of logic that gets her into trouble every single time. Still, I'm willing to play devil's advocate.

"Enough dollars not to feel like you're selling your soul? After all, you'll be spreading your legs and getting fucked by strange, dirty men." I purse my lips. "Sugarcoat it as much as you want, you're still a prostitute."

"Not that I'm class-shaming my counterparts, but the difference between a prostitute and a high-end escort is spreading open your legs for a hundred to two-hundred dollars a fuck versus *fifteen-hundred dollars* an hour, with a minimum of three hours booked."

Blink.

Blink.

Blink.

"A high-end escort gets paid one-thousand-five-hundred dollars an hour?"

"*Or more*, depending on the client's kinks."

"Jesus."

"The most in demand girls are booked up five days a week. Multiply that by four weeks."

My jaw drops as I compute the numbers in my head.

"Yup!" Arya pops the P. "They make more a month than most people earn in a year. And then there's another level." She gestures with a hand. "When a client wants to book you for a weekend, a week, *or* a month, it's like winning the Powerball."

Dear God.

"Being just arm candy doesn't mean you end up with chump change. The rate is seven hundred fifty dollars per hour." The staggering number is like getting splashed in the face with a bucket of ice-cold water. "*Cha-ching!*" She starts doing this ridiculous dance, her booty sticking out, her hands wiggling over her head, and shouting at the top of her lungs, "Show me the money!"

"Stop it!" I chastise her.

She puts an end to her circus. "You asked," she says with a one-shoulder shrug.

"A simple answer would've sufficed. You didn't need to put on a show."

"Count yourself lucky. You got a two for one special." She grins from ear to ear. "All that to say"—she soldiers on—"that kind of money solves *a lot* of problems—"

"But then you'll have other problems." One of us has to be the voice of reason, and of course, that job seems to always fall squarely on my shoulders.

"Name one."

I accept the challenge. "Well... you'll have to live with yourself after."

"Trust me, it won't keep me awake at night as I sleep on my pillow stuffed with *dolla bills*."

She's a rapper now?

I give her my best resting bitch face.

"Ange, any problems that arise for me becoming a high-end escort can be easily solved by throwing money at it."

I shake my head.

"Working for Todd isn't like walking into McDonald's and ordering a Happy Meal. Do you know how many women apply and never get a call back? The competition is fierce for this kind of coveted position. And I'm one of the lucky few who got selected." She points at her chest. Not that I'm willing to admit this to her, but that kind of money would be a gamechanger. "But since life decided to be a bitch today, she threw a wrench into my plans." She points at her lady parts.

"If you're just going to be arm candy for the evening, why would your infection be an issue?"

"Todd has a few ironclad policies, and I quote, *If you feel a sniffle coming, contact me pronto, so I can find a replacement. If Aunt Flo comes knocking, same thing, unless it's one of the client's kinks. Any vaginal infections—mild or severe, stay the fuck home. Ditto for STDs. Our premium clients pay way too much to catch nasties.*" Arya lets out a dramatic sigh. "For my first gig, Todd booked me with a prominent plastic surgeon for four hours—a charity fundraiser. *Four hours*, Ange. That's *three thousand dollars* for a few hours of *work*."

"Holy shit!"

"I know, right?" That is a lot of money. "It's way too easy-peasy to be called work." She pulls her lips down into that sad puppy face she uses when she wants to wrangle something from me. "But I have to kiss all that money goodbye. I can't violate one of my boss's cardinal rules on the first gig. That's the equivalent of kissing my career as an escort bye-bye before it even starts."

Her eyes bore into mine and the energy in the kitchen shifts.

The other shoe is about to drop... I feel it in every fiber of my being.

"I got a loan from someone."

"A loan from someone?"

"Yes."

"From who?" My tone conveys genuine trepidation.

"He only goes by Yevsei. His Russian last name is unpronounceable."

My hands go flying in the air before landing on my thighs in a loud thump. "Good grief, Arya, when does it end?"

"I'm doing something about it!" Her tone drips with as much impatience as mine.

"Why the fuck did you get involved with this Yevsei?"

"Ramsey—"

"Ramsey this. Ramsey that. And now Ramsey is nowhere to be found because he skipped town after stealing every dime we had to our names."

"You asked for an explanation, and when I give one to you, you attack me. How was I supposed to know Ramsey was a bad apple?"

"He wasn't a bad apple, he was like a terminal cancer!"

We engage in a Mexican standoff, our nostrils flared, our eyes squinted.

Until Ramsey came into our lives, we never had these types of virulent fights.

I coax myself to suppress the rage bubbling inside me. "What's the deal with this Russian?"

"If I tell you, you have to promise not to lose your shit."

I doubt I'm capable of such restraint, but I'll humor her. "I'll keep my cool."

"Promise?"

"Just spit it out, already!"

"I topped off our investment with Ramsey."

"Why did you do you that, and more importantly, why am I only finding out about it now?"

"Ramsey said"—it takes everything in me not to roll my eyes—"we'd be guaranteed an eye-popping return if we invested a certain minimum. I knew you wouldn't go for it, so he hooked me up with Yevsei."

My gut churns.

"If Ramsey had told you to jump off a fucking cliff, you would've done it like a fool. You had that much blind faith in the guy."

"You came along in the end." The smug expression on her face irritates me to no end.

I glare at her.

She cocks an eyebrow, the smirk still tilting her lips.

"Yes, because you and that scumbag kept badgering me about not missing out on an opportunity of a lifetime that would set us up for life before we celebrated our twenty-fifth birthday!"

"I just wanted a better life for us!" My sister yells her response.

"Yeah, well, now, our life is a fucking nightmare!" I yell right back.

"It won't be once I'm able to pay off Yevsei!"

"That still won't account for the money Ramsey stole from us!"

I'm certain people living in buildings two streets down can hear us shout.

"The police will find him." That blind optimism again.

Since there isn't anything I can do about Ramsey, I focus on the new clusterfuck of a mess she got herself into. "How much do you owe Yevsei?"

She averts her gaze.

"Arya!"

"A lot." I rub my hands over my face, praying to God to give me patience so I don't end up strangling my twin. "The thing is Yevsei is a scary looking motherfucker who walks around with beefy guys who wear scars on their faces and tattoos on their necks and knuckles."

Fear beats at my chest. Great. The friendly Russian monster has henchmen. "A loan shark who only goes by his first name and who walks around with tattooed goons sounds a bit Bratva, don't you think?"

She rolls her eyes. "This isn't a mafia romance novel. Yevsei is a legit businessman. He owns several dry cleaners and a few restaurants, so he gets a constant flow of cash sales—hence, the beefy security guards. The heavy flow of large cash amounts allows him to give out loans to people who need it."

"What kind of interest is he charging you?" I ask.

She averts her gaze.

"Arya, I asked you a question."

Her green eyes train on my face. "Fifteen percent—"

"Fifteen percent interest a month on a loan isn't bad—"

"Fifteen percent interest *a week*."

My insides plummet with dread. "Mother of God, that's sixty percent a month. That's outrageous!"

"It's a bit high, but beggars can't be choosers." Great logic. Not. "In any case, I'm late on my payments by two weeks, and now Yevsei is demanding I make a payment within the next forty-eight hours."

"Un-fucking-believable." I shake my head. "The hole just keeps getting deeper and deeper. And you don't even have a shovel to dig us out of this shit."

"But I *have* a shovel!" She says that like a toddler who went wee-wee on her own for the first time and now expects a lollipop. "Which is why I was crossing my fingers, toes, and hair, praying to become one of Todd's girls. Mission accomplished!" she says, flinging her long ponytail.

"I'm sinking deeper into this fucking nightmare, like I'm being sucked into the Bermuda triangle during a catastrophic hurricane," I say, picking up steam. "May I remind you, I never signed up for any of this."

"How was I supposed to know behind the handsome face, custom-made suits, Rolex watch, Italian shoes, and pricey sports cars, Ramsey was a piece of shit, scam artist?" I fold my lips between my teeth to avoid answering. It's called not falling for assholes. Again. "In my defense, I just wanted us to have a better life—"

"By gambling the little we had left from Dad's life insurance after his death?"

"Investments are all about timing, Ange." She lectures me

like she's a Wall Street Wolf. "I figured getting in first would set us up for life." Well, it didn't. It ruined us. "I have it all under control." The famous last words that landed her ass, and mine by proxy, knee deep in shit. "Working for Todd is *our*"—she waves a finger between us—"ticket to freedom. One evening hanging from a rich dude's arm, and I'll have the money I need to make a payment on my debt with Yevsei."

"Except, you can't be arm candy to your first client."

An expression that should trigger fear in my heart and have me running for the hills veils her eyes. "No, but *you* can."

Chapter 2

Hudson

A knock at my door breaks my concentration.

My eyes lift from my computer screen. "Come in!"

The door opens and a head of long, blonde hair pokes into my office.

"Do you have a minute?" Marine asks.

I rest back against my seat. "I'll take any excuse not to have to pour over this spreadsheet."

She steps inside and sashays her way to my desk, looking as chic as she always does.

Men or women. Fashion is an Olympic sport in the Big Apple. That was a big adjustment for a poor kid from Summerville, Texas whose parents considered Target stores high-end, and therefore, out of reach. I've upped my game, but some people were born with an impeccable sense of style—like thirty-four-year-old, Toulouse born, Marine Renault. My director of French communications takes fashion seriously. Today she's decked out in a light-blue pant suit, a low-cut white blouse, and white sky-high heels. Her makeup is perfectly applied. Like always.

"*Bonjour*," she says, placing a cardboard tray on my desk.

"*Bonjour*." It's one of the rare French words I know.

"I stopped by Project Espresso on the way from my meeting," she says. "I thought I'd bring you a late morning pick me up. An extra hot, double espresso latte." She points to the tall cup. "I also popped by next door at Sugar Lane for a slice of sugar high. Lucky me. They had your favorite."

My gaze drops to the cup and brown paper bag.

Someone is buttering me up.

"What is it that you want from me?"

"What makes you think I want something?" She feigns innocence. "Is it a crime to bring your boss coffee and dessert?"

I make a show of stretching my arm before checking the time on my Cartier Ballon Bleu watch. "It's not even lunchtime yet. Don't you think it's a bit early for dessert?"

"*Mais non*." She shrugs. "Why be so restrictive?"

What game is she playing?

"We have a kickass coffee machine imported from Italy in the kitchen."

"Pods will never be the same as freshly brewed."

"There are many, more than acceptable coffee and pastry shops right at our door. You had to make a detour for these?"

Her expression is a pure annoyance. "I thought I would be able to ease you into what I have to tell you by bringing you your favorites."

I motion my hand in a circle. "Don't beat around the bush. You know I hate surprises."

With elegance and grace, she lowers herself into one of the guest chairs. Leaning back, she crosses one leg over the other, and brushes off fictitious lint from her pants.

"Come on, Marine, lay it on me."

She sighs. "Well, I know tomorrow night's launch party at

the Bymark Hotel is the opening we've been waiting for to land this LA prospect, but I can't be your date."

Shit.

"I thought we were on?"

"We were, but my girlfriend just informed me a reporter from New York Times Style Magazine will drop by at the art gallery for tomorrow night's exhibit." Impressive. "The reporter will be accompanied by a photographer and a camera crew for photos and videos for their website. I was planning on only staying an hour at the event before making my way to the gallery, but given the big news..." Her words trail. "We just started seeing each other, but things are going well. I want to be there the whole evening to support her."

"I get it. That's a big deal."

"It is." Pride shines bright in her eyes. "That's the only reason why I would ditch you at such short notice. I know how much you hate showing up at these functions alone."

Even after five years living in New York and my colossal wealth, I always feel out of place at these parties.

"I can find someone else to accompany you," Marine says. "There are a few female employees who don't have a significant other or kid to go home to."

"It wouldn't be the same dynamic with another employee. You and I have a good thing going on at these events. We play off each other." Until she met her girlfriend two months ago, Marine was a serial dater, so she was happy to accompany me to these shindigs. My grueling work schedule prevents me from having long-term relationships.

Marine's blue eyes widen. "Are you saying you're willing to do the impossible, Hudson Kincaid? You're willing to fly solo?"

I shake my head. "No way I'm showing up without a wingman. I need someone who can handle vapid conversations better than I can. My fuse is short, I'm blunt, my bullshit meter is set at zero, and I take pleasure in ruffling people's overly sensitive natures."

She laughs, clapping at the same time. "All this time, I thought it was my personality, but you were using me as a buffer so you wouldn't get kicked out of those chichi events, or worse, beat up someone who rubbed you the wrong way."

"Pretty much."

She shakes her head and waves a motherly finger at me.

"That, and you're gorgeous, smart, you seem to never run out of conversation, and your debating skills are impressive."

"It's a byproduct of being French. We learn how to debate in kindergarten," she says. "About the event. If you don't intend on showing up alone— Wait." She lifts a hand up. "Are you seeing someone?"

"No, I'm still very much single. Since your girlfriend came into your life, I knew my days were numbered. So, I made sure to have a contingency plan."

She cocks her head. "Meaning?"

I snatch my Montblanc pen from my desk and tap it against my chin. "If I play my cards right, tomorrow night's event could be a turning point towards closing a huge account that's slipped through our fingers for far too long." I shake my head, disappointed by our past failed attempts at landing this prospect. "I know exactly how to find a last-minute date that has far better social graces than I do. Someone who, like you, knows how to charm the pants off any sucker."

~

I might only be twenty-eight, but it's not like I was born yesterday. I was well aware escort services existed, but until recently, I didn't know how many high-powered men preferred to avoid the hassle and unpredictable nature of taking a random date to an important event by hiring a professional. It's the best way to nix the drama factor. Sometimes sex is involved. But sometimes, it's strictly for arm candy purposes. Given Marine's relationship status, it's very likely I'll have to rely more and more on Elite Encounters Escorts' services. Good thing I became a member not long ago.

Right after my director of French communications left my office, I placed a call.

Many hours later, I'm catching up on emails, when my phone rings. I snatch it off my desk.

"Todd," I say, answering.

"Mr. Kincaid. How are you?"

"No complaints. And you?"

"Ditto," he says. "I'm sure you must hear this all the time, but your deep twang is damn sexy."

"Thank you?!"

"Don't worry, I can read the neon signs. You don't swing my way. That said, it needed to be said. Again." I don't have anything to add to that. "Back to business," he says with a heavy sigh. "We met a month ago. I rarely have clients wait that long to enquire about companionship with one of my girls."

I keep my answer brief. "Until today, I didn't need the companionship of one of your girls. However, things changed on my end."

"Change is my friend," he says. "Well, I'd like to officially welcome you to the club. I'm certain you'll be very happy with my girls."

"I have no doubt," I say. "I know my request is last-minute—"

"Please, Mr. Kincaid, we specialize in last-minute. Since you left it up to me to select a girl on your behalf—and may I say it's a huge honor that you place such trust in me—"

"You know your girls better than I do."

"I picked the perfect girl for your first date." There's pride in his tone. "She's a tall, model thin, natural blonde with big amber eyes. She has a college degree in international studies. She speaks fluent Norwegian and knows basic French."

"I'm sure she's gorgeous."

"All my girls are stunning beauties. I'm very picky. Very, very picky." Good to know. "Should I send you her photo, just to be one-hundred percent sure she fits the bill?"

"I trust your judgement, but I'd love to see a photo."

Chapter 3

Angelica

I'm still staring at my sister, dumbfounded by her declaration.

"We need this money, Ange." Arya soldiers on. "No one will know. You just need to be charming and smile a lot for four hours and collect three thousand dollars from the plastic surgeon. It won't erase my loan with Yevsei, but it will help a lot."

I'm still incapable of finding my voice.

"Please, big sis." She summons her hurt puppy face. The one that tugs at my protective side. "I need your help." She pouts, her green eyes shimmering.

Damn her for using the oldest trick in the book.

I let out a suffering sigh.

"Let me get this straight. Either I become *Pretty Woman* for one night or my twin sister will be in trouble with Yevsei, who I'm certain works with the Bratva, unless he's the head honcho of the Manhattan Russian mafia? Good times all around."

"You don't have to put out like Vivian in *Pretty Woman*." Of course, she ignores the Russian mafia part.

I level her with a hard stare.

Let it be known identical twins have their own distinct personalities. In Arya's case, she's made it her mission to be as different from me as possible. I can't even begin to comprehend where she got this wild child streak.

Then, she pulls out the big guns. "This"—she tugs at the hem of my *Life Is A Highway* t-shirt—"is your definition of edgy. You have a collection of these faded t-shirts with inspirational quotes." I do, although the one I'm wearing is the title of a song. As much as I'd like to buy new t-shirts, my shopping budget is a big fat zero. "That's not living, Ange. Same for your hobbies—"

"What's wrong with my hobbies?"

"Even when you're not completely lost in one of the manuscripts you're editing for a client, fiction is still your safe place." Book boyfriends do it better. "You live vicariously through the characters in the books you read or listen to for pleasure, while remaining behind the closed doors of our apartment."

I cross my arms over my chest. "I go out for walks—"

"While re-listening to an audiobook you've already listened to countless times."

"I can't afford to buy new ones," I argue.

She sighs. "This is your chance to step out of your comfort zone—"

"What you're asking me to do isn't stepping out of my comfort zone. It's more like jumping in the deep end."

"It's called *safe* danger," she counters. "Like I said, you'll be dealing with very rich men who have been thoroughly vetted."

"I'm sure someone will know."

"We've done tons of twin swaps before."

"This is different."

"How so?"

"You met Todd in person, so he knows what you look like—"

"We literally have the same eye color and face. We have the same everything."

"Until you started at the bar, you were a natural blonde." I point to my head. "You're a brunette now."

"It's called hair color."

"There's no money for a hairdresser."

"Lucky for us, there's a Walmart right here in Queens."

"I bet you've been plotting this since leaving the doctor's office."

"Ride life. Don't just read about it."

"Easy for you to say. You're the exuberant twin."

"And tomorrow night, we swap places, so you"—she points at me—"get to walk in my shoes."

"I don't have your self-confidence."

She places her hands on my shoulders, her eyes locking onto mine. "Here's a little secret Todd shared with me. Being an escort is like being an actress—you step into a role every time you're out with a new client. Like they say in Hollywood... fake it till you make it..."

For a long beat, we just stare at each other.

I bite the inside of my cheek, replaying this far-fetched conversation in my head with the playback mode set up at twice the speed.

"Don't men prefer tall, skinny girls as arm candy?"

"Todd says there's a huge demand for women with slender curves. Not all men want skinny minis."

"Aren't those men looking for Amazonians?"

"My height wasn't an issue with Todd and it shouldn't be an issue for you since we're the same height."

I nod.

"You're one-hundred percent certain the plastic surgeon won't expect sex?" I blame desperation for prompting the question.

Arya's face breaks into a huge smile.

"Thank you, thank you, thank you," she chants, doing the happy dance.

"I haven't agreed yet!"

She grins. "Okay, sis, I'm willing to pretend with you." Damn her. "To answer your question, I am certain. Unless he requests a little dirty on the side and commits to paying the higher rate, there won't be any exchange of genital fluids."

I respond with a grimace.

"What does he look like?"

The expression on her face is smug as she pulls out her phone from her pocket. She swipes a few times before turning the screen towards me. "This is *our* first client. He's a prominent plastic surgeon."

I grimace again.

He clearly drinks his own Kool-Aid, because he looks like he's performed one too many surgeries on his own face.

"He's only hiring you as arm candy. It's not a date," Arya says.

"What if he tries to feel me up?"

"Todd has a strict pay to play policy. A chaste goodnight kiss on the cheek is the most he can expect. More than that, and it could lead to getting down and dirty... and the client would have to fork out more *dinero*."

Yuck.

I know I'm going to regret this. "I'll do it."

"Yay!—"

"On one condition."

Her happy face turns into a frowny one. "What?"

"You quit this job before you have to have sex with a client."

"But Todd is going to be pissed off for grooming me, just so I quit on him."

I cross my arms over my chest and adopt a defiant stance. "Take it or leave it."

Chapter 4

Angelica

As I make my way to meet my sister's first client, I silently curse asshole Ramsey for putting Arya and me in this fucked up situation. Since he came sweeping into my sister's life like the angel of death, leaving a trail of destruction behind him, we've been living hand to mouth. The only reason I can even afford to have my ass grace the backseat of a taxi is because Todd has a corporate account for his girls. Thank God, because I can't imagine riding the subway decked out in this glam frock. If I wasn't so fuming at how the asshole left us practically destitute, I'd be able to appreciate the sparkling light ahead. These days, unless I absolutely have to make the trip from Queens to Manhattan, I avoid it at all costs. Too many temptations that could part me from the little money we have lurk in the city. It's safer to stay locked up in our apartment.

Thanks for nothing, Ramsey.

My phone chimes in my hand, putting an end to my recurring fantasy of tracking down the thief to make him pay for what he did to us. Forget about waterboarding. I'd much rather pull his pubic hairs out one by one with a tweezer until he agrees to return all the money he stole from us.

Arya: Change of plans.

Angelica: The venue for the charity gala changed?

Arya: You're no longer meeting the plastic surgeon.

Angelica: Why not?

Arya: His car just got rear-ended. It's really bad.

Angelica: Oh shit. I get to come home?

Arya: No. Todd has assigned me—you, really—a new client.

My heart drops.

Arya: Another newbie at the agency can't make her shift. Her five-year-old daughter is coming down with a fever and possibly an ear infection.

Angelica: Poor thing. And poor mom.

Arya: Yeah. Todd asked me to fill in for her.

Angelica: Who's the client?

Arya: Some rich guy. He's attending an event to celebrate an upcoming TV series for a big streaming company. It sounds a hell of a lot more fun than the charity event.

Angelica: Any photos of the rich guy?

Arya: Todd didn't send me one yet. I'm sure he's juggling a lot. Just show up.

Angelica: How will I recognize the client if I don't know what he looks like?

Arya: Hudson Kincaid, the client, will meet you at the Crawford Lounge inside the Bymark Hotel on 57th Street. He'll have the latest edition of CEOs & Moguls magazine on the table. And he's given the heads up to the maître d'. Ask for him when you get there.

Angelica: Got it.

Arya: The event starts at seven, but the client wants a face-to-face beforehand. Probably to give you the lay of the land. You're—we're—booked for three hours.

Angelica: Okay. Still no sex, right?

Arya: Strictly arm candy.

Angelica: Thank God.

Arya: About *our* fee... Todd is a firm believer in first impressions. He hates last-minute kerfuffle. Since this is a first-time client, he'll comp the client by footing the bill. I'll pick up the money tomorrow. No need for you to collect it from the client.

Angelica: One less thing to worry about.

Arya: Yup!

Angelica: You're going to make a payment on your debt with Yevsei, right? Don't go on a shopping spree.

Arya: Relax. I will. He's first on the list after I get *our* money.

Angelica: Okay. Good.

Arya: Text me when you get there.

Angelica: Copy that.

Arya: Break a leg. And don't forget, you got this.

Right.

Arya: If I call, answer. That means, we have to coordinate our stories with Todd.

Angelica: If I hear your ringtone, I'll answer for sure.

Chapter 5

Angelica

Forty nail-biting minutes later, the taxi drops me off in front of a hotel, located in a coveted zip code, I never thought I'd ever step into. Instead of heading to the lounge where I'm supposed to meet the client, I stand in the lobby, awestruck. My eyes bounce to every which corner, taking it all in.

Talk about being a fish out of water.

The Bymark Hotel is the height of opulence. Even the air smells expensive. So far, I've only been able to experience this kind of luxury within the pages of a good steamy romance novel.

Wow.

Reality trumps fiction.

A commotion somewhere in the lobby, jolts me back to the moment.

I can't be late for my first gig. I mean, Arya's first gig.

Speaking of which, I forgot to text her. I fire off a quick message, to tell her I've arrived.

Done.

Six o'clock.

Get a move on.

I take a step forward, but nearly trip.

Shit.

Arya worships sky-high heels. Even though, I practiced walking before leaving the apartment, this isn't the same. These polished granite floors are like an ice rink.

I compose myself and take a deep breath.

Don't twist an ankle. We need this money.

With careful steps, I trail to the concierge's desk to find out where I'm going.

Armed with directions, I head towards the elevators.

I step into a car filled with beautiful people, dressed head to toe in designer wear.

I send a silent prayer to God.

Along with heading an escort agency, Todd doubles as a fairy godmother. That's the only reason why I'm able to show up at this luxury hotel, dressed like I belong here.

Todd's contacts are golden.

He's among the first to be made aware of sample sales, he has contacts at every second-hand shop in the city, he's on first name terms with personal shoppers of the big luxury retailers, and if there's a shoe sale going on anywhere in Manhattan, he'll get a notification. Thank God Arya was able to score a dress that looks like it cost a million bucks for a steal. That was a good use of the advance from her first gig.

When I reach the floor to the lounge, I exit the elevator.

As I stride down the corridor, I'm hit with a wave of panic. Fear and adrenaline spike through me. It's violent. Destabilizing me to the point I have to grip the wall to avoid collapsing to my knees. The pounding in my ears is so loud, it's deafening. The stars dancing in front of my eyes are blinding. The realization of what I'm about to do washes over me like a tsunami, making it a struggle to breathe.

Holy shit.

This isn't a 90s romcom. This is my life. Sad. Tragic. Overwhelming.

The thought of pulling off this charade without being outed, and landing Arya and me in even more trouble than we already are, makes me want to puke.

I cringe.

Okay, perhaps not the sexiest thought just before meeting a client, even if sex is off the table.

I place a calming hand on my tummy.

I can't have cold feet now.

Breathe.

There are times in your life when you have to take one for the team. I need to suck it up and make the ultimate sacrifice to save my twin's misguided ass.

The thought pushes me forward.

I swallow against the greasy feeling crawling up my throat, as I repeat *You got this* over and over in my head.

As I step inside the Crawford Lounge, I catch the lyrics of the song playing.

I twist my face, unimpressed by God's cruel sense of humor.

It's a remix with a lounge vibe of *"Take me to church"*.

Forgive me heavenly father, for I'm about to sin. In my defense, my hands are tied.

"Good evening, ma'am," the maître d'hôtel says.

I muster up my most dazzling smile, freezing it on my lips. "Good evening." There's nothing I can do about the trembling in my voice.

"Will you be enjoying the evening alone or are you meeting someone?" he asks in a hoity tone.

"I'm meeting Mr. Hudson Kincaid."

His demeanor changes. His standoffish smile is replaced with a warmer one. "Please, follow me."

Mr. Kincaid must be big shit.

I follow the maître d', as we weave our way through table upon table of patrons involved in animated conversations. Just like the lobby of the hotel, the lounge's décor is sleek and modern.

Fingers crossed Hudson Kincaid isn't hideous, or addicted to plastic surgery, or a hundred years old, or creepy, or his breath won't smell like rotten garlic.

Please, God, make him decent looking with a pleasant personality.

When we reach the far corner of the lounge, the maître d' stops and extends a hand.

My eyes spot the *CEOs & Moguls* magazine before shifting to the man with brown hair wearing a black suit. His eyes are glued to the phone he's holding, a look of quiet concentration visible in his profile, as his long finger quickly drags whatever he's reading up the screen. Even from this angle, I can tell he looks nothing like the plastic surgeon.

Trepidation is replaced with excitement.

I can definitely wrap my head around being arm candy to a handsome man for an evening.

I blame a gust of excitement I have no business feeling for pushing me forward.

"Mr. Kincaid?" I say, approaching his table.

He looks up, his eyes locking onto mine.

I'm momentarily paralyzed.

So is he.

For a few beats, we stare at each other.

A shiver runs through me.

Slowly, because he's clearly a man who knows the dizzying

effect he has on women, the blue-eyed god pushes his chair back and stands to his full height. Nothing turns me on more than height on a man. The sight of him unraveling like an Adonis god who's used to having New York at his feet makes my mouth go dry and my lady parts go wet.

Even in my five-inch heels, this man towers over me.

I look way up into the most beautiful blue eyes I've ever seen. Even under the low light, there's no mistaking, those eyes can be used as a weapon of mass seduction.

Holy shitzballs!

And talk about sharp dresser. The man wears a suit like he was born in one.

Basically, my—I mean, Arya's—first client is utterly, stupidly, infuriatingly gorgeous. And not the universal kind of gorgeous that almost dulls itself into the background in a city like New York where rich, handsome men in suits are a dime a dozen. Nope. His kind of gorgeous is next level hot because of the raw magnetism he emanates.

He's a poster child for suit porn perfection in his tailored black suit that fits his athletic body like a second skin. His white shirt is crisp and offsets his black tie. His silver cufflinks scream money and power. He looks in control... like a bossman. I brush a fictitious strand of my freshly dyed brown hair behind my ear as I furtively glance down at his expensive looking black shoes.

Damn.

Lucky me—

This isn't a date, Angelica.

"Brinley," he extends a hand.

Huh?

I'm just about to look over my shoulder, certain he's talking to someone behind me, when I remember Brinley is my sister's working girl name. Todd takes his girls' privacy and protection very seriously.

"Yes!" I say, with a little too much force. "I'm Brinley!" I add, more to convince myself than him.

When I place my hand into his large one, an electric current zaps through me.

Great balls of fire.

He flinches, then frowns, his eyes lowering to our joined hands.

"It's a pleasure to meet you, Mr. Kincaid."

He leans into me, his lips flirting with my earlobe. *Sweet baby Jesus.* "I know I'm not allowed to know your real name, but you can call me Hudson. Mr. Kincaid might give us away."

"Hudson."

"Much better."

His deep voice is sexy as fuck, and that Matthew McConaughey twang does something to me.

I'm a jumble of nerves. Not only because I'm stepping into a role Arya was born to play, but also because this man exudes such potent masculinity, it's intoxicating.

Chapter 6

Hudson

I take a step back from the beauty in red.

From the photos Todd sent, his first selection embodies so many women I meet at functions—tall and model thin. Nothing wrong with that, but a woman with slender curves is my kryptonite. And the one staring up at me with wide eyes hits all the right buttons.

You can take the man out of Texas, but you can't take the Texan out of the man.

I don't know the first thing about jewelry, but I bet my fortune her green eyes are more beautiful than rare stones. It's not only her eyes that are captivating. It's every delectable inch of her. And then there's her alabaster skin. It's mid-July. Most New Yorkers worship the short summer months, sporting a tan like it's a badge of honor.

Not her.

My date's pale skin looks like it's been barely touched by rays of sunshine. Her hair is pulled back in a long braid, which makes it easy to appreciate her slender neck. Her face is delicate, pointy chin, fine cheekbones, large eyes, and bow-shaped lips painted in a delicate nude shade. Her sinful mouth draws me in, sensual lips that beg to be kissed. And that dress...

Red.

Formfitting.

A real show-stopper.

With a low-cut front that showcases the kind of tits that would fit perfectly in my large hands.

She's temptation on legs.

"I was heading to a charity event with a doctor when Todd informed me there was a change of plans"—she waves a finger up and down her form—"hence the sequins. I hope I'm not overdressed for your event."

"Not at all, darlin'." You look like a wet dream. "That dress on you could stop traffic."

"Thank you."

"No, thank *you*."

A small, shy smile lifts her mouth.

I'm completely transfixed by her lips.

Scratch that.

I want to kiss her, so I know how she tastes... before tasting her other set of lips.

My tailored pants suddenly feel a little too tight. Same for my boxer briefs.

Looking up from under her long, dark lashes, Brinley pretends to brush a strand of brown hair behind her ear.

What is her real name? And why does it matter so much?

She clears her throat. "You're staring." Damn right I am.

"It's your fault." I say. I haven't heard that voice in far too long. It's the one that gets women to drop to their knees and reach for my belt without me having to issue a command.

"Oh."

My eyes shift from hers and trail down the long braid that falls over her shoulder, cascading over her generous breast. And fuck if I don't have visions of fisting it as I drive into her from behind.

Going for the arm candy package was a mistake.

I soften my approach. "You make it hard not to stare."

She responds with a broad smile, flashing me perfect white teeth.

I don't know if that touch of shyness is an act, but her reaction sends a jolt straight to my cock.

"You aren't from New York."

Five years in the Big Apple has done nothing to soften my Texan drawl. Not that I'd ever want to erase it. It would be like giving up a part of me.

"There's no pulling the wool over your eyes."

She blushes.

It won't be long before the bulge between my legs becomes noticeable. Only a thin line of self-control prevents me from bending her over one of these tables and spanking her creamy white ass in front of all these people for making me hard. "Let's sit down and order a drink, and we can talk about tonight."

She lets out a sigh of relief. "That sounds good."

Chapter 7

Angelica

You aren't from New York?

No shit, Sherlock.

That's your conversation opener?

If I don't get my head into the game, I'm going to blow my cover.

Conversation comes so easily to my twin sister. I've never been great at breaking the ice.

I need to channel Arya if I'm going to pull this off.

The drop-dead gorgeous hunk gallantly pulls out the chair for me. "Please, sit down."

I barely have time to drop my clutch on top of the magazine when a waiter appears to take our drink order.

"What's your poison?" Hudson asks, taking a seat across from me.

A hundred different drinks collide in my head all at once.

White wine is lame and screams of 'you don't get out much'.

Along with the long list of things we had to cut out of our

lives, going out tops the list. With her waitressing job I'm sure Arya would be able to come up with an original drink.

The pressure is on.

I settle for the drink of choice of the heroine of the last billionaire romance novel I read, because, hello! I'm living large tonight. "I'll have a lychee martini, please."

The waiter nods before turning his attention to Hudson.

"Three fingers of whiskey—Irish or Scotch, I don't care. But neat, please."

With a head bow, the waiter scurries off.

Hudson's dazzling blue eyes shift to mine.

I flash him a shy smile, but he remains stoic.

I lean into the table. "Can I ask a question?"

"Of course."

"Why three fingers?"

He cocks an eyebrow. "Because one finger isn't enough and two would be playing it too safe. You *feel* three fingers." He delivers his answer in a raspy voice that suggests we're no longer talking about whiskey.

A blush rushes to my face and I'm certain my cheeks match the color of my dress.

Holy hotter than hell.

"You asked," he says with a lopsided grin.

It takes everything in me not to fan myself... and I'm not talking about my face.

I need to change the conversation before I burst into flames.

I shift in my seat. "Everything is next level amazing at the Bymark Hotel."

"Your first time here?"

"Yes. I gather you've been here before."

"It's kind of a stomping ground for me. I'm a member of a private business club located on the forty-first floor of this hotel." He points to the ceiling.

"I see."

He reaches for the magazine. "May I?"

"Oh, sorry." I grab my clutch and place it on the other side.

"Here's another reason why I like this hotel." He taps a finger on the cover of CEOs & Moguls. "The CEO, Logan Ellison, is a buddy of mine." Talk about knowing people in high places. "To your point, everything here is impeccable, but then again, the clientele demands it. Furthermore, Logan wouldn't have it any other way."

The disparity in our tax bracket slaps me in the face.

Hudson is just about to say something when our waiter returns with our drinks, placing them in front of us.

Lifting his tumbler, Hudson says, "Here's to new friends."

I'm taken aback. "Are we friends?"

"Tonight, we're really good friends." The way he says that turns something inside me into the consistency of molten lava cake.

Be brave.

I lift my martini glass. "To new friends."

We clink before taking a sip of our drinks, eyeing each other from over the rims of our glasses.

Holy delicious cocktail.

A hum of pleasure escapes me.

Oops.

"I gather the drink meets your standards?" Hudson asks.

It blows it out of the water. "This is delicious."

"Top-shelf vodka makes all the difference."

It does.

He drops his glass on the table.

I do the same.

"When Todd told me there was a last-minute change of plans and he found a replacement that was sure to knock my socks off, he wasn't lying." Hudson gives me a onceover. "The other girl Todd had paired me with looked gorgeous in her photo, but you"—another onceover—"you're stunning."

I'm dumfounded.

I'm blinking so fast, I'm certain I'll take flight.

After a *'Pretty Woman'* worthy transformation, I barely recognized the well put together woman that was staring at me in the mirror. The dress, heels, expertly applied makeup, and perfectly coiffed, slicked back hair could fool anyone.

From the outside, I look like my twin. But inside, I'm still lil' ol' me—shy, a bit socially awkward, and uncomfortable being the center of attention. I almost cried when Arya pulled out the dress I had to wear. Red? No way can I melt into the walls wearing such a vibrant color. Hudson Kincaid's words just gave lil' ol' me wings.

As I gather my wits to say something—anything—I catch the lyrics of the sultry song playing, *I've got a burning desire for you, baby.* That's exactly how I feel about this stranger—

This. Is. Not. A. Date!

"You're going to make me blush." That's the best I can come up with.

"Don't look so damn sexy if you don't want compliments, Brinley."

I place the back of my hand against my cheek.

Dammit, his pantie-melting drawl is going straight to my head and my lady parts.

"I'll do my best next time." I mumble my answer.

Something indecipherable passes over his face. Anger? Annoyance? Irritation? Is he pissed off?

Then, it vanishes.

"Let me go over how the evening is going to unfold," he says.

I sit a little straighter in my chair. "We're heading to a launch party."

"Yes and no."

I frown my confusion.

"We're *crashing* a launch party."

And just like that I graduate from escort to criminal.

This night keeps getting better and better.

"Come again?" I ask.

"Let me start from the beginning," he says. "I'm the CEO of Pay Gateway. My company makes it easy for top apps to offer their users with multiple safe transaction options on both iPhone and Android smartphones."

"Wow. You're so young."

"My journey is an interesting one, but that story is for another day."

"Okay." I hope I didn't say the wrong thing.

"UTV.com—"

"I'm a subscriber!" Canceling our streaming subscription would've been like cutting off a limb.

"Good," he says. "Their headquarters are in LA, but they're hosting a party at this hotel to start creating buzz for an upcoming action thriller series that will air next February to the east coast press."

"I see."

"The streaming service is owned by two brothers. CEO Rory Wolfe will be attending with his wife Isobel. I've been courting him and his brother for a while now, but I can't seem to get my foot in the door. This is my chance. In my experience, a more casual setting is often a better way to connect than a more formal meeting."

I nod.

"For tonight, I need you to be the Bonnie to my Clyde, so I can get close and personal with the CEO."

"You're luring me into connivance?"

"You're putting a poetic spin on it."

It's a professional hazard.

I word my question differently. "Aren't we going to get caught? And if we do, won't we get in trouble?"

"It pays to know the owners of the hotel."

"They'll post bail when we get arrested?"

"Good one, but you don't have to worry. It's unlikely we'll end up in the slammer."

A gust of excitement rushes through me at the thought of being this powerful man's partner in crime.

"What's the plan?"

"Logan is on the list of invites," he says. He checks his watch. It's a beautiful timepiece with a rose gold bezel and a black leather strap that must cost as much as a down payment on an apartment in a pricey zip code. "As we speak, his executive assistant's assistant"—*Holy crap!*—"should've contacted the event's coordinator to tell her he regretfully won't be able to make it, but will be sending someone on his behalf."

"That someone is you!"

"Bingo." He pretends to fire a gun at me.

"What do you expect from me?"

"Your only job will be to look charming, which you're already acing."

I blush again.

"One last thing."

"I'm all ears."

He holds my gaze.

The intensity of his blue eyes is unsettling.

Everything about this man leaves me weak in the knees.

It's a struggle to remember the reason I'm sitting across from him tonight.

He's hiring you by the hour.

"Even though Todd is picking up the bill for this evening, I want you glued to my side during the entire evening."

Like that's going to be a hardship. "Absolutely."

"You arrive at the event with me, you leave with me."

"Of course. Can I ask you a question?"

"Shoot."

"What if someone asks about our relationship? What do I say?"

He leans into the table. Since he's tall, his handsome face is dangerously close. His gaze bounces from the low V-neck of my dress, up to my lips, before his dreamy blue eyes land on mine. "Tell them your fine, curvy ass is mine," he says in a suggestive voice I feel down to my clit.

I'm pretty sure I just came.

Chapter 8

Hudson

I might have to give Todd a big fat bonus, a box of Cuban cigars, a case of the finest whiskey on the market—unless he prefers wine—and season tickets to his favorite sport or Broadway show.

I'm certain Todd's first selection is good at what she does, but for some reason, I doubt she would've been able to charm the pants off Isobel Wolfe. After forty minutes of animated conversation, our hosts excuse themselves to continue working the room.

For the first hour upon our arrival, Rory and his wife were busy greeting guests, while I strategized a plan to butt into a conversation without being too obvious. I needn't have bothered. Brinley overheard Isobel talk about a book I had never heard of in my life, and just like that, the gates to Heaven opened up to me.

I grab Brinley by the hand and drag her to an isolated corner of the room.

I whirl around to face her. "Holy shit! You were fucking amazing."

"Really?"

"I was blown away." She's grinning from ear to ear, her gorgeous green eyes sparkling. "And I wasn't the only one."

"It felt like I couldn't shut up." And it paid off in dividends. "I tried to contain my enthusiasm, but it was impossible. I hope it didn't come off like I had verbal diarrhea." She was nothing like the shy woman I met in the lounge.

"You achieved more in forty minutes of conversation than I've been able to accomplish in two months."

"With a gun to my head, I wouldn't have been able to shut up about last year's biggest fantasy romance series because it was a well-deserved runaway success. Finding out UTV's CEO's wife is as much of a diehard fan as I am, was like dying and going to heaven."

"You two were going at it like you were long-lost friends. Rory and I could've stepped out of the room for a cigar."

She laughs. "What can I say? Women bond over romance."

"No kidding. You knew every detail of that book as if you had written it yourself."

Her head jerks back. Her joyful expression is replaced by a horrified one.

"What did I say?"

She shakes her head. "Nothing."

Why do I have the feeling she's hiding something?

"I know *The Court Games* series very well because I read it multiple times."

"That was obvious. You"—I tap the tip of her nose—"are my good luck charm."

She dances from one foot to the other. "You're giving me too much credit."

I shake my head. "No. Thanks to you, I have a confirmed dinner date with UTV's CEO before he leaves New York."

She drops her gaze and pulls her lower lip between her

teeth. "Glad I could be of service," she says, looking up from under her curtain of long lashes.

"You went above and beyond."

"I hope I didn't step on your toes. After all, it's your business—"

I place two fingers against her lips, silencing her. "Not at all. You won the Wolfes over with your exuberant personality—"

"Me, exuberant?"

"Did you notice another hot brunette hanging from my arm?"

She giggles.

Fuck, I love her laugh.

"I was in my element, I guess," she says.

Her voice is sexy. Her laugh is even sexier. But both pale in comparison to her beautiful face.

I want my dick in that mouth.

An inexplainable wave of anger washes over me at the thought of how many men have kissed those lips or how many times she's wrapped them around an asshole's cock.

I snap out of my foul mood. "You knocked it out of the park."

She doesn't seem convinced.

"There's usually a lot of mingling at these events," I say. "In other words, conversations tend to mirror speed dating—superficial chitchat for five minutes before moving onto the next victim. I mean, prospect."

There she goes laughing again.

"You managed to hold the Wolfes' attention long enough for me to get a foot in the door. And let's not forget, this is an event they were hosting in a room with three hundred other guests who all would've killed to monopolize their attention for that long. I don't know how to repay you."

"I was just doing my job," she says in a sheepish tone.

"You underestimate yourself, Brinley."

She responds with a one-shoulder shrug.

Damn, I'm dying to know her real name, but that goes against Todd's cardinal rules.

What the fuck is wrong with you, Kincaid?

I have little experience hiring an escort for the evening, but this woman is nothing like I expected. There's something almost innocent about her. Perhaps I'm judging, but I would've expected an escort to be a lot more jaded. She was like a kid hitting Disney World for the first time.

I step closer, crowding her space. The pull towards her is too strong.

I can't even start to make sense of the host of implausible desires that crowd my mind or why I'm so attracted to the woman staring up at me with captivating green eyes.

"Since I caught sight of you at the Crawford Lounge, I've been wondering how I was going to manage to focus on business without being distracted by the way you wear this form-fitting red dress that hugs every single one of your curves to perfection. I never expected you'd distract me by stealing the show."

"You said you didn't mind." Her tone is accusatory.

"I'm not complaining. I'm just telling you what's been going on in my mind since I first laid eyes on you."

"Oh."

I check my watch. "Are you up for another adventure?"

Her eyes widen, pupils dilating. And then she has the audacity to take the seduction factor to another level by biting into that full lower lip.

Between the drinks, the finger food, and the animated conversation, her nude lipstick has vanished, leaving her natural pinkish lips.

Christ.

It could just be an act, Kincaid. After all, she's still on the clock.

Fuck it. I don't care.

My body is having an unprecedented response to this woman—

It hits me how long it's been since I've been putting my company's—and employees'—needs before my own.

Not tonight.

"Want to get out of here?"

She scours the room. "There's no one else you need to meet?"

"Nope. I got what I came here for."

"What did you have in mind?"

"Remember that private business club I told you about earlier?"

She nods.

"Why don't I give you a tour?"

"I'd love that."

"Just so we're clear, giving you a tour is codeword for alone time with you."

She swallows hard. "Okay."

Chapter 9

Angelica

I could die as I stroll in front of Hudson towards the elevator.

Arya frowned at me as I was shimmying my ass into my trusted body shaper. When she told me to ditch it, I nearly broke out in hives. Something about men relishing what us women consider imperfections. I fought her at first, but relinquished. To her point, it's unlikely I'll ever see any of the people I'll meet tonight again. Still, it doesn't make this any easier. I'm an editor. I sit all day. I have a love affair with ice cream and I'm addicted to all forms of potato. I don't believe in discriminating.

Translation: I don't have buns of steel.

What if my jiggly butt repulses Hudson? It's completely irrational why I would give this man's opinion of me any importance, but here I am, holding in my breath, as if that's enough to firm my ass.

When we arrive at the elevators, he leans into me. "The gentlemanly way would've been to walk by your side, but trailing you from behind... what a view."

My eyes widen.

"I nearly tripped over my feet, I was so mesmerized by the fabric of your dress caressing your ass cheeks with each step."

Holy hell!

My face bursts into flames as if the heat of a thousand suns is burning me up; my neck, chest, legs, and every other exposed part of my body. Even the parts that aren't exposed feel like a brush fire just blazed through.

"Watching you move was a feast for the eyes." He places both hands in front of his crotch. I'm sure my complexion goes from pinkish-red lobster to fire-engine red. "And other parts."

Did he just shield his cock?!

My heart gallops in my chest.

No fucking way.

I might never wear a body shaper for the rest of my life.

Arya was onto something. Not that I'd ever fess up because I'll never hear the end of it.

The elevator door opens and Hudson invites me in first.

What I read in his eyes thrills me and scares me in equal measure.

It's just a tour and a little conversation.

Right before the elevator door closes, a crowd of people gets in, forcing us to huddle close. A wave of heat ripples through me, as the warmth emanating from his body seeps into mine. I close my eyes for a beat.

I dreaded tonight, but I must admit, there's something freeing about being an escort, even if it's one who is hired as arm candy. That's the only way I can explain the Angelica that was chatting up a storm to the wife of a CEO of a multibillion-dollar company. I still can't believe something I'm passionate about could help a man as powerful as Hudson Kincaid.

My eyes pop open and I look up.

Sure enough, his eyes are on me.

Not even in my wildest dreams could I ever have imagined a man who looks like that could look at me the way he is right now.

Tonight is a one and done. You can be anyone you want, Angelica.

Chapter 10

Hudson

We ride the last three floors to the forty-first floor in silence. The doors open. I'm just about to invite my date to exit, when I freeze. A group of four men who are also members of the private business club are standing there, evidently waiting for a car.

I gesture Brinley to step out and follow her.

After a round of introductions, greetings, and backslapping, the men are on their way.

"Wow, those are heads of major corporations," Brinley says.

"The VIP Den is where some of the most influential executives in the city strike a deal or two."

"I believe you."

With my hand in hers, we stroll towards the concierge desk. As I scan my membership card, I strike a casual conversation with the guy sitting behind the desk. Without me having to ask, he divulges the information I'm looking for.

It's a quiet night.

Good.

I give Brinley the grand tour before guiding her to a

meeting room that's recently been renovated. Just like she did in every single room, she runs towards the floor-to-ceiling windows, places her fingertips against the glass, and takes in the view of New York at her feet.

Her reaction is unfiltered.

"I've only seen aerial views of New York on the internet, and shows and movies." She turns around. "Since I've never been on a plane before, this is the highest up I've ever been. The view is breathtaking."

"I agree. The view *is* breathtaking. Stunning, even."

She lets out a little laugh. "Like you can see anything standing from way over there."

"I see exactly what I need to see," I set her straight.

Step.

"And I very much like the view."

Step.

"But you're right, Brinley, it would be much better up close and personal."

Step.

"*Very* up close and personal."

One last step and I'm standing in front of her.

I'm unable to keep my gaze from raking over her body, over her sexy dress, over her fantastic tits, over her slender neck, over her gorgeous face, until I lock eyes with her.

She looks up at me, her eyelashes fluttering like crazy.

Her green eyes, wide and innocent are enchanting.

"From this vantage point," I say, "the view is even better." I reach out and trace a finger between her breasts. "What if I told you I'm dying to taste your lips?"

She blinks, shakes her head and places a hand against my chest.

"Should I take that as a no?"

"I just had to make sure I heard you correctly and you were real."

"Baby, I'm as real as whatever's playing between us." I take her free hand into mine and place it over my cock. "And as real as my hard-on."

She lets out a shuddering exhale. "Oh, my God. I can't believe this."

"You better believe it because it's for you." That's the only warning she gets before I crash my lips against hers.

The moment my mouth touches hers it's like something detonates inside me.

Not that the kiss started soft and gentle, but now, my lips become merciless—the result of months of not being with a woman. I grip the back of her head hard, pressing her face to mine. Tilting my hips into her, I rub myself against her, and use my free hand to palm her breasts.

Fuck, these feel amazing.

The mix of abstinence and arousal for this woman coursing through my body is making me eager, impatient, and hasty. As my hunger for her grows, my touch becomes more forceful. Perhaps a little too much.

She groans.

Slowly, oh so slowly, her mouth opens up to me.

Good girl.

I slip my tongue into her mouth, tangling with hers.

I ratchet the kiss to blazing levels.

Her mouth is as greedy as mine.

Her hand travels to the back of my head, fisting my hair.

I fucking devour her.

My hand itches to fuck up her slick hairstyle, but I resist. Barely.

With each tongue stroke, her hips jerk against my body.

Her soft curves under my hands feel like heaven.

I take, and take, and take.

She matches my fervor tongue stroke for tongue stroke.

In a jerking move, I pull away from her.

Huge green eyes stare at me surprised.

"Fuck!" I grab her face in my hands and press my lips against hers like a man possessed.

She throws her arms around my neck, fusing her body against mine.

I swear, this is the most electrifying kiss of my entire life.

When I finally break our kiss, she's panting.

I'm out of breath, but I'm only getting started.

I need more of this woman.

I grasp her chin and lift her head up, forcing her to hold my gaze. I can only assume the intensity I read in her face is reflected on mine. "I'm hard as a fucking rock, and it's taking everything in me not to tackle you right here on the floor. So, we're going to have to compromise."

She furrows her eyebrows.

"I need to taste your lips."

"You just did."

"Your *other* set of lips."

An audible sound drops from her lips.

"It might be asking too much. And it's not the arrangement I have with Todd, but I swear to God, I can't leave here without knowing what you taste like."

She stares at me like a deer caught in headlights.

I lean into her, my mouth flirting with her earlobe. "This can be our little secret." I murmur the proposal low, as if we weren't the only people in this room.

"Yes." One word. Her submission. It comes out so faint, if I wasn't this close, I would've missed it.

I'm so desperate to claim this woman. That one word has the same effect as shooting my veins with a shot of adrenaline.

"Give me your clutch," I say.

She hands it over.

I step over to the long conference table, drop it there, and return to her.

"Turn around."

She hesitates.

After a long beat, she does as she's told.

"Hands on the glass."

She looks over her shoulder, her eyebrows knitted together.

"I don't make a habit of repeating myself."

She obeys.

I wrap my hand around her braid, twisting the long strands of brown hair around my wrist multiple times before pulling.

She hitches a breath.

I lean in and press my cheek against hers. "Let's get one thing straight. We play this game my way or not at all. Got that?"

She nods.

"Words please."

"Got it."

I let go of her hair. "We're on the same page."

"Yes." I wasn't expecting an answer, but it pleases me that she's a quick learner.

I press myself against her back, wedging my cock between her ass cheeks, allowing her to feel what she does to me.

"Oh, God." She gasps. "You're so hard." There's a quiver to her voice. Excitement? Apprehension? A bit of both?

"I already told you. I've been like this since watching you walk in front of me." My eyes bore into hers. "Is this attraction mutual?"

She places her hands on the window and pushes back against me. "You're the most gorgeous man I've ever seen in my life."

"That's a tall order."

"I mean it."

I let out a ragged groan.

My fingers skim the sides of her breasts before cupping and groping them. "Fuck, these are beautiful."

She hitches a breath.

I slide my finger under her bra until my fingertips skate over her nipple. *Fuck.* "I doubt there's a part of you that isn't perfect," I say, pinching her hard peak.

She lets out the tiniest of cries.

I press my lips against the back of her neck.

She tilts her head to the side, leaving her neck exposed. I accept the invitation and trail the side of her neck with slow kisses that become quicker and rougher as my fingers tease her hard nipples with more fervor.

Her hands slide down the glass.

"I want you to keep your hands where they are."

I don't have to repeat myself.

"Fuck, your hard nipples are amazing." I'm overcome by the desire to cover her tits with my cum. To punish her for making me want her this much, I twist her nipples between my fingers eliciting desperate sobs from her.

"Are you dripping wet for me?"

My freehand travels down her soft belly, until I reach the hem of the showstopper she wears so well. I slide my hand under her dress and up between her thighs until my fingers flirt with the crotch of her underwear. In a languorous motion, I trace her bare pussy from clit to hole. "You're drenched."

"I don't think any woman on the planet could resist you."

"Baby, I don't care about all the other women on the planet. I only care about you."

Her head whips to the side.

Even at this angle, I can read the thousands of questions in her eyes.

"I'm not bullshitting you."

She responds with a shy smile.

"Eyes upfront."

She does as she's told, holding my gaze in the reflection in the window.

I grip the seam of her lacy panties. "What is it about you?"

"I—I don't even know how to answer that."

Rip.

Her eyes widen to the size of dinner plates as her mouth drops open.

For a long beat, she's speechless.

"You tore my panties right off me!" she says when she finds her voice.

"How else am I going to be able to taste your lips?"

She opens her mouth to say something. Then closes it. She does that a few times before giving up.

I bring her shredded, wet panties to my nose and inhale her heady scent.

"You're dangerous," she says.

"Everything about you turns me into a fucking animal."

"You're going to make me combust."

"Not before I make you come."

She lets out a shuddering breath.

I tuck her panties in my pants pocket.

Time to play.

I slide my hand under her dress, feeling my way around. "A landing strip… I approve."

She giggles.

I cup her pussy and give it a squeeze.

She gasps.

"Tonight, this pussy belongs to me. And when I make you come, I better hear my name on your lips."

"OhmyGod," she says. "Your touch makes me lose my mind."

"I don't believe in half measures."

I slide a finger between her pussy lips.

A moan pours out of her.

A growl pours out of me.

"Shit," she says.

She turns her head to the side, pressing her cheek against the window as she curves her back and lifts her ass higher.

"What do you want?" My voice is rough.

"More."

"More of what?"

"Your touch."

Satisfaction swells my chest.

"But I am touching you."

"More."

I oblige.

"Your fucking clit is amazing. You're going to come hard for me?"

"God, yes." The words rush from her lips.

"Good girl. You've earned your reward."

I focus on her clit, skating over it in dizzying circles and her moans are divine.

"It's that good?" I ask as I push against her clit, trapping all the blood there.

"Oh, God, Hudson!"

"Think of this as a way of showing my appreciation for what you did for me earlier," I say. "Now, it's your turn to show me appreciation for what my hand is doing to you. Ride my finger, dirty girl."

And she does.

She starts rocking against my finger.

It's slow at first, but in no time, she picks up the pace, her hips swaying faster.

Back and forth.

Back and forth.

She grinds, and grinds, and grinds.

"Good girl. That's it."

"Dear God." Her legs tremble, her hands sliding down the window.

My gaze meets hers in the glass. "What did I tell you?"

She corrects the errors of her way. "It's like I know longer have control of my body."

My lips flirt with her earlobe. "That's because I've taken over the reins. Still, when I give you a command, I expect you to obey."

She nods in a jerky motion.

I rub her clit faster.

Her forehead drops against the window, and she juts her hips back.

I don't even bother taunting her. I give her what she needs, focusing all my attention on her clit.

She's shaking like a leaf now.

"Don't hold back." My hand tightens around her waist, holding her in place. "Take what's yours. Use me for your pleasure." I grind my hard cock against her more forcefully.

The fucker is so hard it could punch through concrete.

Her body starts convulsing, as if an earthquake just hit New York City.

"Oh. Yes. Hudson. God. Jesus—"

Her whole body goes rigid and then, a little helpless cry drops from her lips as she comes undone, shuddering all over my fingers.

She drops her head back against my chest, her eyes

catching my gaze. The veil of desire coating her green eyes is such a turn on.

Fuck.

There's no way of describing the way she comes so beautifully for me.

I bring my fingers, dripping with her pussy juices to my mouth, and lick them clean.

"Jesus!" She closes her eyes.

"No way was I going to waste a drop of your sweet juices."

She lets out a low grunt. "I stand by my word. You, Mr. Kincaid, are a dangerous man."

"If you only knew."

I turn her in my arms, pressing her close to my body.

She gasps.

"God, you're still—"

I don't let her finish her sentence.

I take her mouth in an all-encompassing kiss, leaving her no choice but to taste herself on my tongue.

She grinds herself into the hard bulge in my pants and I let out a loud groan.

I cup her face in my hands, deepening the kiss.

Never in my life have I made it a priority to thoroughly kiss a woman like this.

She slides a hand between us, groping my cock.

"Fuck, you're a hot little thing," I say, breaking the kiss.

Her lips curl up in a hesitant smile. "What about... you?"

That intoxicating shyness, it's such a turn on.

To my surprise, Todd offered to compensate me for tonight. I would've been a fool to argue. I wasn't planning on going all the way when I came up here with Brinley.

Damn.

Using her fake name is annoying the fuck out of me.

I just needed a taste. Not to mention, the VIP Den isn't set up for a night of hard fucking. After a long drought, the beast inside me is raging.

"We've already pushed the envelope quite far, angel."

Her eyes grow as wide as saucers.

From her expression, you'd think I just sprouted a second head.

She had that same look of shock earlier when I was talking about the book she seems to know like the back of her hand, but now, she's even more freaked out.

"What?"

"Nothing," she shakes her head.

I narrow my eyes. "I don't buy it."

"It's just—" She shakes her head again.

"What is it?"

"I didn't expect a nickname from a client."

Ah.

Her other fucking clients.

The reminder has the same effect as snuffing a campfire with a fireman's hose.

I'm an idiot for forgetting who this woman is.

I hired her for three hours.

This isn't a date.

I'm just another John with deep pockets.

She opens her mouth to say something, but her phone rings.

"Err... maybe I should take that. It might be Todd."

My mouth twists.

I step to the side.

"Sorry about the bad timing," she says.

There it is again, that weird anger—a non-familiar corkscrew of jealousy spiraling in me with the same devastating fury as a tornado sweeping across the Jackson Prairie.

She's one of Todd's girls—an escort paid to be with different men.

He's probably calling to line up her next John. Who knows? It could even be for tonight.

You paid for her services for three hours. Not a lifetime.

"You wouldn't want to make Todd wait," I say.

"No."

I extend a hand in an exaggerated way. "Go for it."

She smooths her dress, then brushes a hand over her hair before rushing to her clutch, running on her tiptoes.

The thought of her fucking other men makes me want to commit a murder.

I suppress this irrational rage before I do something I'll regret.

I almost laugh at the absurdity of my train of thought.

Months of abstinence, and I'm losing my goddamn mind over this woman. A stranger.

Chapter 11

Angelica

When I crossed the Queensboro Bridge earlier, I was too preoccupied to soak in the view at night. Now that I'm returning to the apartment, my mind is spinning for another reason.

Hudson Kincaid.

I haven't been able to stop replaying our naughty encounter—from the exhilarating excitement of kissing him and finding out what he tastes like, to what he did to me...

Damn, that man's fingers deserve an award.

Note to self: Apologize to the Eastern European esthetician for calling her every name in the book while she was ripping the hair off my pussy.

It was all in my head, but still.

Todd insists all his girls landscape religiously, so I passed as Arya for the Brazilian wax appointment he had booked for her. When I bother landscaping, I tend to prefer shaving. In my humble opinion, waxing was probably invented by a grooming Nazi without a soul. Every strip of wax ripped, felt like torture.

Turns out, it was a gift. Not sure my hot as hell client would've liked to find Chewbacca hiding in my panties.

It was a mind-blowing night, until it all came to a screeching halt.

When I heard Arya's ringtone, I cursed under my breath.

The sexiest man alive had just made me come so hard, I saw stars, but I had to break the moment. It felt awkward, but I had no choice. I made a promise to my sister. In my world, my word is gold.

Since my twin and I are already walking a tightrope by swapping places, and therefore, lying to her new boss, I didn't want to take any chances. I had to rush to the table where Hudson had dropped my clutch. By the time I fished for my phone, the call had gone to voicemail.

Arya followed up with a text.

Todd was looking for an update.

With quick fingers, I responded to my sister's text. When I was done, I returned my full attention to Hudson, but the hotter than hell man who brought me up to the forty-first floor of the Bymark Hotel to corrupt me was replaced by an aloof and standoffish one. And then, he was walking me to the taxi area.

Crap.

By the time I reach our apartment building, I'm still sulking, mortification still looming over my head. I get a few side glances from other tenants as I ride the elevator to the fourth floor, but I'm too bummed out to care.

When I slide my key into the lock of the corner suite we live in, the door flies open.

"How was it?" Arya fires off her question at me.

"Can I at least come in?" My annoyance is audible.

She frowns. "Your text suggested everything was A-okay. What's up with the attitude?"

"I live in flats. You prefer heels. My feet are killing me." It's a partial lie. There's a lot more to my pissy mood, but I'm not willing to go down that road. Not yet.

"Sorry! Come in." She's practically vibrating with excitement. "Why don't you go change and tell me all about it." I open my mouth to tell her I'm pooped and suggest we wait until tomorrow, but she reads me. "You *have* to give me the play-by-play just in case Todd calls or texts."

I let out a heavy sigh.

I pop into my bedroom to change into my nightgown before joining my sister on the couch. She's already in her pyjamas—shorts and a t-shirt. I'm sure if I take the time to remove my makeup, she'll have a shit fit. Might as well get it out of the way now.

She folds her legs underneath her, shimmying her ass on the cushion until she's comfortable. She taps the one next to her. "Sit!" I plop down next to her. "So?"

"The Bymark Hotel is stunning and so well decorated—"

"Seriously?" She purses her lips. "*Our* first gig as an escort, and you're harping on about the décor? What about the client? What was he like? Tall? Short? A bore? Did you meet anyone rich and famous? Details. I want details."

"It goes without saying, most people at the event were rich or ultra-rich."

She nods.

"As for the client, there was nothing boring about him. He was decisively more handsome than the plastic surgeon. And a lot younger."

"Ooooh, a hot, rich top gun. Todd texted me a photo in the end, but glad to hear *our* first client is as sexy in person."

"I'm guessing he's in his late twenties."

"What else? Tell me more about the event?"

I give her the highlights.

She oohs and aahs.

I bypass how the CEO's wife and I geeked out over our common adoration of a fantasy romance I know nearly by heart. My sister prefers TV series and movies to books, even if she can't sit still long enough to finish a movie. Of all the fantasy romance books published, Isobel Wolfe has a fixation on *The Court Games*. Mind-blowing. I don't tell Arya about the euphoric feeling of being a powerful man's partner in crime, either. Of course, I don't touch on how ecstatic I was by Hudson's praise. Lil' ol' me helped a mogul strike a deal. Wow. I still can't get over it.

"That was the easiest and most lucrative three hours work ever," she says. "And to think, you didn't even have to spread your legs, get on all fours, or give anyone a blowjob. Bonus, you didn't even have to kiss a frog."

"No, but a prince kissed me—"

"A goodnight kiss? That's so sweet and very gentlemanly—"

"You didn't let me finish." I angle my body so I'm facing her. "Hudson kissed me so thoroughly, my entire body sizzled like I'd just stuck my finger into a light socket."

My sister's green eyes widen and her jaw drops in shock.

I keep talking. "Granted, I haven't kissed that many men, but I doubt any man on the planet can top tonight's blazing kiss." I shake my head as a flashback hits me. "It was so fiery, I thought I was going to run out of air."

Arya stares at me, dumbfounded.

I don't blame her. I'm still under Hudson's spell.

I know I was supposed to keep this naughty encounter a secret, but if I don't tell someone, I'm going to burst. Not to mention, technically, Arya was supposed to be his date—

Shit.

My twin was supposed to be on the receiving end of that toe-curling kiss, not me.

Jealousy slithers in my belly at the thought.

Arya has always been the life of the party. I tend to watch from the sidelines as my twin bewitches harems of men, wrapping the most gorgeous guys around her pinky finger with just a dazzling smile. It's been like that since we were teenagers. Even though we have the exact same face, when we're in a room together, my sister shines, while I tend to get cast away in the shadows. Had it been the two of us out tonight, Hudson would've probably never noticed me—

What the hell is wrong with me?

Hudson isn't a potential boyfriend.

He's a client who paid for me to hang from his arm.

End of story.

"Holy. Shit." My sister brings me back to the moment.

I keep pouring out my soul. "He also gave me a tour of a private business club he's a member of, which is located on the forty-first floor of the hotel, where he proceeded to rock my world by making me come with his fingers."

Arya's head rears back. What am I talking about? Her whole body jerks.

With exaggerated white eyes that resemble a cartoon character's bewildered expression.

She shrieks. "What?"

"I swear to God, it was the most electrifying kiss—and experience—of my entire life. My body was convulsing uncontrollably from waves of post-climatic pleasure."

Blink.

Blink.

Blink.

"I have no idea how it went from me admiring New York at

my feet from the forty-first floor of a chichi New York City hotel to a starring role in *Fifty Shades of Grey 2.0*."

"Did Hudson want to fuck you?"

My sister, always keeping what's important top of mind.

My cheeks burst into flames.

"Because that's extra." She taps her chin with her finger. "I wonder if there's a premium when you're a—"

"I'm *not* an escort, you are. And as we both agreed, this is a temporary gig for you."

"Yeah, yeah, yeah." She brushes me off. "Let's talk about what's really important here."

"Because everything I've said up to now isn't?"

"It is, but there's something quite monumental here."

"What's that?"

"Escorts are paid to be at the client's beck and call—even if you're only arm candy. And if pleasure is involved, it's usually *one way*. Todd—"

I grip her arm, digging my fingers into her flesh.

"Ouch!"

"Sorry. I didn't mean to hurt you." I let go of her arm. "You can't tell Todd."

She rubs the sore spot. "Jesus, for someone who just got the orgasm of her life, you'd think you would be a lot mellower."

I roll my eyes. "I don't want Hudson to get in trouble. We were swept away... and then everything fizzled because I got freaked out."

"What do you mean?"

I exhale a long sigh, as if I'm carrying the weight of the world on my shoulders. It surely feels like that right now.

"Talk to me."

"He used *angel* as a nickname and I freaked the hell out. For a second, I thought I had blown my cover. And then you called, and it killed the mood."

"I agree that was freaky and a little too close to home."

"When I returned my attention to him, he was no longer the same man."

"Huh?"

"You should've seen the look on his face. He was leveling me with an ice-cold stare. Everything suggested he was pissed off. It was so intimidating. When he suggested we cut the evening short, his tone was resolute. I couldn't muster up the courage to ask him for the panties he ripped off my body. Not that they'd be of any use since they were ruined."

"Are you shitting me right now?!"

I shake my head. "I'm an editor. Not an author. There's no way I would be able to come up with an over the top story like that. In my defense, God was in a good mood when he created Hudson Kincaid." I cross my arms over my chest. "Don't even get me started on the sexy Texan drawl."

Why is my heart squeezing so painfully?

"Jesus, Ange this is the kind of thing fairytales are made of—a working girl falling for her client."

"Newsflash! You and I"—I wave a finger between us—"are living a nightmare. That's why I had to play *Pretty Woman* tonight. Not because I wanted to."

She claps. "What a perfect analogy!"

"Huh? What are you talking about?"

Her lips split in a wide grin. She grabs my hands into hers. "I wanted to know your side of the story first—"

"Oh, no. Did Hudson complain to Todd? Did I get you—us—in trouble? We're not going to get paid? I screwed up by allowing an illegally gorgeous man to finger-fuck me? I threw the whole pay to play commandment out the window. Shit. Shit. Shit."

"Calm down!"

"I am so, so sorry. You told me exactly how to behave, but

I've never been around a man like Hudson. You should've seen the way he was looking at me. No other man has ever looked at me that way. He even loves my jiggly butt."

"Thank God and hallelujah the man loves your jiggly butt. Your body shaper would've been a mood killer."

"I'm not going to argue with that."

"Say it." She motions with her fingers.

"Say, what?"

"I was right."

"Stop acting like a child!"

She turns her head to the side and places two fingers near her ear, tilting her head slightly.

"Fine." I grumble. "You were right."

"Well, your sexy, jiggly butt worked overtime tonight."

"What is that supposed to mean?"

"We got paid twice tonight."

"Huh?"

"Mr. Kincaid will pay you for tonight."

"But I thought Todd was footing the bill."

"He is. Hence, why I said, we got paid twice tonight."

"Seriously?"

She nods.

"That's amazing!"

"But there's more!"

"More money?"

"Todd texted to let me know tomorrow I'll also receive a big fat bonus compliments of the client. Apparently, Mr. Kincaid was *extremely* pleased with how the evening unfolded."

I'm incredulous. "Really?"

She nods, a knowing smile twisting her lips. "There's more."

"Even more money?"

"You could say that." Her grin takes over her face. "Mr.

Kincaid booked us—you, really, because my va-jay-jay is still smelling funky—for..."—she does a drum roll movement with her hands—"the entire week!"

"What?!"

"Not a word of a lie. He's booked you for the next seven days *and* he'll head to Todd's office tomorrow to pay for the week in advance. Todd says it's rare for arm candy girls to get booked by the same clients, let alone back-to-back, let alone with advanced payment in full. So, this is kind of monumental for his agency. Kudos to you, sis!"

I'm dead.

Chapter 12

Angelica

Hudson's gorgeous face flashing behind my closed lids awakes me from a restless sleep.

With a jolt, my eyes fly open.

As if my sheets were engulfed in flames, I fling them off my body before sitting upright.

Holy shit.

The dream was so vivid.

"You're going to come hard for me, angel."

God, the man has such a hold on me.

I check the time on the nightstand.

Two in the morning?!

I'm going to feel like crap if I don't get some rest.

I lie back in bed, flipping to the side before closing my eyes.

With each deep breath, I coax myself to fall back asleep.

My body betrays me by remaining wide awake.

Arousal courses through me, firing up every cell in my body.

He's not even in the room, yet I'm as turned on as if he were lying in bed with me.

I have to do something with myself before I combust.

I bypass the idea of getting out of bed and fishing through my drawer for a toy. Instead, I turn on my back, lift my nightgown, and sink two fingers into my wet and aching pussy. Breaking from convention, I'm pantie-less. I blame Hudson Kincaid for turning a good girl, bad.

I'm so wet, it's ridiculous.

With my eyelids closed tight, I try to remember how Hudson touched me.

It's not the same, but that doesn't prevent me from pleasuring myself, as I chase after my orgasm.

I work my pussy, remembering the feel of Hudson's erection pressing against my ass, imagining that my wandering fingers are his own.

In record time, the familiar build up bubbles at my core.

Oh God.

With my clit pinched between my fingers, and two fingers fucking me, while thinking of the drop-dead gorgeous man with the Matthew McConaughey drawl and Paul Newman blue eyes, I come all over my hand.

I come so hard, I have to bite my lower lip to stifle a cry.

Holy hell.

For a few long minutes, I bask in a sublime post-orgasm glow.

Even though my body is humming with satisfaction, my climax was nowhere near as earth-shattering as the one Hudson gave me, but it was toe-curling enough to make me lose my mind.

I don't know what to expect tomorrow with Hudson, but I pray it's a repeat of last night.

Damn.

I just might be addicted to my first client.

Chapter 13

Angelica

I'm usually an early riser, and my internal body clock never fails me.

That's until this morning.

I was lost to sleep.

Concerned, Arya woke me at nine o'clock as she was trailing back to her bedroom, still half asleep, and found me passed out in bed like a starfish. She had to shake me hard to rouse me.

When she did and told me what time it was, I freaked the hell out.

I blame Hudson for the best sleep of my life.

After my middle of the night blissful orgasm, I laid in the dark for what seemed like an eternity, reliving every minute of my naughty encounter. Eventually, everything faded to black. I guess too many powerful orgasms in a row knocked me out dead.

Even though I'm fully rested, I'm stressed out like crazy.

I had planned on knocking off five thousand words of a manuscript I'm editing before heading out to lunch. I barely had time to catch up on emails before I had to jump into the shower, get dressed, and make my way to Manhattan. I can spend weeks without coming into the city, and now I'm here two days in a row. The only difference is today, I'm no longer playing Cinderella. No prepaid taxi rides. I had to take the subway like the broke girl I am.

When I reach my stop, I rush out of the subway.

After double checking the address where I'm supposed to have lunch, I race to my appointment, weaving through crowds of hurried New Yorkers so I don't arrive late. Given who I'm meeting and the posh hotel for our lunch date, I had to up my fashion game.

Translation: I had to spend extra time on makeup, hair, and wardrobe.

So now, I'm really cutting it short. By the time I reach the Pompadour Hotel, I'm out of breath and I'm hot.

You really need to start exercising.

But if you do, you'll lose your jiggly butt.

I grin like a loon as the angel and demon sitting on each of my shoulders debate.

Given how broke I am, a gym membership isn't a consideration.

No danger my jiggly butt will firm up anytime soon.

And just like that, I'm thinking of Hudson again.

I really have to stop doing that.

I cannot allow him to take over my thoughts.

There's no future for us. Not only because he's a client, but because we're from totally opposite sides of the track. It was a lucky coincidence I was able to help with the Wolfes, but I have nothing to offer a billionaire.

I search the lobby and find a spot where I park myself to swap shoes.

I admire women who can navigate through New York's

subway system in heels, I'm not one of them. Once I put my budget friendly heels on, I check my reflection in the mirror one last time, before dashing off towards the restaurant.

As I'm checking in with the maître d'hôtel, my phone chimes.

Shit.

I politely excuse myself before checking the message.

Grace: Look up. I'm here!

I do.

A tall brunette standing in the middle of the chic restaurant is waving at me like a crazy person, a ridiculous grin stretching her lips.

I smile wide and respond with a more contained wave.

The maître d' looks over his shoulder, before returning his gaze to me.

Without further preamble, he invites me in.

After thanking him, I rush to Grace's table.

She steps towards me and takes me in a bear hug, swaying me side to side.

This woman gives the best hugs.

"You look amazing," she says, breaking our embrace.

"Thank you."

"Seriously, Angelica, had you not told me you were a brunette like *moi*, I would never have recognized you. What brought on the change?" I'm just about to answer, but she keeps talking. "Honey, if I had your beautiful, natural blonde hair, never—I mean, never—in a million years, would I have dyed my golden locks. Well, unless a lot of money was involved." She explodes in laughter.

I don't.

She has no idea how she hit the nail square on the head.

"Change is good," I say with a smile.

"Great attitude," she says. "I love your dress, by the way."

I selected a pink floral dress I scored on a discount rack at a discount store.

Yup, I'm that broke.

"Thank you. You look pretty chic yourself."

"Sit," she says.

I take a seat.

She circles the table and sits across from me, that ridiculous grin still plastered on her face.

Her elation is contagious.

Thirty-one-year-old Grace Halcyon, who writes under the pen name Melanie Heywood, is a successful self-published author. You'd never know a few years ago she was on the verge of giving up on her dream and she was as flat broke as I was.

Her life has dramatically changed.

Mine has as well, but for the worse.

"I got so lost in my current story, I didn't have time for breakfast. I'm starved," Grace says. "Let's order."

"I'm famished as well."

She grabs a menu and points a manicured finger to an item. "Even though I'm not a vegetarian, the special of the day—Italian Fix—is calling out my name."

One glance at the ingredients and my mouth waters.

I meet her brown eyes. "Sold! I'll have the same."

"You're sure?"

"Yes!"

She narrows her eyes at me. "You're not just saying that because lunch is on me?"

That's partially it.

I'm not one to make a fuss in general, but when someone

else is paying for a meal at an upscale restaurant I'm too broke to even walk by, I won't go all diva on them. "Are you kidding me? Sundried tomatoes, artichokes, sweet roasted peppers, arugula, and melted sharp provolone on ciabatta bread? You don't need to twist my arm."

She nods, seemingly satisfied. "A side of frites and sweet potato fries?"

Thank you, Heavenly Father, for this woman who will allow me to indulge in frites drizzled with truffle oil.

"You're speaking my language," I say.

She laughs.

She catches the attention of a waiter who rushes to our table.

"How's the hubby?" I ask, once the waiter finishes taking our order and scurries off.

"Dreamy. Loving. Perfect. One year later, and we're still in the honeymoon phase." She cups her mouth with her hands. "We can't keep our hands off each other. It's better than any romance book I've ever written or read."

Lucky bitch.

If I didn't like her this much and if she wasn't such an incredible human being, I'd hate her.

She reaches out for my hands. "I know I sound like a broken record, but without you, *The Court Games* would never have seen the light of day, and I sure as hell would never afford to be able to treat you to lunch at this five-star eatery."

"I just gave you a push in the right direction."

It took a little convincing, but Grace took my advice, and split her epic story into four parts. I also convinced her to self-publish instead of waiting for someone to validate her work.

The stars were aligned for Grace Halcyon.

A couple months after she published the second part of her series, an influential book blogger, who has an eye-popping following on all social media platforms, gave her a glowing review that changed the course of her life. All four books of *The Court Games* series hit the New York Times Bestseller's list and it now boasts over seventy thousand reviews for each book.

When she made it big, she made do on her IOU in spades. That's the only reason Arya and I are aren't homeless after being scammed. Thanks to Grace's generosity, I was able to stash away four months' worth of rent. Sadly, that money is gone.

She shakes her head. "No, you changed my life." I wish I had that kind of super power to change mine and my sister's. "Not only my career, but thanks to you, I met the man who stole my heart."

At least one of us has a dream life.

"I'm humbled to have played a small part in your happy ever after."

"More like a huge part," she says with a grin.

I smile.

It didn't take long for a top book publicist to contact Grace after she exploded all over the Internet. She was doing a book signing at a local independently owned bookstore, when she met the love of her life. Kevin Halcyon—a thirty-four-year-old former Wall Street broker turned tattooed barber—had accompanied his niece to a book signing, when their eyes locked. He lingered around, and after the book signing, he invited her out for dessert. The rest is history.

Our waiter returns, her arms weighed down with plates piled high with yummy food.

My mouth waters, and my stomach does a happy dance. I'm so used to rationing portions, this is such a treat.

"*Bon appétit!*" Grace says.

"*Bon appétit!*"

When I bite into the sandwich, I moan.

"I know, right?" Grace says around a mouth full of food. "Amazing!"

For a few long minutes, we're too busy devouring our delicious sandwiches to talk. When I finish the last bite of the first half of my scrumptious sandwich, I'm stuffed. My belly is so content right now.

"I had a *very* important late breakfast meeting," she says, popping a *frite* in her mouth after dipping it in aioli.

I cock an eyebrow. "Anything you can share?"

She leans into the table.

Her eyes shift left, then right, before fixing onto mine.

"You have to keep this a secret."

"Oooohhhh! It sounds like it's big news."

"It is," she says.

"You'll never guess who I met this morning."

"Probably not."

"You'll never guess who's a huge fan of *The Court Games*."

I actually know someone who—

No way.

"Who?" I ask.

"UTV.com!" My jaw drops. "It's still preliminary talks, but I met with the CEO's wife who brokers in this type of deal—by the way, she's the most adorable person on the face of the planet. So approachable." *Yes, she is.* "In any case, she'd love to explore the possibility of adapting the series for the small screen."

"Oh. My. God."

"I know. I called Kevin to share the good news, but he thought I was pulling his leg. When I was finally able to convince him I wasn't joking, he freaked out."

When Isobel Wolfe started gushing all over *The Court Games*, it took everything in me not to start jumping up and down like an excited kid. I was already counting the hours to today's lunch so I could share the mind-blowing news with Grace. Now I know why Isobel was so passionate about the book. I'm just about to tell Grace about last night's event, but it hits me. I'd have to explain why I was in the same room as UTV's CEO and his wife.

Nope. Not going there.

"That's insane, Grace."

"It's totally surreal," she says. "We can't get too excited, because I haven't signed a contract yet—"

"If they weren't serious, they wouldn't have approached you."

She nods. "That's what I keep telling myself. In any case, Kevin landed not long ago. He's just back from a three-day barbers' convention in Orlando. His staff is manning the shop, so instead of heading there straight from the airport, he's going to swing by here. I hope that's okay?"

"Absolutely. The more the merrier!"

"You're such a trooper. I miss Kevin so much. And he doesn't want to wait until tonight to congratulate me. He says he needs a little sugar so he can make it through the day. I'm the sugar." She giggles.

Like I said, lucky bitch.

"Oh, I forgot to tell you." She lifts a hand up. "Isobel met one of my cheerleaders at her launch party last night." She places both hands against her heart. "God, I love my readers. Apparently, Isobel and this Good Samaritan bonded over my book and couldn't shut up about it. Can you imagine?"

I'm dying to punch my arm in the air and shout, *It's me! I'm the Good Samaritan!* But I don't. "Of course, you have thousands of loyal fans who gladly gobble up every word you write."

She responds with a one-shoulder shrug. "Yeah, I'm blessed."

"That, and you're a wildly talented author. That story needed to be told."

She responds with a warm smile.

She's just about to say something, but her mouth hangs open, her eyes wide as her gaze travels over my head. "Holy hotness."

I don't have a chance to turn around to see what—or who—captured Grace's attention.

"I'm sorry to disturb you, but I believe I know your lunch date," a deep, smokey voice with a sexy ass Texan drawl says.

My head whips around.

The vision of Hudson standing there hits me with the force of a cannon blast, nearly knocking me off my chair. My heart starts beating in erratic staccato thumps, bringing the clamoring around us to a deafening silence.

No, no, no.

This can't be happening.

God, how can you do this to me?

The man who brought me unbridled pleasure last night places a strong hand on my shoulder.

"I didn't expect to see you this soon," he says.

Neither did I.

Slowly, I turn around on my seat to face him.

I'm temporary blinded by his gorgeousness, but remember my precarious situation.

Forcing a tight smile, I say, "Oh, hi. Hello there."

His gaze travels to Grace, then back to me.

I'm so freaked out right now, I'm tongue-tied.

My two worlds are colliding without my permission.

This could turn into a spectacular train wreck.

"I'm Hudson Kincaid." He extends a hand to my lunch companion.

"Pleased to meet you, Mr. Kincaid. I'm Grace Halcyon."

"Pleased to meet you, Grace."

They shake hands, deepening my mortification.

"You must be one of her lucky clients," Grace says from over my shoulder.

I turn on my seat, reach out for some of the sweet potato fries, grab a handful, and stuff them in my mouth.

I feel Hudson's gaze burning a hole in the top of my head. I chew with more gusto.

"Yes... I am." This man exudes extreme confidence, but there's a touch of uncertainty in his tone.

Yeah, this is quickly becoming a cluster fuck.

"So am I!" Grace says. "She's been my go-to person for two and a half years."

"Really?" The shock in Hudson's voice is unmistakable.

Dear God, the man thinks I'm an escort who swings both ways.

The onset of a painful migraine starts throbbing at my temple.

"Really." Grace is oblivious to what she's agreeing to. "Isn't she the best?"

My eyes scour the distance, searching for an exit.

If I bolt out of here like an Olympic sprinter, maybe I can still save face.

"I agree," Hudson says, "she's pretty amazing." He tightens his grip around my shoulder.

I wince internally. Not from pain, but from the absurdity that is my life.

"You'll find professionals who offer cheaper rates, but you'll never—*and I mean, never*—find anyone who has so much dedication to her vocation."

"Is that so?" Hudson asks.

"I can guarantee it!"

It would be easier for me to march to the kitchen and dunk

my head in the same oil the kitchen staff used to cook the fries than endure this uncomfortable situation that's quickly on its way to becoming very humiliating.

"I'll be using her services for as long as I—" The expression on Grace's face changes, and the next thing I know, she shoots to her feet. "I'm sorry," she says, her voice giddy. "It's my husband. I'll be right back."

With that, she dashes off.

I close my eyes, praying to God and all the saints up above that they might grant me one wish.

Please make Hudson Kincaid disappear.

Please, please, please.

"Pretend as much as you want, but I'm still standing here," he says.

I knew all this bullshit about visualization was crap.

He taps my shoulder.

I refuse to face reality.

That doesn't prevent him from forging ahead. "It seems there's *a lot* I didn't know about you, angel."

At least he didn't call me Brinley.

Slowly, I open my eyes and look up at him.

"Hey, you," he says.

I lose my ability to speak.

Under the lights of the lounge, the ones at the bar room, and the city lights shining through the window on the forty-first floor, it was impossible to appreciate this man's pantie-melting blue eyes.

"Hudson—"

"We're back!" Grace interrupts me midsentence. She's holding her husband like a koala bear hugs a tree. "This tall, strapping, blond is Kevin. My hubby," she says. "Babe, this is Hudson Kincaid. We share the same secret weapon." She gives me an exaggerated wink.

The two men shake hands and exchange polite greetings.

Despite the AC, I'm sweating bullets.

This is the point where my life could unravel at the same speed as a cat claws its way through a roll of toilet paper.

"How's life treating you these days, An—"

"Good. Great. Fantastic. Couldn't be better. Life is a cabaret." I blabber on, interrupting Kevin before he blurts out my real name. "And you?" I'm sure I must sound like a complete idiot.

He looks at his wife with adoration shining bright from his hazel-brown eyes and says, "Now that I'm back near my little honey, life is pretty damn sweet."

"Aww... hot stuff," Grace coos. Her eyes shift from her husband to Hudson, then me. "Not to be rude," Grace says, "but we have to dash."

"What happened?" I ask.

"Nothing." She looks at her husband and they do lovey-dovey eyes at each other. She returns her attention to me. "The hubby and I are heading upstairs." She leans forward. "He was able to snag a cancellation on his way from the airport." Another exaggerated wink. "We're going to hang out in a room for a few hours."

Translation: They're going to fuck like rabbits.

"We probably won't go back to Bushwick until much, much later. No rush to go back to Brooklyn."

"I see," I say.

"Anyhoo, the bill is paid, and I kept the tab running just in case you and Mr. Kincaid want to have dessert and coffee, or a little *vino*." More exaggerated winking. "Whatever you fancy, it's on me!" She cups her mouth. "He's so hot!" At least she mouths her words.

Kill me now, God.

"Thank you," Hudson says.

"All right now, have fun you two," Grace says.

"See you," Kevin says with a wave.

Hudson and me wave back.

And they're off.

"Let's skip dessert. I'd like to talk," Hudson says.

"I really had my heart set on a big piece of chocolate cake." If there's ever been a time where I needed comfort food, it's now.

"Brinley, or whatever your name is, that wasn't a suggestion."

Chapter 14

Hudson

I always look forward to lunch with my fellow VIP Den members and buddies—Max Keller, and his cousins Xavier and Zane Keller. As we were engaged in an animated conversation over espressos at the tail end of our meal, I did a double take. I couldn't believe my eyes when the sexy, curvy brunette who came all over my fingers last night sashayed into the restaurant.

The Kellers went back to their office.

I stayed back.

Even though I've booked her for tonight, I wanted to stop by her table. I'm not sure what I was expecting, but what her client Grace insinuated nearly knocked me off my feet. I thought Brinley gave off an air of innocence, when in reality, it's a well-practiced act.

With my hand resting on the small of her back, I guide her further inside the hotel. I try my luck with a few doors in the lobby, but I strike out. Frustrated, I drag her towards the gardens. Since there's an army of travelers, I have to weave through bodies.

"You're walking too fast."

She has the audacity to complain.

"You have a lot of explaining to do."

She curses under her breath.

Too bad, cupcake.

We're just about to cross the threshold to the gardens when I notice a door that's ajar.

Bingo!

I poke my head inside to get the lay of the land.

It's a linen closet. It'll do.

I look over my shoulder. "Get inside."

She has the good sense not to argue.

I follow after her.

I turn on the lights and survey our surroundings.

It's a crammed space, but it offers privacy.

To be on the safe side, I lock the door behind me.

I turn around and level Brinley with a long, hard stare.

She dances from one foot to the other under my scrutiny.

"That was quite the five-star review from your client," I say.

She averts her gaze.

"You must be really tight with her and her husband to have lunch together. Is he the one who usually hires you, or is it her?" There's a sharp edge to my voice I don't bother softening.

"It's not what you think."

"She couldn't stop singing your praises. It's *exactly* what I think."

"It's not."

"Why don't you enlighten me?"

She lifts a defiant chin. "I don't have to tell you anything."

I study her for a long beat.

Her warrior princess stance hasn't changed.

"You're right." I nod. "If a client wants to hire you for a

threesome with his wife, that's none of my business. There's nothing wrong with kinks among consenting adults."

"I've never had sex with Grace."

"She prefers watching while her husband fucks you?" I'm fully aware I'm completely out of line. I have no business claiming her time unless I'm paying for it. Yet, I can't help this out-of-control Neanderthal raging inside me.

"I've never slept with Kevin, either."

"He hires you to watch *them* fuck?"

She shakes her head. "No."

What kind of kink are these two into?

"They hire you so they can watch you fuck yourself with your fingers, toys, or edgier things like a cucumber or a Coke can? Unless Kevin prefers fisting you?"

She looks at me like I've lost my goddamn mind. "You're way off."

"Then, stop beating around the fucking bush! Spit it out!"

She flinches.

"I've never done any of the... things you suggested. And I've never slept with Grace or Kevin. In fact, I've never had sex. Ever."

"What?" *Did I hear her right?*

"I'm a virgin."

My eyebrows lift high. "You're a virgin?"

"It wasn't my intention to divulge that much about me, but you're looking at me like I'm the bad guy."

"You're starting to look like a really shady character," I say. "Circling back to what you just said. You're a virgin escort?!"

"I'm a virgin, but I'm *not* an escort."

"What the hell are you talking about?"

"I'm not an escort."

"You don't work for Todd?"

She shakes her head.

I rub my face with one hand in frustration. "I'm confused as hell. I hired your services through Todd. What are you saying? You're an imposter?"

She pinches the bridge of her nose and rubs the area there for a few long beats.

"I'm waiting," I say.

"This is awkward—"

"I don't take kindly to people who try to con me. The sooner you start talking, the less awkward it will be for both of us."

Her lips pinch together in a thin line.

"Start talkin', sweetheart, or else I'll be callin' Todd real quick." My Texan accent is pronounced.

She hesitates.

"Maybe it'll be faster if I call the police, then you won't have a choice but to reveal your real identity and come clean about what kind of trickery you're up to."

Her hands fly in the air, waving in a pleading manner. "Please. Don't." The words come rushing out of her mouth.

I cross my arms over my chest. "I'm listening."

"My—"

"Before you say anything, what's your name? Your *real* name."

She pulls her teeth between her lips and stares up at me from under her long lashes. Even through my haze of confusion over the real identity of this woman and her possible deception, my cock goes hard as fucking steel.

"My name is Angelica McQuinley."

"Angelica—" It hits me all at once. "That explains last night's weird reaction to your nickname."

She responds with a small nod.

"How come you were my date last night, Angelica McQuinley, if you aren't even an escort?"

"My identical twin sister was supposed to be your date last night." My jaw drops. "She's the one who works for Todd."

Well, hell.

"Why did you swap places with your sister if you're not on Todd's payroll?"

"It's a long story—"

"Aren't they always?"

"We weren't trying to trick or dupe anyone. It's just... we desperately needed the money. My sister, Arya, wasn't feeling well... so she begged me to swap places with her. You're her first client, by the way. Since you were hiring her as arm candy, we figured we could pull it off."

I nod slowly.

"What brought on your financial difficulties?"

"I'd rather not talk about it."

I don't push.

Now that my anger has ebbed, I can take her in.

My eyes rake down the length of her body.

Last night, she looked like a glamorous starlet.

Even though she isn't dressed to walk the red carpet, she still radiates.

Damn her for having a perfect body. It's like God himself designed her just for me—curvy, short, with long hair to her round, supple butt.

She's gone easy on the makeup, which only showcases her beautiful features.

Unlike yesterday, her long hair cascades over her shoulders.

I continue my shameless inspection.

Not that she was an Amazonian last night, but in her more sensible heels, she's tiny. Barefoot, she can't be more than five-two. Quite the height difference compared to my six-feet-three-inch frame.

My gaze travels to her face.

Apologetic green eyes stare back at me.

"You're a virgin, Angelica?" I ask again because I can't believe my ears.

Her name on my lips tastes as sweet as honey.

"Yes," she says before lowering her gaze to the floor.

My cock is throbbing with the need to be the first to fuck her virgin pussy. The caveman inside me wants to claim her right here and ruin her for all others. That part that I've been forced to suppress for the last year and a half. That same part that had me twisted inside, so jealous and possessive, I had to book her for the entire week.

I close the space between us.

Her eyes remain downcast.

I brush a strand of hair behind her ear. "From what I hear, Todd is thorough in his vetting process, but it's not like he's the Secret Service or the CIA," I say, "What if you'd ended up with an asshole?" Or worse, a predator?

Her eyes widen in surprise.

"It never crossed your mind, angel?"

Her gaze drops again.

Looking at me from under her long lashes in a way that's so fucking debilitating to my ability not to want to keep her locked up in my home all to myself, she says with a one-shoulder shrug, "Desperate times call for desperate measures."

Chapter 15

Angelica

My best friend Sadie is doing a stellar impersonation of the shocked emoji—the one with the mouth gaping open–on our video chat.

I get it.

First, she couldn't believe her eyes when my face popped on her screen and I was no longer a blonde. Then, I word vomited my misadventures, sharing every detail since my sister announced she was moonlighting as a high-end escort and the reason that pushed her to consider the unthinkable.

"You asked what I was up to."

"I thought you were going to bitch about a manuscript that was kicking your butt or even about a loser Arya was seeing," Sadie says. "What you just shared, is so out of character."

"Of course it is. I swapped places with Arya. Only my twin would think becoming *Pretty Woman* would be her ticket out of the colossal mess we're already in."

"How that girl always manages to get herself into trouble is beyond me."

"And the irony of it all is, I always end up having to clean up her mess."

"It shouldn't be like that." Outrage shines in Sadie's brown eyes.

"That ship has long sailed. It is what it is, and I have to make the best of it. As much as I hate siding with Arya, seven-hundred-and-fifty-dollars per hour to be a rich guy's arm candy is the kind of work a lot of women would kill for."

"Had it not been for Arya, you wouldn't be in this predicament."

It's not like I can dispute that.

Sadie Kent and I met in high school. After we graduated from college, we ended up working at the same publishing company. She got laid off a couple months before I did. Just like me, it was a struggle for her to find another job. In an unbelievable twist of fate, her grandmother saw a casting call posted on social media for Hallmark Channel. They were looking for coordinators to join their programming team. It had nothing to do with editing scripts, but it was a foot in the door. We both applied. She got a spot. I didn't. Although it's a one-year contract and she's crumbling under student debt, Sadie jumped in with both feet. Three months ago, she packed and moved to LA. Having Hallmark Channel on your CV opens doors. Because of the time difference, we don't video chat nearly as often as we'd like. Today, I'm lucky. God knows I needed to talk to her.

"How did Arya react to you bumping into Hudson or you going to his place later tonight?" Sadie asks.

"As far as she's concerned, I'm accompanying him to a charity event. She doesn't know Hudson will be sending a couple of his directors as stand-ins instead."

"She's not at the apartment?"

I shake my head. "She texted me to let me know her boss

needed her to cover a shift at the bar. She can't work as arm candy, but she can serve drinks. She was already gone when I got here."

"I'm sure she'll curse that guy who gave her the infection. She's going to be on her feet all evening, dealing with drunk idiots, while a rich guy will wine and dine you."

"We're just going to talk," I say.

Given the deception my sister and I dragged Hudson into—and the fact he's been kind enough not to blow the whistle on our sorry asses with Todd—it's the least I can do. Not to mention, I'd welcome any opportunity to spend time with sexy Hudson Kincaid.

"Like there aren't a million restaurants, bars, lounges, coffee shops, and dessert spots in New York City to talk?" She rolls her eyes. "The fact he wants to do it at his place speaks volumes."

"You're reading too much into this. He's just a client."

She cocks an eyebrow in response. "Maybe after dinner, your sexy, filthy-rich client could punch your V card."

"You're crazy." It has crossed my mind.

"It would be a hell of a lot better than the way your sister lost her virginity."

"Arya's standards are much lower than mine."

Sadie scoffs. "More like nonexistent. She needs to learn to be a lot pickier."

"That'll be the day."

"So, yesterday you were rubbing elbows with the rich and famous. Tonight, you're having dinner at a filthy-rich guy's multi-million-dollar abode, savoring caviar and sipping on Dom Perignon champagne... what's in store for the rest of the week?"

"In all fairness, I'm not privy to the menu. So, it might not be Dom."

"You sound like you're auditioning for a part on the *Real Housewives of New York*," Sadie says with a laugh.

"That's funny." I join her. "To answer your question, I'm not sure what Hudson has planned for the rest of the week, but tomorrow night, he wants me to be his plus one at a black-tie event. Something about an upcoming Broadway show. He was planning on going with one of his directors, but he'd prefer it if I accompany him."

Sadie whistles. "Forget about auditioning. Sounds like you have the part. Hudson Kincaid likes you." She singsongs that like a five-year-old. "Hudson and Angelica sitting in a tree—"

The alarm I set so I'm not late rings, interrupting Sadie's teasing.

"I have to go. I need to get ready."

"For the record, I'm totally picturing that scene in *Pretty Woman* where Vivian's alarm clock rings and she has to get ready for her shift."

"Unlike Vivian, I won't be bussing it, nor will I be walking to Hudson's place. He's sending a chauffeured car to pick me up."

"Ooohhh! Look at you, living *la vida rica*."

"In my defense, I was forced into this life."

~

For someone who never takes taxis, I'm on a roll. Actually, I've upgraded my ride. Hudson called the chauffeured car service he used earlier to drive me back to my apartment in Queens. He had to go back to the office to play CEO, so he took a different car. I had to work for at least a few hours. After getting all dolled up, another car was waiting for me.

So here I am, sitting in the back of a car, on my way to Hudson's place.

My stomach has been a jumble of nerves for the past forty-five minutes. As the driver turns onto a street lined with beautiful homes, well-manicured greenery, and expensive cars, I hitch a breath.

This is how the other half lives!

I peer out the window, my eyes jumping from one luxury home to the next. It's been years since my sister and I played tourist in the Upper West Side with our parents. And even then, we never ventured into these chic neighborhoods. We stayed where the shops were located. We didn't have the money to buy anything in this zip code. Thank God, window shopping was free.

A momentary pang of sadness hits me.

It was the four of us against the world.

Now, it's just the two of us. Arya is the only family I have left.

It crushes my soul to know I can't talk to or see my parents ever again.

The car comes to a stop, cutting short the memories of better days.

"We're here, ma'am," the driver says.

"Thank you."

Just as I'm about to check my phone for Hudson's address, someone taps on the window. I look up, and a gorgeous man with dreamy blue eyes is staring at me.

With a huge grin stretching my lips, I wave with the enthusiasm of a kid seeing Mickey Mouse at Disney World for the first time.

He winks, but he doesn't smile.

Come to think of it, Hudson Kincaid is a very serious man.

Granted, it's only been twenty-four hours since we met. Still, in that time, I haven't seen him crack a smile once.

He opens the door.

"You made it," he says, helping me out.

"I did." I accept his outstretched hand.

With my feet on *terra firma*, I check him out from head to toe.

The man is so handsome, it's unfair to other men on the planet.

The elegant plaid navy suit he was wearing earlier has been replaced with a more casual look—a form-fitted black t-shirt that showcases his wide chest, broad shoulders, and muscular arms, paired with dark wash jeans. He traded his laced-up dress shoes for black loafers. Dressed down like this, he looks like a young, handsome guy instead of the fierce CEO who grilled me earlier in a storage room. Both versions of him could make me lose my mind.

"You like what you see, angel?"

Busted.

I struggle to get my wits back. "Not bad."

He shakes his head.

"You look incredible, as always."

I'm kind of giddy from the compliment. "Thank you."

"The ride was to your satisfaction?"

"Absolutely. Bonus, there was no way I was going to get lost." I laugh at my own joke. "It's not every day I get to ride in the back of a Lincoln. It beats New York taxis and share rides any day of the week."

"Good." Hudson leans into the car to thank the driver before closing the door. "Let's go," he says, lacing his fingers with mine. "I live in that brownstone across the street." He points.

Hudson Kincaid is made of money. "It's beautiful."

"It's comfortable and I'm close to the ground."

"That's funny."

"It wasn't meant as a joke," he sets me straight. *Awkward.*

"I work in a building. One of the stipulations I had when my business partner and I were looking for a space was that we wouldn't be hanging in the sky. I can't handle being too far up from the ground. Although, I could've bought a penthouse or apartment on Billionaires' Row"—*Holy. Shit. Hudson Kincaid is filthy rich*—"I chose not to. I want to open my door, run down a few steps and have my feet firmly planted on concrete."

"I understand. My sister and I live on the fourth floor of a six-story building. I can't imagine living on the sixty-third floor of a building."

"Neither can I. Now that we've established that, let's go inside so we can find out what else we have in common."

Other than the fact we're both humans, speak English, and we're both Americans, I doubt we have anything else in common. Still, I'm his guest, so obviously, I humor him. "That sounds good to me."

When we get inside his home, he locks the door, grabs my hand, and pulls me towards him. "It's good to see you again, angel."

The heat burning in his eyes nearly sets me on fire. It's as all-encompassing as it was yesterday. A world apart from the guarded and intimidating way he was glowering at me in that linen closet when he thought I was an imposter.

Well, technically I am.

"You saw me only a few hours ago," I say.

He leans into me until his lips flirt with my ear, his hot breath pulling goosebumps up the side of my neck. I catch a whiff of cologne. It smells expensive and manly, and appeals to my senses... and lady parts.

"Yeah, but there was so much going on, I couldn't do the one thing I was dying to do when I saw you walking into that restaurant."

"What?" My question comes out breathy.

Swallowing hard, I can't figure out if I'm nervous or aroused.

His eyes flash as his hands grope my ass and pull me closer to him, forcing my body against his hard-on.

Aroused. Definitely aroused.

Hot desire stirs between my legs.

"This," he says.

I pant.

The heat of his body spreads to my core, setting my lady parts ablaze.

The rise and fall of my chest is so exaggerated, I could give any steamy regency romance heroine a run for her money. It's like my hormones are silently screaming out his name.

He runs the tip of his nose up the column of my neck.

I shiver.

It's so sensual.

"And this..." I expect him to say something, but when he doesn't, I pull away from him.

"And what?" I ask, even as his lips touch mine.

The first soft press sends sparks in every direction, like fireworks on the Fourth of July. My legs can barely hold me. His grip tightens on my ass as the kiss deepens. His tongue slips between my lips, engaging in a passionate dance with mine.

Kissing Hudson is about one hundred thousand times better than last night, and our first kiss was pretty unbelievable.

My nipples harden, scratching at the fabric of my bra, pleading to be pressed against his naked chest.

His fingers tangle in my hair, yanking my head back as he deepens the kiss. He devours me with the desperate fervor of a drowning man.

I'm not faring any better. I'm on the verge of losing myself as well.

Our kiss is frenzied, wild, and frantic, our teeth clashing

and our tongues dancing as he explores every part of my mouth. I have to get on my tiptoes to lock my arms around his neck, clinging, and pulling him closer.

I don't ever want to stop kissing this man.

A low moan escapes me, and I feel his smile—the first one since I've known him. Of course, it would be because he's satisfied with himself for making me melt like marshmallows over fire.

He breaks the kiss.

I grunt my dissatisfaction.

My fingers clench with the need to keep him pressed against me.

"First things first," he says, pulling away from me so our eyes meet. His gaze flashes with unmistakable desire. Long, tanned fingers reach out to caress my cheek. "Let me feed you before I feast on you."

Dear God.

Chapter 16

Hudson

As much as I wanted to, it would've been ungentlemanly of me to devour her in the foyer of my house. My head understood that, my other head... not so much. I'm still sporting a hard-on as I give Angelica a tour of my house.

"The renovation of your brownstone is better than anything I've seen online," she says when we reach the threshold of the kitchen.

"I'm extremely happy with the end result, despite the inconvenience," I say.

"It must've been quite distracting living here with a construction crew on site. The noise and dust must've driven you crazy."

"It was an extensive renovation, so I couldn't stay here. I ended up renting the apartment of an actor for the fourteen months it took to complete the work. Since the guy got a role in Los Angeles that was going to keep him on the west coast for a year and a half, on the heel of an acting job in New Zealand, it worked out for both of us."

Her eyes bulge out of her head. "You had to pay rent for fourteen months on top of a mortgage?"

"Yes." I nod. "And let's not forget, the renovation cost me a pretty penny."

"Wow. My sister and I can barely manage rent."

Her cheeks redden, her embarrassment evident.

I'm guessing she didn't mean to say that out loud.

"Let's get started on dinner."

"That sounds good!" Her tone suggests she's happy for the change of subject.

If she only knew I'm giving her a temporary respite.

I don't know what's going on in her life that's put her in such a dire situation, but I'm determined to find out. No way am I allowing her to leave my house without getting to the bottom of it.

"Let's see what's cookin'," I say, cocking my head towards the kitchen.

"You cook?"

"I had to learn how to take care of myself at a young age, so I know the basics. I'm grateful I'm at a stage in my life where I can afford to leave the cooking to professionals. My personal chef has my fridge and freezer well stocked, but I decided to share a little of myself. Tonight, we're going all Texan cookin'!"

"I've never had Texan cuisine before."

"Allow me to introduce you to some of the best food on God's green earth." I extend a hand in a ceremonial gesture.

She places her small hand into mine, and I guide her to the granite island, laden with bags of food.

"Holy Jesus! Did you raid a restaurant?"

"You could say that. I bought a little of everything."

"A little of everything to feed an army."

"I wanted to give you the full home-cooking experience."

"What did you get?" Her excitement is palpable.

"The food was delivered not long ago, so it's still hot." I open the bags. "Cowgirl in the West Village offers an unpretentious menu, but it's pretty good."

"I'm already salivating."

"So am I, but I'm sure for different reasons."

"You said you need to feed me first."

Slap.

"Ouch!" She yelps. "What the hell was that for?" she asks, rubbing the sore spot.

"I want to make sure you keep your attitude in check."

She squints her eyes at me, her lips pursed.

"Back to the food," I say. "For appetizers, I got us a few of my favorites and I also got Fritos pie."

She frowns. "What's that?"

"A bag of Fritos, topped with homemade beef brisket chili, cheddar, onions, sour cream, and jalapeños."

"Seriously?"

"It's a Texan culinary delight. You don't know what you're missing till you try it."

"I'll take your word for it."

"I also got us some rattlesnake bites—"

"Say what?" She looks horrified.

"Don't worry, we aren't going to be eating reptiles. These" —I open the container—"are roasted jalapeños, stuffed with grilled shrimp and wrapped in bacon."

"I think I'm going to eat several rattlesnake bites."

I wink. "That's my girl."

We stare at each other and something passes between us.

It's crazy to say that about someone I've only known for twenty-four hours, but Angelica McQuinley has a hold on me.

Shaking out of the trance, I rattle off the other appetizers I bought. "For the main, I got us some staples—a rack of baby back ribs with all the fixings and chicken fried steak. The name is a little misleading. There's no chicken. Just a pound steak, battered and fried, topped with gravy."

"Oh my God, I'm going to weigh a ton by the time I leave here."

"Suits me just fine, since I love your curves."

"You're such a smooth talker."

"I'm not trying to butter you up, angel. When I caught sight of you yesterday, your slender curves nearly brought me to my knees."

She blushes.

"Here I thought rich men living in New York preferred skinny model types who survive on air and kale juice."

"There are tons of New Yorkers who prefer curves on a woman. Many of my buddies do. Maybe you've been hanging out with the wrong rich men."

She explodes in laughter. "That was just my assumption based on what I've been able to observe. This is the first time I've dipped my toes into the world of the rich and famous."

"Rich? Definitely. Famous? Not so much," I say.

I finish telling her about the menu. "Finally, a Texan meal wouldn't be complete without something sweet. I got us a variety of pies."

She shakes her head.

"You don't like pie?" Maybe I shouldn't have assumed everyone loves pie.

She stares up at me with an expression I can't decipher.

"I can get you any dessert you want. Just name it."

"The dessert selection isn't an issue."

"In that case, what's up with the sad face?"

She places a hand over her heart. "I've been in survival mode since our dad died. Since I'm the oldest—"

"I thought you were a twin."

"I am, but I came into the world first and that kind of set the order of things between my sister and me." She shakes her head again. "All that to say"—her voice chokes up—"I'm not used to someone fussing over lil' ol' me."

"Good thing I don't mind fussing over lil' ol' you."

Chapter 17

Angelica

I lean back against the chair, clench my tummy, drop my head back, and let out a suffering moan.

"You're going to need a construction crane to lift me off this terrace and transport me back to my apartment in Queens."

"What are you saying?"

"I'm so full, I'm about to burst. That second serving of the Big Ol' Mac 'N' Cheese did me in."

"Are you saying you're too full for dessert?"

"Wash your mouth out with soap, mister. There's always room for dessert."

"Glad to hear it. I'll be right back," he says, pushing his chair back and getting up to his feet.

"Let me help. That way, I can exercise a little before dessert." Calories in and calories out.

"You're my guest. Your butt better remain on that chair."

"I insist," I say. "Not to mention, it's hot out here and the mosquitoes seem to like my blood a bit too much."

"Sure is a hot night," he says. "And you're right, the mosquitoes are assholes tonight. Let's go inside, then." He helps me up.

It's a struggle to get out of my chair. You'd think I was eight months pregnant with quintuplets. I wobble behind him all the way to the kitchen.

"Do you want coffee or a shot of whiskey with dessert?"

"I can't handle the hard stuff."

"What about espresso with a shot of Grand Marnier, topped with whipped cream? It's the best of both worlds, and it's sweet."

"I'm game!"

I help Hudson display the pies on the white granite kitchen island. Everything looks so delicious. I just want to deep dive at the bottom of each one of those pies with a fork in hand.

"Make yourself comfortable at the island while I take care of the coffee," he says, heading towards the refrigerator.

So far, I've only seen a kitchen like Hudson's on TV, in magazines, and on the Internet. If I had a restaurant grade eight-burner stove and a refrigerator you'd expect to find in a five-star restaurant, I'd cook and bake my way through the *Food Network* website.

It's not only the kitchen that's unbelievable. Every square inch of Hudson's home is something else. And it's decorated so beautifully.

And holy-black-forest-chocolate-cherry-milkshake-with-whipped-cream-on-top, the man has an actual elevator leading to the top floors. In his home. Mind explosion! Never in a million years did I think I'd ever be setting foot in such a luxurious house, unless things got so dire for Arya and me, I'd have to moonlight as a cleaning lady.

With my eyes glued to his firm butt, I yank my little body onto one of the stools.

After preparing the coffee, using an expensive looking coffee machine, and dropping the cups on the countertop, he slides onto the high stool next to me. The height difference is comical. My feet are dangling. His are firmly planted on the floor.

He points to a glass bottle with a pour top. "This is liquid sugar. You can sweeten at will."

I nod. "Okay."

He points to my glass cup. "Let me know if you want more Grand Marnier."

"Thank you." I take a sip, bracing myself to be knocked out by the booze. "I'm pleasantly surprised," I say. "This is delicious."

"Glad you like it," he says. "Which pie flavor do you want to start with?"

"I only recognize the pecan pie. What are the others?"

"That's key lime pie." He points at the third pie. "And that's..." He purses his lips and shakes his head. The expression on his face is somber. "I don't think you can handle that one."

I frown. *How dare he underestimate me?* "I'll have you know, there isn't a dessert I can't handle."

He shakes his head again. "This one is different."

Puh-lease. "Try me."

"All right, but it will be your demise."

"Whatever."

"That is red velvet pie."

My eyes widen. "As in red velvet batter poured into a pie crust?"

"Yes."

God is good. "No disrespect to the two other pies, which I'm sure are delicious, but I'm definitely starting with that one!"

"Don't say I didn't warn you."

"Stop being so dramatic."

Hudson serves me a slice and hands me the plate. "Thank you. What about you?"

"I'll wait until you've tested yours." I frown my confusion. "Just in case I need to call 911."

I roll my eyes. "It's just pie."

Shaking my head, I take a bite.

Oh.

My.

God.

Someone needs to call 911. Now!

This is so out of this world scrumptious, I moan around a delicious forkful of the most amazing thing I've ever tasted in my life.

"Told you." Hudson shrugs. "It's a slice of pure magic, right?"

"Huh-uh." I nod, chewing.

He cuts up a piece of pecan pie and places it on a dessert plate.

"You're not having the red velvet pie?"

"I bought a second one. It's in the freezer. I bought this one just for you. You can take the rest back to Queens to share with your sister. In fact, you can take all the leftovers as well."

"You didn't have to."

"Remember what I told you about taking care of lil' ol' you?"

I smile. "I'm touched."

He winks.

For a long beat, we enjoy our desserts in silence, the scraping of my fork on the plate as I attempt to scoop up every last bite, the only sound against the soft lounge music playing in the background.

This pie is so decadent, it's ridiculous.

"As an only child, I'm always fascinated by sibling dynamics," Hudson says. "Especially twins. I assume identical twins swap places all the time?"

I place my empty dessert plate on the counter.

He does the same.

"We used to do it all the time when we were kids and as teenagers," I say. "As adults, we have different personalities, so it doesn't take much to differentiate us. Not to mention, until yesterday, I was a blonde—"

He reaches for a lock of hair, twisting it around his finger. "No shit."

I nod. "Arya and I are natural blondes, but a few months ago, she decided she wanted to know what life was like as a brunette. In order to pull off last night's swap, I had to dye my hair. It'll wash out eventually, but in the meantime, I'm back to looking exactly like my sister."

"So, looking at her is like looking in a mirror?"

"Yup."

"That's wild."

"It's been my reality since day one. When my sister is standing next to me in front of a mirror, I see double."

He chuckles.

I turn on my seat so I'm facing him. "That's what you sound like when you laugh."

His eyebrows knit together. "Why would you say that?"

"Because yesterday, you were all serious, broody, and shit—"

"You think I'm serious, broody, and shit?"

"Until now, that's what I thought," I tell him. "I figured you were one of those grumpy CEOs who was all business all the time. I don't know what to do with this lighthearted, not as stuffy side of you, Mr. Kincaid."

Without warning, he reaches out and twists my nipple.

"Ouch!" I yelp.

"That was for your smart mouth."

"You're a sadist!"

"No, sweetheart," he says with a pronounced twang. "Just an alpha."

"Good one."

"Just managing your expectations."

"I was paying you a compliment. I didn't expect to get punished."

He leans into me. "I haven't even started punishing you."

I swallow hard. *Note to self.*

"I'm curious," he says. "How did your parents manage not to get you confused?"

"Color coding," I say. "We each had our designated colors—pink for Arya and purple for me—well, lavender, really. Mom went as far as buying identical toys in pink and purple. Same for pacifiers and hair accessories. Until I became a teenager, I never wore pink."

"What happened during bath time?"

"As babies, it was easy—one baby at a time. As we grew, we each had our color-coded bath seats. As we became toddlers, Mom would put color-coded floaters on one arm."

"That's funny. Your mom is a clever one."

"*Was.*"

He flinches. "I'm sorry."

"You didn't know."

His eyebrows dip low. "You lost both parents?"

I nod.

"Shit."

"It's just Arya and me."

"Unlike me, you're not a one-person army."

My head jerks back. "You lost your parents?"

"Yes," he says. "I'm an orphan. Have been for a little over a decade now. I lost both parents six months shy of turning eighteen."

My heart goes out to him. I know first-hand what it's like to lose both parents. My sister has a knack for finding trouble, but at least I'm not alone in the world. "Arya and I lost Mom when we were nineteen. Dad passed away a year later."

"How old are you?"

"I'm twenty-two," I say. "And you?"

"I'm twenty-eight."

My eyes bulge out of my skull.

"You're so young to be this successful. For the love of God, you have an actual elevator in your house. I didn't even know that was possible—" The words spout from my mouth without my permission. Horrified, I clamp both hands over my mouth, my eyes widening in shock.

Crap.

Too much, Angelica.

"Sorry," I say. "That was supposed to be my inner voice."

"Allow me to answer her." Thank God he's such a good sport about my faux pas. "This"—he opens his arms—"was built on the back of champions. I didn't become a billionaire before the age of twenty-five alone. I had help."

Holy.

Shit.

He's a billionaire?

I knew he was rich—a blind person could see that—but a billionaire?

That's a lot of moolah.

Yup, he could afford to buy a place on Billionaire Row.

To avoid embarrassing myself any further, I keep it simple. He doesn't need to know I've never been this close to a filthy rich man. "It's very impressive."

"It's the result of a lot of work, dedication, and sacrifice."

"I can imagine." I really can't, but it seems like the right thing to say.

"As for the elevator, I thought it was over the top when the agent showed me the house, but she was quick to school me. This brownstone is five stories high. Schlepping up and down stairs all day long is a bitch. The same goes for having furniture delivered. She was right. The elevator is worth its weight in gold."

I bob my head up and down. "Makes sense."

I hold my breath, hoping he'll tell me more about his background and rise to success, but he veers the conversation back to me. "Do you have uncles, aunts, grandparents?"

I hide my disappointment. "Mom was an orphan and Dad was an only child to a single mom. My grandma died when Arya and I were fifteen. Dad is from Oregon. He had cousins there, but he was never close to them. We never really had money to fly to Oregon, so we never established a relationship with dad's cousins. That's why when he passed away, we didn't even know how to get a hold of them."

"My mom was an only child and my dad had an older brother. My uncle died five years ago. Both my parents had single moms who passed away when I was a teenager." I can't believe how much we share in common. "Were your parents... sick?"

"No." I shake my head. "They both died in car accidents—different car accidents."

"Not that losing someone you love to a disease is easier, but you can at least say goodbye. My parents also died in a car accident. They died at the same time."

"Oh my God, Hudson."

He nods. "If you don't mind me asking, how did you lose your parents?"

"Mom worked as a production warehouse packer at a pharmaceutical company in the Bronx. On the day she died, there was a little snowfall on her way to work, but nothing crazy. During the day, a little snow turned into a blizzard. Mom waited it out until she felt she could handle the road. She promised Dad she'd drive carefully." I fiddle with my fingers on my lap. "She never made it home. The roads were really icy." I breathe in a lungful of air. "Ashlyn Dempsey McQuinley lost control of her car and died on impact."

Hudson squeezes my hand. "I'm so sorry for your loss, angel."

I nod, old emotions choking me. "Dad was devastated after Mom's death. He retreated in his shell, only emerging from his bedroom to go to work. He was a high-rise window cleaner—"

"That's a hell of a job."

"It's a dangerous job, but the irony is, dad died on the ground, not hanging from a skyscraper. He died on his way to Manhattan. You know how morning radio shows have contests?"

"I don't listen to radio much these days, but I know what you're talking about."

"On her way to work, a twenty-year-old woman heard her name called out for a chance to win ten thousand dollars if she called back the radio station within half an hour—"

"No!" Hudson shakes his head.

"Yes!" I nod.

"Instead of pulling off the road or pulling over, she called in while she was driving. The radio hosts asked her if she was on the road. She lied and said she was parked on the side of the road. She won the contest, and I guess in her excitement, she swerved into Dad's lane." I place a hand against my heart. "The horrific accident played out live on the radio. Christopher McQuinley died. Same for the girl."

"Jesus."

"Arya and I were lost. Devastated. Broken. Sad. And without parents. In an ironic twist of fate, we were the same age as that girl."

"Did you sue her parents?"

"No. It never crossed our mind." I cover my face with both hands. "It's been a really rough two years."

He rubs my back in soothing circles. "Is that why your sister got involved with Todd?"

I look up at him. "Yes and no." I let out a heavy sigh. "My sister used to work at a coffee shop before she started working at a sports bar. This guy with bespoke suits, cufflinks, expensive shoes, and a gold Rolex watch started paying her attention. Since she suffers from erotomania—"

"What does that mean?"

"She tends to fall in love fast, easily, and often with men of a higher social status."

"She only has eyes for rich guys."

I nod. "Her customer was exactly her type—blue-eyed, tall, dripping with money, with a suffix to his name, which suggested old money. It started out with a little flirting, and then the guy asked her out. She came back from that first date on cloud nine because her rich date owned a Bugatti *and* a Lamborghini, and he had a Black American Express card. Overnight, she couldn't start or end a sentence without referring to her *boyfriend*," I say, grimacing. "It's like she became a marionette, and every time she opened her mouth, I could hear him."

"Your sister's boyfriend introduced her to Todd?"

"No, he's the reason why she was desperate for him to hire her."

"What was weighing her down?"

"It's only when Dad died, we found out he had an online gambling addiction. I'm not sure if it started before Mom died or as a way to cope with her passing, but he owed a lot of money. As a result, there wasn't much left from his life insurance or Mom's once his creditors were paid off. Even his car was repossessed. Arya's boyfriend—a broker—was branching out on his own. Long story short, he convinced my sister to invest what we had left from the insurance and money my parents had stashed away for college for us."

"How long had she been dating this guy?"

"About six months."

"And you went along with it?"

"Not at first. The thing is, I knew nothing about investments. This guy cut his teeth on Wall Street and he was setting up shop. Over several dinners he paid for, he convinced me to use the money we had left to guarantee we'd be multimillionaires by the age of twenty-five. He said it was the same life-changing opportunity as being one of Google's first investors."

"I gather it wasn't."

"It was at first."

"What do you mean?"

"Overnight, the guy was able to quadruple our money. It was too good to be true, but the numbers were staring at me in the face. Big numbers. Life-changing numbers." I hesitate. "Still, I agonized over my decision to agree to give him what we had left from the insurance money. That first statement transformed me into a believer. Maybe this was our gold rush, after all."

"What happened to the money?"

"Two things lowered my guard going into this—the fantasy of being able to erase my student loan instead of it being a noose around my neck and the dream of being a home owner. Money was tight. My parents were blue-collar workers. Mom never bought anything at full price. If an item wasn't discounted, we had to learn to live without it. Owning a house was never on my parents' radar. It was too much of a longshot to even consider. I wanted that for myself and my sister, and I wanted that as a way of honoring their memory. I figured they would be so proud of us."

"That never happened."

"No. I tried to pull the profits... like they say in Vegas, you have to know when to fold 'em. I was ready to take my winnings and run."

"What stopped you?"

"My sister."

His eyebrows dip. "Why?"

"Arya pleaded with me to ride the wave a little longer, assuring me her boyfriend could make it such that our kids would never have to work a day in their lives. She even pulled out the big guns—we each could own a house without being burdened by a mortgage because we would be able to buy our house with cash. Few people are wealthy enough to pull off that *tour de force* in New York."

"She knew how to sweeten the pot."

"She knows me well," I say. "Our investment kept growing, and growing, and growing. So much so, I started feeling like an idiot because I almost caused us to miss out on such an amazing opportunity. My sister and I started counting our chickens before they hatched, then Armageddon descended upon us."

"What happened?"

"Out of the blue, Arya's boyfriend announced he was heading to Singapore to expand his business—lots of rich people in Asia. The first week he was gone, he was in constant contact with Arya. The second week, he claimed things were on fire, so communication might be infrequent as he closed deals. The third week, Arya didn't hear a word. She figured he was too busy to call, but he'd be in touch. I was starting to get worried. The fourth week without a word from this guy, I started to panic. Arya was determined to stand by her man. By the fifth week, *she* started to panic—"

"The money was still in your account?"

"It was. I was watching it like a hawk," I say. "Arya finally got a call from him. He told her to check our recent profits. I couldn't believe my eyes. Once again, I tried to pressure Arya into pulling out our money—"

"Let me guess, she wanted to ride it a little longer."

"Yes. I told her that was her prerogative, but I was pulling out my share. She told me I was making a big mistake. I didn't care. That was more money than I thought I'd ever see in my lifetime. Since I knew nothing about trading, I needed her boyfriend's help. I sent him a flurry of text messages without ever receiving a response. I tried to convince myself he was busy with new clients, but something in the pit of my stomach... my gut knew something was terribly wrong." My eyes meet his. "Then just like that." I snap my fingers. "It was all gone."

Hudson frowns in confusion. "What do you mean?"

"A couple days after he called, I tried logging into our accounts, but I couldn't. After numerous attempts, I asked my sister to try. She couldn't either. Don't ask me why, but it occurred to me that in her blind faith Arya might've shared our logins and passwords with her boyfriend."

"Did she?"

"She assured me she hadn't. For a week after that, we lived in terror. Eventually, we called the police to report a fraud. We were told someone would get back to us. Eventually. I don't remember setting the Google alert, but I guess I did. I was just about to email one of my clients when Ramsey's name appeared in my inbox. When I clicked on the link, I nearly died. The screaming headline answered all of my questions. My sister and I had been unknowingly wrapped up in a big cryptocurrency scam—"

Hudson's head jerks back. "You and your sister were involved with Ramsey Kenyon III?"

My eyes widen in shock. "Were you one of his victims?"

"No, but the news was all over the place. That guy was a master manipulator. He scammed billions from hard-working, gullible people—"

I lift a hand in admission. "I was part of the bunch of gullible people—"

"You can't outwit the devil, angel."

I hang my head low.

"Angelica, look at me."

Slowly, I lift my gaze.

"It might have been under the cryptocurrency banner," he says with air quotes, "but at the end of the day, Ramsey ran a Ponzi scheme—he lured his victims knowing full well he'd end up defrauding them because there would be no profits for anyone other than him."

"I paid the price for being greedy."

Hudson ducks down to meet my gaze. "I'm sorry you trusted someone who didn't deserve your trust, angel. And I'm sorry you got conned. This has nothing to do with you being greedy. Ramsey is a snake oil salesman. He traded in lies, deception, and inflated data. Like any good Ponzi con artist, he paid profits to earlier investors with funds from more recent ones. Those earlier investors became his cheerleaders, opening doors to their friends with deep pockets. This would allow Ramsey to dupe people with less money to spare but who had big dreams—"

"Like Arya and me." My voice trembles. "I feel like the village idiot."

Hudson stares at me.

I've never seen such a blatant expression of shock.

I keep talking. "I should've listened to my gut." My throat

squeezes tight, strangling my voice. Tears well in my eyes. "I should've been firmer and pulled my money out right after Ramsey had quadrupled it. Even if Arya had lost her half, we'd still have something to show for it. Now, we have nothing. I'll have to live with this guilt for the rest of my life."

"Stop!" Hudson says. "Just stop!"

I flinch.

Don't cry.

Don't cry.

Don't cry in front of him.

And... I'm crying.

"Fuck, angel, I didn't mean to make you cry." He cups my face, holding my tear-filled gaze to his and places a gentle kiss on my lips. That only makes me cry even harder. "You have to stop self-flagellating yourself. You weren't to know," he says. "Ramsey is a predator. Manipulating people is an Olympic sport to him."

I respond with a pathetic one-shoulder shrug.

When a fresh tear slips down my cheek, Hudson catches it with his thumb.

I place a hand on top of his, holding onto him for dear life.

He brushes a strand of hair behind my ear, and the sweetness of the gesture only makes me tear up even more. "Don't cry, angel." His voice is as soft as a caress. "There's nothing you could've done." He kisses my tear-streaked cheek. "Nothing at all," he says and catches another falling tear.

The tension in my body seems to ease.

It's almost ridiculous, considering I've only met this guy, but right now, I feel safe—like the Ramseys of this world can't get to me.

"Assholes like Ramsey keep spinning their deceptive web of lies until someone starts asking hard questions," Hudson says. "That's probably what happened to cause him to run and then disappear."

"I wanted to scream at my sister for getting us involved with that monster, but all I could do was cry. I cried for days. Not even Arya's signature sad puppy face or the guilt I could read in her eyes were enough to shake me out of my agony. If it wasn't for the fact I was afraid we'd end up homeless, I probably would've stopped working altogether, hiding under my covers for the foreseeable future." I'm surprised I still have tears left after all those weeks of crying. I pinch my lips together, doing my best to contain the rage bubbling inside me. "I'm not a violent person, but the number of times I've had dreams of tracking Ramsey down and choking him with my bare hands for what he did to us..."

"I'd want to strangle the asswipe as well."

"To make matter worse, Arya got tangled up with this Russian loan shark—"

"What?"

I tell him everything.

"That was the final straw that pushed her to become one of Todd's girls."

"Christ."

"Yeah." I nod.

"I guess the Russian guy Arya owes money to doesn't know where Ramsey is, or else the police would've pulled it out of him."

My eyebrows hit my forehead. "I didn't even think of that."

"This is an international case. I'm sure the police have eyes on him."

"I guess you're right."

"Now that we've established you aren't an escort, what do you do for a living?"

I laugh.

"What's so funny?"

"Remember Grace?"

"The woman you were having lunch with today at the Pompadour Hotel who's probably still getting it on with her husband as we speak? Yes, I remember her very well."

I laugh even harder.

"I'd much rather see you laugh than cry, but I feel like I'm missing a piece of the puzzle."

"The reason I know *The Court Games* like the back of my hand is because I edited the manuscript. I'm a freelance editor."

"No way."

"Yup!"

"How did you two connect?"

"I used to work for a big publisher as an editor, specializing in epic fantasy and fairytale fantasy novels."

"Got it."

"Two and a half years ago, when the publisher *restructured*—God, I hate that R word—my head was on the chopping block. They also dropped a bunch of authors. Grace was one of them."

"That sucks."

"Big time."

"How did she go from losing her publishing deal to writing *The Court Games*? That's a huge leap."

"On the heel of her dismissal, she sent out multiple query letters, pitching a series she was hoping would get her name on the map, but she ended up with a string of soul-crushing rejections."

"Getting rejected chips away at your confidence."

"Even more so for an artist."

He nods. "I can imagine."

I cross a leg over the other. "I bumped into Grace after an

interview for a job I really didn't want, but since I desperately needed the money, I was considering it. Grace and I were both tight on funds—obscenely expensive New York rents and all—so we ended up sitting in Central Park, where we commiserated for hours. I offered to take a look at her manuscript and polish it up for her on an IOU. I figured if I kept myself busy, I wouldn't have time to fret over my lack of job prospects doing what I love for a living. Within the first two chapters, I was hooked. Even though she'd only given me a nominal fee, I edited *The Court Games* with as much dedication as if she had paid me a million dollars. To this day, it's the best fantasy romance book I've ever read, and I'm not just saying that because I edited it. It's truly a masterpiece."

"Talk about serendipity," he says. "Does Grace know you were her cheerleader last night?"

I shake my head. "I couldn't divulge that without telling her why I was at one of UTV.com's parties. That conversation would've been an awkward one."

"Makes sense. You'll have to tell her one day."

"She doesn't need me to pimp her talent."

Hudson's blue eyes turn stormy.

What did I say?

Chapter 18

Hudson

Angelica is too selfless.

Forget about her unwillingness to recognize her huge contribution to Grace's skyrocketing career, but she stepped in to save her sister's ass without a second thought.

It isn't my place to say, but Angelica has been shouldering too many responsibilities. She's been acting like her twin's surrogate parent when they're the same age. The way she stuck her head out and swapped places with her twin last night is admirable.

There was something lighthearted about Angelica that didn't fit the profile of a high-end Manhattan escort. Heck, she doesn't even fit the profile of most women I meet at events. She wasn't guarded enough. Her unbridled reaction to things people who are accustomed to hanging out at these types of shindigs no longer bat an eyelash to, was a dead giveaway she was a fish out of water.

Now I know why I could smell the innocence of her...

She's a study in contrasts—she's young and sheltered, but at the same time she's brave and strong.

She's been dealing with heartache over losing her parents and keeping her head above water because of douchebag Ramsey. After listening to her story, I'd pay whatever it takes to take away her pain. I also want to hunt down that piece of shit Ramsey like a rabid dog and end his miserable life. Assholes like that don't deserve to live. Despite it all, Angelica maintains a sunny disposition that's quite remarkable.

And there's that darn dangling carrot. She's a virgin.

There was too much going on earlier at the Pompadour Hotel for my cock to react at that revelation, but the fucker is reacting to having her all to myself in my home.

As much as I'm turned on, her virginity has my head spinning and my protective alpha streak flaring. It also brings out the caveman in me. As God is my witness, I'm going to be the one to claim her.

Another client, and last night could've played out very differently for her.

She took a huge risk.

What if I had been a rich jerk willing to pay to pop her cherry? Or worse, what if I had forced myself on her or spiked her drinks to get what I wanted without her consent?

The thought makes my blood boil.

It's a good thing I ended up being her sister's first client, and this twin swap put her my way. Not only is she a delight, she's also good for business.

"Why are you looking at me like that?" she asks.

"You're shortchanging yourself again."

She squirms in her seat. "It's a bad habit."

"One you can change."

She shrugs. "My sister is the complete opposite. She basks in supreme confidence twenty-four-seven."

Maybe this will force her to see what she brings to the table. "Rory Wolfe called me."

Her eyebrows knit together. "Don't tell me he canceled dinner with you before he leaves for LA?" The concern is clear in her voice and etched on her beautiful features.

"We're still on."

"Oof." She swipes the back of her hand over her forehead. "All that bonding with the CEO's wife for nothing."

There's that lightheartedness I find so intoxicating.

"Our meeting prompted him to ask his accounting department for a breakdown of the fees they pay to their current online shopping cart provider. His brother and partner, Roark, will be flying in from LA for the meeting. The Wolfe brothers are very interested in what I can offer."

"That's good news, right?"

"That's fucking good news, angel."

She claps and does a happy dance on her seat.

"Without you, last night would've ended with me leaving the party emptyhanded."

She brushes her shoulders off. "I may not wear a cape, but I have superpowers."

"You certainly do." My finger grazes the creamy skin of her neck. "How will I ever repay you?"

Her eyes shift to her empty dessert plate before bouncing back to meet mine. "I think you already have."

I shake my head. "I disagree."

"The meal was delicious and the red velvet pie made me see God."

"I know of another way that can make you see God."

She swallows hard. "We're not talking about dessert anymore?"

"What do you think?"

"We aren't?!" Her voice goes up by several octaves.

I stand up.

"That was the wrong answer?" she asks.

I clear the kitchen island, moving the dessert plate and coffee cups, and dropping them into the sink.

"That was the right answer." I come and stand in front of her. "Time for *my* dessert."

Big, green eyes widen as long, dark lashes flutter furiously.

"I want you on the countertop," I say, helping her off the stool and dropping her ass on the granite surface.

I lean into her and get right in her face. "You captivated me at first glance, Angelica."

She shifts on the countertop. "It seems surreal I'd have that kind of power."

"Are you doubting yourself, angel?" She furrows her eyebrows. "A minute ago, you were boasting about your badass superpowers. Now, you're backtracking. Was that false advertising?"

She tilts her head back, exposing her slender neck, and smiles.

"Okay, you got me," she says.

"After I put you in the car to drive you back to your place, I stood in front of the hotel, stewing."

"Why?"

"The thought of another man hiring your services and touching you..." My nostrils flare. "I wanted to murder someone."

"Really?"

"Why do you think I booked you for the week? I'm completely obsessed with you."

Her jaw drops. "You—you are?"

"Fuck yeah. I wasn't sure how I was going to keep hiring your services for as long as necessary, but I figured I'd cross that bridge at the end of this week."

"You would've been willing to spend that kind of money on me?"

"Abso-fucking-lutely."

"I don't know what to say."

"I'm crazy about you, Angelica. I didn't expect you'd flare up a possessiveness I didn't recognize after meeting you just once." I pause. "But here I am... all wrapped up in you."

"But—" She shakes her head. "There are so many worldly women in New York City. Taller, too. Thinner, as well. With trust funds and high-powered careers. Women who don't have messy lives like me."

"Good for them," I say. "I like you just the way you are."

She's at a loss for words.

After a few heartbeats, she shakes her head, as if breaking from a trance. "You're everything I never had the courage to dream about, Hudson."

"I'm just a guy from Texas who made it big in the Big Apple, but I'll take the compliment."

She swats my chest. "Cocky much?"

"You opened the door."

She rolls her eyes. "All that to say, I can't believe you'd say that about me."

I cup her gorgeous face in my hands and kiss her lips. "Believe it, angel. You have no idea how much I want you."

"Me, too."

"But I can't have you."

"Why not?"

"I don't want our first time to be a transaction," I say. "That's exactly what would happen if I were to fuck you before the end of the week."

"Oh."

"So, for the first week of us dating, we're going to have to be creative."

"We're dating?"

"I'd like that."

She blushes. "I'd like that, too."

"We're on the same page?"

She nods. "We are."

"Bring on the kinky!"

"Kinky? You just talked about being creative."

"I don't do vanilla sex. Same for foreplay. It's kinky all the way, or I keep it in my pants."

She pulls her lower lip between her teeth and gnaws at it.

"What is it?"

"Just in case you don't remember our earlier conversation, I'm a virgin. I fooled around with the one and only boyfriend I've had..." Her words trail.

"That's another reason why I want to take my time with you."

"I wouldn't know how to spell kinky even with Google and an old-fashioned dictionary. I don't want to disappoint you with my inexperience."

"The only way you could disappoint me is if you didn't submit fully to me. Last night, you proved yourself *very* capable of doing that."

An unconvincing smile breaks across her face.

I set her mind at ease. "I mean it, Angelica."

She considers me. "What about returning the favor? I'm no porn star adept at deepthroating."

She watches porn? Fuck, my cock twitches. "The fact you even know what deep-throating is tells me you're not as inept as you think. Not to mention, tonight is about you. There's plenty of time for you to suck my cock."

Her cheeks redden. "O—okay."

I grab her hand and place it on my hard cock. "You have no idea how much it turns me on to coerce the sex kitten in you to come out and play."

She hitches a breath.

I forge ahead. "Let me take care of you. Spread your legs for me."

She obeys beautifully.

"This outfit doesn't only look fucking hot on you, it also makes it easier for me to take what I want."

I grab her by the hips, sliding her forward to the edge of the counter before grinding my hard cock against her. I force her to feel every hard inch of me.

"You drive me fucking wild, Angelica."

"It's the same for me."

I grind my cock with more determination.

"Naughty, naughty girl. You're going to leave a wet spot on the front of my jeans."

"I—I can do kinky."

"Now you're speaking my language."

My hands slide to her waist, lifting her white top, and I close my fingers around her nipples poking through the fabric of her bra.

She bites hard against her lower lip, her eyes rolling to the back of her head.

Needing more, I yank the satin cups of her bra down, exposing her beautiful tits.

"Fuck, those are amazing," I say, my eyes fixed on her breasts. I lower my head and latch my mouth onto one of her rock hard nipples, flicking it with my tongue.

She moans as I suck, nip, graze, and toy with her peak.

Her fingers tangle with my hair as her ass writhes against the counter.

She's a hot little one and so responsive.

Fucking perfect.

Unable to resist, I bite down hard on her nipple.

She cries out.

To make it better, my hand travels under her skirt, up her thighs, and I stroke her pussy through her wet lacy panties.

Her free hand clamps around mine.

I let her nipple drop from my mouth. "What is it?"

"This is too good."

"Let me make it better."

"I don't know if I can handle anymore."

"Silly angel. Hands off."

"You're going to make me lose my mind."

"That's the point. Anything else and I'd be wasting your time and mine. And angel, wasting time isn't a currency I trade in."

She lets go.

"Good girl." I resume my mission.

My mouth is back, latching around her nipple.

She stares down at me through hooded eyes.

A feral grin crosses my lips around her nipple right before I open my mouth and bite down hard enough to make her cry out.

A whimpering moan escapes her and my cock swells for her.

I stroke her clit through her panties with more ardor.

"Oh, oh, oh. Dear God. Hudson. Yes."

Everything stops.

"Why—why did you stop?" Her breath is labored.

I lift my gaze. "Because yesterday, I made you come with my fingers. Today, I want you to come all over my tongue."

Her lips form an 'O'.

I take a step back and place a hand against her chest. "On your back."

She doesn't budge.

"I gave you an order, angel."

"There something you should know."

I furrow my brows. "What is it?"

"I'm going to put it out there." She hesitates. "It's not you. It's me."

"Well, that didn't make a lick of sense to me."

"My ex could never—" She inhales a deep breath. "It never really worked..." She pinches her lips together. "You know," she points to her pussy, "I become numb after a while."

My poor little angel.

That's a crying shame.

Not that I'm interested in knowing much about her ex, but I have to ask. "How old were you when you had a boyfriend?"

"Before Mom died."

"So, nineteen?"

"Yes."

"Was he your age?"

She nods. "Yes."

"Not all guys up their game, but I can assure you, most of us become better lovers with age."

She giggles.

"Do you wanna ride my tongue or not?"

"Jesus, your mouth."

"A mouth that would very much like to make acquaintance with your sweet pussy."

She shakes her head. "You're so out of my league."

"Something tells me you're a fast learner."

She rewards me with a beaming smile.

I don't have to ask twice.

She lowers her body against the countertop.

Her tits are still exposed and her light-blue skirt bunches around her waist, offering a peek of her white lacy panties.

She looks like a goddamn feast.

My goddamn feast.

I cup my balls and squeeze tight. It does little to tame my hungry cock. I doubt anything will until I claim her.

She tilts her head to the side, staring at me with wide, innocent eyes.

Damn those eyes.

I want to protect her and fuck her like a wild animal at the same time. As much as it's going to kill me—and it will—I have to stay the course.

Only six more days to go.

I inhale her headiness.

The mixture of her arousal and her floral perfume has me all riled up.

She's begging to be touched and sucked.

And I'm the man for the job.

My hands run down one leg until I reach her feet. I remove one strappy heel, letting it fall on the granite floor. The other leg receives the same treatment.

I lean forward and drop a soft kiss against her exposed tummy.

Her abs contract, quivering underneath my lips.

I kiss the smooth rise of her pubic bone.

"Hudson." My name comes soft and prayer-like.

My balls throb.

I tap between her thighs, and she parts her legs.

I kiss the inside of her right thigh. Then the left.

Sliding my hands up her legs, my fingers latch around the waistband of her panties. With my eyes fixed onto hers, I drag them all the way down to her painted toes before removing them.

"You aren't ripping them off today? Lucky me. I don't have to go home commando." Her tone is mocking.

"You're lucky your ass is on the countertop or else I'd be reddening it right now for that smart mouth."

"The first time we met, you kidnapped my panties. I'm allowed to ask the question."

"Even though I'm not ripping these"—I dangle her panties in the air—"I'm still keeping them as part of my collection."

"Is that your MO? Pantie-kidnapper?"

"Until you, I was a pantie-ripper, but never a pantie-kidnapper. You're the only woman I've ever wanted to take a piece of with me."

"You're just saying that."

I shake my head. "I'd never bullshit you."

She responds with a shy smile.

I tuck her panties into the pocket of my jeans.

"Do you have a special drawer for them?"

"Not yet." I wink. "At this rate, I'll have one by the end of the week."

She laughs.

Back to the program.

I lick my lips in anticipation.

I'm just about to lower my head, but freeze.

"That's not how this game is played, angel." Her eyes pop open. *Better.* "I want you to watch me lick your pussy." I dip my head and drop a kiss on her tummy. "I want you to watch me fuck you with my tongue." Her eyelashes flutter like crazy, but her eyes remain open. "I want your eyes locked onto mine when you come your head off."

Her body is already shaking and I haven't even touched her yet.

"Got that?"

She stares at me from under hooded eyes. "Yes."

"Yes, what?"

"I'll keep my eyes open."

"I'm not convinced. Try again."

"I'll keep my eyes open while you... while you... lick my pussy."

"Good girl."

I dip my head.

Her heady scent is even more intoxicating now.

I can't help a smile of satisfaction.

She's as turned on as a light switch.

I press my tongue against her pussy lips and lick all the way to her hard clit.

She arches her back, letting out a loud cry of pleasure.

She clamps both hands over her mouth, muffling the sound as my tongue laps and probes, over and over, applying just the right pressure.

Fuck, she's sweeter than I ever imagined.

Lick.

She tastes so good.

Lick.

She squeezes her fist tight, folding her legs, so her feet are planted against the countertop.

Her parted legs are like an invitation.

Lick.

She lets out a sensual sigh.

Lick.

She swivels her hips, as if begging for more.

I grant her wish.

Lick.

She seems entirely lost right now, so I'm stunned when I hear her quiet plea. "More."

Lick.

No other man will taste this pussy.

Lick.

The thought sparks something in me.

I'm ravenous, devouring her, licking from clit to hole like a gluttonous man.

When she presses against my mouth, it detonates something inside me.

I swirl my tongue around her entrance before plunging it deep inside her warmth.

Her body starts writhing uncontrollably against the cool surface.

That's it, greedy girl, take your pleasure.

Each one of her desperate mewls, travel straight to my cock.

The fucker swells inside my boxer briefs, desperate to come out and play.

"Oh, God."

Slap!

Her hand hits the countertop with a resounding thud.

"Sweet Jesus."

Slap!

"Mother Mary."

Slap!

"God, Hudson, your mouth."

Slap!

That last one is music to my ears.

She swings a leg over my shoulder, pressing hard against my mouth.

Fuck, yeah.

I reward her by plunging my tongue deeper into her warmth.

I can't wait to be balls deep inside her tight pussy.

Her head turns right, then left.

She's unhinged.

I place my hands on her hips to keep her in place.

I lick back up to her clit and slide two fingers deep, stretching her.

"You asked me a question when we met," I say.

She lifts her head and stares down at me with dazed eyes.

She opens her mouth, then closes it.

She does that a few times.

She's stumped.

"You asked me why three fingers. Here's why."

I plunge a third finger inside her as I latch on her clit.

Her cry is deafening.

Heck, I wouldn't be surprised if they heard her across town.

I curl my fingers, fucking her in a relentless rhythm as my tongue laps at her clit.

A groaned string of curses falls from her lips, her legs shaking as her needy pussy clenches around my fingers.

She struggles against my grip.

I won't have it.

I clamp my hand tighter against her hip.

She's going to be bruised tomorrow.

Lightning shoots through my veins at the thought.

"I can't take it anymore. I'm going to die." Her voice shakes as much as her body. "This is too good. Please, I need your mouth."

It takes everything in me not to chuckle at the contradiction.

I lap harder, faster, pumping my fingers in and out of her as I take her clit between my lips and suck hard.

She struggles like a hellcat, but my grip is unyielding.

I close my lips around her clit, applying just the right pressure as I curl my fingers inside her.

"Hud—"

She closes her eyes tight, and shatters with a cry, coming so beautifully over my wicked tongue until she's gasping for air.

I should punish her for disobeying me, but she came so

well, it makes up for her robbing me from seeing the look in her eyes.

I'm addicted to making her lose her mind.

Her gasping breaths reverberate around the kitchen walls as she struggles to get her feet back on the ground.

Yeah, you came hard.

And I'm as hard as steel.

My balls ache with the need to release.

This is going to be the longest week of my life.

I've gone without sex for months at a time, too focused on work and adjusting to the tragic curveball life threw at me a year and a half ago. If you had asked me yesterday, I would've said it's unfathomable to be with a woman without fucking her, considering how long it's been. That's before Angelica came sweeping into my life.

I pull my fingers out of her pussy, bring them still dripping with her juices to my mouth, and lick them clean.

Damn.

I want my mouth on her pussy every day of the week.

If the blissful expression on her face is any indication, she's fully satiated.

I admire her, unwilling to rush her to come down from her high.

I caress her thigh in languorous strokes, coaxing her back to reality.

Her body stiffens, her eyes fly open. She sits straight up on the countertop, huge, green eyes blinking furiously at me.

What the hell? "Are you in pain?"

She shakes her head, brown strands flying all over the place. "What do I tell my sister about us?"

Chapter 19

Hudson

I couldn't even wait for the chauffeured car I hired for Angelica to disappear from sight before rushing back to my house, need coursing through my veins.

I slam the door a little too hard, lock it, and take the stairs two-by-two to my bedroom.

Making my sweet angel come without expecting her to reciprocate is going to give me a serious case of blue balls. I have no one else to blame but me. After all, it was my idea to wait until the week-long arrangement runs its course before sinking my cock inside her sweet, tight pussy. Problem is, this week might kill me.

I want this woman something fierce.

When I reach the second floor, I'm like a restless beast.

I bolt towards my bedroom, heading straight for the bathroom.

I turn on the light with my elbow before heading towards the counter.

With quick hands, I undress, dumping my clothes in a pile at my feet.

I catch my reflection in the tall mirror, and freeze.

My balls are swollen and heavy, and my cock is so hard, angry veins line my shaft. The look in my eyes is that of a man possessed.

My desperate need for this woman will be my undoing.

I'm gonna lose my fucking mind if I don't do something about this big problem between my legs.

I reach for my body cream and pump a few squirts into the palm of my hand before slicking up my cock, and then I'm jacking myself hard and fast, nothing in my mind but release.

Visions of Angelica's pink, virgin pussy flashes in front of my eyes, as I work my cock faster.

That pussy is mine and only mine.

I close my eyes, relishing every wave of pleasure.

It was so dirty, the way her skirt was still hitched up to her hips as I brought her to orgasm, a real feast for the eyes, right on my countertop. It wouldn't have been nearly as perverted if she were naked. The way she shamelessly angled her body so my thumb would press on her clit just right, as I finger-fucked her real deep.

Damn.

My climax is at the tip of my fingers. I feel it building, taut in my pelvis. Chasing after it, I thrust into my hand fast and furious, imagining I'm fucking Angelica's pouty mouth.

Every cell in my body is buzzing.

I need to mark her mouth, then punch her V card... and then, I'll take her sweet ass.

I plan on claiming every fucking last inch of her.

I pick up my pace, working my cock with single-minded focus.

I want her pussy milking my cock for everything it's worth. I want to own her, take her, claim her, ruin her for all others.

The caveman in me wants my cock to be the one and only she ever takes.

My movements quicken, and my thighs tense, my forearm flexing with every stroke.

My breathing is ragged, my nostrils flared, my jaw so tight, I'm surprised my teeth don't crack.

The memory of her taste and her heady smell do me in.

"Shit!"

I take a step closer to the sink and aim my cock, my fist still working in earnest.

My climax washes over me like a tidal wave. "Christ!" I grunt. I shoot my load, pulsing and spurting as I imagine each and every drop filling her.

I release so much cum, it's embarrassing.

Too many months of celibacy will do that to a guy.

My climax abates, my hand stills, my breathing slows, and reality comes crashing back down.

Six more days...

Six more days of fantasizing about losing myself between her legs.

Six more days of jerking myself raw.

Six more days of wanting her, but not being able to have her.

My lips curve in an evil smile.

Six more days of corrupting my little angel...

Chapter 20

Angelica

As I step inside my apartment, my phone vibrates in my hand. I dump my handbag on the couch and read my sister's message.

Arya: Hey. How was the event? As exciting as last night's event?

Angelica: Hey. There was a change of plan. I'm back at the apartment. I expected to find you here. Where are you?

There's too much for me to share over text. Best to keep it short and sweet. My sister gave me the address for tonight's event, so in her mind, that's where I was. She doesn't know I've been in direct contact with Hudson.

Arya: Worked a second shift. I made a ton of money in tips because it was super busy, but my feet are killing me.

I can't help but think of what Sadie said earlier.

Angelica: That's good. The tips, that is. Not your feet killing you.

Arya: As good as the tips are, it's hard-earned money. Way harder than being arm candy to a rich dude.

It's not like I can dispute that. My evening with Hudson was a dream. And it ended on such a depraved note, I'm still floating.

Angelica: When do you think you'll get home?

Arya: I might end up spending the night at Vanna's. Her boyfriend dumped her on a voicemail while she was having dinner with co-workers. He didn't even have the decency to speak to her over the phone or tell her face to face. My best friend is devastated, so I'm going to spend the night at her parents' place, comforting her, and convincing her she's better off without that asshole.

Angelica: Poor thing. It's best if she isn't alone. You'll come back tomorrow?

Arya: Yes. I don't have a shift tomorrow night, so I'll play it out and see how Vanna is feeling. She was so distraught, she cut her time short with her co-workers and came to the bar. I sent her to the coffee shop up the street, so I could finish my shift. We're probably going to head out to a bar—one I don't work at—to knock off a few drinks. She needs it. She was crying her eyes out.

Angelica: Oh, gosh. Tell her that idiot doesn't deserve her.

Arya: #FACT. Do you have another event with Hudson tomorrow night?

Angelica: I do.

Arya: We should be able to swap places before the end of the week. My va-jay-jay should be back in action! No more nasty smells. Just in the nick of time, too. If Todd has questions, it's best if I meet **my/our** first client and hang out with him. Speaking of my boss, he's lining up my next client.

My sister's next message prevents me from having to comment.

Arya: Got to go. See you tomorrow, sis.

Angelica: See you tomorrow.

I stare at my screen.

She wants to meet Hudson?

That scenario never crossed my mind.

Bile rises in my throat.

Fuck. Fuck. Fuck.

As I head to my bedroom, my phone rings.

Perfect timing.

"Sadie!" I say, accepting the video call.

She's sporting a huge grin.

Her head shifts, left to right.

She swore up and down LA would never chase the New Yorker out of her, but the hot pink strands framing her face say otherwise.

"What are you wearing? I want to see."

I oblige by moving my phone up and down the length of my body.

"Nice."

"It's a discount find," I say.

"That may be the case, but you wear it well."

"Thanks."

"You didn't have a good time with your client?"

"I did. It was an amazing evening."

"You could've fooled me. What's up with that weird expression on your face? It's as if someone kicked your puppy."

I sigh. "Someone did."

She frowns. "What are you talking about?" I don't have time to answer before she fires off another question at me. "Don't tell me Hudson Kincaid went from charming, debonair billionaire to a frog overnight?"

I shake my head. "No, he's still dreamy."

"Which begs the question, what's up with that expression on your face?"

"It's Arya."

My best friend rolls her eyes. "What kind of trouble did she get into now?"

"It's about Hudson."

"What about him?"

"Let me start with how the evening unfolded."

"I'm all ears."

I kick off my heels, slide my feet into my house slippers, walk to the couch, and take a seat.

I tell my best friend all about tonight.

"Holy shit, Angelica!" my best friend says, fanning herself. "That was five-alarm hot."

"I swear, I couldn't remember my name," I say. "The way his skillful fingers brought me to orgasm… it was like an out-of-body experience. Hudson has given me the most thrilling, dirty, sexual experience of my life. Twice in less than twenty-four hours—"

"Did you return the favor?"

I shake my head. "Even though, I know I'd be awkward at

it, I tried, but he keeps telling me it's about me and there will be plenty of time for me to return the favor."

"What a man..."

"And it's not only about his kinky streak or how he pushes me out of my comfort zone. It's also about his praise. A guy like Hudson doesn't need a girl like me. I mean, what do I have to offer him? But he insists on making a big deal about how I connected with Isobel Wolfe and how that resulted in opening doors for him. Every time he brings that up, my insides feel like an explosion of confetti." I shrug. "Not even in my wildest dreams did I ever think I could catch the attention of a man like that."

"But you did. You're gorgeous, smart, and you're an amazing person. You've lost a lot over the last few years. Even in your darkest moments, you've sacrificed so much to make it easier for your twin to handle the pain of losing both parents, and having to adult. It's about time something good happened to you."

I nod, moved by her words.

"I still think a guy like that is out of my league."

"If he were, you wouldn't have spent an evening of debauchery with him."

I smile.

"Seriously, Angelica. New York City is the land of opportunity for a rich man—even more so for a billionaire. If he wasn't into you, it would've ended last night."

A part of me wants to believe her, but my insecurities have me convinced the other shoe is about to drop.

"It scares me—and thrills me—how my body responds to Hudson. How my good sense goes flying out the window when he looks at me with those beautiful blue eyes. I've never felt anything like it, and God, that freaks me out."

"You're so used to thinking for two, you're overthinking this."

"Arya is usually the one who loses her head—and good sense—over a guy after meeting him. It's not that my standards are too high, it's just that I don't want to repeat the same mistakes as her."

"I'd hardly call Hudson Kincaid a mistake."

"That's not what I meant. It's just fast... and furious."

"But it's amazing?"

"It's fucking amazing."

"So, what's the problem?"

"Arya."

"Huh?"

"Before I left Hudson's, we agreed we'd keep things quiet until the end of the week—"

"Why does it matter? You're not the escort. Your sister is."

"Yes, but Todd doesn't know we swapped places. If he ever found out, he'd fire Arya on the spot."

"This isn't going to be a long-term gig for your sister since you gave her an ultimatum."

I bite my lower lip. "I did." I hesitate. "She'd still be able to work as arm candy for three months. That's a lot of money, Sadie. We desperately need that money."

"Okay. You don't want to ruin a good thing because the money is out of this world. What does it matter if you tell her?"

"First, Hudson hired me this week as arm candy. Everything we did last night and tonight fall under a more expensive bracket. If Todd were to find out, he'd slap Hudson with a hefty penalty—"

"Since your sister can't keep a secret to save her life."

"Arya is like a colander."

"So, what she doesn't know, can't just come blurting out of her mouth when she isn't thinking."

"Which she tends to do a lot."

"By keeping her in the dark, she won't get her ass into more trouble than she already is, and sexy Hudson won't get slapped with a penalty."

"Exactly!" I nod. "There's just one problem with that plan."

"Which one?"

I share my sister's parting words.

"Crap!" my best friend says.

"I'm so swept away in this fantasy, it didn't even occur to me Arya would want—or need—to swap places. In my defense, how was I supposed to know a rich guy would be obsessed with me after meeting me once? Considering how apprehensive I was about going along with my sister's shenanigans, it took me by surprise how fast I fell head over heels for him."

"I know I said it earlier, but this is the kind of stuff fairytales are made of."

"Yeah, well, my fairytale will blow up in my face when Hudson meets Arya—"

"That's preposterous," Sadie says.

"You've met my sister and you know her as well as I do. She can get any guy wrapped around her pinky finger by batting her eyelashes." I pinch my lips together. "She's the exciting twin. It wouldn't take much for Hudson to succumb to her charms... not to mention she's far more experienced in bed than I am. I don't want her to get her claws into Hudson."

Chapter 21

Hudson

I'm pacing back and forth, my hands dug deep in the pockets of my suit pants, my mood as grouchy as it was when I first stepped into my office.

I come to a stop in front of the floor-to-ceiling window, my eyes lost in the horizon.

Goddammit.

I know I'm giving off a don't-fucking-breathe-the-wrong-way-around-me-unless-you-want-me-to-bite-your-head-off vibe, but I can't help it. I'm bone tired and frustrated from a restless night.

There's no doubt, Arya's blind faith caused the McQuinley twins to get entangled with a human leech. She's one loose cannon, but Ramsey manipulated them like a puppet master.

Piece of shit Ramsey Kenyon III.

I can't believe I ended up emptyhanded after hours of research online.

Sleuth detective, I'm not.

I might've failed my mission, but I know someone who wouldn't.

I walk to my desk, snatch up my phone, and compose a quick text to a buddy of mine who might have some insight on Angelica's situation. It's only seven in the morning, but hopefully, he can get back to me soon.

Even though it's likely Angelica is still asleep, I send her a quick text.

Hudson: Morning! Text or call when you wake up. I have a question for you.

Angelica: Morning! I'm up!

Hudson: You're an early riser.

Angelica: I'm not used to going out in the evening two nights in a row. On top of that, I had lunch with Grace yesterday. Translation: I had to wake up early to catch up.

Hudson: Got it.

Angelica: What did you want to ask me?

Hudson: Do you have anything to wear for tonight?

Angelica: I was planning on wearing the red dress I wore a couple nights ago.

Hudson: It looked fucking hot on you, but there's a color theme for tonight.

Angelica: What is it?

Hudson: Black and white.

Angelica: Oh. Shit.

Angelica: I don't think I have anything to wear that won't embarrass you with my basic wardrobe. I don't own anything that's gala-appropriate.

Hudson: You won't embarrass me, angel. That said, I don't want you to feel uncomfortable tonight.

Angelica: The red dress is the nicest dress my sister owns.

Hudson: It's not yours?

Angelica: No. She bought it with an advance from Todd. I'd have to ask her if she can get another advance.

Hudson: Forget about Todd and Arya. I'll buy you a dress.

Angelica: No, I can't accept that.

Hudson: In that case, we got ourselves a problem. I want you to accompany me tonight, but you don't have a dress. What do you suggest?

Three little dots jump around.

Angelica: Well, I guess I'll have to accept your generous offer, but on one condition.

Hudson: I'm buying you a dress, but you have conditions? I'll humor you. Let's hear it.

Angelica: It has to be budget friendly.

An evil grin slits my lips.

Hudson: You got yourself a deal, little lady.

Angelica: You're not going to fight me on this?

Hudson: Your terms are clear.

Angelica: Okay. Good. All right. Excellent.

Innocent little lamb.

Hudson: See you tonight.

Angelica: See you tonight!

Just as I drop my ass in my chair, my phone rings.

"Hey, Bryce," I say, accepting the call.

"Hudson, how are you?"

"Good. Can't complain. And you?"

"Same. What's up? Your text message said you're chasing down an asshole?"

If Ramsey is still alive, Bryce Van Der Linden can track him down.

"I am indeed."

"Did someone con you?"

"Not me. A dipshit bamboozled someone... close to me."

"Close, as in a friend?"

"A lot more than a friend."

"Got it. How can I help you?"

"I need to track down the whereabouts of a guy by the name of Ramsey Kenyon III—"

"Your friend got involved with that asswipe?"

"It's really her sister... but it's a long story. Suffice to say, my friend and her identical twin lost a lot of money they didn't have to lose in the first place."

"Stories like this make my blood boil."

"Same. I couldn't sleep last night after hearing how my friend got conned. I was so consumed, I got out of bed and trudged to my home office. In my delusion, I figured a few keystrokes and some in-depth Google searches would give me answers. That's how I found myself playing detective until four o'clock in the morning. Hours of research amounted to nothing at all. It's like Ramsey disappeared." I rub a hand over my face. "I'm told there's a possible connection between Ramsey and the Russian mob. Maybe he's under their protection?"

Bryce lets out a sigh. "After Ramsey's cryptocurrency Ponzi scheme scandal broke, five of his victims with deep pockets hired my firm to track the degenerate down."

"And?"

"And, this case has more spikes than a porcupine."

This doesn't sound good. "May I ask what you found out about the asshole?"

"This isn't the kind of conversation I can have over the phone, Hudson."

"I understand. Can we meet?" Before he can answer, I tack on another question. "I know you have an empire to run and your schedule is tight, but I'd be grateful for fifteen minutes of your time if you could squeeze me in."

"You're right. I'm slammed, but then again, I always am. Same as you. I was planning on having lunch tomorrow with my brother-in-law, but I'll cancel. Why don't we meet instead?"

Yes! I fist pump. "That sounds great. I really appreciate it."

"One thing, Hudson."

"What?"

"You should bring your friend to lunch. She should hear what I have to say first-hand. Come to my office and I'll get my executive assistant to order lunch in. What I have to share is best kept behind closed doors."

My eyebrows hit my forehead. "That bad?"

"Yes."

Shit.

Chapter 22

Angelica

The chauffeured Mercedes-Benz Hudson hired to take me shopping stops in front of a posh address I've walked plenty of times in front of, but never dared to step inside, not even to window shop.

No, he didn't.

No. No. No.

There must be a mistake.

There has to be.

I slide forward on the seat, my eyes locking onto the chauffeur's dark brown eyes. "I think you have the wrong address," I say. "I'm sure you were supposed to drop me off at an overstock or a secondhand shop. You know, a budget friendly shop."

He checks his iPad. "This is the right address," he says in a heavy Spanish accent.

"You're sure?"

"Mr. Kincaid gave clear instructions to drop you off at Saks Fifth Avenue. There is only one Saks Fifth Avenue in Manhattan."

The little devil.

"Can you give me one second? I'm just going to shoot Mr. Kincaid a quick text."

"Yes, ma'am. Take your time," the chauffeur says.

My thumbs fly on the screen as I compose a message.

Angelica: Why am I sitting in front of Saks Fifth Avenue?

Hudson: You need a dress.

Angelica: Are you kidding me right now?

Hudson: You said so yourself earlier. I figured, might as well go all the way by including shoes and everything else women wear to attend formal events.

Angelica: Two can play this game, buddy. I'm going to go to the discount store.

Hudson: Don't even think of stepping inside Saks Off 5th. I already called them and instructed the manager NOT to charge any purchases from their shop to my account. You'll have to shop in the **main** store.

Angelica: I thought you agreed to **budget friendly**.

Hudson: In my world, Saks Fifth Avenue **is** budget friendly.

Angelica: That's why you were so agreeable. You tricked me.

Hudson: I didn't. You didn't say **which** budget shop you were referring to.

Angelica: You're impossible.

Hudson: Why are you arguing?

Angelica: It's a question of principle. I don't want you to think I'm taking advantage of you.

Hudson: I don't.

Angelica: New York is the motherland a fashion. Surely there are some more budget friendly options.

Hudson: I'm sure there are, but I don't have an account with those budget-friendly options.

Angelica: I won't win this argument?

Hudson: Nope.

Angelica: You're impossible.

Hudson: You're repeating yourself, darling.

Angelica: Arghhh!!!

Hudson: Stop fighting me. Let me take care of you.

Angelica: The only reason I'm accepting is because I want to look the part.

Hudson: You already do. Except tonight, you'll look the part in a pretty black—or white—dress **I** bought you.

Angelica: I surrender. You win.

Hudson: That was a given.

Angelica: Cocky, much?

Hudson: Always. But that's beside the point. I had my executive assistant hire a personal shopper for the day for you. His name is Trenner. I'll send you instructions on how to find him and I'll tell him to expect you momentarily.

Angelica: OhmyGod! A personal shopper? Are you crazy?

Hudson: I already told you last night, I'm crazy about you.

I roll my eyes, but secretly I'm tickled pink.

Hudson: I also had my executive assistant reserve a table for you at L'Avenue. All shopping and no eating? That's a bad combination. Oh, don't be surprised if champagne is served.

Angelica: Hudson?!

Hudson: One last thing.

Angelica: WHAT?

Hudson: Are you shouting at me?

Angelica: YES!

Angelica: I'm not used to being treated like… like… Arghhh!!!

Hudson: Like what?

Angelica: Like a princess. I'm not used to this lifestyle.

Hudson: Go back to what I said earlier. Let me take care of you.

For someone who's been thinking for two and carrying way

too much on her shoulders, his willingness to take care of me touches my heart.

Angelica: What's the last thing I need to know? You hired flight time on a helicopter to take me to the event?

Hudson: No. But that can be arranged.

Angelica: Please, don't.

Hudson: Cool your jets. It's not far enough to warrant a helicopter ride.

Angelica: Okay. You had me worried there.

Hudson: To answer your question, I want you to look so fucking good tonight, my cock will be jumping out of my pants, begging to say hello.

Angelica: Holy shit! Your mouth. I guess in this case, I should say your fingers…

Hudson: THREE fingers, darling! Have a fun shopping day!

Saks Fifth Avenue from the inside is everything I could never have possibly imagined. Although I've lived in New York my entire life, I didn't even know there was a restaurant located inside Saks Fifth Avenue. L'Avenue at Saks—so appropriately named—isn't a run-of-the-mill eatery, it's French cuisine at its finest. Granted, I've only eaten at a French bistro when I was working corporate, but I'm certain this restaurant ranks way up there.

When I opened the menu, I nearly hyperventilated when I

saw the prices. I was so overwhelmed and intimidated by the selections—and accompanying eye-popping price tags—I played it safe. I was expecting a burger, but Saks's bacon cheese burger was so moist and juicy, I nearly wept at the first bite. My addiction to all things potato was satisfied when I bit into the crispy fries. The *fleur de sel* salt makes all the difference. I was a little more adventurous with the appetizer and selected the Neapolitan stack of eggplant burrata. Holy scrumptious. I might've gone a little crazy on the selfies and Instagram-worthy shots. I want to freeze-frame every little detail of this day forever.

I finish the last gulp of my lip-smacking champagne and drop the flute on the table when a waiter appears. The service here is impeccable.

"More champagne, madame?"

I shake my head. "No. Two glasses are more than enough."

"Everything was to your liking?"

"Everything was chef kiss!" And I do the chef kiss for emphasis.

"We aim to please," he says with a slight bow. "Dessert? Coffee?"

"I shouldn't."

"Ah, madame would be missing out."

"I guess... I could hear the selections." I mean, it can't hurt.

With a ceremonial flourish, he produces a menu from behind his back and places it on the table in front of me. "Everything on the menu is delicious, of course, but once a month the pastry chef makes his award-winning profiteroles." *Be still my beating heart.* "Today is the day."

"Really?"

"Oui."

This day keeps getting better.

"Let's do it! You only live once and all—" My phone chimes. I lift a finger. "Excuse me one moment."

The waiter responds with a bow.

The message from Trenner, the personal shopper, reminds me why I am here and why I need to limit my calories.

I respond to his text.

I lift my eyes, meeting the waiter's hazel-brown eyes. "I have to go. The personal shopper is ready for me."

"In that case, I'll send the profiteroles upstairs to the dressing room with coffee or espresso, whichever you prefer."

If you're going to twist my arm. "That would be lovely."

"Mr. Kincaid suggests I also tempt you to try *la tarte infiniment vanille*, aka the *very* vanilla tart. It's a crowd favorite. I'll include that one as well?"

Good grief, this waiter is a tyrant. "I've never tasted vanilla tart before."

"Then, it is settled."

~

After a half hour consultation, Trenner suggested I go for lunch while he pulled out a few selections that would stop traffic, as he says. Forty-five minutes later, and I've tried four dresses—all stunning designs that looked better on the rack than on my body.

I slip into design number five—a flowy white dress with abstract black flowers printed on the fabric. I made the mistake of looking at the price tag on the first dress I tried on and nearly collapsed to the floor. To preserve my sanity, I decided not to peek at the price tag anymore.

I finish the look with a pair of black heels I brought along with me, and step outside the dressing room, where Trenner is waiting for me, arms crossed over his wide chest.

"Hmmm." He scrutinizes me, tapping his chin with his finger. "Better. Give me a twirl." He motions with his finger.

I oblige.

"Not bad, but we're not going for not bad, are we?"

I shake my head. "We're going for fabulous." I borrow his words.

An appreciative smile stretches his lips. "You're a quick learner."

Trenner is tall, bald, and wears a pair of thick-framed, fashionable black glasses. The black man pulls off wearing a light-blue double-breasted suit with a white shirt, slim pants, and white cowboy boots, adorned with a gold tip, like it's nobody's business.

"I'm going to veto that last dress I selected earlier. While you were changing out of design number four, I pulled another design that will suit you better. You have breasts." His fingers gesture in that vicinity of my body. "Hips." He waggles his fingers. "And a butt. We need to accentuate all of that and take into consideration your petite frame." He walks to a chair, picks up a black dress, and strolls towards me. "This dress was designed with your body in mind," he says, extending his arms.

My eyes widen. "It's... stunning."

"It's an Italian designer, of course." *Of course.*

"What kind of fabric is this?" I ask, reaching out for the black dress. I've never seen anything like this before. Then again, I never shop at high-end stores.

"It's a sequined croc-effect," he says. "It's strapless, so it will showcase your beautiful neck while containing the girls, and the midi length will elongate your body."

For a girl who prides herself on being able to find the best discounted clothing in New York, this is a major upgrade.

Trenner walks past me and hooks the dress inside the

dressing room. "I also grabbed shoes and jewelry. Give me a second." He's back in a flash.

My jaw drops when I spot the red sole.

Holy shit!

"Are those Christian Louboutin?!"

He looks incredulous.

Fluttering his eyelashes, he recovers. "Of course they are." I've offended him. "This is Saks Fifth Avenue, not a knockoff store."

Embarrassment warms my cheeks. "Sorry. It's my first time playing a princess for an evening," I say, my tone sheepish. "All this is a little surreal." *And overwhelming.*

His expression softens.

"Count your lucky stars a man is willing to treat you like one, girl."

"I'm trying really hard to go with the flow."

"I know exactly what would help." He drops the white skyscraper heels on the floor. "Follow me."

I'm right on his heels.

We enter an office.

I hang out at the threshold, while he walks towards a safe?!

I crane my neck.

Oh, it is a safe.

He opens it, pulls something out, and turns around to face me as he hides his hands behind his back.

"You can't play a proper princess without jewelry. Ear bling." One hand produces a pair of dazzling hoop earrings from behind his back. "And wrist bling." The other hand produces a stunning bracelet dangling from two fingers.

"Those are beautiful!" I say. "It's amazing how they can make Swarovski crystals look like real diamonds."

Trenner stares at me with a scandalized expression on his

face. I've offended him again. "Girl, these are the *real* deal," he says.

They are?

"Mr. Kincaid didn't skimp. The diamond hoops cost ten thousand dollars."

Holy fuck!

His eyes drop to the bracelet before he locks his gaze onto mine. "Times that by *seven* for the BVLGARI Serpenti Viper 18K white gold and diamond bangle."

I'm dead.

Chapter 23

Angelica

Hudson Kincaid doesn't believe in half measures.

To top off the Made in Italy dress, French designer shoes, and expensive jewelry, Hudson also threw in a hair appointment at the Saks Fifth Avenue salon for hair, makeup, and a mini manicure. When I left Saks Fifth Avenue, I was in makeover heaven. That's until the driver announced there was one more stop. An hour later, I left a store I only knew about because it's featured regularly in one of my favorite romance author's books, with an enviable collection of luxury lingerie, courtesy of Agent Provocateur.

Forget about looking like a princess. I look like an empress.

I wish I felt more regal, though.

I might scrub up nicely—not that it's hard to do when you're wearing high-end everything—inside, I'm still a broke girl from Queens.

Translation: I'm a ball of nerves and worried I'll make a monumental faux pas tonight.

I don't want to embarrass Hudson.

Freaked out I might not know which cutlery to use, I spent

a whole damn hour watching proper etiquette videos on YouTube. I also checked out videos on how to eat oysters and snails. I hope neither of those delicacies will be on the menu. I don't think there's a proper or polite way to barf at the table. But like the Girl Scout motto dictates, "Be prepared". I doubt it will be required, but just in case, I also know how to curtsy.

Go, me!

The same Hispanic man that's been playing the role of my personal chauffeur all day drives me to the venue for tonight's gala in the Lower East Side. When we arrive, there's a long procession of luxury vehicles and limousines. By the time we reach the lineup of doormen, I'm practically jumping in my seat with a mixture of nerves and excitement. A young man opens the door and helps me out.

I'm standing among a swarm of extremely well-dressed people buzzing about on their way to the entrance.

Then it hits me.

I'm standing among a swarm of extremely well-dressed people.

A laugh escapes me.

How the hell did I end up among New York's elite?

I don't belong here. Don't fit in. Completely out of my element. And probably out of my mind. I'm so going to get exposed as the imposter I am.

My gaze bounces frantically as I search for Hudson.

I can't see him anywhere.

Crap.

Trepidation runs through me.

I get on my tiptoes, pretending that'll give me enough height to look over a crowd.

He said he'd wait for me outside, but I don't see him.

Taking a shaky breath, I place a hand on my tummy, my stomach doing somersaults as I search for my date.

Where is he?

Clenching my designer white clutch with my other hand like an anchor, I turn around to see if he'll emerge from one of the many cars slowing down in front of the venue.

A large hand finds the small of my back.

I jump and yelp at the same time.

"It's me," Hudson says. "I didn't mean to startle you."

His deep voice and Texan drawl are a dead giveaway. So is his distinct manly cologne emanating a dizzying amount of pheromones.

My tummy quivers.

I look up.

Dear God.

He's so handsome, I nearly swallow my tongue.

Hudson is porn suit perfection. Dressed down, he's sexy as hell. Dressed in a tuxedo that fits him to perfection, he looks... frankly, like he's way out of my league. That was clear from the moment I met him, but now realization is slapping me across the face. With his model-good looks, he belongs with all these beautiful people getting out of chauffeured luxury cars, partying on a yacht, jet-setting on private planes, or shopping on 5th Avenue or Rodeo Drive. He doesn't look like a guy I'd ever be lucky enough to date. Yet, here I am...

I shake my head, breaking out of my trance.

"You... you look so fucking hot." The words drop from my mouth without my permission.

Hudson barks out a genuine laugh.

God, his laugh is the best sound... and the way it softens his features causes my knees to buckle.

"You stole my line," he says, when he regains his composure.

"I expected you in a suit, but this..." I motion my finger up and down the length of his body. He oozes power. "Honestly, if

CEOs and Moguls don't feature you on their cover in one of their upcoming editions, I'll be picketing in front of their offices. Scratch that. You look so fine, I might start a riot."

He laughs again.

Don't ask me why, but eliciting laughter from a man who doesn't often crack a smile, makes me feel like a superhero.

"If we're exchanging compliments." He gives me a languorous onceover. "Trenner was certainly the man for the job."

"Look, pockets!"

Hudson knits his brows in confusion.

"Men always have pockets, regardless of what they wear," I say. "Women, on the other hand, never have pockets in cocktail or evening dresses. This is a big deal for formalwear."

"I'll take your word for it. Should I assume you like the dress?"

"I love the dress. I love everything."

"Good. And I must say, I like your hair pulled back."

I turn my head to show off my low chignon.

"Real classy," he says.

For years, I've watched the red-carpet events leading to awards shows. Never in a million years did I ever think I'd be decked out head to toe in couture, accompanying a rich man to one of those events.

Mind explosion.

"I gather you had a good day?"

I smile up at my hot date. "A full day of eating, shopping, and pampering at Saks Fifth Avenue? It was ah-mazing!" I say in a theatrical way. "For a girl like me, it was like receiving the A-lister star treatment."

He leans into me, his lips flirting with my earlobe. "Without having to see the other women attending, I already know my date will be the hottest woman in the room."

That's a tall order, but okay.

The best part about tonight isn't all the stuff or the bling. It's hanging from Hudson's arm as his date... not an arm candy escort for hire.

"You look good enough to eat, angel."

Oh, boy.

"I'm going to be the envy of every man here tonight. They'll wish they knew what you taste like... I'm the lucky bastard who knows."

Heat whooshes to my lady parts.

I clear my throat.

"On a more PG note," he says, "you do look the part. But then again, I knew you would."

I beam up at him.

"Thank you for saying that."

"You say that like I'm slicker than a slop jar."

I laugh. "That's a funny expression."

"It's as Texan as I am. It means you think I'm just giving lip service. I'm not. I tend to tell it like it is."

"You can give me lip service any time you want." I grin.

"You see," he says, dropping a kiss on my neck, "that's what I love about you, dirty girl. You'll get lip service soon enough."

Another woosh of heat.

I'll hold you to that!

"Thank you so much for a day I'll never forget," I say to change the topic.

"It's my pleasure." He taps the tip of my nose. "You wear the earrings and bracelet well."

"Hudson, you shouldn't have."

"Are you saying you don't like them?"

Worry slams into me. "No! That's not what I'm saying. I love them!" I don't want to come across as ungrateful. "Other than a few sentimental treasured mementos to remind me of my parents, they're my most treasured possessions." Even more so than my MAC laptop that took me three years to pay off.

"What are you complaining about, then?"

"It's a lot of money to spend on me."

"Why don't you let me be the judge of that?"

I blush.

"I feel like I should be walking around with a pair of bodyguards, given how expensive this is." I lift my arm, flashing him my bracelet, the constellation of diamonds glittering in the night.

"Darlin', I'll be the one guarding your sexy little body tonight."

It's so cheesy—and so totally adorable—I can't help but sigh.

"I don't think we're talking about the same thing," I say.

He stares at me with an intensity that shakes me to my core. "My version of guarding you is a whole lot better."

I purse my lips, feigning being unimpressed.

He drops a soft kiss on my forehead. "I really want to ravish your lips, but I don't want to fuck up your perfect makeup." His revelation ratchets my arousal. "Let's go inside before I decide to hightail it out of here and drag you back to my place for a repeat of last night." His voice is a deep, smoky rumble of sexiness. Beneath my Agent Provocateur strapless bra, my breasts grow tender, my nipples prickling against the satin fabric.

Good God.

Every time I'm near this man, it's like I'm one breath away from combusting like a volcano.

I'm tempted to pressure him to make do on his promise, but after so many hours of primping and prepping, I'd like to at least step inside this iconic venue. As much as I love getting down and dirty with Hudson, it would be a shame to come all the way here and not peek inside.

I hold his gaze. "What kind of gala are we attending?"

"My company, Pay Gateway, takes care of all the transactions flowing through www.nyc.com, aka New York's and Broadway online box office."

"That's so exciting!"

"It gets better."

I lean into him. "Do tell."

"This is a party to announce an anticipated Broadway show kicking off next season."

Dear God. It's like attending the Oscars.

I keep my cool, even though inside a marching band is giving the performance of a lifetime. "I see." My eyes land on a couple dressed to kill, heading to the entrance. "It's well-attended."

"Always is," he says. "Fixin' to mingle?"

Huh?

I guess my expression must give me away because he says, "Ready to mingle?"

"Hell yeah. I'm ready!"

Chapter 24

Hudson

The moment I set foot inside the Angel Orensanz Foundation, I was accosted by clients. After wrapping up a round of animated conversations, I have a minute to myself.

Although the party is going strong, I park myself near a window, place a hand over my heart, and lift my gaze to the ceiling.

I miss you, buddy.

For a few long seconds, I give into melancholy.

Someone bumps into me, jolting me back to the present.

"Sorry," a tall black man says.

"Don't worry about it."

I scan the crowd for my date.

Angelica has been gone for a while.

Since I was engrossed in shop talk, she excused herself to go to the bathroom. I get that the wait time for women is longer, but she's been gone a long time.

Concerned, I set off to find her. As I weave myself through

the crowd, I lift my head to see if I can spot her through the sea of people.

Did she get lost?

Nah. She's a smart cookie.

I pull out my phone and shoot her a text.

I clench the device in my hands and wait for a response.

A long minute ticks by.

An unease I can't quash builds at the pit of my stomach.

I lift my head and spot a waiter.

With *pardon me, I'm sorry,* and *excuse me,* I make my way towards him. After checking with the guy, I head towards the ladies' bathrooms. There are six bathrooms, two on each level, each with two stalls. Given the crowd, Angelica is probably in line waiting her turn.

Considering her sexy as fuck sky high heels, I'll start with the bathrooms on this level.

Just as I'm about to turn a corner, I hear a man's boisterous laughter.

My hackles rise.

I quicken my step.

When I turn the corner, I stop dead in my tracks.

My eyes drop to the floor, and I recognize Angelica's heels.

My heart freezes.

She's standing against a wall, and a man is caging her, his hands pressed against the wall on either side of her head. The guy isn't that tall, but he's wide.

What the fuck?

Jealousy floods through me like a shot of adrenaline, red filling my vision.

Anger fires through me in a rush of heat that could bring down this building in flames as my feet eat the floor beneath me.

When I come to stand near the asshole I'm about to send back to his maker, the man turns his head. Brown eyes lock onto me, and I'm hurtled back to seven years ago.

Shocked, I stagger back.

I blink in rapid succession, as if I just conjured a ghost.

The shock dissipates, replaced with disgust.

Baylor Tilney?!

A chill runs down my spine.

Unfinished business causes a storm of anger to whirl through me. It's as potent and destabilizing as the last time I was in the same room as this clown.

My gaze shifts to Angelica. "Come here." I point to the spot next to me.

She ducks underneath Baylor's outstretched arm and comes to stand near me.

I return my attention to a man I was hoping never to see again in this lifetime or the next.

"If it isn't Hudson Kincaid," Baylor says with a smirk.

Motherfucker.

My jaw clenches so tight, I'm certain my teeth will crack.

He straightens and adjusts his tuxedo jacket. "Long time, no see, old boy." He extends a hand. "Put it here."

The skin around his mouth and eyes looks too tight for his face.

Plastic surgery?

My gaze travels to his extended hand before meeting his eyes.

"What the fuck is going on here?" Manners go flying out the window when it comes to this dipshit. He doesn't deserve politeness or niceties.

He lowers his hand. "Just because you have a little money now, you think you're too good to shake my hand?"

Ignoring him, I turn my attention to Angelica. "What's going on here?"

Red blotches cover her chest and neck. "Baylor was trying to convince me that I had arrived at the event with the wrong guy, But I still had time to save my soul."

Rage grows so thick in my throat, it nearly chokes me. It's a miracle I manage to get any words out.

"By associating yourself with the devil?" Sarcasm drips from my question.

She shakes her head. "I was politely trying to tell him I wasn't interested, but he's... persistent."

A snarl rumbles in my chest.

My gaze travels to Baylor. "Leeches usually are."

"What language is that, Kincaid? Country bumpkin?" he says with a sneer.

I laugh without humor, shaking my head.

Unfazed, he keeps running his mouth. "With all that money I helped you amass, you think you would've hired a vocal coach to help you sound less... back country." His tone is imperious, as if he were a British Royal.

Without thought or care of my surroundings, I lash out. "You can kiss my ass, fuckface."

He takes a step closer, a bold move, considering I tower over him. He tilts his head back to look up at me, his beady brown eyes shooting daggers at me.

"You're such an ungrateful bastard. I made you, Kincaid." He waves a menacing finger at me. "Without me, you'd still be clinging on to your uncle's cleaning company—"

"Fuck you, Tilney!" I cut in. "I made myself."

Angelica must have a thousand questions, but Baylor Tilney's unexpected presence here has the same effect as a matador waving a red cape in front of an angry bull. No way am I moving my eyes away from the target.

His nostrils flare. "Without me, you would've never met Yonas."

"You're delusional! Whatever prescriptions you're getting from your doctor, change them."

"You stole that partnership from me." Another threatening finger waves.

"More like I rescued Yonas from a shark like you." I jab a finger right back in his ugly mug.

He levels me with the cool, smug gaze of a snake.

I keep drilling into him. "There's nothing admirable about conning people, Tilney."

"You don't know what you're talking about."

"You trade in lies and manipulations."

"Jealous people constantly try to bring down people who've achieved greatness. I'm an easy target."

"And I'm the fucking pope."

He takes a step back, readjusting his bowtie. "I don't con people." He makes a noise that sounds pitying. "They come to me, desperate, and eager to sign the contract I present them with. It's not like I have a gun pointed to their heads." A protracted laugh slips from his lying mouth. "What can I say? People believe what they wanna believe. It's not my fault if they can't read between the lines or don't read the fine print."

"They're chumps, right?"

"You said it."

I narrow my eyes at him. "You're as glossy as Texas asphalt on a hot as Hades day, spotted with motor oil."

"Can't get the Texas out of you, old boy."

I shake my head at the pitiful asswipe.

"I must say you surprised me, Kincaid."

I frown my confusion.

"Since you barely graduated from high school, I didn't

think you had the mental capacity to keep going on without the real brains of your operation."

His low blow sets me off.

We aren't alone in the hallway, and I'm aware people are staring, but fuck if that stops me. "Keep talking shit, and I'll make sure you're only able to consume liquefied foods for the next month."

He makes a show of looking around us. "Is that a threat?"

"What can I say? People believe what they wanna believe. It's not my fault if they read between the lines." I borrow his words.

He narrows his eyes at me.

I close the gap between us.

Startled, he takes a step back.

We do this song and dance a few times until his back hits a wall.

A scavenger caught in a mouse trap.

"One more thing," I say, lowering my voice. "You so much as breathe the same air as my girl again and I'll snap you like a fucking twig. You get in her face again, and I'll rearrange yours." I jab a finger in his face. "Don't look at her." *Jab.* "Don't talk to her." *Jab.* "You got that, or do you need me to repeat myself? With my country bumpkin pronunciation and all, I wouldn't want you to miss the goddamn message."

He lifts his hands in a truce. "She's all yours, buddy. I saw her arriving with you—"

"Then why the fuck were you trying it on?"

"To piss you off," he says.

My fingers curl into a fist, itching to punch his lights out.

"But she's so not my type—"

"You're begging for me to rearrange your face, Tilney."

"Ah!" He smirks. "Mission accomplished!" He's really pissing me off. "I had one goal in approaching your date—poke the fucking bear. I wasn't going to miss out on the chance to rattle your chain." If eyes could kill, the fucker would be lying in a pool of his own blood. "I prefer tall, model-thin girls... like the date who's waiting for me."

My brows go sky high. "You're here with a woman and you're hitting on another? You're two-faced in business and in relationships. Some things never change."

He shrugs. "I like to keep my options open in both arenas of my life."

Just as I'm debating if I shouldn't punch his teeth out, a man speaks. "Break it up, you guys."

I look at him.

Must be a security guard.

I don't budge.

"I mean it." He points a finger at me. "Step away. Now."

Fume is billowing from my nostrils as I take a step back, my eyes still glued to Baylor.

He smirks, and it takes everything in me not to let my fist fly.

"You"—the security guard points to Baylor—"move."

The weasel shuffles away.

The security guard gives me a hard look before turning on his heel.

A small hand presses against my back. "Hudson, what was that about?" Angelica asks.

I look over my shoulder.

I'm just about to answer her, but a voice announces dinner will be served momentarily, inviting us to make our way to our table.

"It's too heavy for me to explain right now," I say.

"Okay." Concern radiates from her big, gorgeous eyes. "Why don't we go eat? Maybe you need a stiff drink... or *five*."

I pull her into my arms. "You're right. A couple of drinks,

and I'll be like a new man." I lace our fingers together. "Let's go."

As we head towards our seats, my eyes land on a slim brunette sitting at our table. Her lips painted bright red part in a huge smile, revealing too-white teeth. With a hand pressed against her chest, above breasts the size of watermelons, she laughs. It's forced. Everything about her lacks sincerity. She catches me staring and flashes me a come-hither smile before flinging her long hair over her shoulder.

I don't think so, sweetheart.

My gaze shifts to the man accompanying her.

There are times in life when everything sort of slows down like they do in the movies. Your fight-or-flight instinct goes on high alert, and you see everything from a distance, as if you're looking through a telescopic lens.

This is one of those moments.

Baylor Tilney.

The man's presence rubs over me like a pervasive itch up my butt crack that won't go away. One you can't scratch in public without coming across as rude and crass.

My upper lip twitches, pulsating with anger.

For a few long seconds, Baylor and I enter a Mexican standoff.

"Howdy, cowboy." He gestures to the seats—*our seats*—across from him. "Take a load off. Same for the little lady." His mocking tone and appalling Southern accent grate at my last nerve.

I pin him to his seat with a glare.

When his lips part in an arrogant smirk, I have to hold back the urge to leap across the table Jack Reacher style and tackle him to the ground.

I've already put on a show. No need to embarrass Angelica further.

Fuck this.

I'd rather drink cyanide than sit down at the same table as this asswipe.

I turn to Angelica. "We're out of here."

Chapter 25

Angelica

Baylor Tilney is a primo jerk.

The only reason I didn't knee him in the balls is because I was afraid of making a scene that would've embarrassed Hudson.

Everything that came flying out of his mouth painted Hudson in such a negative light. I haven't known Hudson for long, but deep down, I knew this Baylor guy was talking shit.

That standoff confirmed it.

It's no wonder Hudson wanted to punch his lights out.

I don't condone violence, but if I was taller, I would've taken a swing at him for talking shit about my boyfriend.

I let out a sigh of relief when Hudson came to my rescue.

I wasn't ready for the storm veiling his eyes. His blue eyes were dark and menacing. I swear, I've never seen such rage radiating from a person in my life.

Scratch that.

That's probably how I look when I'm thinking of strangling Ramsey Kenyon III.

The ride from the Angel Orensanz Foundation is tense, to say the least.

As much as I'm dying to bombard Hudson with questions, I keep my mouth shut.

Other than to bark orders at the driver and make reservations somewhere else, he hasn't spoken a word.

I'm too chicken to speak.

He's been staring out the window. I have no doubt he's reliving that unpleasant scene.

My gaze drops to our joined hands. His fingers are laced with mine in a possessive way.

My eyes drift up to his tense profile again and I recall his words...

...I rescued Yonas from a shark like you.

Who the hell is Yonas?

Chapter 26

Hudson

It takes the entire ride to our destination to quell the anger that nearly caused me to do something that would've landed my ass in jail.

I have a lot more self-control than that, unless I'm confronted with a scum of the earth like Baylor Tilney.

When the car pulls in front of The Fifth rooftop bar on 5th Avenue, located just a few blocks from the Empire State Building, I've had time to swallow down my irritation over seeing the lying, cheating idiot.

I tap the chauffeur's shoulder. "No need to get out."

"Very well, sir."

I open the door, step onto the pavement, circle the front of the vehicle to Angelica's side to help her out.

She emerges from the car like a graceful black swan.

Draping my arm around her shoulder, I pull her close and guide her towards the building's entrance.

"Sorry I cut the evening short, angel."

She looks up at me. "It's not over yet. That's why we're here."

"I love your attitude, kid."

She responds with an exaggerated wink. "I've never been here, so for me, the adventure continues."

"You're going to love it," I say. "The rooftop offers one of the best views in New York."

"Better than the view from the forty-first floor of the Bymark Hotel?"

The mention of that night causes my cock to twitch in my pants.

I lean into her. "This setting won't allow for a repeat of a couple of nights ago." I run the tip of my nose along her cheek. She shivers. "But if you want, we can go there instead."

She clears her throat. "I wasn't suggesting that... but now that you mentioned it..."

My hand is itching to slap her ass, but I settle for something more acceptable. "Dirty girl."

She looks up at me from under her dark lashes. "If you weren't as talented with your fingers... and your mouth..." She lets her words trail.

I study her for a beat. "If I didn't feel obligated to make it up to you for tonight, I'd drag you out of here, fireman style, while dialing my driver with my free hand, so we could finish this evening at my place." I arch a brow. "I'm dying to find out what kind of lingerie you're hiding underneath the dress. But I'm a gentleman. I wouldn't want to shortchange you more than I already have. You look too fucking sexy not to enjoy you a little while longer in this dress."

She's at a loss for words.

"Don't start something you can't finish, angel."

"Noted."

"To answer your question, the view is different here because the rooftop isn't as high."

"Got it."

"If it were higher, it would be impossible to enjoy the rooftop in the winter."

Big green eyes widen in shock. "It's open during the winter?"

I nod. "This isn't Montana, but it's still cold in the winter."

"Don't people freeze?"

"You can reserve a heated custom built igloo, complete with fake fur blankets."

Her eyes practically take over her face.

"It's quite the experience. It's pretty cool when it's snowing. Same for the outdoor movie nights in the winter."

"It's like a reverse snow globe."

I chuckle. "You're right. The snow is outside the globe."

"Are the movies on a big screen?"

"No. Each igloo has a flat screen TV encased in a box, made to look like an old-fashioned 60s style television. It's set on top of a fireplace that's nothing more than a wooden box with a flat screen TV, featuring a nonstop video of crackling flames."

"That is so cool."

"It's wicked."

"Sounds like you come here often."

"This is another one of my haunts, yes."

"Don't tell me one of your friends owns this rooftop bar?"

I shake my head. "He owns the whole building."

Her jaw drops.

"Man, you know people in high places." It's not like I can deny knowing New York's movers and shakers.

"We'll come back this summer, and for sure this winter."

She flinches.

"What?"

"We're in July."

"I know."

"Coming back in the winter implies we'll still know each other six months from now."

"You plan on moving out of state?" My tone is teasing.

"No, silly." She laughs. "I just... didn't think we'd be seeing each other for that far out in the future."

"Unless you're done with me, I'm not done with you."

She rewards me with a beaming smile. "Deal! We'll come back this winter."

The doorman opens the door, and I invite Angelica to enter the building first.

She freezes on the spot, her eyes bouncing all over the place. "This is magnificent."

"It is. Remember my friend Logan Ellison?"

"The cover model on this month's CEO & Moguls magazine?"

I nod. "This is part of his empire. His sister oversaw the renovation. The woman has an eye for design."

Angelica nods, taking it all in. "Is this a residential building?"

"No, it's a commercial one. The building was converted into the headquarters of wholesale showrooms for the home décor industry. There are over two hundred showrooms."

"Wow!" Her eyes drift to the ceiling. "Holy gorgeousness!"

I lift my gaze. "The custom crystal chandeliers here are something else."

"Everything in your world is something else."

"In that case, let's go dive deeper into my world."

"Sounds good to me."

Sandwiched between other patrons, we ride the elevator to the top floor.

Hand in hand, I guide her towards the maître d'hôtel's station.

A few keystrokes later, and a waiter is walking us to our table, near a floor-to-ceiling window, overlooking the rooftop.

"We're not sitting outside?" Angelica asks as I help her into her seat.

"It was too last-minute to get a table," I say. "Not to mention, this is a lot more private." This works well for me. I owe her an explanation, and I'd rather not air my dirty laundry for all to hear. "We can take a tour when we're done, then we can park ourselves at one of the standing-only high tables and order a drink and dessert."

"That works for me."

I circle the table, unbutton my tuxedo jacket, and take a seat across from her. "We might be a little overdressed for the venue, but who the hell cares, right?"

She responds with a complicit grin.

Our waiter returns with glasses of water as we peruse the menu. A few minutes later, he's back to take our drink and food order. He doesn't waste time returning with our drinks. A French 75 with rosé for her and a Rusty Nail for me.

Thank the fuck God.

We clink glasses and I take a long swig of my drink. I welcome the burn of the alcohol trailing down my throat.

Angelica gulps down a generous amount of her cocktail.

I'm sure she's as troubled as I am by my hostile attitude tonight.

"Although not nearly as fancy as what we would've been eating had we stayed at the Broadway event, the food here is outstanding."

"I have no doubt it is."

She's so easy-going.

I drop my tumbler on the table and address the elephant in the room.

"About tonight—"

"I wasn't flirting with that guy, Hudson. After taking care of business, I stepped out of the bathroom and there he was. He told me he was waiting for me. At first, I was confused, because I didn't know him. He suggested we get out of the way, so I did. That's when I found myself caged in against the wall."

I open my mouth to speak, but she lifts a hand, stopping me.

"Please let me explain. Even before stepping into the venue, I didn't feel like I belonged. The last thing I wanted to do was bring attention to myself, embarrassing you in the process. That's why I didn't knee the jerk in the junk."

"Baylor loves stirring trouble," I say. "I'm sure the minute he saw us arriving, he had already devised a plan to rattle my cage."

She leans into the table. "Who is he?"

I'm just about to answer when our waiter returns with our appetizer.

Before he scurries off, I ask him to hold off on our main meal until I give him the okay.

"Wow, these look amazing," Angelica says, her eyes fixed on the appetizer platter.

"It tastes even better than it looks."

"I've never had chorizo sausage before."

"I'd never steer you wrong when it comes to sausages."

"Why, Mr. Kincaid, was that a very inappropriate joke about your package?" She bats her eyelashes coquettishly.

"Why, Miss McQuinley, I believe it was."

She giggles.

"Eat up now."

Angelica grabs a grilled shrimp and chorizo kabob, pops it into her mouth, and chews.

Her eyes roll to the back of her head and she moans.

She brings a hand in front of her mouth and says, "Ooohhh. This is out of this world."

She grabs another kabob.

"You're not wrong." I place a few on a small plate and dive in.

"If the appetizer is this delicious, I can just imagine how mouthwatering the main dish will be."

"It certainly is. Every time I come here, I tell myself I'll try something else on the menu, but I always fail."

"The dry-aged New York steak frites is that good?"

I nod. "Can I tell you a little secret?"

"Yes!" She's practically bouncing in her chair.

I feel like I've known her for a long time, but then I remember, we only met forty-eight hours ago. I've shared a few things about my past, but for the most part, I've been a closed book.

"Until making it big, I didn't know rich people—or the French—ate their fries with fancy, garlicky mayo. I thought everybody on the planet ate their fries with ketchup."

She laughs.

"Nowadays, I have to have both to dip my fries in—aioli and ketchup."

"Same!"

Her expression changes.

I frown. "What is it?"

She bites the inside of her cheek. "I'm dying to know how you made it big, but I'm afraid to ask for fear of overstepping my boundaries."

"Well, I guess this is as good time as any to explain what went down between Baylor and me."

"I don't want to pry."

"That was an over the top display of testosterone. You deserve an explanation."

"If you're willing to share, I'll gobble it up."

"You already know I'm an orphan." She nods. "I also told you my uncle died eight years ago."

"Yes, but you never mentioned how they died."

"Let me start with my parents."

She sits a little straighter in her chair.

"After a devastating hurricane in Louisiana, my parents' church organized a convoy to help the people who had been most affected. My parents—Nora and Lander Kincaid—volunteered, leaving me behind. My dad was a superintendent of the 6-plex building we lived in. My best friend and his single dad were tenants, so I stayed with them while my parents were gone. Three days into their trip, my best friend's dad got a call. During a bad post-hurricane storm, my dad lost control of his car."

"Oh my God."

"It wasn't the crash that caused my parents' fatal injuries. It was their exposure to high voltage electricity that occurs when a crash results in electrical lines being downed."

Angelica places a hand over her heart. "I'm so sorry."

"It never occurred to me my parents wouldn't come back from their trip."

"I get it. You see your mom or dad in the morning, and the next thing you know, you get a call from the police." She knows what's it like. "Sorry, I didn't mean to interrupt."

I shake my head. "Don't be." I inhale a deep breath, calming my trepidation. Only one other person knows my story. And he's hanging out with Mom and Dad. "A few days later, I got a call from an uncle I really didn't know that well, telling me I was moving with him to the Bronx. Since I was six months shy of my eighteenth birthday when my parents died, I didn't have a choice. My dad's older brother was now my guardian. I wished Uncle Macon lived in Summerville—where he was born—so I could be close to my best friend, my buddies, and everything that was familiar to me, but he didn't. From a very young age, my uncle couldn't wait to get out of the small town he was born in. After serving in the army, he settled in New York. He worked a few jobs, and he decided working for the man wasn't for him. He wanted to forge his own path. Since Manhattan is the land of office buildings, he started his own commercial cleaning company—no shortage of work. He never wanted kids, and he didn't attempt to hide his displeasure at becoming a father-figure. He treated me like I was an inconvenience—"

"That's so wrong. He was your uncle."

"It didn't change the way he viewed things," I say. "Since Mama always taught me to pull my own weight, I told him I wanted to work for him to help with bills and put food on the table. He took me up on my offer. Working for my uncle was just as bad as living with him. He was an asshole and never missed a chance to break my balls. His weekend workouts consisted of drinking his way through copious amounts of booze. When he'd get drunk, he'd get violent—"

"Did he hit you?"

I twist my lips.

"Child abuser," Angelica says in a whisper. "What a monster."

"Since I wasn't a scrawny boy, I'd fight back. It got ugly—and bloody. With broken jaws, at times." She looks horrified. "I was miserable living in New York. I hated the Bronx—"

"You were uprooted from your life—from small-town tranquility to the concrete jungle."

I respond with a tight nod. "The adjustment was rough. Downright impossible on some days. I hated the commute to New York. I hated the subway, period. It was dirty, noisy, smelly, crowded, and it was underground. It always felt like I was descending into the bowels of hell. I also hated I had to leave my high school girlfriend behind. And more importantly, I hated breathing the same air as my uncle."

"It must've been a horrible situation to be in."

"It was hell on earth." I fidget with my bowtie. "The minute I celebrated my eighteenth birthday, I packed the little I had to my name, and moved back to Texas."

"Didn't your uncle try to stop you?"

"He was too happy to slam the door on my ass. Since he stopped calling me by my name and referred to me as ungrateful bastard all the time, I was too happy to get the fuck out of New York."

She reaches for my hand. "I'm so sorry you had to go through that. Your uncle sounds like he was a mean grump."

"He wasn't a grump. He was an utter asshole."

Her brows knit together and her lips pull down in a frown.

"My sole living relative wanted nothing to do with me." I sneer.

She holds my gaze for a long beat.

"What happened when you moved back home?"

"Instead of moving back to Summerville, I moved to Dallas. My best friend had scored a job for a prominent construction company that specialized in condos. Those apartments in the sky were popping up all over the place. Since I had years of experience working construction in our small town, it didn't take long for me to get a job, working along with him."

"What kind of work did you do?"

"Neither my best friend or I had a trade degree, so we did grunt work."

"Did your high school girlfriend join you?"

"No. She didn't wait for me. She moved on to another guy. We were young." I shrug. "In any case, it wasn't too bad being single in Dallas. My best friend and I had a good life. We were young. We were working full-time. We made decent money.

We shot the shit with friends on weekends. We lived together. Our fridge was always packed with food and booze. For two years, it was Nirvana. We were twenty years old and living the dream. Then, we decided to rent a house. It was a single level house, but we had more space than the two-bedroom apartment we were renting. More Space. Bigger parties."

She laughs.

"Hey, that's what twenty-year-old guys do."

She rolls her eyes. "If you say so."

"Everything was pretty great until we each started dating..." I let my words trail.

"Uh-oh. Your girlfriends didn't get along?"

"Justin's girlfriend was a bitch. I couldn't stand her. To his credit, Justin lasted three months before calling it quits. On the other hand, my girlfriend was a dream... or so I thought—"

"Was she also a bitch?"

"Worse."

"Yikes."

"Long story short, on Sundays, I'd meet up with a bunch of guys to play football until we were too exhausted to move. Justin was a baseball fan, so he'd sleep in late. On that particular Sunday, it started to rain hard an hour into the game. We cut our play time short. Instead of going out for a hearty breakfast with the guys, I headed home. I figured I'd shower then drive to my girlfriend's place so we could go out for brunch—she loved brunch. To my surprise, when I pulled in front of the house, her car was parked next to my best friend's truck. I was excited until I walked through the front door. I froze in place when I heard an animalistic growl, followed by"—I place a hand in front of my mouth and lean into the table, so only Angelica can hear me—*"You dirty whore. You love my cum even more after I've fucked your slutty ass bareback. Now, open wide."*

"Dear God."

I rest my back on the seat. "Even though I knew exactly what was going on, I still needed to see it with my own two eyes. As quiet as a mouse, I tiptoed to my best friend's bedroom. Since the door was ajar, I was privy to a hell of a grand finale. My naked girlfriend was on her knees as my best friend was releasing himself all over her face."

Angelica's mouth drops open.

"At least they didn't try to insult my intelligence by telling me, *It's not what you think.* I broke things off with my girlfriend and told my best friend I was moving out. While I was looking for a new place to stay, we ignored each other. Same MO at work. Just as I was about to sign a new lease, I got a call from a lawyer in New York. My drunk uncle had drowned in his bathtub—"

"Good God."

"It was a gruesome death. That wasn't the biggest shock. Apparently, I was the only person in his will."

"Even after the way he treated you?"

"That was my reaction. In any case, I quit my job and moved back to the city I promised myself I'd never set foot in again. It took me hours after the will reading to absorb my new reality—my uncle left me his cleaning company, his small house in the Bronx, his debt load, and everything else that made up his miserable life." I rake my hands through my hair. "I was scared shitless. I didn't know the first thing about running a company, and I sure as hell didn't know the first thing about managing employees. The first six months in New York, I didn't sleep. I barely ate. I was a ball of stress. And I worked up to twenty hours a day, often filling in for employees who couldn't make it to their shifts for whatever reason. For the four hours I would lie in bed, staring at the ceiling in the middle of the night, my mind would try to find ways to get out of the situation. I hated the cleaning business, but I couldn't just close shop and move on with my life."

"Because the employees would be left high and dry?"

"Exactly. There were too many people who were depending on me. They had mortgages to pay, weekly grocery bills, and other expenses. They were also counting on the health insurance my uncle offered. The pressure was eating me alive. At three o'clock in the morning one day, I stumbled upon one of Baylor's videos promoting his upcoming Rebooting Your Business event. It was free. From his bio, it sounded like the guy knew what he was talking about. He used to work for a big Wall Street investment firm. What I didn't know at the time was that he worked an admin desk job. He was never a trader."

"No way?"

"Yeah." I nod. "He crafted his persona by emulating a lot of the traders he used to work with. That's why he sounded like he knew his shit. It was all smoke and mirrors."

"Unbelievable."

"He's a great con artist."

"Like someone else I know."

"For the record, until yesterday, when you told me about Ramsey, I didn't think it was possible to hate anyone more than Baylor."

Her shoulders slump. "Did Baylor steal from you?"

"No, but he almost fleeced me."

"What did he do?"

"I signed up real quick for the Rebooting Your Business event. The idea behind Baylor's free evening training is to upgrade participants to a month-long more advanced training. Four weeks for only two-hundred-and-ninety-nine-dollars. Once again, I didn't even question it. I was all in. The first night of training was a bit of a letdown."

"In what sense?"

"It wasn't so much training, but more of a big song and dance show. Right before wrapping up, Baylor told us he'd select ten participants who would become his apprentices—he'd partner up with us to take our business to the next level. He warned us there would be a long questionnaire to answer, but for the selected few, it might be the most important questionnaire of our lives." I pop another kabob in my mouth and chew.

Angelica does the same.

I wipe my mouth with the cloth napkin before continuing. "At the end of the evening, I was just about to race to the front to tell Baylor I was determined to be among those ten people, when the guy sitting next to me asked me a question. English wasn't his first language, so he didn't catch a lot of what Baylor said. One question led to another. Even though his Spanish accent was pronounced, this guy's background was really interesting."

"Baylor mentioned a guy by the name of Yonas. Is that him?"

I nod. "I was at the training to learn the basics of running a business. He was there to gain more insight in business lingo, so when he was ready to go out and pitch his business idea to potential partners, he'd have a better grasp of the language. Eventually, we had to vacate the space. Baylor was long gone, and neither Yonas nor I noticed when he left the room. I suggested we go to a diner that served all-day breakfast to continue our conversation—that was one of the things I loved the most about living in New York back then, and it fit my budget. I didn't have any friends in New York. Yonas was my age and his family lived in Argentina, so, like me, he was alone in the Big Apple. The more we talked, the more it became obvious. Yonas Elmkies was what you call a brainiac. I never stopped teasing him about that."

"Stopped?" She hesitates. "As in past tense?"

"Yes."

Sadness morphs her features. "You've lost a lot of people."

"I have." It takes me a minute to find the courage to continue speaking. "Like I said, Yonas's brain was like a computer. The week that followed changed the dynamic between us. We were in constant contact. Neither of us had siblings. We became fast friends. That's when I learned he was renting a small two-bedroom apartment with four other guys he knew from college who spent most of their free time gaming and partying. I offered him to move in with me since I lived alone in my uncle's house. Even though the mortgage was paid off, I needed help to pay for the taxes and utilities. I also welcomed the company. There's nothing fun about being a lone ranger."

"I can imagine," she says. "My twin is trouble with a capital T, but at least I'm not alone."

"You're lucky that way. You have someone in your camp."

"Even though I didn't feel that lucky two days ago, when I had to pretend to be her."

"But that paid off for everyone involved." I tap the tip of her nose.

She pulls her lower lip between her teeth, peering at me from under her long lashes, blushing from ear to ear.

"Circling back to Baylor."

"Douche canoe Baylor."

"Touché." I chuckle. "Yonas and I made the cut. We were ecstatic. It was as if we had won the Powerball's big win. Baylor was heading to Vegas for two weeks to conduct training out west. During that time, Yonas and I were to fill out a more detailed questionnaire, review the contracts, and sign on the dotted line. We had individual meetings with Baylor, and he told us the same thing in regard to hiring an attorney to go over the contracts. He said usually people who come to him don't have a lot of money. Baylor told us we were welcome to hire a lawyer, but since the contract was fairly standard, why dig ourselves into a bigger hole by pissing good money away? After all, New York lawyers don't come cheap. Yonas was on a student visa and money was tight. At least in his case, he was big on ideas, even though he was short on cash. I was short on both."

Angelica's brow wrinkles. "I'm not an expert, but Baylor's comment sounds shady."

"You're a smart cookie."

Her tense expression softens. "You sweet talker, you."

I wink.

"As much as I hated having inherited my uncle's cleaning company, it was the best thing that could've happened to me."

"How so?"

"There were numerous lawyers' offices on my uncle's roster of clients."

She slaps her forehead with the palm of her hand. "Of course."

"I resisted at first. I didn't want to foot the legal bill to have a lawyer review a stack of documents this thick." I part my fingers, illustrating my point. "I figured I would go over the contract for both Yonas and me, and use Google as a reference as Baylor suggested—"

"That was his cost-saving idea?"

"It was."

"That's as smart as using Google to diagnose your own health issue."

"Baylor was very convincing."

She shakes her head.

"A few pages in, and I knew I was way over my head. Not

even Google could help me make heads or tails of certain legal terms."

"Hence, why lawyers go to law school."

"Right. But it wasn't only the contract. The second questionnaire delved real deep into everything we owned—all assets and liabilities. Don't ask me why, but something just didn't sit right with me."

"Did you listen to your gut?"

I nod. "Yonas and I talked it over. We decided to suck it up and approached one of the law offices my crew cleaned. I went in with plans to report back to him. I was paired off with a junior lawyer who looked like she had graduated from high school that morning. I figured I'd gotten the short end of the stick, but it couldn't be worse than me having to decipher all that legal gibberish on my own. I didn't hear from her for three days. I emailed her, but got a succinct answer, *I'm still working on your case.* When she called me back, she suggested I come in with Yonas because he would require separate representation. My expectations were low. I underestimated that woman."

"She found something in the contract that was suspicious?"

"Yes."

"Good for you."

"My lawyer was young but determined to make her mark. Not only did she go through the contract with a fine-tooth comb, she researched Google like the search engine was her bitch. Conclusion, signing a contract with Baylor was the equivalent of selling your soul to the devil. It wasn't a 50-50 partnership. It was a 55-45 structure that gave him a leg up. Essentially, he became a majority owner, holding all the power."

"Jesus!"

"That five percent doesn't look like much when you're desperate, but when you're trying to get out from under his thumb, it does. In Yonas's case, it was a 70-30 split *and* profits paid for *five* years after the end of the contract."

"That sounds as outrageous as the interest my sister is paying to her loan shark. She's holding onto the short end of the stick."

"Different situation. Same outcome. The person who's desperate gets fucked over."

She shakes her head, disgust twisting her lips.

"Baylor had convinced Yonas he was sitting on a multimillion-dollar business idea, but his English would hold him back. It was better for him to be in the background if he wanted the company to thrive. Even though Yonas was the brainchild behind one of the most innovative payment gateways on the market, Baylor would've been the one cashing in."

"That's bullshit!"

"That's Baylor for you."

"I guess you ended up partnering up with Yonas?"

"I didn't have the courage to suggest it. I was twenty-one, and I only had a high school degree. I thought he would laugh in my face. Imagine my surprise when he brought it up after we left the lawyer's office. We were roommates, and I never made him feel less than worthy because he wasn't fluent in English. In other words, he trusted me. Given my southern roots and Yonas's Hispanic ones, we decided to man up and meet with Baylor at his office upon his return to politely decline his offer and bow out of the mentorship program."

"I can't imagine it went well."

"I didn't expect he was going to be jumping for joy, but I didn't expect his reaction."

"Did he lose it?"

"He went all Jekyll and Hyde on us. Long gone was the polite, smiling man. He went apeshit crazy. He was right in our faces, pointing an aggressive finger, yelling so loud, spit was flying out of his mouth. He was only in his late thirties at the time, but his face was so red and his eyes bugged out of his head to the point where I thought he was going to have a heart attack. He called me a back country hick who'd never fit in—a simple country boy who'd never express himself in a way wealthy people respect—"

"What a vile bully."

"He was—and still is—a piece of shit."

"I agree."

"After a long list of insults, he told us we'd eventually come crawling back to him for help. And when we did, the only job he'd be willing to give us was to wipe the shit from his ass after he was done taking a dump. To drive his point, he added vulgar gestures of him squatting down as if he was taking a dump before wiping his ass. He even forced a loud fart."

"You mean a farting sound he made with his mouth."

"No. I mean, an actual fart."

Angelica's head jerks back. "Are you kidding me?"

"I'm not."

"So rude. And vulgar."

"The man was unhinged. But it gets better—"

"Did he unzip and urinate at your feet?"

"Had he done that, he would've lost his dick, then his teeth."

She laughs.

"After we left his office, he started bombarding us with nasty texts and emails. He was relentless."

"Did you block his number?"

"We did. He kept getting our new numbers."

"Okay, that's freaky."

"It was so unsettling, I went back to the law firm that helped me with the contract to inquire about a restraining order."

"Did you have to get one against him?"

"We changed our numbers and opened new email accounts and waited it out. Either he got tired of pestering us or he set his sight on new victims."

"He finally stopped badgering you?"

"Yes, but when we got our first taste of success with Pay Gateway, he kicked off his campaign again, sending nasty messages to the email we had listed on the website."

"That's harassment." Angelica's indignant expression speaks volumes.

"When Baylor is unable to manipulate you into getting what he wants from you, he turns into a psycho asshole. His second smear campaign lost steam real fast."

"Thank God."

"Actually, the second time around, I was looking forward to going toe to toe with him. We had the money to hire the best lawyers in Manhattan to nail his ass to the wall."

"Speaking of lawyers, that woman saved you from partnering up with one crazy, two-faced asshole."

"She did. She allowed us to see Baylor's true colors. After dodging that bullet, Yonas and I were ready to move forward full speed ahead. The only problem is, we needed capital to get the business off the ground."

"Since things were tight for both of you, how did you manage?"

"You know what other kind of offices my uncle's company used to clean?"

She thinks for a minute, her finger tapping against her chin, as her green eyes search the ceiling. "I got it!" Her gaze fixes onto mine. "Business consultants or accounting firms?"

I point at her and pretend to shoot a gun. "Bingo! I approached a few firms, and I selected the one that made me feel the most comfortable. I wasn't selling a tech sensation. I was selling a commercial cleaning service. It turns out, there was a demand for an established business with a group of employees with good work records. My uncle also had some stocks—to my surprise, they were really great ones. With the help of a trader, I sold the vast majority of them."

"And just like that you were in business!"

"We were."

"Watch out, Manhattan!"

I chuckle.

"Yonas and I worked tirelessly from our first headquarters, aka the living room of the house we shared in the Bronx. I'd teach him English. He'd teach me everything I needed to know, so I'd sound half intelligent about our business. We both spent hours watching so many YouTube videos, reading business blogs, articles, and books we'd go cross-eyed—"

"Did you go to business school or get an MBA?"

"Yonas finished his degree. But I never got any formal education. Over the years, we acquired the skills we needed to stay on top of the business world by taking online classes, attending seminars, conferences, and weekend specialized training."

"Very impressive."

"At the end of the day, my highest degree is still a high school degree I barely managed to earn. I was never great at school. For many years, it made me feel less than so many other successful New Yorkers, but then I became a member of the VIP Den, and I was surrounded by kickass men and women who held a *real-life* MBA," I say that last part in air quotes.

"You're self-taught and a self-made billionaire. That's nothing to sniff at."

"Given my humble beginnings, I never thought I'd get this far in my life. Certainly not at such a young age."

"I'm sure your parents must be watching you from Heaven with such pride."

"Since their deaths, I vowed not to let them down."

"I think you've achieved that in spades," she says.

I send a silent prayer to Mom and Dad.

"Sorry, I interrupted you. Please continue. I'm fascinated by your story."

It does something to me to hear her say that.

"When Yonas and I weren't cramming our brains with knowledge, we were securing appointments with prospects. Then, we'd adorn cheap suits we bought at discount stores and ride the subway to make our presentations in Manhattan. One client at a time, and a year and a half after we met at Baylor's training event, we were able to move our operations to a bona fide office in the Bronx. Granted, it was a shoebox—a room in a shared office space. Still, it was a place for us to hang our shingles and hire an executive assistant. As a reward for our achievement, we headed to Vegas for a week-long vacay."

"Viva Las Vegas!"

"One of your favorite party places?"

She shakes her head. "No. Remember, I've never been on a plane before."

"We're going to have to change that."

"It's okay."

I cock an eyebrow. "You don't want to live out the adventure?"

She lifts her wrist, pointing at her bracelet. "You've been more than generous."

"What did we agree on?"

"*Hudson.*" She draws out my name, shifting uncomfortably on her chair.

"I expect an answer."

"To let you take care of me."

"Exactly."

"But—"

"No Buts." My tone brooks no argument.

She rolls her eyes, a small smile stretching her lips.

"How was the trip to Vegas?" she asks.

"After checking into our hotel, we decided to walk The Strip. We passed in front of a venue that was hosting the biggest yearly adult entertainment industry expo. We weren't planning on going in, but the two gorgeous—and scantily clad—hostesses at the entrance informed us there were still tickets left. It was more curiosity than anything else—"

She snorts. "Right."

I lift one hand and place the other over my heart. "I swear on a stack of Bibles."

Her dubious expression hasn't changed.

"Four hours later—"

"And you had seen enough T and A, small and big Ds, and God knows what else to last you a lifetime?"

"Yes, smartass. We saw a lot of tits, ass, dicks of all sizes, and a few other freaky things. *And* we found out how much money adult toys pulled in every single year."

"I bet it's a lot."

"At the time, the amount seemed obscene. But then, it got even better when we found out most of those sales were through online stores."

"And online stores require payment carts."

"They require *very secure* payment carts."

"Of course."

"Since it was the first day of the four-day expo, Yonas and I went back every single day. We talked to three-hundred-plus exhibitors. Nothing beats face to face."

"So much for a vaca. You guys worked most of the week."

"And it was worth every single handshake. Vegas was a game changer."

"You got a lot of clients from that expo?"

"When we got back to New York, we followed up like our lives depended on it. We didn't close everyone we spoke to, but we signed up a considerable number of clients. Word of mouth got out that the technology behind our shopping carts was more secure than most on the market. More clients came knocking at our door. From then on, we grew in leaps and bounds. We could barely keep up. Forget about hitting milestones, we were smashing them. We were even able to rent an office in Manhattan, which we had to expand to two floors within a year.

"Amazing!"

"It was wild," I say, flashing back to those days. "When we had our first billion-dollar year, we gave gargantuan bonuses to every employee, and we threw a party that would've made rock stars proud. After that, everything snowballed. Billions of dollars in sales kept pouring in every single year. We upgraded our lifestyle, our houses, our wheels, our watches, we were no longer buying suits or shoes off the rack, you name it. Nothing was out of reach. Not a damn thing. It's like we were on a rocket, traveling through space at lightspeed. There were so many great articles about us in business magazines. All that buzz was keeping us busy and filthy rich."

"Life was good," she says.

"Life was fucking good. Then, life took a cruel turn." I let out a sigh. "The Angel Orensanz Center is known as an art and performance center, but it was originally built as a synagogue."

"I didn't know that."

"Yonas got married there to the woman of his dreams—"

She reaches out for my hand and squeezes it. "It must've been so hard for you to return to that venue."

"I've attended other events there since his death, but every time I'm there, I'm flooded with images of Yonas's big day. Inevitably, sadness washes over me. A year and a half ago, he was celebrating his one-year anniversary. Him and his wife decided to visit the motherland."

"Argentina?"

"Israel. Yonas and his wife were Sephardic Jews, aka Hispanic Jews. Since his wife was expecting twins, they wanted to make the long trip before the babies arrived."

"Oh God, they never came back?"

I shake my head. "No. They died in a terrorist attack."

Angelica gasps.

"I was distraught. Yonas was more than a business partner. We were as close as brothers. To honor his parents' wish to have him buried where he was born, I paid to get his body and his wife's flown to Argentina. I flew down for the funeral with a bunch of our directors and VPs. It goes without saying, I made sure Yonas's family was set for life, but the money wouldn't replace their son, daughter-in-law, or unborn grandkids."

Angelica squeezes my hand.

I squeeze back.

"Even in my grief, I had to keep moving forward because we had so many employees who counted on me. I couldn't drop the ball."

"That must've been so much pressure." Her expression is sorrowful.

"I'll be honest, I didn't think I could carry the business on my shoulders alone. I didn't think I had what it took. I was no longer the twenty-going-on-twenty-one-year-old young man who had inherited a cleaning company he had no business running, but old insecurities crept in. I was a small-town boy without a college degree, let alone an ivy league education, running a multibillion-dollar company on my own. I was certain I was going to fuck it all up—"

"But you didn't."

I shake my head. "Thank God. That would've been a horrible way to honor my best friend's memory. No one jumped ship. Every staff member was one hundred percent behind me. I also had a lot of support from my buddies at the VIP Den and their contacts."

"And here you are, standing strong, Mr. CEO." She punctuates her sentence with an exaggerated wink.

"I didn't do it alone."

"But you're the captain of the ship."

"A captain with a kickass crew."

"The nerve of Baylor Tilney for thinking you owe him anything."

"In essence, I owe him for putting Yonas and me in the same room. But that's as far as it goes."

"I wish Arya and I had consulted with a lawyer before signing our lives away to the devil—"

"Speaking of Ramsey. I was going to tell you, but seeing Baylor again, threw me off."

"Tell me what?"

"I called a buddy of mine. We're both members of the VIP Den—so is his brother-in-law. Bryce is a native New Yorker who lived in Silicon Valley for a few years. He's back in the Big Apple."

"Were we supposed to meet him tonight?"

"No," I say. "Bryce runs one of the most important internet security companies in the world."

"You're one of his clients?"

"I am. The man is a secret weapon. Any breach of security in my business could bring me down. Given the daily volume of transactions my company deals with, he and his team save me several millions of dollars every single *week* with his cyber-intelligence."

"Whoa."

"It cost an eye-popping amount to work with Bryce, but he's worth every penny." I fold and unfold my white napkin before locking my gaze onto hers.

"Why do you look so intense?"

"Because Bryce Van Der Linden might be the answer to your prayers."

She scrunches her nose. "I don't have an internet company. I'm an editor."

"He's branched out to white-collar crimes for his clients—hacking, siphoning funds, and such. He and his team of experts can track anyone, anywhere."

Her brows hit her forehead.

"I talked to him earlier today, and he told me five of Ramsey's victims hired him to track down the weasel. Apparently, he stole several millions from them—"

"Your friend knows where he is?"

"I'm not sure yet. But my understanding is, he might give us some insight on Ramsey. We'll know more tomorrow. We're meeting him for lunch."

"Are you serious?"

"I'm as serious as a heart attack."

"Oh, my God." She claps. "I can't believe this. We might get a chance to get our money back—" She cuts her sentence short, and her shoulders drop.

"What is it?"

"I'm sure your friend doesn't work for free."

"Of course not."

Her lips twist. "I don't have the money to pay for his services."

"Don't worry about that. If there's a sliver of hope Bryce can get back your money—even a portion of it—I'll foot the bill."

"Hudson—"

"What have I told you?"

Tears well in her eyes and her lower lip trembles. "There are no words to thank you."

I reach out and caress her cheek, wiping a tear away. "Let me take care of you, angel."

Chapter 27

Angelica

My eyes are fixed on my dessert plate as I contemplate licking the last few cookie crumbs.

"You look like you're about to perform brain surgery," Hudson says. "There's an easy way out of this. Just have another slice."

I lift my gaze. "I shouldn't."

Hudson was right. The steak at The Fifth was outstanding. And the thinly cut fries were out of this world delicious. I thought the ones at L'Avenue were incredible, but these take the cake. For someone who can't resist potatoes in any form, today was like Christmas, the Fourth of July, and my birthday all wrapped up in one.

After dinner, Hudson guided me to the rooftop for a tour. It was crowded, lively, and buzzing with excitement. Loud music vibrated through my body. It was an experience to watch people letting go, their inhibitions freed. After a while, Hudson suggested we take dessert to go. I didn't complain. It would've been fun to hang out a little longer, but spending alone time with Hudson is a lot more tempting.

So here we are, back at his place, enjoying the most amazing dessert I've ever had. We're sitting in his beautifully decorated living room, kicking back on his comfy oversized couch. He ditched the tuxedo jacket and bowtie, but he's still wearing his crisp white shirt and beautifully tailored pants. I'm still in my pretty dress. I love it so much, I might have to sleep in it.

"There's a reason I bought a whole tart, instead of just a couple of slices," he says. "One slice just isn't enough."

"Another slice would allow me to appreciate The Fifth's lip-smacking creamy chocolate filling in a crumbly Oreo crust with a giant dollop of whipped cream on top a lot more." The first bite of the pie was like an out-of-body experience.

"So much fanfare just to indulge in a lil' sugar."

Says the guy who already had two slices.

It's so unfair how men metabolize fat better than us.

"Easy for you to say, Mr. Wall of Muscle—"

"How would you know?" A husky note enters his voice. "You haven't touched my body yet."

Heat surges between my legs.

"Um... in my defense, I couldn't when we were at the Bymark Hotel, and last night, your mouth was doing things to me that caused me to forget my name."

"Fair enough," he says with a slow nod. "That was then. This is now." His blue eyes are smoldering, darkening to an indigo color, a contrast to the usual ocean-blue. "Instead of making assumptions about my body, why not find out firsthand?"

His expression is all, *I dare you.*

I drop my dessert plate on the coffee table next to the fifteen-hundred-dollar bottle of Pappy Van Winkle's 15 Year Family Reserve.

I still can't believe the too boozy for my palate Kentucky bourbon whiskey could be that expensive.

I focus my attention on the sexy Texan sitting next to me.

He's waiting for me to take him up on his challenge.

I poke a finger against his chest, as if I'm trying to evaluate the springiness of a mattress.

Yup, the wall of muscle from Summerville, Texas.

The man is hiding a ripped body under a sharp suit.

I meet his expectant gaze. Every time I stare in his eyes, I could lose myself in that mesmerizing ocean. It takes everything in me to keep my cool.

"Hmmm..." I hum.

He knits his eyebrows together. "What is that supposed to mean?"

"It's not as hard as I expected." *Lies.* "Might I suggest a few more reps at the gym," I say, patting his hard chest.

In one swift movement, Hudson's long fingers grasp my wrist. "Oh, yeah?"

The contact jumpstarts all my senses.

"Yes." I squeak, my voice going up several octaves.

He lowers my hand.

It happens so fast, my brain doesn't register what's happening.

"What about this?" He presses my hand against the bulge between his legs. My startled eyes meet his. "Is this hard enough for you?"

Mother of God.

The man's gaze is nothing but smoldering hotness.

I'm at such a loss, I can only blink.

He grinds his cock against my palm.

Oh.

My.

God.

Every cell in my body sparks to life.

Still unable to find my voice, I stare in his eyes.

Even if I wanted to avert my gaze, I couldn't. His gaze enthralls me.

Electricity crackles through the dense air, vibrating throughout my body.

"You haven't answered me yet."

That's because I can't lust and talk at the same time.

He closes his hand over mine.

Great balls of fire.

"Not bad."

He's incredulous. "Not bad?"

"Tell me, angel, when was the last time you handled this much meat?"

Err... never.

"I've... only... been... with... one... guy..." It's a struggle to string together a cohesive sentence. Hence why I sound like a complete moron. My ex's cock didn't feel nearly this impressive.

"So, you only know what a boy's cock looks like and you wouldn't know what to do with this." He grinds against my hand.

My teeth dig into my lower lip so hard, I swear I'm close to drawing blood.

I have no business feeling like that was a personal affront, but my mouth moves before my brain can rein it in. "Who says I can't handle it?" And then I dig a deeper grave for myself. "As far as you know, I could deepthroat like any porn star."

Hudson's brows raise high.

For a long beat, he studies me, his nostrils flaring. It's as if I'm staring at a tiger hungry for fresh meat. Pun unintended.

The words are out there, cowardice is out of the question, so I lift a defiant chin.

His lips part in a slow, calculated grin.

The warning is there. It's staring at me in the face.

I should jump to my feet and bolt out the door, running as fast as my heels can handle, putting as much distance as humanly possible between me and the Big Bad Wolf, but like an idiot, I say, "That's right. I have skills."

"Skills?"

Ah... the perils of being an overachiever.

Those fierce eyes shear through me for a few uncomfortable beats before he drags them down to my quivering throat, before locking onto my gaze.

As my brain tries to come up with a sassy response, he speaks. "Let's see what you got."

"You... want me to..." My eyes lower to where my hand is still resting. His cock seems to have doubled in size. "Um—"

"I want you to demonstrate your mad skills. You wouldn't boast about them unless you could deliver. I want to find out for myself."

And that's what you get for running your mouth.

I'm just about to admit I might've been a little overconfident, but I don't want to come across as all talk and no action. Not to mention, given how he made me see God two nights in a row, it's only fair I reciprocate.

He pulls me tight and kisses me.

I. Cannot. Breathe.

Every time this man ravages my lips, I'm lost to ecstasy. I melt into him, moaning in pleasure. His tongue slips between my lips, and I open my mouth to greet it. He kisses me until I run out of air. When he breaks our embrace, I groan my protest.

He pulls away and points to the floor. "On your knees, angel."

The urge to pleasure him is all-encompassing.

I rub my nervous hands a few times over my dress for courage and get up.

I can do this.

I'm just about to kneel in front of him, but he stops me with a tsk and a raised hand. "I want to see the Agent Provocateur lingerie I bought you."

My heart skips a beat.

"You want me to get undressed?"

"I don't have x-ray vision, Angelica."

Of course he doesn't, you nitwit.

I ready myself to fold my arms behind my back but stop when he lifts a finger up in the air.

"Turn around," he says.

I obey.

Slowly, very slowly, he inches the zipper of my dress down.

I close my eyes, tuning out the soft music playing from the speakers in the ceiling, focusing all my attention on the feel of his hands on my body. He trails a finger against my skin and flames scream up my spine, igniting a blaze rumbling deep in my core.

I gasp.

He pulls down the fabric off my body until it's pooling at my feet.

"Step out of the dress."

I do as I'm told.

I'm just about to kick off my heels, but he stops me. "No, those stay on. Same for the lingerie."

"Okay."

Hudson drops a soft kiss on the small of my back. He trails down to my ass with a flurry of kisses. The sensation causes my nipples to pebble, grazing against the satin of my strapless bustier.

I gasp when he bites into my ass cheek.

"Fuck, that ass. It's as ripe as a peach," he says.

His compliment boosts my ego to the stratosphere.

He stands up.

His hands find my chignon. He plays with my hair, removing bobby pin after bobby pin until my hair cascades, falling to my waist.

I peer at him from over my shoulder.

"I can't wait to find out what you look like as a blonde."

When he says things like that, I want to believe. He keeps saying we'll see each other well past the end of our one-week arrangement, but a part of me struggles to believe a man like Hudson would want more.

His eyes rake the length of my body, pausing for a long beat, admiring my ass. "Money well spent," he says. I can't help my smile. "Turn around."

I tense up.

My stomach churns with dread.

I haven't been this exposed in front of a man in... well, forever. The last guy I was with was a teenager. Hudson is all man. A mogul who's probably slept with the most beautiful women in Manhattan—women who don't have a love affair with potatoes and ice cream, and who don't have their asses parked in a chair all day.

"I said, turn around." Hudson repeats his command.

I don't budge.

"Angelica." His tone is impatient.

I cross my arms over my soft tummy and slowly turn around to face him.

"Drop your arms."

I inhale a fortifying breath and let my arms fall to my side.

"I only caught glimpses of you yesterday when you were spread on my kitchen island, but now, I get to take it all in." He shakes his head. "Goddammit, you're gorgeous."

The lust I read in his eyes is unsettling. It's as if he's oblivious to my imperfections.

His reaction gives me wings.

Lifting the middle finger to my insecurities, I strike a pose.

Surprised blue eyes fly up to meet mine. "That sure of yourself, huh?"

I respond by striking another pose.

Slap!

I didn't see that coming.

I yelp.

"Did you just spank me?"

"I did," he says. "Keep up the sass and I'll put you over my knee and redden your fine ass."

The editor inside me wants to give him two thumbs up for rhyming, but the depraved girl inside me wonders what it would be like to get spanked, his big strong hand leaving an imprint on my ass.

"You're curious," Hudson says, as if he could hear my inward yearnings.

"You're putting words in my mouth."

"We'll add it to the list."

"What list?"

The corners of his eyes crinkle with wicked amusement. "The list of ways I want to corrupt you."

And if my pussy doesn't tingle in response.

He returns to the couch, his arms stretched out over the backrest before parting his legs. The look in his eyes is pure sin, a promise of depravity.

And there he sits like a king in his crisp white shirt and tailored pants.

"My cock is waiting."

"Aren't you going to get undressed?" I ask him.

He shakes his head. "You're going to take care of pulling my cock from my boxer briefs, but for the rest, I'll remain dressed.

The few times I'd given my one and only boyfriend a blowjob, we were both naked. Maybe this is part of his plan to corrupt me. Secretly, I find the idea of him remaining dressed with only his cock exposed, hot as hell.

I kneel between his parted legs.

His eyes lower. "Get to work, sweetness. My cock is aching to be introduced to your hot mouth."

His filthy words ratchet my arousal.

I fumble with his belt and the button of his tuxedo pants before inching down the zipper. My hands slide underneath his pants. I'm all thumbs. It's as if the slit at the front of his boxer briefs isn't big enough to pull out his cock. Either that, or my hands are shaking so badly, making it that much harder.

His hand circles my wrist, forcing me to halt all movement. "Let me pull down my pants. It will be more comfortable for both of us."

I nod, sending God a silent thanks.

When he pulls his pants and boxer briefs down to his knees, his long cock snaps against his stomach.

My eyes widen in shock.

Holy hugeness.

Hudson Kincaid is packing some serious meat.

Chapter 28

Hudson

I have to suppress a grin as Angelica takes in my huge cock, her red-painted lips parted.

"Still up for the challenge?" I ask.

She swallows hard and lifts her gaze to meet mine.

Her eyelashes bat like crazy.

She's like a deer caught in headlights.

"When I ask you a question, I expect an answer."

"Yes." Her voice is a near whisper.

Let's see if she puts her money where her mouth is.

I undo the buttons of my shirt, so it's more comfortable for both of us.

Big green eyes widen as they zoom in on my chest.

"You have a tattoo?" she asks.

I look down at my chest.

It's hard to believe it's the first time she's seen my bare chest, even though I've made her come multiple times. The last time I was with a virgin, I was a virgin. Things are moving at a different pace with Angelica than they were with my high school girlfriend. As much as it's killing me, I remain steadfast in my decision not to fuck her until the end of this arrangement. Popping her cherry while she's still, technically an escort, would taint what we share.

"Does it have any meaning?" she asks.

"It's a Celtic cross. I got it when I moved to Dallas. The tattoo commemorates the memory of my mom and my dad, and how they died in servitude of others. They had strong Christian values when it came to helping those in need and those who had less than they did. They were the first to raise their hands to go down to Louisiana."

"What a beautiful way to remember them." She lifts her gaze. "Can I touch?"

"Of course."

She traces a delicate finger, outlining the Celtic cross. "I don't know anything about tattoos, but it's striking."

"I wanted an intricate design. The tattoo artist delivered." My eyes drop to where she's touching me. "Every time I look at myself in the mirror or take a shower, I know I'm not alone."

She pulls her hand away, sits on her haunches, and looks up at me from behind a curtain of lashes. In that position, she looks like the perfect little submissive. *My* perfect little submissive.

"As much as I loved my parents," she says, "I would've been too chicken to go to that extreme."

I tap two fingers against my heart. "As long as they're here, it's all good."

She responds with a warm smile.

Her eyes travel up and down my torso.

"I could tell even in your suit, your body was something else. It was obvious yesterday in the way your t-shirt clung to your muscular chest..." She lets her words trail. She gives me another onceover and shakes her head. "Seeing you in the flesh... you could easily double as a fitness model."

"You like what you see, angel?"

Her eyes bounce up to meet mine. "Do you even have to ask?"

"Yesterday, you said I was okay."

"I was downplaying it," she says. "You're hot."

"Now you know how I feel when I look at your heavenly body."

She responds with a lop-sided smile.

Her eyes zoom in on my huge erection.

My cock is still on full alert.

I fist the fucker, squeezing it hard. "Too much?" I taunt her.

"You're... a lot bigger than I ever imagined."

"You'll control the cadence at first. When you're comfortable, I'll fuck your face."

She flinches. "You don't believe in training wheels."

"Nah, I have faith you'll blow me away with your deepthroating skills."

"About that—"

"We'll take it one inch at a time."

She looks up at me and something flashes in her eyes I can't read.

"What is it?"

"My ex-boyfriend's cock wasn't as long as yours, he didn't have your generous girth... and he wasn't circumcised."

"Like I said, one inch at a time."

The tension on her face softens.

For all her big talk, I could tell she was bullshitting me.

The idea of being the guy she deepthroats is a fucking turn on.

"The more we talk, the closer I am to suffering from a severe case of blue balls," I say. "My cock desperately needs some attention." I fist my cock, squeeze it hard until the head blooms dark red. "Show me what your mouth can do."

Chapter 29

Angelica

Hudson strokes his hard cock nice and slow.

"I can't wait to shoot my load down your throat."

Fever-bright heat engulfs me at his naughty words.

I'm not sure what turns me on the most—his dirty talk, or the way his strong hand fists his cock.

My eyes are glued to his eye-popping erection as he strokes it.

His angry veins are popping like crazy. It's so powerful and manly. I've watched my one and only boyfriend stroke himself, but it never caused my pussy to do Kegel exercises. His rock-hard cock pulses and juts out from under his eight-pack of abs.

I feel his eyes on me. Watching me.

I'm sure my innocence is flashing like a neon sign, but I'm so mesmerized, I don't care if he can read me like an open book.

A thick, white, milky bead of pre-cum glistens at the tip of his cock, and trickles over his swollen head, down his veiny shaft.

Fuck.

I look up at him.

"Ready?" he asks.

I feel the lone word all the way down to my clit.

I nod.

"I want words."

"Yes."

"Better. We're doing this nice and slow."

"Nice and slow," I parrot.

I might be a virgin, but I'm not dumb.

Hudson saw right through my bluff.

There are thousands of women with far more experience than me who know how to bring a man like him pleasure, but knowing he's willing to be patient with me melts my insides.

"Lick," he says, indicating his cock.

His hands rest on his thighs. He doesn't bother holding himself for me. Instead, he sits back and watches.

I reach out for his cock, wrapping my hands around him.

He's hot and thick, and fits between my palms just right.

I bring his massive cock to my lips, stick out my tongue, and run it from his base to his tip in one long motion.

His head falls back and he lets out a low hissing sound.

I do it again.

A tortured groan leaves him.

The sight is so hedonistic, so insanely hot, that my clit pulses and my pussy clenches. I bring my legs together to alleviate the pressure.

His eyes pop open. "Don't you dare." His growl reverberates against the walls.

How the hell did he know?

"Legs apart."

I obey.

"Focus on the underside of my cock."

With my eyes pinned onto his in the dim light, I run my tongue there, as if I was licking a lollipop.

"You're such an obedient, dirty girl. With your small hands and your fingertips painted in red, the matching color lipstick smearing my cock, and the way your pink tongue is licking me, it's enough to make me come."

I throw a quick flash of a smile his way.

His praise does something to me.

I lick him like that for a few long beats, relishing the intimacy we share.

"Good girl, but I need more." He presents his cock like an offering. "Wrap those pretty lips around me and suck me off."

I part my lips.

"Open wider."

I do as I'm told.

He slides his cock inside my expectant mouth, and I struggle to adjust to his girth.

I moan at the saltiness of him against my tongue.

When he lifts his hips off the couch and feeds me a few more inches of his cock, I lower my gaze, too intrigued.

"Eyes up!"

My eyes bounce up to his.

"Don't look away. I want you to watch what you do to me. I want our gazes locked onto each other when I spill my seed in your pretty little mouth."

A frisson runs through me at the low rumbling of Hudson's voice and his filthy command.

I nod and mumble a muffled *okay* around his cock.

"Can I go deeper?"

I nod again.

He feeds me more of his throbbing cock.

My eyes widen at the invasion.

He's so hard.

He moves his hips back and forth in a slow and calculated cadence.

When his cock pulses against my tongue, I moan around him.

"Fuck, the vibration of your moan feels so fucking good."

To hear a billionaire who could have any woman he wants just by snapping his fingers say that is such an ego boost.

Mission: Bring Hudson as much pleasure as he brings me, commences.

His hips thrust with more determination.

"You okay, angel?"

"Hmmm."

"More?"

I nod.

He's a lot to handle, but I manage.

"I want your hands on my cock."

There I go stumbling on a hurdle, putting a kink in my mission.

Crap.

"Now, use your mouth and your hands."

On it.

"Good girl."

I grip his cock and bob my head, meeting his thrusts.

His hips and legs are practically vibrating.

"Fuck... yeah." His words come out strained.

He peers down at me from underneath heavy lids, his heated gaze searing through me.

With a grunt, he fists my hair.

The sharp tug catches me off guard.

I hitch a breath.

"You're right where you're meant to be. At my feet, worshiping my huge cock."

Sweet baby Jesus.

Without warning, he swings his hips back and plunges his

cock into my mouth in one single stroke and hits the back of my throat with such force, I gag.

Holy fuck.

He pulls free while I cough up drool.

"Sorry, angel, I got carried away. Your mouth feels so good, I just couldn't help it." His breathing is labored. "You need a minute?"

He's staring at me with such raw sexuality, I don't want it to stop. I'm determined to give him a happy ending.

I shake my head, ignore the drool on my chin, and lick my lips at him.

"You're sure?"

"Hell yeah."

He threads his hands through my hair. "Fuck, you're perfect."

His words fuel me.

With my lips wrapped around his tip, I suck softly and flick my tongue over his slit.

"Dirty girl." He holds me down over his cock and pushes up with his hips. My saliva drips down his shaft in my attempt to take more of him inside my mouth. "That's it, suck me hard, my little slut."

This man's dirty mouth.

"Force me to come in your pretty mouth."

I close my lips around his cock and suck hard.

"My little slut wasn't lying. You have skills, angel."

I'm dizzy from how he called me slut and angel in the same breath.

"I've never been harder than this before. You do that to me."

I can't believe he said that.

Empowered by his words, I grip his cock tightly and pick up the pace, my head bobbing up and down with more determination. Now that my fear of choking around his cock has somewhat subsided, I don't hold back.

He yanks my hair, pulling my lips off his cock.

For a second, I fear I'm doing it all wrong.

"My balls. Don't you dare ignore them." There's such authority in his husky voice.

His balls. Right.

Just like the size of his cock, the swell of his balls is impressive.

"Feel their weight in your hand." I'm just about to cup them, but he pulls my hair hard, the tingling sensation sending a rush throughout my tits. "Careful. You have to go nice and easy." He flashes me a salacious grin. "The family jewels are precious."

I can't help my giggle.

I slide my hand down and close it over his balls.

I meet his gaze and squeeze just a little.

His upper lip twitches.

For a second, I fear I've hurt him, but then he says, "Do it again."

I oblige.

He tilts his head back and lets out a low groan.

This is fifty shades of hotter than hell.

He loosens his grip on my hair. "Kiss them."

I lift his cock, lean in and drop hot kisses on his balls.

This is positively filthy.

"Gentle!"

Oops.

I kiss his balls with more tenderness this time. Forget filthy. This is as erotic as it gets.

"Feel how heavy they are?"

"Yes," I say between soft kisses.

And then I go for it, suck one ball into my mouth and run

my tongue around it. Hudson rewards me by gripping my hair tight and moaning, the straining hardness of his cock pressing against my brow.

"Christ," he says, my cue to pay attention to his other ball, sucking it in and swirling my tongue.

"Christ almighty," he says, "the beautiful woman who caught my attention at first sight is kneeling in front of me, worshiping my balls. I can die a happy man."

I was just hoping not to disappoint him due to my lack of practice. It's been a long time since I've given a guy a blowjob, and I'm not sure it was that great. The flurry of compliments is completely unexpected.

All those raunchy romance books really paid off.

"I need to come, angel. I want those lips wrapped around my cock again."

I grip the base of his cock with one hand and suck him into my mouth, bobbing my head up and down with more resolve.

His grip on my hair stops me.

"I can't hold back any longer, angel," he says. "I need to fuck your mouth."

Translation: The training wheels are coming off.

I brace myself.

With a steady hand gripping my hair, Hudson makes do on his promise.

Each forceful thrust is accompanied by a loud grunt.

It's raw. Animalistic, even.

And damn, is it ever sexy.

Hudson is relentless as he chases after his release.

When he thrusts deep inside my mouth and hits the back of my throat, my gag reflex doesn't kick in this time.

"Fuck!" His growl reverberates around the walls.

My clit is in desperate need of attention. I rotate my hips, grinding my clit between my pussy lips, but it isn't enough.

"I can smell you," he says, his voice hoarse. "Is your sweet little pussy dripping for me?"

Yes. Yes, it is.

I moan and nod in response.

"Touch yourself, slut," he says. "I want you to come with me."

He doesn't have to tell me twice.

I obey his command.

One hand holds his cock as the other travels down my tummy until my fingers pass the elastic of my panties.

Hudson brushes off the hand holding his cock, taking control.

I place a hand on his muscular thigh, and go to town with the other, my fingers skating around my hard clit.

Jesus.

I'll never be able to bring myself to orgasm again without remembering this moment and how debauched it is.

"Look at you, desperate to come, with my big fat cock between your lips and your fingers rubbing your clit. So beautiful!"

I can only whimper in response.

I'm close. So, so close.

Hudson's hand jerks his cock. Since he isn't buried as deep as before, he doesn't hit the back of my throat. Not that I'd object, but I welcome the reprieve.

"My dirty angel is sucking my cock like the good little slut she is."

As much as my nipples are scratching my strapless bra, begging to be fondled, my release is the only thing that matters.

The pressure builds at my core and my fingers move faster over my sensitive clit.

My eyes water but I don't blink. The hedonistic expression on Hudson's gorgeous face keeps my eyes locked onto him.

"Jesus, your mouth. You're going to make me lose my fucking mind."

The ecstasy I read on his face leaves me in awe.

"Fuck, I'm gonna fucking come." He sounds frantic. Unhinged, even.

That makes two of us.

"I need to shoot my load down your throat."

Oh boy!

"Mm-hmm." With the tip of his cock buried inside my mouth, I hum an eager moan.

His breathing is heavy as he jerks his cock faster and more of my juices drip between my thighs.

His cock swells in my mouth and my eyes fly up.

The tips of his fingers turn white as he grips the couch's armrest. All the finely wrought muscles of his eight-pack clench.

He's so fucking gorgeous.

My head is spinning. I can't believe I've reduced this strong, powerful man to this trembling mass.

"Oh, shit, angel!"

He clamps the back of my head with one hand as he christens my mouth with a savage cry and his pulsing cock spurts warm cum down my throat in a hot gush as pleasure ripples through me.

My pussy starts to pulsate in staccato beats. I squeeze my legs together and tilt my hips back and forth a few times with my finger trapped between my lips.

Ahhhh!

That's all it takes for me to freefall.

Letting his cock drop out of my mouth, I cry out, "Oh, Hudson—"

Dear God.

A powerful climax slams through me. My body shakes as

ripples, upon ripples of pleasure wash over me. It's so strong and so blissful, it takes my breath away. Even though, there's no danger I'll tumble to the side and fall since I'm on my knees, I still hold on to his strong, muscular thighs for support. That was one hellava core-shaking orgasm.

Hudson slides his hands under my armpits, and lifts me onto his lap, my dripping panties sitting right on top of his still-hard cock.

He cups my face in his large hands.

I meet his gaze.

"My dirty angel has quite the mouth on her. You made it so fucking good for me, I might need your mouth on my cock every single day of the week. Twice on Sundays," he says with a wry grin.

His admission causes my pussy to flutter.

"To make it even better, my perfect little slut came all over her fingers as I was shooting my load down her throat. That was so hot, I think I'm going to have to keep you."

I'm so stunned, words fail me.

There's so much I want to tell him.

You boost my ego like crazy.

You don't seem to mind my imperfections.

You make me feel so sexy.

You give me wings.

You're the most wonderful man on the planet.

You're a formidable lover.

Instead, I blurt out, "I love being your dirty angel and your perfect little slut."

"Fuck." He growls, before crushing my lips in a bruising kiss.

He kisses me long and deep, his cock rubbing against my pussy through my soaked panties and I'm in heaven all over again.

It takes me a second to register his cum is still coating my mouth as I return his kiss with as much passion as he bestows on me.

Holy Jesus!

Today has been a day of filthy firsts.

He sucks my tongue, stealing every one of my whimpers, swallowing them like he owns them.

Too soon, he breaks the kiss, pulling away from me.

His ocean-blue eyes are loaded with lust.

"Fuck, angel," he says, "You're so fucking mine."

Chapter 30

Angelica

Three days ago, had someone told me my life would be better than a romance novel, I would've snort-laughed in their face. Yet, here I am, living *la vida rica.* Although these past two days have been such a whirlwind, it feels more like *la vida loca.* Since it's one a.m. in the morning by the time the chauffeured Mercedes Benz comes to a stop in front of my apartment complex, most of my neighbors are fast asleep. And it's a good thing. At this rate, someone will start wondering if the McQuinley twins won the lottery.

I only ever had animosity and hatred towards Ramsey Kenyon III. After stealing everything to our names and leaving us hanging out to dry, he's the last person I ever thought I'd thank for anything. Without that asshole, I would never have met a man that's quickly turning my life upside down, in the best possible way. If Greek Gods Eros and Aphrodite had a baby together, Hudson Kincaid would be it.

His handsome face.

His Paul Newman blue eyes.

His chiseled body.

His washboard abs, complete with lickable V.

His edgy tattoo.

And his happy trail of dark hair leading to the promised land—his eye-popping cock.

What a combination.

Blowjobs with my ex felt like a chore.

I do you and you do me.

A blowjob with Hudson is a hedonistic experience I'm unlikely to forget anytime soon. It was like I was kneeling at the altar of temptation while my Texan Adonis leaned back with the confidence—and arrogance—of a king while he watched me service his magnificent cock.

My nipples tighten at the thought.

Not once did I think of my ex-boyfriend's cock unless it was staring me in the face. I already know Hudson's massive cock will be the star feature of my dreams every single time I make myself come from now on.

It wouldn't have taken much for him to convince me to go all the way. I was willing and ready for Hudson to corrupt me all night long. Alas, you don't always get what you want in life. He's determined to wait until there isn't an arrangement between us. To avoid getting swept away in more naughtiness, he had his chauffeur drive me back to Queens.

So, here I am, back at my place, which could easily fit in Hudson's kitchen.

I'm still engulfed in fever-bright heat after our scorching night when I enter the apartment. I turn on a few lights and drop my clutch on a chair near the door. Since Arya is staying at her best friend's parents' place, I slide the security chain into place. I kick off my Christian Louboutin heels. I still can't believe I own a pair of these. Between this financial fiasco with Ramsey and my crushing student loans, I wouldn't even be able to afford to buy an empty Louboutin box on eBay.

"Time to count sheep," I say, using the same soothing voice Mom would use when Arya and I would whine about watching five more minutes of a show or movie.

My heart clenches like it always does when memories come flooding in.

God, I miss her. I miss them both so much.

With that heart-breaking flashback prodding my memory, I resume my mission.

I need a good night's sleep, so tomorrow I can catch up and make up for today. I loved my day of pampering, but those manuscripts sitting on my laptop aren't going to edit themselves. I might be living the life of a socialite, but it's all make-believe. If I don't get some work done tomorrow before the lunch meeting with Hudson's friend, I won't earn enough money this month to pay the rent. I guess this is when Cinderella's gold carriage reverts back to being a lowly pumpkin.

Back to reality.

With a heavy sigh, I slip my feet into a pair of flip-flops I use instead of house slippers and let out a sigh of relief. I'm not used to living in heels, so my feet hurt. I bend down and arrange my shoes so they're nice and neat. I smile down at them as if they'll smile back. I'll hide them tomorrow or else the next thing I know, my twin will take ownership of them.

I set off to do my bedtime routine. Just as I'm about to reach the door to my bedroom, I freeze.

I need water.

That's what happens when you indulge in too much expensive champagne and wine.

I amble to the kitchen, a smile coming out as I hum.

I turn on the light and stroll to the refrigerator.

I squint when I notice a piece of paper taped to the fridge with my name written on it. Frowning, I grab it and unfold it.

Not that I need to confirm the identity of the person who wrote the note, but I read the signature before reading the message.

My stomach bottoms out.

Hey sis!

So, a funny thing happened while I was out with Vanna. Instead of a non-descript bar (so boring), we decided to go to a place that would lift her spirits. That's how we ended up at the Crosby Bar, the chic lounge inside the Crosby Hotel.

We just so happen to be sitting next to this hot and famous DJ from Vegas, who was in town for a couple of nights, before heading to Miami. One thing led to another, and Bromley (his name is Bromley Scott, just in case you want to Google him) invited Vanna and me to party with him for the next three days while he DJs. He wants us to be his DJ bunnies.

We're flying on a private jet!!!

I rushed back home, packed a few things, and Vanna and I headed to the airport. You have the Todd gig covered.

Yay!

One of the benefits of being an identical twin.

Since my pockets are lined with tips and I'm not working for the next few days, I might as well live it up. Am I right or am I right?

I'm going old school with the note, because I

didn't want to text or call and interrupt at an importune time. Miami is exactly what the doctor ordered to help Vanna get over her douchebag ex. What kind of friend would I be if I let her go by herself? Not to mention, Bromley invited both of us. Toodles.

PS: Yes, I'm totally bringing you a cool t-shirt and PJs.

See you soon. XOXO Arya.

I'm so shook up, I stare at the piece of paper I'm holding for a solid minute, my mouth agape.

I reread the note.

My lips twist as if I'm sucking on a lemon, my fingers curling hard around the paper.

As if I haven't already memorized each word, I read the note a third time.

It doesn't soften the blow.

"Un-fucking-believable." I mutter under my breath. "She's so full of bullshit. She didn't get in touch with me because she knew I'd rip her a new one and forbid her to go to Miami." I'm so infuriated, I keep talking to myself. "She can be such a coward! And an airhead!"

When Arya McQuinley is given a choice between A (a decision any rational person would make) and B (a decision that will inevitably end up in a shitshow that will cause her twin sister to shave off ten years from her life), she will undoubtedly select B.

Instead of paying off that Russian dude, she's off partying in another city.

Argh!

Pinching the bridge of my nose, I breathe in and out to calm down.

I just can't sometimes with my sister.

She's always a breath away from making a bad decision.

What if DJ Famous isn't who he pretends to be? What if the guy is a pimp who lures women with his private jet just to enslave them? It's not like Arya doesn't have experience with fraudsters. That's how she ended up working for Todd as an escort, after all.

I have half a mind to Google "Divorcing your twin sister". And "Can I legally emancipate myself from my sister?"

I huff out a humorless laugh.

This is my cross to bear.

It's my fault she's like that. I'm too overprotective.

So far, I've been hell-bent on taking on Arya's sins as my own. I went as far as stepping in to save her ass by playing *Pretty Woman*, and she's fucking jet-setting?!

She doesn't take anything seriously.

I shake my head.

Fuck. My. Life.

I close my eyes, praying for calm.

One.

Two.

Three.

Four.

Five.

I reach twenty, but I'm still agitated.

Counting usually grounds me, but I could count to a thousand, and it wouldn't make a difference.

My heart rate is five times faster than the ticking of the kitchen clock.

I'm fuming.

Sadie is going to freak out when I tell her how careless my sister is.

"Damn it all!"

I swear to God, Arya is a lost cause.

You give her an inch, and she bites your arm off.

I'm in no financial position to move out, but I need to establish better boundaries. Once this twin swap subterfuge is over, she's on her own. I'm done rolling over and playing doormat. The next time she digs herself into a hole, she better not come crying to me.

I tear up the note and send the pieces of paper flying over my head like confetti.

My sister is officially on my shit list.

Chapter 31

Hudson

The traffic is a bitch. It takes forever to get to Bryce's Brooklyn office. It doesn't help I had back-to-back meetings this morning and I was cutting it short to begin with. Just when I thought I was going to murder someone, the traffic cleared up on the Brooklyn Bridge.

I trail behind one of Bryce's staff members on the way to the conference room. When she opens the door, Bryce and Angelica are chatting over lunch like old friends.

"I'm sorry I'm late," I say, entering the conference room. Even though I've apologized via text, I'm compelled to repeat myself. I hate tardiness.

Bryce stands and extends a hand.

I give him a firm handshake, patting his shoulder.

Bryce Van Der Linden is tall, but I tower over him by a couple of inches.

"You made it," he says.

"You mean I made it without killing anyone?"

"It's summer in New York, aka construction season."

I shake my head, grumbling under my breath.

"Since I needed the space, having an office in Brooklyn was the way to go. It's usually smooth sailing," Bryce says, "but every time I'm stuck in traffic on the bridge, it makes me reconsider."

My eyes shift to Angelica, who's standing now, before locking onto Bryce's gaze. "I guess introductions are no longer necessary."

He shakes his head. "We can skip to the good part."

"You won't hear any objections from me."

I walk up to Angelica.

She looks so different from yesterday.

Staring into her eyes, I'm assaulted by filthy images of last night when she was in a sexy black bustier and panties combo, with her pretty mouth stuffed full of my huge cock. And afterwards, when I pulled her onto my lap, my still-hard cock pressed against her wetness.

I give myself a shake.

Today, she's all business in a light-gray suit and white shirt. Her pulled-back hair and subdued makeup add to the professional look. I much prefer her in a dress. The suit looks amazing on her, but it hides her curves. My eyes drop to her feet. I cock an eyebrow in appreciation of the bright pink heels that match the color of her lipstick.

Nice touch.

She frowns, as if she can read my thoughts.

I rein it in because flipping her onto Bryce's conference table and eating her out isn't an option.

"Hey, you," I say before placing a soft kiss on her cheek.

"Hey, you," she says.

"I hope Bryce hasn't been trying to pull out your deepest, darkest secrets."

She laughs. "No chance of that ever happening. My life is boring."

"Not that boring or else you wouldn't be here," Bryce says.

Touché.

Angelica cringes. "Like I said earlier, I would've loved to have met you under different circumstances."

Bryce nods, a solemn expression on his face.

"Have a seat, Hudson. Hungry?"

I unbutton my suit jacket, pull out the chair next to Angelica, and take a seat. "Famished."

"Help yourself." He points to the assortment of gourmet sandwiches placed on a tray in the middle of the table. "Let's eat in peace before we talk shop."

"Sounds good to me," I say.

I grab a plate and reach for what looks like a grilled roast beef sandwich with some sort of melted cheese. Right up my alley.

Bryce, Angelica, and I enjoy a scrumptious lunch. The conversation is pleasant and light. It's so casual, it's easy to forget why we're here in the first place.

Bryce crumples a paper napkin and drops it on his empty plate. "While you enjoy your dessert, I'll start talking."

I nod before biting into said dessert. "Holy shit!" I place a hand in front of my mouth and chew quickly. "Sorry," I say. "I didn't mean to be that vocal about a dessert bar."

Angelica shoots me an inquisitive look. "They're that good?" She doesn't give me a chance to answer. She takes a big bite out of hers. "Dear God!" she says over a bite. "This is like biting into a slice of heaven."

"I couldn't have said it better," Bryce says. "These dulce de leche and white chocolate snickerdoodle bars are an addiction. When I invite family and friends to our offices for lunch, those are a staple." He points to the plate.

"I could totally become addicted to this," Angelica says.

"Same here," I say.

"I wish a tasty dessert was enough to make up for what I'm about to share with you, but I'm afraid it isn't."

Leave it to Bryce not to sugarcoat things.

Angelica drops her bar on her plate.

I mimic her move. "What do you know?"

"First, I'd like for Angelica to share her experience with Ramsey," Bryce says.

She clears her throat and shares her tale of woes.

"How much did he steal from you?" Bryce asks at the tail end of her story.

"It's only after my dad died, we found out he had a serious online gambling addiction problem. So, after paying off what he owed, a good chunk of the insurance money was gone. Whatever we had left, we gave to Ramsey." She concludes by blurting out a number.

Bryce nods. "Your concerns were justified, but I understand how Ramsey pulled the wool over your eyes. Obviously, your sister campaigning on his behalf didn't help matters and made the water murky," Bryce says. "Your gut was telling you danger, danger, but Ramsey was seducing your base nature. Who the hell doesn't want to be financially free by the age of twenty-five by riding a lucrative wave?"

"I hate myself for not having listened to my gut. I should've stood my ground and pulled out our initial investment and the profits," Angelica says. She pinches her lips and shakes her head. "Greed is one of the seven deadly sins. I was so blinded, I ignored the warning signs."

"You're not the only one," Bryce says. "Not to mention, it's hard to outwit a professional fraudster. Think of them as Oscar-worthy actors. They know how to play their audience like a fiddle."

"Well, Ramsey played us like a virtuoso," Angelica says.

"I don't want to downplay how much you and your sister

lost, but like I've mentioned to Hudson, the victims who approached us lost several millions of dollars."

"It's small potatoes for someone who is wealthy, but for us, it was everything."

"Understandably," Bryce says.

"Given these victims have deeper pockets than I do, were you able to get their money back?" Angelica asks.

"I pride myself on hiring the best. My staff has a stellar record tracking bad guys. You can run, but you can't hide—"

"You found him?" I ask.

Bryce's gaze meets mine. "I was going to say that *was* our motto until recently." *Dammit.* "In this electronic era, everyone leaves a trace. Except Ramsey."

"How can that be?" I ask.

"I'm stumped," Bryce says. "So is the rest of the team."

"Where did he go after leaving Indonesia?" Angelica asks.

"We tracked him under a fake ID as far as Finland— By the way, Ramsey Kenyon III isn't his real name."

"It's not?" Angelica asks.

"No. His real name is Syarhey Vladimirovich Nyakhaychyk."

Holy fuck, that's unpronounceable.

"Is he Russian?" I ask.

Bryce shakes his head. "He was born in Belarus. Grew up in Poland before coming to the United States with his parents when he was twelve years old."

"No wonder the motherfucker was able to dodge the authorities," I say. "While they were looking for Ramsey Kenyon III, Syar, whatever-his-name is, was bouncing around the globe, slipping through the police's fingers."

"You forgot his other fake identity," Bryce says.

"Right." My tone is sarcastic.

"And I wouldn't be surprised if he had more."

I just shake my head.

Bryce holds my gaze for a beat. "Going back to what I was saying, not long after he arrived in Loviisa, a coastal town in Finland, Ramsey's trace went cold. It's like he vanished into thin air."

Angelica sinks into her chair, her shoulders slumping.

I reach for her hand, interlacing our fingers together.

She looks up at me, sadness veiling her eyes.

I squeeze her hand.

She squeezes back.

The tense set of her shoulders eases a bit.

"So, he could still be hiding in Loviisa or somewhere else in Finland?" I ask.

"I have contacts there, and after weeks of searching, they came up emptyhanded. They reached out to contacts in Sweden. Zilch. Like I said, it's like Ramsey vanished into thin air."

"And if he were dead, the police would've found his remains?" I chance a guess.

"Exactly," Bryce says.

"Were you able to tap into his bank accounts?" I ask. "I'm sure a criminal like that must have a few if he has multiple IDs."

"That's a great question," Angelica says, her voice perking up. "He probably has offshore accounts."

"Isn't there some kind of treaty with the United States where you can freeze his accounts?" I piggyback on what Angelica said.

"The first three victims who hired us, approached us for that exact same reason. Ramsey had a complicated transaction web, where he was moving money around different offshore accounts across the globe. We cracked his code and figured out where he had stashed the bulk of the nearly billion dollars he stole—"

"Oh my God, you found the money?" Angelica asks.

"We found the money," Bryce says. "In international cases like this one, a lot of things can be expedited to freeze the bad guy's funds and cut off his or her lifeline, minimizing a flight risk—"

"That's great news!" I say.

Bryce's expression suggests otherwise. "It was fucking great news until the money vanished in front of our eyes."

"What?" I ask at the same time as Angelica says, "No, no, no."

"I had one of my guys tracking that account like a hawk," Bryce says. "One second the money was there, then he blinked, and the money was gone. Hours of work, and we had nothing to show for it." He blows out of breath. "I felt like I had failed my clients. Since I'm a sore loser, I asked my team to go back to the drawing board. I demanded they go over everything we had collected. They were to leave no stone unturned."

"Did they find anything new?" I ask.

Bryce's eyes are stone cold. "We found a key piece of information. As a result, we had to halt our investigation."

I frown. "What did you find?"

Bryce's jaw works, tensing and releasing as if determining what he's willing to share. His blue eyes turn dark and cold. There's nothing in his expression that's reassuring. Not that anything he's shared so far has been.

I lean into the table. "Bryce?"

Angelica shifts in her seat. "Please tell us, Bryce."

Bryce's eyes bounce from mine to Angelica's.

Can it get worse than it already is?

Bryce places his elbows on the table and steeples his fingers together. "The money bounced around in Russia under a numbered company—those types of corporation names aren't very memorable. When we cross referenced that company name with the ones that fell under Ramsey's umbrella, it wasn't on the list. And we checked twice. That was the first clue we needed to tread carefully. Then, the money—and I'm talking about nearly a billion dollars here—moved to a bank in Cyprus with the reputation for welcoming the Bratva's money."

That revelation hits me like a sledgehammer.

My eyebrows hit my forehead. "As in the Russian mob?"

"Yes." Bryce nods.

From the corner of my eye, I notice Angelica visibly jolting in her seat.

"Seriously?" I press.

"Trust me, Hudson, we dotted our i's and crossed our t's."

"Jesus," I grumble.

"Good God," Angelica says.

Arya surely knows how to pick 'em.

Forget about Ramsey being an asshole or fraudster. He was in bed with the Bratva?!

Christ on a cracker.

My gaze shifts to Angelica.

She glances back. Her green eyes are wide when they land on mine, radiating fear.

"The assholes we usually track down are involved in cyber, corporate, or white-collar crimes, which makes them certifiable greedy douchebags," Bryce says, his expression grim. "Is there a chance some might resort to violence to get away with their crimes?" It's a rhetorical question, since he keeps talking. "Yes. That's why we work with experts who are former military, or we work with local police to corner said assholes. Ramsey is a whole other level of assholery—a lethal one." He clenches his jaw. "We weren't able to find out what ties he has with the Russian mob, but for me, this is where it stops." He does a throat-slashing motion that sends chills up my spine. "I'm unwilling to put my staff's safety, my pregnant wife's, my family's, or mine in danger. No amount of money in the world is worth poking the hornets' nest—and that's exactly what would happen if we kept digging around and tripped one of the Bratva's warning signals. My guys and girls have kickass computer skills, but it's not like the mob can't fight fire with fire." His gaze shifts between mine and Angelica's. "And when they do, usually, someone dies." Angelica's legs start trembling. Horror prickles over my skin, and my tie feels as tight as a noose. "We erased our footprints and informed the clients who had hired us we were closing the case because the stakes were too high."

A long silence ensues.

Angelica's back slams against her seat. "Mother of God!"

"What?" I ask at the same time as Bryce asks, "What is it?"

"My sister could be in grave danger. *I* could be in danger since she's my identical twin."

My breath catches in my throat.

"What are you talking about?" Concern etches Bryce's face.

"Arya owes a shit ton of money to a man who goes by the name of Yevsei, I think. Is he involved with the Russian mob?"

"Ah," Bryce nods slowly. "Yevsei Dzhikiya..."

Chapter 32

Angelica

After the meeting with Bryce, my whole day went up in flames.

Since returning to the apartment, I haven't been able to focus on work. Every time I sit in front of my laptop, it's as if the words go blurry. I'm still struggling to make sense of everything Bryce revealed. It was like drinking a glass of water from a fireman's hose. It was way too much to handle. I was so not ready for that bombshell.

I swear to God, my heart stopped beating when Bryce said the word Bratva. I expected bad news. After all, Ramsey is no choirboy. But a connection to the mob? That's just insanity. Interestingly enough, the Russian mafia in romance books is a hell of a lot sexier and much less like a death sentence than it is in real life.

Hudson had meetings after our lunch. He apologized for not being able to comfort me, but he had to go. The man has already done so much for me. I told him I'd be fine.

Lies.

All lies.

I'm anything but fine.

The ride back to the apartment was agonizing. I was left replaying in my mind all the unsettling details Bryce shared with us.

So here I am back at my place, still in a state of shock.

Wine hasn't been on the budget for months, but given the state of emergency, it became essential. I never made it a habit to drink in the middle of the day. That's just asking for trouble. Yet, here I am, drinking. Nerves are eating up the lining of my stomach. It's the only thing keeping me together until my best friend calls me back so I can spill my guts to her.

I pour myself another glass of sauvignon—the third one since I got back twenty minutes ago—and swallow a generous gulp.

"Damn you, Arya. You make fucking up an Olympic sport." If she were here, I'd shake her senseless. I can't blame her for not knowing Ramsey's deep, dark secrets, or knowing his ill intentions from the get go, but she's doing it again.

She meets a guy.

She falls hard and fast.

And then she willingly follows a near stranger to the end of the world.

I'm sure when she gets back, it will be *Famous DJ this, Famous DJ that, Famous DJ knows this famous person, Famous DJ knows that famous person.*

Blah. Blah. Blah.

Same shit. Different asshole.

Ugh.

My phone rings.

I accept my best friend's video call.

"Sadie." Her name comes out as a prayer.

"You sent me like twenty texts and left me as many voicemails." I did. Desperate times and all. "You do realize there's a time difference between New York and LA, and since it's a weekday, I'm at work. I had to wait for my lunch break before calling you."

"Thank you. You're the best."

"What's up?" she asks.

"Arya."

Sadie rolls her eyes. "What has that girl done to give you premature grays?" I'm just about to answer, but she goes on, "Before we go down that rabbit hole, which I'm sure is another train wreck, let's talk about something I've been dying to know."

"What?"

"How was your evening with the sexy Hudson Kincaid?"

Last night seems so far away after the meeting with Bryce, but maybe reliving something drool-worthy is exactly what the doctor ordered.

"It was *fuck*-tastic."

My best friend's eyebrows disappear under her bangs. "You mean..."

I shake my head. "No, no one's punched my V card."

"Should I assume there was more dirty action?"

I tell her everything.

When I conclude my naughty tale, Sadie stares at me, her long eyelashes batting a mile a minute, her expression incredulous.

"You savage slut," she says when she recovers.

"It's Hudson's fault. He brings out a side of me I didn't even know existed."

"He has the magic touch when it comes to coaxing the sex kitten out of you, that's for sure."

"You're right. When he touches me, I come alive," I say. "Heck, when he looks at me, I combust. My body is so attuned to his, and I can't get enough of his domineering streak. Even his kisses are commanding. Every time we're together, he confiscates a little part of me. And I'm perfectly okay with that. Don't get me started on the nickname he has for me."

"Do tell."

"Angel," I say. "And that's when he thought my name was Brinley."

"Awww." Sadie places a hand over her heart. "Totally swoon-worthy."

"His sexy Matthew McConaughey drawl, combined with his deep and resonant voice, makes my nickname that much more arousing."

"My ovaries!" Sadie fans herself. "Matthew could read passages from an instruction manual, and he would make it so, so hot. Have I told you how many times I've listened to his audiobook?"

"Yes, you have."

Her grin is epic.

Just like me, Sadie is still a virgin. Before leaving for LA, she had been dating this guy for a year. He said he was okay waiting. On the night she decided she was ready to have him pop her cherry, a guy showed up at his apartment door just as things were about to get hot and heavy. Her boyfriend was batting for both teams. He just never mentioned it to her *or* the guy he was fucking.

"And then there's the side of Hudson he hides," I say.

"What do you mean?"

"He's been this super serious Mr. CEO since I met him, but then, I made him laugh"—I shake my head—"and oh, boy, the heady feeling that engulfed me just hearing the deep rumble in his chest was the most hedonistic thing ever."

She gives me a, *oh my God, this guy walks on water expression.*

I nod, a knowing smile stretching my lips.

"Girl, you scored! Usually, your sister's vagina gets her in trouble, but in this case, her *vagina trouble* paid off big-time..." —she points at the screen—"for you."

I dissolve in a fit of wine-fueled laughter.

She joins me.

"You should wrap up your virginity in a big red bow and offer it to him on a silver platter when the time comes," she says when she regains her composure. I laugh harder. "Hudson Kincaid is a godsend. Seriously, I want one of those for Christmas *and* my birthday."

"You're crazy," I say, still laughing.

"Seriously, Ange, think about it. Out of all the rich men who happen to be Pimp Daddy Todd's clients, you ended up with the Mack Daddy of them all, and a perfect Southern gentleman, to boot. I want me some of that."

"Technically, Arya ended up with him."

"I guess this is as good as any time to talk about the hot mess that brought you two together," Sadie says, veering the conversation. "What has Arya done now?"

Without revealing Bryce's identity, I tell my best friend everything he shared. As I recount the story, Sadie goes white as a sheet.

She sits back against her chair.

I give her time to process it all.

She opens her mouth to say something, but closes it.

She does it again.

"When you said you needed to talk urgently, what just came flying out of your mouth wasn't even on the radar. No wonder you sounded frantic on the voice messages."

"Until I started day drinking, I thought I was going to lose it."

"Wait. What? You're day drinking?"

I lift my glass up. "I was in a serious state of freakout."

"Let me circle back to that," she says, lifting a hand. "Let's start with Hudson. This guy has known you for three days, and already, he's made it his mission to become your knight in shining armor? Just when I thought he couldn't score more brownie points."

"I can't tell you how much I appreciate what he did for me. Ramsey's case hit a brick wall, but before knowing that, Hudson was willing to pay his friends to track Ramsey down."

"That speaks volumes about the kind of man he is," she says.

"I couldn't have said it better."

"Let's move on to your day drinking."

I tell her about the note my sister left me.

"Clearly, Arya is drinking as we speak, but I suspect it's for different reasons," Sadie says.

"Ya think?"

"Her disappearance to Miami isn't as bad as the time she blew a semester's worth of college tuition three months after your dad died on a weekend in Vegas with Vanna—her forevermore partner in crime, but once again, she gets to live it up, get shitfaced, party like life is a non-stop spring break, while you hold the fort."

I sigh.

After that crazy weekend, Arya came slinking back home, and declared college wasn't in the cards for her. Of course, she failed to mention she had lost a boat load of money gambling, partying, and buying drinks for strangers' bachelorette parties. I wanted to kill her, but refrained. Everyone deals with grief differently, so I thought. It took me a while to accept her careless behavior was just Arya being Arya.

"You're left in New York dealing with the saga that is Ramsey the potential mobster's story. Your twin is in Miami with a so-called famous DJ for three days, completely oblivious to the fact she fucked someone who breaks bread with the Russian mafia and could've put you two in serious danger—"

"In all fairness, Arya doesn't know of Ramsey's Bratva's connection yet—"

"You're making excuses for her again, Angelica!"

I wince.

She's right.

We don't speak for a long beat.

She stares at me with a hard, serious face, her brown eyes a mirror of determination.

"Call me biased, but even if you two hadn't done a twin swap, I doubt Hudson would stick his neck out for Arya like he is for you. And had he gone the distance, your sister would've found a way to make him regret his decision. I don't mean to be a bitch, but Arya is full of herself and she's an ungrateful brat. You're the same age, but in your relationship, she's elevated you to the role of parent. The worst part is, you accept it." I don't have a comeback. "That stunt she pulled with the note speaks volumes it's so lame." Sadie shakes her head like a pissed off school teacher. "She doesn't need to watch her back, and she doesn't need to be careful because you'll always be there to pick up the shattered pieces."

"I'm done picking up after her mess."

Sadie tilts her head to the side and levels me with an incredulous stare. "You were just about to give her another get out of jail free card because she was oblivious to scumbag Ramsey's many layers of duplicity. *She's* the one who got entangled with Ramsey in the first place. Not you."

"I mean it this time." Sadie doesn't seem convinced. "I do."

Unexpected tears prickle behind my lids.

I wipe my eyes with the back of my hand.

"Sorry, Ange." Guilt shines bright in her eyes. "I didn't

mean to be that hard on you, but you're my best friend and I'm tired of seeing you taken advantage of."

Her expression changes.

"Why do you look so freaked out?" I ask.

"If Ramsey is connected to the mob, does that mean Arya's loan shark—Yevsei-whatever—is a mob boss or has mafia ties?"

"That was the only good news that came out of the meeting. Her loan shark is a businessman who's a little shady, but he's not involved with the mob."

Sadie lets out an audible sigh. "Thank God."

"Yeah," I nod. "Had he been, we probably would've had to register in the witness protection program."

"Well, shy of being an accessory to murder, I'm not sure there's much you'd refuse your twin."

I twist my lips.

Easy to say for someone who doesn't have a twin.

"She knows it and she'll always use it to her advantage unless you put your big girl panties on. Talk is cheap, Angelica. Don't let Arya's sad, puppy-eyed manipulative tactics suck you in. She's a grown ass woman, and she needs to take responsibility for her actions."

Chapter 33

Hudson

I enter the Madison Avenue restaurant where I'm about to meet a prospect for drinks, followed by a late-night dinner, when my phone rings.

I answer the call as I step outside.

"Bryce," I say.

"Hey, Hudson," he says. "I hope I'm not catching you at a bad time."

"I'm just about to enter Eleven Madison Park. For the first time today, I'm early."

"Since I already know Angelica isn't a vegan, I assume it's a business meeting."

"It is. I've been in back-to-back meetings all day. And now, my day concludes with yet another meeting."

"I hope you close the deal because your dinner is going to set you back." That's a strange statement coming from a multi-billionaire.

"Isn't it just another expensive New York restaurant?"

"The prime porterhouse for three *and* the chateaubriand

steak for two at Keens—one of the city's most expensive steakhouses—won't cost as much as Eleven Madison Park's three-hundred-and-thirty-five-dollars *per person* plant-based menu. With tax, tips, and drinks, you're looking at well over a thousand dollars for veggies for two people."

"What?"

Bryce chuckles. "I had no idea vegetables cost that much until I had a dinner meeting there last week."

"Not that I intended on leaving the meeting without it being beneficial for both parties, but now I have an added incentive. Those damn vegetables better work in my favor," I say in an exaggerated Texan drawl. "Holy shit, vegan food is expensive."

"Only in Manhattan," he says. "Since I don't want to hold you on the phone longer than necessary, let me get right to the point. How's Angelica holding up? She looked distraught when she left my office."

After lunch, both Bryce and I had to rush to other meetings, so we kept the farewells succinct.

"I don't think I'll see her tonight since it's already ten, but we've been texting back and forth. She's still in shock."

"Understandably so. I hope it's clear now why I couldn't divulge that kind of information over the phone."

"I don't blame you for wanting to keep that kind of explosive information behind closed doors."

"How are you doing?"

"Me?"

"Yes. I could feel the anger rolling off you."

I rake my fingers through my hair. "Given my experience with Baylor, I have zero tolerance for unscrupulous assholes who try to con people by promising them diamonds in the sky just to leave them hanging dry."

"You're preaching to the choir. My entire business is based on that same model."

"I don't know what it is about Angelica that flares my protective nature and makes me want to take her burden as mine."

"I understand where you're coming from."

"Before walking into your office, I was out for blood. I was willing to throw as much money as necessary your way to flip the world upside down and bring chaos to it to search for Ramsey like the fucking rabid dog he is." My nostrils flare and a muscle in my cheek twitches. "But the Bratva..." I shake my head. "Your revelations put things into perspective real quick." The knowledge of Angelica having any kind of dealings with a lowlife who has ties to the Russian mafia wraps itself around my throat and squeezes hard. "I'm man enough to admit that that shit scared the ever-loving hell out of me. Like you said, you cross those motherfuckers and you die."

"That's why I put the brakes on everything," he says. "I know I'm much older, but I feel you and I are forged from the same metal, so I wanted to reach out." Bryce is in his mid-forties. He's fit, and his brown hair is streaked with only a few strands of gray at the temple. "I don't accept defeat easily, and it pisses me off to no end that I'm not able to get Angelica—and Ramsey's other victims—retribution. I just wanted to make sure you knew that."

"The call is unnecessary, but I appreciate it. I would love for the asshole to pay, but if he's in bed with the Russian mafia, he might as well have a bullseye tattooed on his forehead."

"My thought exactly," Bryce says. "How did Angelica's sister react to all of this?"

I groan. "She doesn't know yet."

"She doesn't?"

"Don't get me started on Arya."

"You two don't get along?"

"I haven't met her yet, but from everything I know about her, she's trouble with a capital T."

"It's unfortunate for the McQuinley twins Ramsey didn't set his attention on someone else."

"From what I understand, Arya would've bent over backwards to catch his eye. She has a thing for train wrecks."

"Not good."

"Not for Angelica, it isn't. She keeps coddling her twin, when she should force her sister to grow up. Her determination to protect Arya only makes me want to protect her from her sister even more. Angelica and I sit on opposite sides when it comes to dealing with her twin."

"Family. That's a slippery slope."

"I'm starting to understand that."

"Tread carefully," Bryce says. "When broken, some sibling relationships are irreparable."

"I'm trying my damnedest not to butt in."

"But it's hard."

"It's fucking hard."

"Now that Ramsey is no longer in the picture, that's one less thing to worry about. And one less thing for you to disagree about." *Until the next asshole comes Arya's way.* "In any case," he says, changing the subject, "I hope to meet Angelica again. The meeting was brief, and the circumstances weren't ideal."

"I'm sure you will."

"You never mentioned how the two of you met."

I laugh. "We met in the most unorthodox way."

I tell him all about it.

"Good old Todd," Bryce says. "Since I'm not the one who referred you to him, who did?"

"The Ellison brothers," I say.

"I'm not surprised. The Ellisons prefer to keep their relationships... uncomplicated."

Until recently, I adhered to the same philosophy. "What's your experience with Todd?"

"That's a story for another day." Bryce is guarded about his private life. A professional hazard, no doubt.

"I'll hold you to it."

"You do that," he says, humor coloring his words. "Back to Angelica. Given the fact you asked for my help and you took time out of your busy day to make it to Brooklyn, I'm going to go out on a limb and assume things with her aren't casual." I'm just about to respond, but he keeps talking. "I say that because you haven't so much as looked at another woman since..."

"Yonas died."

"Yes."

I let out a sigh. "You're right. Other than my high school girlfriend, I've never been so hot for a woman that I lose my head. When Yonas died, my cock and my sexual needs took back seat as I was swimming upstream against the current to ensure everything didn't explode in my face."

"I understand that," he says. "Sometimes, your dick is out of commission... until someone comes along and jolts it back to life."

"That's exactly what happened when I met Angelica. Before I knew about the twin swap, I booked her sexy ass for a week so no other fucker could even look at her. I was obsessed with her at first sight. She's the only one who's made me feel truly awake in months, hell, years. Things are moving fast between us, but I have no intention of putting the brakes on. And then, there's this fierce protectiveness that makes me feel like I've reverted to being a fucking caveman."

Bryce laughs.

"What's so funny?"

"Like I said, you and I are forged from the same metal. I know too well about irrational obsessions, and when it comes to reverting to a Neanderthal over a woman, I wrote the fucking guidebook."

It's my turn to laugh.

Chapter 34

Angelica

I woke up bright and early this morning with the intent to *carpe diem*, but like so many things in my life, Loki, the God of Mischief, is behind the wheel.

I was fully immersed in my work, proud of the progress I've made over the last day and a half to catch up since I've been spending too much time living the life of a socialite, when my phone rang. Elated, I picked up when I saw Hudson's name flash on my screen. My joy quickly fizzled when he told me to get my ass to Brooklyn asap. There were new developments in Ramsey's disappearance.

I'm a ball of nerves during the ride from my apartment to Bryce's office. On one hand, I'm apprehensive of what Bryce might have to share, on the other, I'm hopeful that authorities in Finland might have tracked Ramsey down. If the money he stole is lining the bank account of someone inside the Russian mob, it's unlikely I'll see any of it, but I pray to God the weasel will be brought to justice.

I trail behind the receptionist on my way to the same conference room where I met Bryce a couple of days ago.

When we turn a corner, my phone chimes. I check my screen, expecting a text from Hudson, but it's my sister.

I lift my eyes to the receptionist. "I'm sorry. I need to respond to this text. I'll only be a minute."

"No problem," she says.

Arya: Hey, sis. You must've read my note by now. Miami is so, so awesome.

Angelica: A note? Really?

Arya: I wanted to leave you a message to let you know where I would be without interrupting your evening. I think that's considerate.

Angelica: I call bullshit.

Arya: Whatever. You can't accuse me of not telling you I was going to be out of town.

Angelica: You're missing the point. You should've texted or called to let me know you were hopping on a plane with a stranger.

Arya: Well, I'm letting you know now, my Miami trip has been extended. I'll be here for another day.

Angelica: R U FUCKING KIDDING ME?

Arya: It's not every day you get to party with a famous DJ **and** famous people.

I roll my eyes at the phone.

Angelica: Here we fucking go again.

Arya: Don't get your knickers in a bunch. I **have** to be in Manhattan in two days. Todd wants to meet to brief me about my next client. I guess he'll officially be my first. LOL! It's a good thing I'm staying an extra day. Sexy DJ Bromley has something special planned for tomorrow night. He's being all secretive. I bet it's something big. He's so, so cool. So totally different from Ramsey.

Angelica: Speaking of which, there are certain things you need to know about Ramsey.

Arya: Please don't ruin my mini vacay by talking about that douchebag. He's part of my past.

Angelica: Your past? What about me?

Arya: Ramsey is also part of your past, which is another reason for you to never think about him again. Bromley is my **now guy**. He said he'll fly me to Vegas to hang out with him. And he's so, so dreamy. He thinks it's badass I work for Todd.

I press my lips into a thin line, my annoyance growing in spades.

Angelica: Fuck Bromley.

Arya: Rude.

Angelica: Damn it. Stop obsessing over another guy who's just going to screw you over.

Arya: You don't know Bromley. Stop talking about him that way.

Angelica: Then, let's talk about another asshole who rear-ended you. There are certain things you need to know about Ramsey. We need to talk.

Arya: Vanna is doing tequila body shots, and the guy is really hot. Good chat, sis. See you soon. Turning my phone off now. Tootles.

Angelica: Arya.

Angelica: ARYA!

Angelica: Fucking turn your phone back on.

Angelica: I mean it. I need to talk to you.

She shut me out?!

Rage colors my world in blinding bursts of white light.

I'm so pissed off. If I could reach through the phone and shake her, I would.

With a huff of frustration, I tuck my phone inside my handbag.

She's managed to ruin my morning and leave a sick, ugly feeling in my stomach.

"Ready?" the receptionist asks.

"I'm sorry about that. Yes, I'm ready now."

With a nod, she starts walking.

I'm right on her heels.

Agitated heat blooms over my cheeks with each step.

What an ungrateful brat.

When we reach the conference room, the receptionist opens the door and invites me in, but doesn't follow behind me. I watch her close the door and take the opportunity to compose myself.

Breathe in.

Breathe out.

I inhale a last fortifying breath, plaster a forced smile on my lips and turn around to face the two men who are waiting for me.

Since Hudson was heading to Manhattan from the airport, he asked his chauffeur to change course.

After the customary greetings, I take a seat next to him.

I glance his way and cock an eyebrow.

He didn't know why Bryce called us in, but I'm hoping since he got here before I did, his friend might've clued him in.

He responds to my unanswered question with a head shake.

Crap.

He reaches out and touches my elbow. "You okay?"

"Yes."

"Your cheeks are flushed," he says.

I bring the back of my hand against my cheek as if that's enough to tamper the redness. "I was rushing to get here." It's a partial truth.

He nods slowly, but his furrowed eyebrows suggest he doesn't believe me.

"Thanks a lot for coming in," Bryce says, pulling our attention to him.

I sit a little straighter in my chair.

"No problem," Hudson says. "Ramsey's trail went cold for a while, and two days after meeting with you, you get a lead. I'm hoping this is a sign."

"Same here," I echo.

Bryce nods, but his stoic face doesn't reveal a thing. "Normally, I'd make sure we had snacks and refreshments, but this isn't that kind of meeting."

Translation: This isn't a tea party.

"That doesn't sound too good," Hudson says.

"Nothing so far concerning Ramsey has been good, Kincaid."

"Touché," Hudson says.

It's on the tip of my tongue to jump in with a thousand questions, but I bite them down.

Patience.

"The Finnish police found Ramsey—"

"It's about time!" Hudson says at the same time as my gratitude spills from my lips, "Finally!"

"You two didn't let me finish," Bryce says, his expression ominous.

"We got a little carried away," Hudson says.

"Sorry," I say.

Bryce adjusts his tie. "They didn't find him alive."

An arctic air sweeps across the conference room.

To curtail my nervousness, I twist my fingers together and ask, "He's dead?"

Bryce's blue eyes hold my gaze. "Yes."

I was hoping the asshole would stand trial, face his victims, and hear how his callous actions destroyed lives. The only silver lining is, he'll never be able to take advantage of anyone else, ever.

"Do you think it was the Russian mob?" Hudson asks.

Panic claws up my throat.

"The Finnish police believe it is. The way Ramsey died had Bratva 101 all over it."

"What does that mean?" Hudson asks.

Bryce catches my eye. When he speaks, his words come out measured. "I'm not sure you want to hear this, Angelica. It's pretty gruesome."

I swallow hard. "I'd like to know."

"You're sure?" Hudson asks.

My gaze meets his. "I want closure."

Bryce shifts his attention to Hudson.

The two men exchange a silent conversation and a nod.

"Very well," Bryce says. "The Bratva made sure it would be nearly impossible to identify Ramsey. His mouth, fingertips, and private parts... were mutilated. I'm going to leave it at that." *Dear God, that sounds gruesome.* "Then, his killer—or killers—froze his body in an industrial freezer for a few months. A couple of days ago, they thawed and dumped his body in a construction zone. The strategy behind freezing his body is to obscure the actual date of death. Of course, the killers got rid of his wallet and keys—"

"How the hell were they able to identify him?" Hudson asks.

"Ramsey must've known his days were numbered—"

"What do you mean?"

Bryce zooms his attention to the knight in shining armor sitting next to me. "The medical examiner found a note hidden in one of his socks, identifying him with his birth name and assumed identity. Syarhey Vladimirovich Nyakhaychyk, aka, Ramsey Kenyon III, is dead." *Mother of God.* "He wasn't stabbed or shot. He probably bled to death. The Finnish police say it ticks all the boxes of a Bratva vendetta killing."

Holy shit.

Holy shit.

Holy shit.

My heart beats like crazy and I can hardly breathe. It's like the immensity of this news is choking me.

"I guess there's no retrieving the money?"

Thank God Hudson has the presence of mind to ask that question.

I'm too much in freakout mode to speak, let alone think.

"We checked Ramsey's accounts, just in case. They're still all at zero. As far as my team and I are concerned, the money is in Cypress, in the mob's bank account. As I explained a couple days ago, we're steering clear of that bank, so we can't confirm one hundred percent. That said, it's safe to assume none of Ramsey's victims will ever see their money."

Case closed.

The bad guys win.

I bite on my lower lip to curtail the tears threatening to erupt.

I'm all shook up about this news surrounding Ramsey, but what has my nerves jumping and sizzling like hot oil in a fryer is my twin sister.

The woman whose face and DNA I share and who couldn't deign to take five minutes from her stupid mini vacay to find out why I urgently needed to talk to her. Why deal with reality when you can do shots instead and leave it to your twin to be the adult?

Chapter 35

Hudson

I didn't think twice. After that meeting with Bryce, I called my executive assistant and asked her to cancel the rest of my day. As Bryce was sharing the latest findings about Ramsey's disappearance, Angelica kept getting increasingly paler. By the end of it, she was as white as a ghost. I suggested we hang out. She didn't argue. After guiding her to my chauffeured car, I went back inside. There was one thing I needed to talk to Bryce about.

When we got to my Upper West Side brownstone, I asked Angelica what she wanted to do. In a weary voice, she said she needed to sit down for a minute. The next thing I knew, she was passed out under an umbrella-covered lounge chair. Three hours later, sleeping beauty woke up as famished as a grizzly bear who had spent winter hibernating. Neither of us usually eat this early, but if you're going to have an early dinner, you might as well make it count.

It's a beautiful evening, so we're still sitting outside on the terrace. Since Angelica was wearing the same light-gray suit she wore a couple days ago, I gave her one of my white t-shirts.

It's huge on her, but at least she's comfortable. I ditched my navy pinstripe suit for some shorts and an undershirt. We're both barefoot and carefree. It's almost as if the meeting with Bryce never happened.

Right.

As we were enjoying an Italian charcuterie platter with a beautiful bottle of Chianti, we talked about Ramsey. It's safe to say, it's going to take her days—if not weeks—to get over the shock. Same for me.

"I'll never buy frozen lasagna. Ever!" Angelica says, placing her knife and fork on her empty plate. "That was insanely delicious." She does a chef's kiss. "*Molto bene!*" She ate her meal with such gusto, I was certain she was going to lick the plate clean.

"When I lived in Texas, I ate Italian food at restaurants I could afford. Most times, it was either frozen or from the prepared food section at my local grocery store. I'm not saying there aren't amazing Italian restaurants in Dallas. I just couldn't afford them back then. When I moved to New York and started making a little money, I realized there was a whole other level of Italian cuisine. Having my own chef elevated the experience since he's from Bologna."

"Did he teach you how to make the salad?" She points to the empty salad plate, referring to the insalata tricolore con formaggio di capra. A personal favorite.

"I can't take credit for the salad. Everything was in the fridge, well labeled. I just had to coordinate things by tossing arugula, endive, radicchio, and crumbled goat cheese together. The dressing was already prepared. As for the grilled veggies, sure, I worked the barbecue, but my chef cut and marinated the vegetables."

She tilts her head back and says to the sky, "It's good to be Hudson Kincaid."

I shake my head.

She meets my gaze, her eyes gleaming with amusement. "What? I'm stating a fact."

"I'm not even going to be bashful about it. It is good to be me. The only reason I know that is because"—I open my arms wide—"I had to work my butt off to get this."

"Success looks good on you, mister," she says.

I tap the tip of her nose. "Here's the other good thing about being me. I get to invite whoever I want to share all this with."

"And I'm the lucky girl?"

"You are."

She pulls her bottom lip between her teeth. "Lucky me."

I brush a strand of hair behind her ear.

"No, lucky *me*."

She flashes me a warm smile. "Let's agree we're both lucky."

"Let's."

"I know I'm being cocky, but thank you, Hudson."

"For the meal?"

She shakes her head. "No, for everything. For the unforgettable Saks Fifth Avenue spa day, to the designer wardrobe, shoes, and jewelry, to some of the best food I've eaten in forever. Let it be known, I'm not the best chef and my sister can't cook to save her life. The only restaurant food we eat is whatever my sister buys with her employee discount from the pub she works at."

"I know what it's like to have humble beginnings."

She nods. "And more importantly, thank you for Bryce."

"Don't mention it." There's a question that's been nagging at me since we started eating the antipasto. "What does your sister have to say about all this? I assume you filled her in."

Her jaw tightens and her eyes harden.

"My sister doesn't know yet."

"How come? I thought you two lived together."

Angelica tells me all about Arya skipping town to spend a mini vacay in Miami with DJ Bromley—whoever the fuck he is to lift *her* best friend's spirit after *she* got dumped. Then, she tells me about the text messages she exchanged with her sister before today's meeting.

Arya is a freaking train wreck.

It's not my place to come between her and her twin. After all, we just met. She's known her sister her whole life. But Arya needs a good spanking, and I'm not talking in a *Call me Daddy or I'll spank your ass* kind of way.

"Let me get this straight, she's enjoying a vacation on Mr. Famous DJ's dime," I say in quotation marks, "a stranger," I stress, "completely oblivious to the development around an asshole *she* brought into your life and who screwed you blind?"

"Pretty much."

"Is that you taking one for the team like you did for the gig with Todd?" My tone is more biting than I intended.

She hangs her head low and shrugs.

I rub my hand over my face in frustration.

It irks me to no end that Arya takes advantage of her like this.

"Do you have a passport?" I ask, changing the subject.

Her gaze snaps up to meet mine. "What does a passport have to do with my sister or Ramsey?"

"Nothing. There's not much more we can say about that douchebag. As for your sister... it's best if I don't touch that one."

She sighs. "I wish I could do that sometimes."

"You haven't answered my question."

"Yes, I have a passport. I've never used it, but I figured having one was manifesting my intentions of traveling the world one day. The universe hasn't granted my wish yet."

"I'm about to become your fairy godmother."

She scrunches up her adorable little nose.

"We're flying to Bermuda."

Her head jerks back.

Then, her face contorts in this comical expression.

She opens her mouth and closes it a few times, doing a darn good impression of a guppy fish.

"As in Bermuda, the island?" she asks. That bewildered expression remains firmly on her beautiful face.

"Yes, Bermuda, the island."

"Holy shit!"

Chapter 36

Angelica

I was excited at the idea of stepping into JFK Airport for the first time in my life, but the private jet service we're flying with departs from Long Island MacArthur Airport, New Jersey.

So here we are, cruising across the sky.

My first time flying on a plane is on a private jet.

Holy mind-blowing!

Hudson and I are sitting on camel-colored leather armchairs. The smell of the buttery soft leather is unmistakable, as memorable as the scent of my Louboutin shoes. The chairs are set side by side, forming an L shape and there's a small coffee table in front of us. It's literally like being in a luxurious living room. Right behind us, there's another area with leather chairs that look like the type you'd expect to find on an airplane—with seatbelts—and there's a three-seater couch. Not that I know firsthand, but Hudson assures me the extra legroom is a huge bonus. Tall people's problems.

My eyes nearly popped out of my skull when the flight attendant informed us the "airplane seats" have footrests and they're fully reclinable, just in case we wanted to take a catnap. No way am I closing my eyes. I have no intention of missing a minute of this adventure.

On top of that, we don't have to worry about crying babies, five hundred people using the same bathroom, rude people breaking wind, airborne germs, or any of the other concerns you have when you fly coach.

"Like I said last night, it's good to be you, Hudson Kincaid," I say, bouncing in my seat as if I'm a five-year-old doped up with sugar.

"Evidently, it's good to be you too, Angelica McQuinley, since you're sitting here with me."

"Yeah, but you made this happen."

"Technically, my friend Bryce made it happen."

"Whatever, Mr. I Know People in High Places. Maybe it's no biggie to you because all your friends have vacation homes on a Caribbean Island, but for lil' ol' me, it's a big fucking deal."

I was touched beyond belief when Hudson told me Bryce called him to make sure I was okay after hearing about the news of Ramsey's death. A stranger cared more about me than my own identical twin sister. My stupor deepened when Hudson informed me Bryce offered his Bermuda villa to us for a short getaway.

"Not all my friends have vacation homes on a Caribbean Island," Hudson says, "Some have cabins in Aspen. Others have homes in the Hamptons. Martha's Vineyard is also a popular destination. Same for Miami. And of course, Hawaii is also a coveted spot. Many also have a European home, just in case they fancy a culture change."

"Are you mocking me?"

"You make it easy to tease you, angel."

"Are you going to sit there and tell me the first time you

were able to afford to fly on a private jet, you weren't blown away?"

He considers me. "I'm not that blasé. I was just pulling your leg. Actually, I was blown away the first time I was able to afford a first-class ticket." I didn't expect that answer. "It's impossible to comprehend what money can buy until you become filthy rich."

"Either that, or you hang out with filthy rich Samaritans."

His head jerks back. "Samaritans? Who else have you been hanging out with?"

"It was a figure of speech. You're the only filthy rich guy I'm hanging out with."

The indignation vanishes from his handsome features. "Good to know. I wouldn't want to have to break anyone's jaw."

"No need to go that far, Mr. Alpha Macho."

"If you're trying to say I'm irrationally possessive when it comes to you. You better fucking believe it."

His words travel straight to my heart.

Don't make me like you any more than I already do, sexy Texan.

The flight attendant approaches us with a tray.

"Mr. Kincaid, I assume this is a good time?"

"Yes," he says, sliding forward on his seat.

I do the same.

The flight attendant drops the tray on the table and places a black box in front of Hudson and one in front of me. She also places flutes in front of us.

"I'll be right back with the champagne," she says, before scurrying off.

"What's inside the box?" I ask Hudson.

"Patience."

His smug expression suggests he has something up his sleeve.

In no time, the flight attendant returns with a bottle of champagne, dunked in a bucket of ice. She pours some of the effervescent nectar in each glass, and she's off after Hudson and I thank her.

Hudson places the tips of his fingers on top of the box, his eyes downcast. "While playing tourist in Manhattan when I first came to New York to live with my uncle, I passed by this swanky pastry shop." His gaze meets mine. "My mouth was salivating. Everything looked so good. There was a big chalkboard with the selections, but there were no prices. I figured since it was New York, the cookies were three dollars each. It was way more than what I'd pay back home, but I just had to have one. I nearly swallowed my tongue when the woman behind the counter told me they were six dollars and fifty cents a pop, before tax. I remember looking around, my mind computing it all. People were dropping over eleven dollars for coffee and a cookie. Dejected, I walked out. When we hit our first profitable month, I dragged Yonas to Chocolate Chunk. The first time I set foot in that shop, I was wearing worn clothes and I had maybe ten dollars in my pocket. My parents didn't have much. They were working-class folks. I think I mentioned my dad was the superintendent of the six-plex we lived in?"

I nod. "Yes, you did."

"Mom cooked and cleaned for a rich family in town," he says. "I'd end up with their sons' hand-me-downs. They were good to us, especially over Christmas. They always made sure Mom had enough to buy food to prepare a real nice Christmas dinner and buy gifts." He rakes his fingers through his hair. "When my parents died, the insurance money went to my uncle, so he could take care of me. After his death, I found out he had put that money into a trust fund for me. Considering how much he seemed to despise my existence, the fact I left New York the second I was of legal age to be on my own, and he was the beneficiary, I figured I had kissed that money goodbye."

"Wow."

"I was shocked."

"Maybe he felt guilty about how badly he treated you?"

"I'll never know."

"Right."

"Back to Chocolate Chunk," he says. "The second time I walked into the shop, I was in a proper suit. Maybe not tailored, but I looked and felt the part. And I had a hell of a lot more than ten dollars in my pocket. Yonas and I left the shop with two of everything to eat when we got home, and tons more to freeze—"

"Talk about the comeback kid."

"Yeah." A smile stretches his lips. "We took a cab to Brooklyn. No subway for us on that day. When we returned to the house, we ate so many chocolate cookies, we were nearly drunk from the sugar high. Of course, we washed it all down with champagne, so maybe we were drunk, period."

I laugh.

"Since that milestone, I've discovered tons of amazing pastry shops in Manhattan, but I keep going back to Chocolate Chunk because it's a reminder of how far I've come." His eyes bore into mine. "I stopped by the shop before picking you up. I had them place the cookies in airtight containers, to prolong the surprise. Other than my best friend and business partner, I've never wanted to share that little gem with anyone..."

I squirm in my seat.

"Until you, angel."

I bring a hand to my chest. My heart is beating like a metronome cranked up to the highest BPM.

I can't breathe.

I clear the thickness from my throat. "Thank you." I'm so

taken aback by his words, I can't come up with anything better to say.

"I hope to meet your twin soon"—that has the same effect as jumping naked in a frozen lake—"so I can thank her in person for putting you in my path."

My stomach does a weird lurch at the mention of the possibility of Arya meeting Hudson. Conflicting emotions swim through me and jealousy sits heavy on my chest.

I try to smile, but I can't. Instead, I pinch my lips together.

He frowns, as if asking a silent question.

I respond with a small head shake and a noncommittal shrug.

He reaches out for my arm.

My eyes drop.

I watch, riveted as the tips of his fingers stroke a soft path from my wrist to my elbow. He touches me as if he can't stop himself.

I fucking love the way he touches me.

"You wanna know what I got us?" he asks.

I swallow with effort. "Yes!"

"I went with the Chocolate Heaven Box."

"Oh, that sounds serious."

"Very serious. Only pros can handle this level of decadence."

"I'm up for the challenge."

"I wouldn't have expected anything less of you."

He lifts the lid of the box in front of me, pulls out a second transparent box, and places it on the coffee table.

I gasp.

Oh.

My.

Freaking.

God.

He opens the box. "I got us one of each." He points to each treat. "Dark chocolate brownie, chocolate explosion cookies, chocolate and hazelnut barks, and nutty chocolate chip cookies—we're talking about cookies stuffed with macadamia nuts, almond, walnuts, and French chocolate. Those are among my favorites and they're staples. But I didn't stop there... I also bought one of each of their daily special treats."

I'm dead. And I've gone to chocolate heaven.

~

We all have a scene from a favorite movie or TV show we'd love to recreate. The thing is, how many of us will ever get that chance?

For instance, the scene in *The Titanic* with Jack and Rose standing on the bow of the boat, Rose with her arms outstretched, is still on my bucket list. Same for the famous "*The Time of My Life*" scene from *Dirty Dancing*. I've watched *The Thomas Crown Affair 1999* a thousand times and I know every scene by heart. I never expected to recreate one of them. When Bryce's majordomo came to pick us up at the airport in a Jeep, no way was I going to miss a chance of a lifetime. This might not be Martinique, but it's close enough.

I lift my hands above my head. "Hello, Bermuda!"

I'm totally channeling heroine Catherine Banning in the movie. Just like her, I'm standing in the convertible vehicle as we race down the road.

I've thrown caution to the wind.

The black man behind the wheel, maneuvering the jeep like a Formula One racing driver, looks up at me and flashes me his white teeth.

My smile is as epic.

"Jesus, woman, we barely landed on the island, and already, you're unleashed," Hudson says.

"You bet your bottom dollar I am!" I say before resuming my mission. "Bermuda, I love you!"

"Sheesh. You get the girl out of New York, and she turns into a wild thing," Hudson says.

"*Born to be wild!*" I belt out the bridge of a song that was popular well before my parents were even born. Once a classic, always a classic. "Come on, sing along with me," I say to Hudson.

He just shakes his head.

I'm not sure if it's from my outrageous behavior or the fact I can't sing for shit, but whatever.

Fuck being the responsible one. For the next three days, I get to live it up.

I get to be silly.

I get to be carefree.

No adulting for me!

I don't have to worry about my sister *or* her fuckups.

And the best part is, I don't have to think for two.

For once, I get to be selfish.

I'm going to drink some of my sister's Kool-Aid. *Me first!*

My eyes drift to the gorgeous man staring up at me.

Okay, maybe not.

I'm incapable of being exactly like my sister. After all, I wouldn't be here without Hudson or his friend.

So maybe it's more like *us first*!

I texted Sadie and told her I was turning my phone off while I was on the island. I could use roaming charges as an excuse, but I was upfront and told her I just wanted to shut the world out. As for my twin, I texted her a succinct message, borrowing her words.

Angelica: You won't be able to reach me for the next few days. Sadie knows where I am. No need to contact her. She won't tell you unless there's an emergency. Turning my phone off now. Tootles.

Anyone can fly down to Miami for a getaway, but not everyone gets to fly on a private plane to an island where they'll be staying in a billionaire's luxury villa located on a secluded part of the island.

Take that, Arya.

"I should demand you sit your ass back down, but that smile on your face is too contagious for me to ruin the mood. Not to mention, your ass looks amazing."

My God, this man is wonderful.

I stop clowning around and sit my amazing ass next to Hudson.

I put my seatbelt on and look at him. "Shy of a cataclysmic hurricane, nothing will ruin my mood over the next three days."

"I like the sound of that," he says, before planting a passionate kiss on my lips.

There's no tongue or anything X-rated, but still, he takes ownership of my mouth and I'm seriously melting.

If cleaning up my sister's mess always means I'd end up with a man like Hudson, I'd do it over and over again.

An unsettling thought crosses my mind.

I wouldn't want to meet another man like Hudson.

I just want Hudson.

Chapter 37

Hudson

This is my first time in Bermuda, and given it's less than three hours from New York, it's no wonder Bryce and his wife come here whenever they can.

This is paradise.

Bryce's property is impressive. The view is outstanding. And the exterior is a dream. Not only because of the hot weather, but because everything is so meticulously groomed. I swear, I could live in that big, beautiful pool. And the abundance of flowers and the greenery are postcard-worthy.

Right after dropping our suitcases in our room, we traded our clothing for something more appropriate—a sexy as fuck red bikini for Angelica she bought at a shop before we made it to the villa, and swim trunks for me.

We spent all afternoon at the beach. I've been swimming in rivers running along Summerville since I was a kid. Although the sea is a lot more unforgiving, I never miss a chance to jump in. Angelica looked at the water with the same wariness as a kitten, only choosing to dip a toe in the water. She wouldn't even allow the water to go up to her ankles.

We walked along the beach for the greater part of the afternoon before lying down on beach chairs. Outraged I didn't pack sunscreen, Angelica, the forever caretaker, lathered my body with SPF 50. It would've been foolish of me to refuse her hands all over me.

Now, we're enjoying dinner outside.

The glowing sun is dipping below the horizon, almost as if it's disappearing into the ocean. It's a treat for me to watch the sunset. Since Yonas's death, I've been operating in one mode—go, go, go. I never have time just to kick back and watch as Mother Nature paints the sky in golden, pink, and crimson tones, mixed with spots of light blue. A mesmerizing symphony of magnificent colors. God's palette. It's calming and wondrous at the same time. The perfect conclusion to our first day in Bermuda.

It's no longer hot as Hades. Strings of lights illuminate where we're sitting, making the experience enchanting. A beautiful breeze causes Angelica's long brown hair to dance around her face. Since meeting her, it's the first time I've seen her without any makeup on. She's radiant. And judging from her long blonde lashes, she *is* a natural blonde. I wouldn't say she's sporting a tan, but she has some nice color as a result of our time spent in the sun. Even though it broke my heart, she covered her heavenly body in a pretty sundress in a similar shade to the thousands of bougainvillea flowers growing on Bryce's property.

"These sandwiches are so delicious, I might have to ask Bryce's chef to prepare them every day," I say, wiping my mouth with a cloth napkin.

"You won't hear me complaining." Angelica pops the last bite of her sandwich into her mouth. "I'd totally eat the crab cakes every day as well."

"Same!"

The meal was excellent.

Nothing fancy, just good island food.

I can't say I've eaten too many fish sandwiches in my life, but the Bermuda fish sandwich is something else. Angelica was only able to manage half of hers. Those babies are colossal, easily the size of a triple decker sandwich, layered with goodness. I finished the half she was too stuffed to eat, along with my sandwich. I was famished.

"I'm still struggling with the concept of mixing raisin bread and fish, but it works," she says.

The thick slices of raisin bread threw me off. Curious mind and all, I asked the chef to enlighten us. He explained the raisin bread satisfies the sweet-savoury taste combo preferred by most Bermudians. By God, it works. It's one of those things you have to try to believe it.

"I hope it's okay if we wait a bit before we attack the rum cake and homemade Bailey's ice cream." She pats her tummy. "I need to digest before I take another bite."

"The good thing about being on a vacation is we don't have to do anything we don't want to."

She grins wide.

"More wine?" I ask.

"That would be lovely."

I reach for the bottle, top up her glass before serving myself.

We take a long sip of the chardonnay Bryce imported from California.

"This is truly exceptional," she says, "just like everything here."

"I agree."

"You're going to make it hard for me to go back to reality, you know that?" Her tone is accusatory.

I take hold of her hand. "Stop thinking of when you get back to New York. This"—I stretch an arm out—"is as close as you'll get to Paradise. We're only here for a few days. Enjoy every single moment of it."

She bites against her lower lip. "You're right. I guess my mind is constantly churning."

"Flip the switch," I say. "I want your mind to focus only on the here and now. Anything else has no business on this island."

From the way her lips form a line, I'm guessing she's still not ready to let go.

I arch a brow. "Let's make this a challenge."

She shoots me a dubious glance. "What did you have in mind?"

"Every time you think of something that might drag you down, there will be consequences."

"What kind of consequences?"

"The *pleasurable* kind."

"Pleasure and consequences don't usually go hand in hand."

"In my world they do."

"What does that mean?" Her question is guarded.

"I get a blowjob."

She nearly chokes. "What?"

"If you're on your knees while I fuck your face, you're forced to be present."

"Wouldn't you be the one benefiting the most?"

I shake my head. "You came hard the last time with my cock between your lips. So, we'll both be benefiting."

Lust veils her eyes. "Ah... it's a win-win all around..."

Dirty girl.

I tilt my head from side to side. "Yes and no."

"I don't follow."

"Once I'm done fucking your face and coming down your throat, I'll put you over my knee and redden that beautiful ass of yours to the point where you won't be able to sit comfortably. That'll keep you focused on the moment, preventing your mind from wandering."

"Tyrant!"

"It's for your own good, darlin'."

She throws her head back and laughs.

When her green eyes meet mine, all levity dissipates.

"What is it?" I ask.

She shakes her head. "Nothing."

"I don't buy it."

"I'm having... fun."

There's more to it. "Sounds like you're unsure."

"It's just that... fun hasn't been in my vocabulary for so long, I almost forgot how to spell the word."

I can sympathize. Until she came into my life, I was too focused on work to take time off, let alone have fun. "Well, it's priority number one until we fly home."

"I'm on board!"

"Do you know what day this is?" I ask, changing the subject.

"I'm guessing you're not referring to the day of the week?"

"No."

Her eyes shift left to right. "I'm stumped."

"At midnight, the arrangement I have with *Brinley* expires."

She blushes, peering at me from under her lashes.

It's been torture watching her prance around in a bikini. The only thing I wanted to do was lose myself inside her, but my word is golden. I don't renege on a promise. However, it didn't prevent my mind from coming up with all sorts of lewd ways for me to get my fill of her.

"I can't wait to claim you, angel." I reach out for her hair, twisting my fingers in her strands. Soon, nothing will prevent me from fisting all that silky hair while driving my hard cock inside her tight pussy as I take her from behind. "Say yes." I tug gently on her mane, making her gasp.

"Yes."

Good answer.

She opens her mouth to say something, but closes it.

"What's going on in that pretty little head of yours?"

"There are a few hours left before the clock strikes midnight," she says. "What are we going to do until then?" The hunger in her eyes betrays the innocence of her question.

The corner of my mouth curls. "Glad you asked."

I untangle my fingers from her hair, stand up and extend a hand.

"Where are we going?" she asks.

"The bathroom."

Confusion causes her eyebrows to touch. "I thought only women went to the bathroom together."

"This has nothing to do with nature calling." My voice is deep and low. "It has everything to do with pleasure."

"I'm all in!" Her lascivious grin makes her response that much sweeter.

When someone is staying in Bryce's two-story villa, the majordomo returns to his home for the night. So, we get the place all to ourselves. I guide Angelica upstairs to the ensuite bathroom of the bedroom we share.

I turn on the light, invite her inside, and follow right behind her.

I close the door, leaning against it.

"Strip!" I deliver my command with a finger wave.

She pulls her dress over her head and drops it to the floor.

I approve of the strapless pale-pink bra and matching panties.

My mouth waters and tingles dance through my balls.

What a thing of beauty.

She brings her hands to her stomach.

"What are you doing?" I ask.

Shyness radiates off her.

"Err... the way you're looking at me?!"

"I'm not looking at you. I'm *admiring* you. Big difference."

She's struck mute, her eyelashes fluttering.

If it wasn't for the glint of disbelief shining bright in her eyes, I wouldn't feel compelled to soldier on. "You were sprawled on my kitchen countertop like a feast a few nights ago. I've already seen you in lingerie. Not to mention, you spent the day in a bikini."

"True." The pulse at the base of her neck visibly beats. "But you've never seen me fully naked before."

"And it's about fucking time we rectified that."

She stares at me, speechless.

"Usually, men stare at my sister that way," she says in a near whisper.

I hate the insecurity in her voice.

"In what way?"

"Like... you want to eat me alive."

"First, that's exactly what I want to do. Second, the first part of your statement doesn't even make any sense if you're identical twins."

"That may be the case, but Arya always shines. I tend to live in her shadow."

The dynamic between her and her sister is so imbalanced.

She's completely oblivious to her beauty. When she grows into herself, she'll be a force to be reckoned with.

"Good for Arya for always shinin'," I say in a pronounced Texas drawl, "but you glow like the fuckin' sun, darlin' and I'm all about worshippin' the sun."

She giggles.

"Lower your hands."

She obeys my command.

"Get rid of the lingerie."

The bra and panties come off.

She's not putting on a show, but goddammit, she's so fucking hot.

I step closer.

With my eyes locked onto hers, I trail a finger up the length of her arm, relishing the feel of her smooth, silky skin under my touch. My finger travels to her full breasts, tracing a circle around her pert nipple with the perfect pink areola. Her other nipple receives the same treatment.

She hitches a breath, her chest heaving.

A wicked grin splits my lips.

Determined to commit every inch of her skin to memory, I place my finger at the base of her neck, and in a languorous motion, I run my fingertip down between her tits, down her stomach until I reach her bare pussy.

"Every part of you is fucking perfect."

"You make me feel so pretty."

I shake my head. "No, angel, you did that on your own."

She rewards me with a beaming smile.

"I want you to stand before the mirror."

She flinches. "Why?"

"Because I want you to see what I see."

"Are you going to...?"

"Don't be vague. Spell it out."

"Are we going to have... sex?"

"Not today." I want to ease the tight ache in my balls, but we're here for another couple of days. I want to prolong the pleasure for her. "I need to corrupt you a little more before I claim you."

An unreadable expression flashes in her eyes. "Right." She

accentuates that single word with a firm nod and repeats, "Right."

I cock an eyebrow.

"I'm a bit nervous, that's all," she says.

I can't promise her it won't hurt. "We'll take it nice and slow."

"I want you to be my first, Hudson."

A thick, heavy feeling pushes through my chest.

I blame the foreign feeling on the way she's looking at me, all vulnerable and trusting.

The tips of my fingers trace her cheek, and she leans into the touch. "I'll make it good for you, angel."

"I know you will."

"Even if I don't pop your cherry today, we can still have a lot of kinky fun."

"I don't know if I can handle kinky."

"You have so far. I came gushing at the back of your throat and you didn't blink an eyelash. We're well past kinky."

Her cheeks blush.

"I gave you a command, angel."

She strolls to the counter and positions herself in front of the mirror.

Since Bryce's bathroom is as expansive as the rest of the villa, I get an eyeful of hips swaying side to side, her biteable, round, peachy ass in full display.

"Hands on the countertop," I order from my position near the door.

She leans against it.

With her body angled, her full tits hang seductively, begging for my hands to cup them.

Fuck.

Licking my lips, I stalk in her direction.

I catch her gaze in the mirror.

I run a slow hand down her back and around to her breasts.

She shivers as my palms cup her tits in a firm hold and lift them high, taking their weight and kneading them.

An appreciative growl rumbles from the depths of my chest.

God bless this woman's breasts.

She straightens, as if begging for more.

I'm just getting started, angel.

I toy with her nipples, unrushed.

For a few breaths, she watches me make love to her tits. Her eyelids droop and her lower lip is trapped between her teeth.

Fuck, yeah.

When my thumb sweeps over her nipple, she drops her head against my chest, a soft moan escaping from her lips. The more she melts into my arms, the more my cock swells.

The fucker is desperate.

I let go of her tits and allow her tight nipples to scrape my palms as her heavy globes sink back against her chest.

"Christ." A growl escapes me.

I do it again.

And again.

Her gasp turns into a groan as I prolong the subtle torture.

My lips flirt with her earlobe. "I intend on pushing you way out of your comfort zone."

Her eyes pop open.

She considers me for a beat, our gazes locked onto each other in the mirror.

I don't rush her.

"I'm okay with that."

"You trust me?"

"Yes."

Lust and need make my head swim.

I take a step back and shrug out of my shirt, letting it fall to the floor.

Her eyes are riveted on me. "Your body is a work of art."

I wink at her.

I drop my shorts next.

"You're not wearing any boxer briefs?!"

"I've been hard since you walked out of the bathroom, wearing nothing but a red bikini. Boxer briefs would've been the equivalent of wearing a chastity belt. I had to go commando." Even though her bikini is modest by today's standards, my cock responded favorably.

"I can't believe you feel that way about me."

My lips and nose brush against the soft skin of her slender neck and she shivers. "Believe it."

She shakes her head.

Man, she's a tough sell.

"Look in the mirror, Angelica. Tell me what you see."

"A gorgeous man and me."

"Funny, because I see a gorgeous woman and me."

She lets out a girlish laugh.

I place a hand to the middle of her back. "Lean forward."

She obeys, bracing her palms on the countertop.

I rest my free hand next to hers, fist my cock pointing north with the other, and rest my chest on her back.

She hisses.

I drag the tip of my cock down her backside until I'm nestled between her thighs.

"Oh shit," she says.

"Can you feel how much I want you?" I brush her hard clit with the tip of my cock, barely suppressing a growl. Her hips sway. "From the feel of it, you want me too."

"I do!"

I slide my greedy cock between her lips, teasing her, torturing me.

She lets out a strangled sound.

"I've wanted you something fierce since the moment I laid eyes on you."

"It's the same for me,"

"You're so fucking wet for me."

"You turn me on so much. You just have to look at me, and I'm wet."

Music to my ears.

I pick up the pace, swinging my hips back and forth, slamming through her thighs with more force, my cock sliding beautifully against her soaked pussy lips.

Her eyelids drift shut as she pushes back against my thrusts.

I need more.

I halt all movement.

Her eyes fly open. "Why did you stop?"

"I want to make it real good for you."

I remove my cock from between her legs.

I chuckle at the discontentment I read in her eyes.

"I won't be more than a second, angel."

"It had better be worth it. What you were doing to me was so hot."

"Trust me, it will be, and it will more than make up for the inconvenience."

She purses her lips.

Demanding little slut.

I reach for the bottle of almond oil I spotted earlier, open the cap and pour a generous amount into my palm. I rub my hands together before spreading the oil all over her ass, turning them into shiny globes. Then, I run my hand between the valley of her ass cheeks.

Her eyes widen in surprise at the intrusion.

I pour a bit more oil into my palm, fist my cock, and coat my hard length, making sure it's nice and slick.

Now, I'm ready to play.

"Change of plan," I say. "Turn around."

Her confusion is evident, but she turns to face me.

I place my oily hands underneath her armpits and lift her up and drop her on the countertop. I pull her forward, so she's close to the edge.

"What are you doing?" she asks, laughter coloring her words.

"I changed my mind. I don't want to look at you in the mirror. I want to be staring directly into your eyes when I make you come."

"Oh."

I tap the inside of her thighs.

She spreads them wide.

I step between her parted legs and fist my cock, giving it a few hard thrusts.

"It's so sexy the way you do that," she says, her eyes glued to my cock.

"Your ex never jerked off in front of you?"

She shakes her head. "I can't believe how hard you are."

"Thanks to you, angel."

A slow grin parts her lips. "I like knowing that."

I grab her hand. "Why don't you help me." I close her small hand around my cock.

"Grip it hard."

She does.

I let out a strangled moan.

"Did I hurt you?" The question comes tumbling from her lips.

Through half-lidded eyes I respond, "Not at all."

Together, we stroke my cock.

Our combined hands produce a totally different experience from her jerking me off or when I jack off.

"I love doing it with you," she says.

My gaze lowers to my straining cock. "Me too." Drops of pre-cum forming at my tip are testament.

I scoop them up with a finger.

"Stick your tongue out for me."

She does.

"Lick it clean."

Like a good little girl, she obeys.

I reach between her legs and glide my fingers through her wetness.

The green eyes that were riveted on my cock bounce up to meet my gaze. I scoop up her juices before bringing my fingers to my lips, licking off her slickness.

She's startled by my action.

"You do me, and I do you." My voice is like gravel.

I do that a few times until my tongue is coated with her juices and her sweetness floods my tastebuds.

"I can't wait to fuck your tight pussy."

Her chest heaves, her breathing labored.

Her hand travels between her legs.

"Tsk." I brush away her hand with my free one. "What are you doing?"

"I want to join in."

I shake my head. "*I'll* be the one to make you come."

She frowns. "How is that going to work if we're not going to have sex and you're taking care of business?"

Such innocence.

"This is how we're going to do it." I let go of her hand, taking ownership of my cock. I angle my fat head between her pussy lips, nudging her clit. "Just because I'm not going to fuck you, doesn't mean you can't come all over my cock."

I drop a quick kiss on her lips.

My hand moves, gliding my cock from her clit to her forbidden hole.

"Oh, God, yes."

I keep up the dizzying rhythm.

It's raunchy as fuck.

"I've never done anything like this before," she says.

"We'll be crossing off a lot of firsts from your list."

I squeeze my tip and apply more pressure against her clit.

"This is so hot. I've been missing out."

"Good thing we connected," I say with a wink.

Her eyes bore into mine, and she nods.

I need more.

Just a taste.

I press my cock against her entrance.

"Ah!" She gasps.

I slip the tip of my cock inside her warmth. "Fuck."

My head falls back at the intoxicating sensation.

It's only when I let out a low moan, I realize I was holding my breath.

"I thought you said we weren't..."

"We aren't. We're just having a little fun."

Slowly, I slide in just a bit more.

Damn.

What makes this even better is that our gazes are locked to the place where we're connected, both of us in silent contemplation.

Feeling the heat of her pussy lips wrapped around my cock end awakens a primal need in me I didn't know existed.

Like a greedy bastard, I ease my tip deeper inside her dripping, virgin pussy.

Just another inch. Just to have a taste.

"How does it feel?" It's a struggle to speak.

She responds by clenching around my tip.

I let out a strangled groan.

I didn't see that coming.

"Your pussy is going to be the end of me."

"I love feeling your cock inside me."

I might not survive the day I claim her.

"Are you on the pill or are you getting shots?"

She shakes her head. "Neither."

Noted.

If I keep up this little game, I might accidentally slide in balls deep. Once I do, there's no going back, regardless if she's on the pill or not.

The possibility of her getting pregnant should send me running for the hills, but for some unexplainable reason, it doesn't.

Still, it's best to play it safe. For now, anyway.

I pull my cock out, and resume to teasing her clit in slow circles, stroking her nub with my engorged knob.

Our combined moans rip through the air.

I change things up, rub my slit against her, applying just the right amount of pressure to make me see stars. My hips swing back and forth, my big balls moving in rhythm, her hips swaying to match my cadence.

I'm in fucking heaven.

"In this position, I get to watch you come," she says.

"You like watching me come?"

"It was so fucking hot. I want to do that to you again."

"You will, angel." My voice is husky with lust. "You will."

I pick up speed, gliding my cock in dizzying circles, eliciting sensual moans from her.

An all-encompassing burst of pleasure overtakes me as my pace turns frantic.

No more taking it slow. This is base hunger. Adulterated passion.

One hand snakes around my neck, bringing our foreheads together. Her other hand rests behind her on the countertop. "This is so good."

"Fuck, yeah."

My eyes lift to the mirror, catching a glimpse of my heavy-lidded eyes. My attention shifts to her. I watch, amazed, as she writhes against the surface, her body moving with such velocity.

Then it hits me.

Her ass cheeks are well-oiled.

"Are you going to come all over me?"

Her question catches me off guard.

All the blood in my body pools to my straining cock.

"I plan on defacing your sweet pussy."

Her hips gyrate faster.

Dammit.

She's dripping all over the countertop.

It's such a shame to let her juices go to waste, but I'm barreling down the road to my climax. Switching things up now isn't a consideration.

My gaze lowers to my cock that's hard as a pipe. Purple angry veins lining the fucker let me know I'm close.

Round and round.

The sound of my slickness rubbing against hers bounces off the walls.

"That sound is just pure filth." Her words end in a whimper.

"I promised you depraved."

"I like a man who keeps his promises."

"In that case, you'll fucking love me."

I flinch at the L word.

So does she.

I resume my mission, even though the word is still hanging in the air.

She changes position, putting more of her weight on the hand that's on the counter. Her hips tilt forward. Without missing a beat, I rub the underside of my pulsing cock against her clit.

Even though we're the only two people in the villa, I bite my lower lip to avoid grunting loudly.

My cadence becomes erratic, applying more and more pressure on her clit.

Her body is already pulsing with pleasure.

My balls tug, reminding me they're fully loaded.

"Oh, Hudson, I'm close."

Thank the fuck God.

"You're going to come hard for me?" My breath is ragged.

"Mmm."

"Answer me."

"Yes. Yes, I will." Her breathing is labored.

I grunt.

"Oh, God... I'm coming," she says, panting.

I'm right behind you.

She digs her nails into my shoulders. "Mother of God."

The sweet sounds of her whimpering travel to my balls, igniting a fuse inside me.

"Christ!"

I'm blinded by my need for release.

"Oh, Hudson— I'm— Hudson—"

Her cries combined with her quivering body are my undoing.

I grip my cock and shoot my load.

She gasps as cum spurts.

"Fuck, angel!"

My cum sprays in creamy ribbons across her stomach, her thighs, and her pussy. One final spurt and her tits are sprayed.

There's cum everywhere.

Her head falls on my chest and I take hold of her.

I slap my spent cock against her pussy and she shudders in my arms.

It won't take me long before I'm ready for another round.

As if she could read my thoughts, she says in a low voice, "I want to do that again."

"We will."

Through hooded eyes, I stare at my reflection in the mirror as I drop a soft kiss on the top of her head.

She's completely limp in my arms.

I suspect she came as hard as I did.

We stay like this for several heartbeats, our heavy breathing reverberating against the bathroom walls.

Out of the blue she says, "I like when you mark me." There's such naked honesty in her admission. "It's like I'm yours."

I pull away from her and meet her gaze. "That's because you *are* mine, angel."

She looks up at me with what I can only describe as wonderment.

I place two fingers underneath her chin, tilt her head back, and crush her lips. I kiss her until I can't remember my own fucking name.

That strange, foreign tightness at my chest returns.

Chapter 38

Angelica

Day two in paradise is pretty idyllic.

After a delicious breakfast spread I couldn't get enough of, Hudson and I hit the beach. A few hours after lunch—we requested the chef prepare the delicious Bermuda fish sandwich and crab cakes—the majordomo gave us a tour of the island. We stopped by a favorite local spot to try out the Bermunchie with rum hard sauce, aka Bermuda Dark n' Stormy bread pudding. It was unbelievable. Let's just say, it's a good thing tomorrow is our last day on the island. At this rate, I'll eat my weight in food. Bermuda does wonders for a girl's tan and ranks high up there when it comes to ultimate pampering. However, it's dangerous to a girl's waistline.

After a little R&R on the beach, Hudson and I headed to the spa situated on Bryce's property. I nearly passed out when the majordomo gave us a tour yesterday and stopped at what I thought was a luxury shed. Boy, was I wrong. Bryce converted what could be considered a more than acceptable tiny house into a gym-slash-spa. There are no spa attendants. The home-spa concept designed in Italy is state-of-the-art and fully computer operated. You can even manage the functions with voice commands.

"Please turn on the chichi Himalayan salt sauna."

"Please turn on the posh cold steam and cold storm shower."

"Please set the kickass rain showerhead to x temperature. And please turn on the wicked wall jets."

"Please heat up the really cool green tea bath."

"Please call the main house to request more fruity flavored water from the kitchen staff."

I swear, rich people don't have the same problems as the rest of us.

I'm going to fall hard from heaven when I get back to New York, but like Hudson says, I need to focus on the here and now.

That's exactly what I'm going to do.

Since Saks Fifth Avenue was my first mini spa experience, I couldn't leave the island without indulging. It's everything I expected and so much more.

Hudson and I are kicking back on the spa's comfy lounge chairs near the green tea bath—a mini Jacuzzi pool filled with green tea.

I steal a look at Hudson.

He's on his back, his eyes closed. His long lashes are wet from our last dip in the green tea tub.

I turn to my side, propping my head against my open palm to take full advantage of the moment.

He's wearing nothing more than a white towel cinched around his trim waist. His swim trunks, shorts, and t-shirt, along with my red bikini and sundress, are drying on the electric drying rack. He was naked in the Jacuzzi and steam room. That was a real treat. It's a pity the towel hides his mighty cock.

Six-foot-three—or six-foot-four—inches of sexy as sin,

practically naked, muscled man who made one of my biggest wishes come true. His hair is also wet, and it's slicked back. Droplets of green tea water dot his shoulders and torso. The need to follow those droplets with my tongue is overwhelming. He has chest hair, but it's sexy. It's nothing crazy. Thank God he doesn't have hair on his back or shoulders. My gaze rakes down past a ridged stomach, following the dark trail of hair starting from below his navel and running underneath the white towel wrapped around his waist—the happy trail that leads to the promised land.

My eyes move lower.

I bite the inside of my cheek.

There's no missing the bulge beneath the towel.

If it weren't for the fact I'd had the pleasure of his enormous cock in my mouth, I'd be tempted to believe he had a thick pair of socks stuffed between his legs. But I know better. Hudson Kincaid is packing.

Shamelessly, I continue to devour him.

Long, muscular legs stretch out, slightly parted.

His feet—his size thirteen feet—are gorgeous and perfectly groomed.

He has one arm draped underneath his head. The way his muscles bunch around his biceps is a beautiful thing.

Holy tamales, he's hot.

Adonis hot.

God was in a stellar mood when he created Hudson Kincaid, that's for sure.

And I get to enjoy every scrumptious inch of him all to myself.

I could savor Hudson Kincaid every day of the week, letting his delicious taste melt on my tongue like all those delicious chocolate treats he bought for me. Basically, I wouldn't be opposed to a steady diet of this fine specimen.

Unable to resist, I reach out and trace the Celtic cross tattooed on his left pec.

His eyes pop open and he grabs my hand. "You're done with your inspection?"

Busted.

"What are you talking about?" I flutter my lashes.

"I could feel your eyes on me, angel."

"Well, if you didn't look this good, I wouldn't be ogling," I say, almost offended.

"So, it's my fault you can't keep your eyes off me?"

"Yes!" I nod. "Yours, your mom's, your dad's, and God's. They all conspired together to create..." I wave a frantic finger at him. "What am I supposed to do? Close my eyes?"

He laughs.

"Your lightheartedness is contagious. Before you, I rarely laughed." Those words do things to me. "I was carrying too much on my shoulders. My workload and responsibilities haven't changed, but being around you is a breath of fresh air."

"I aim to please," I say with a shoulder shrug.

He kisses my hand, and I love that he keeps hold of it as he sighs.

"You know," he says, "I could get addicted to this lifestyle."

"But you live this lifestyle," I say.

"Didn't you hear the part of me carrying a lot on my shoulders? Unless I'm sick with a cold *and* a fever, you'll never catch me on my back at this time of the day in New York. And I don't have a majordomo on my staff. Must rectify that when I get back." He winks.

I laugh.

"All that to say..." He brings my hand to his lips once more and drops a soft kiss against it. "...This is as much of a treat for you as it is for me."

"Thank you."

"You're sounding like a broken record, darlin'," he says.

"I know, but I don't know how else to express my gratitude. In my world, I never would've been able to afford to fly to Bermuda, let alone on a private jet. As for the 5-star luxury accommodation with majordomo, full staff, and personal chef, not even in my wildest dreams did I think I'd ever get to live this kind of experience."

With one more kiss, he lets go of my hand. I rest it on his chest, stroking his nipple.

"It's my pleasure," he says, "And Bryce's."

"I feel I need to do something to thank Bryce. The thing is, what do you give to a guy who has everything?"

"Just buy him a lifetime supply of those dulce de leche and white chocolate snickerdoodle bars."

I laugh again.

"I'm not joking. That guy is as impassive as they come. Not much fazes him. I guess you have to be in his line of work. That says a lot about those bars."

"Noted."

My fingers continue their exploration.

"I'm going to miss being able to touch your body at will."

"What did I tell you about thinking about tomorrow?"

"I know, but tomorrow *is* tomorrow."

"We're flying out early the day *after* tomorrow, so that means there's plenty of time for you to have your hands all over my body."

"Lucky me."

"And you know what's sweet about this deal?"

I shake my head. "Something tells me you're about to educate me."

"Damn right I am. I get to have my hands all over you, too."

It's a bit corny, and both of us should be laughing, but we just stare at each other, the air between us sizzling with...

Hudson grabs my hand into his. "Come here."

I hitch a breath when he forces me to straddle him in his lounge chair.

My ass is sitting on his *very* hard cock.

He groans. The sound goes straight to my core.

I adjust myself.

"It's more fun if we get to touch each other at the same time," he says, his warm hands traveling underneath the towel wrapped around my chest.

The heat emanating from them seeps into my stomach.

God, there's so much heat coming off him.

That's all it takes for me to be turned on.

My breasts tingle and my hard nipples press against the towel.

The painful tenderness in my nipples is unbearable.

His hands move to my flanks.

He stares at me, his lips curling into a wicked smile.

I flash him a small smile, oblivious to his evil intentions.

Without warning, his fingers start to torture me.

I choke on laughter.

"Look at that. Someone is ticklish." He says that like he's just discovered a big secret.

I'm laughing and wiggling.

He doubles his effort.

The bastard takes advantage of my weakness.

I'm laughing so hard, I'm crying.

"St—stop! Pl—please!"

I'm howling now.

His hands stop their assault. "On one condition."

It takes me a few seconds to regain my composure. I should be wary to bargain with the devil, but that doesn't stop me from being curious. "What's your condition?"

"I want a kiss."

"That's it?"

"Yes."

I cross my arms over my chest. "What's the catch?"

"There isn't one."

I level him with a dubious gaze. "You expect me to fall for that?"

"Kissing you is everything, angel."

A lump rises in my throat.

How am I going to manage not being with this man twenty-four-seven?

He twists a wet lock between his fingers before grabbing a fistful of my hair and tugging just a little. "You don't want to kiss me?" His tone is playful, as if we were five-year-olds and he was pulling my pigtail. He pulls again. "Aren't you going to answer me?"

I debate whether I should be transparent or keep my cards close to my chest.

His eyebrows knit in concern. "Talk to me, angel."

Here goes nothing. "The more I kiss you, Hudson, the more I become addicted to you."

With me still straddling him, he sits upright.

I weigh a hell of a lot more than a stuffed animal, but from the ease with which he moves, you'd never know.

Damn, the man is strong.

He cups my face with his hands, his ocean-blue eyes sucking me right down into their depths. "Good. That's the way it's supposed to be."

He crushes my mouth in a blazing kiss.

A hum of approval vibrates throughout my body as my fingers intertwine into his thick hair, returning his kiss with fervor.

His hands settle on my hips.

My free one moves to his cheek as he deepens the kiss.

I'm so lost, I let out a little groan into his mouth when his finger drags between my pussy lips.

He growls into my mouth. "You're so fucking wet."

"I can't help it when I'm around you."

"I turn you on?"

"So fucking much."

"Good answer."

His mouth is on mine again.

The madness of our mouths is dizzying. Our tongues are a tangle of need. With each tongue stroke, our kiss turns frantic. Frenzied, even. We're nothing but tongues, teeth, and explosive passion.

It's wild, tumultuous, all-encompassing.

My hips sway back and forth, as I grind against his finger.

"What do you want, angel?" he asks in a gruff voice, breaking the kiss.

I pull away from him. "I want you."

"I want you too, but I won't be happy with just the pieces of you I've already claimed." His blue eyes hood as they lower down my body. "I want *all* of you." His deep, dark, smoky voice works over my skin like warm melted chocolate.

I nod.

"Words."

"I want that too."

He shifts on the lounge chair, swings his legs to the side and gets to his feet, picking me up with ease in the process. In a few steps, he carries me to the lounging area where two chic vinyl black day beds are situated.

He gently lowers me onto one of them.

"I'll be right back," he says.

"Okay." I get on my elbows to see where he's going.

Yesterday was the first day I saw his bubble man-butt naked.

Just like the rest of him, it's a thing of beauty.

Firm and muscular, his ass gives true meaning to the saying, *you could bounce a quarter off it.*

He's back in a flash, his fingers clenching a gold packet and a little bottle.

He lifts both hands. "Lube and protection."

"You expected me to agree?" *Am I that predictable?*

"I was *hoping*. Big difference. In case you agreed, I wanted to be ready," he says. "It would've ruined the moment for me to run back to the villa to hunt for a condom." I laugh a little. "I'm clean, but neither of us is ready for parenthood."

"Okay." My heartbeat is thundering in my ears.

This is really happening.

With the towel still wrapped around his waist, he straddles the day bed.

He places the packet and bottle near my head and lowers himself to his elbows.

He drops his forehead against mine. "I'm going to be as gentle as I can, but if anything hurts, you tell me and everything stops."

I nod.

Shit.

He wants words.

"I really want this, Hudson."

He pulls away from me, so our eyes meet. "That's music to my ears, angel, but I need to make sure we're on the same page."

"If anything hurts, I'll tell you."

"Promise?"

"Yes."

"I want it to be pleasurable. I'm going to use as much lube as possible, but there's probably going to be a little pain. Still, I don't want your first time to be so painful it's a turnoff."

"I understand."

"Good girl."

He kisses me again, but this time it's gentle and quick.

He gets to his knees.

His cock is tenting the towel.

Oh boy.

I watch with rapt attention as he undoes it and lets it drop to the floor.

His cock is on full alert. Thick, straight, ready. His balls hang proudly underneath his cock and his dark purple head is engorged with blood, and yeah, *oh boy* doesn't do it justice. My pussy flutters at the sight of it.

He reaches for the lube and drops it on my tummy. He then grabs the condom and brings it to my mouth. "Use your teeth to open it."

I do as I'm told.

With his eyes locked onto mine, he sheathes his massive erection.

"Let's open up your towel," he says.

"Okay." It's as if I've forgotten all the other words in the English language.

He undoes the knotted towel and peels it open. His eyes rake over my body. "Do you have any idea how fucking beautiful you are, Angelica?"

If I wasn't this freaked out, I wouldn't be this tongue-tied, and my brain would have the capacity to form an answer.

Not for the first time, I stare at him like a deer caught in headlights.

Concern etches his handsome features. "Breathe, baby."

"I am." I take a few quick breaths, as if I'm at a Lamaze class.

He gives me a *do you think I'm stupid look?* "Is my girlfriend lying to me?"

That brings a smile to my face.

My girlfriend.

God, I love those words on his lips.

"Maybe a little."

"Do you remember our agreement?"

I place both hands on his solid thighs. "I do."

"It's going to be even better between us after I make you all mine."

Well, what are you waiting for, mister? Pop my cherry!

Not wanting to sound too overconfident, I settle for a response that's not dripping with cheekiness. "I like the sound of that."

He lathers a generous amount of lube in his hands before coating his cock. He pours more and rubs it between my legs.

I hitch a breath.

"It's just my hand."

"I'm a bit nervous..."

He leans forward and kisses me.

He then drops a kiss on my chin and keeps going down my neck, my chest, one soft kiss at a time.

My nerves melt like snow under a hot sun.

He stops at my breasts and exhales a hot breath that makes me shiver.

I look down as he captures my nipple into his mouth and sucks hard.

He teases me by moving his tongue from one breast to the other.

"I love your tits."

"And I love your hot mouth on my tits," I say with a touch of sass that surprises me.

Since he can't spank me, I expect him to go all alpha on my ass with a stern response. I'm so off the mark.

He bites my nipples.

I gasp, bucking my hips against him wildly.

He does it again. Harder this time.

I clamp both hands over his head, nearly suffocating him. "Oh shit!"

The zing of pain quickly turns into pleasure.

The next thing I know, Hudson plunges three fingers inside my pussy, and I let out a shuddering moan as he finger-fucks me.

The things this man can do with his mouth and fingers...

He slows down his cadence and scoops up my juices. Without warning, he slides a finger into my ass. Just the tip, but it's enough to send my heart hammering in my chest.

"You're going to enter my back door before entering the front door?"

I can't believe I just said that.

He chuckles. "No, I won't claim your sweet ass today." He changes tactic, circling my asshole in a gentle touch and the sensation is... filthy hot. "You're not ready yet."

That loaded statement leaves room for interpretation.

I should be worried. Freaked out. Panicked. But instead, I say, "Oh, okay."

"I like how you're keeping the *back door open*," he says with a grin.

I can't help my nervous laugh.

He winks. "Wrap your legs around my waist."

I do.

He holds my gaze for a beat longer, as if searching for any signs of hesitation.

"I want this," I tell him.

Even though I'm certain of my decision, it doesn't prevent my voice from coming out shaky.

"Tell me what you want, angel."

His hard cock is pressing against my thigh.

Just say the words…

"I want you to fuck me, Hudson…"

I'm not sure what I'm seeing in his eyes… lust… adoration… a heady mix.

"It will be my honor," he says and lowers himself like before, but this time, he has only one elbow resting on the daybed.

My eyes close to the pleasure as he runs his cock end up and down my pussy lips.

Slowly, he pushes the head of his cock into my tight virgin pussy, stretching me.

Jesus.

He pushes in again.

I grit my teeth and wrap my hands around his neck.

He pushes in a little further and it hurts.

I bite my lower lip hard, to prevent a cry from spilling from my lips.

"You're doing great, angel."

"I am?"

"Fuck, yeah."

His words bring me comfort. I want to tell him he's doing great too, but he eases further in and all I can do is grit my teeth.

It's only when he stops moving, I realize my whole body is trembling.

"Holy fuck," he says. "You're a hell of a lot tighter than I expected." *And you're a hell of a lot bigger than I expected.* "I don't want to hurt you—"

It hurts like hell.

I tighten my thighs around his waist. "Don't stop."

"More lube will make it easier for you."

"Okay."

He angles his body, slowly pulls his cock out a little way, and pours the slick liquid where we're joined.

"Nice and easy," he says and pushes back into me.

I gasp. And then I moan.

"Better, angel?"

"God yes."

He resumes his mission, easing his cock into me.

Another shove.

Another inch.

Another prayer this is almost over.

The pain is indescribable. It's almost... pleasure.

"I'm nearly there," he says.

I simply nod.

"Breathe, baby."

I let out the breath I was holding.

Slowly, Hudson pulls out, keeping only his tip inside me.

My legs tighten around his waist.

I know what's coming.

Without warning, he pushes through my resistance.

It feels like I've been impaled by red hot steel.

Mother of God!

Did I say that out loud?

I'm not sure.

"It's over, angel."

Tears well in my eyes, but I blink them away.

"Let me make it good for you now. It might still be a little uncomfortable, but it won't be as painful."

"I want to make it pleasurable for you, too." My voice is trembling.

"You are," he says before kissing me.

He's careful when he draws himself out of me.

He eases in and out in a languorous motion.

To my surprise, the cadence allows me to adjust to his size.

Little by little, he picks up the tempo.

It feels so weird. I can feel him deep inside me. But hell, it's so nice.

I relax, running my hands along his back as I move my hips in rhythm with his.

He lets out a grunt of approval.

That makes me smile.

He pulls out again before burying himself so deep my body bucks off the bed and it takes my breath away.

He fucks me in a steady rhythm.

I match his tempo, our bodies moving together.

We're so in sync.

It's ridiculously hot.

"You can only get your V card punched once." He looks between us.

I follow his gaze.

Oh wow.

I'm surprised by the sight of my blood smeared across his stomach and his thighs. I'm also marked by blood.

"No other man on the planet will be able to claim you like this."

My eyes lift to his. "I wouldn't want it any other way."

"You have no idea what it does to hear you say that."

My declaration seems to trigger something in him.

He starts driving in and out of me, penetrating me with unwavering force. I'm amazed and thrilled all at once. So much slicker now, I'm taking him with ease. I tilt my hips up to meet his frantic thrusts, my greedy pussy swallowing every inch of him.

We're both grunting and breathing hard.

The pain has been replaced by a foreign tingle. It's nothing like when he has his tongue or fingers on me. This sensation ignites something inside me I've never experienced before.

Ignites being the operative word because right now my pussy is on fire!

His heavy breathing caresses my cheek as he fucks the hell out of me. I bring a hand to his handsome face, feeling his 5 o'clock stubble scratch my palm.

"I'm close," he says. "I can't come until you do. You're going to come hard for me, angel?"

"Yes." I answer, even though I doubt I'll be able to have an orgasm without being able to rub my clit. Since we're practically fused together, I don't see how that's going to work.

If I thought Hudson was fucking me with urgency before, I was wrong.

He lets loose.

The wet sounds of sex fill the space.

Eager to hear him lose it again, I clench my pussy around his invading cock.

"Fuck," he says. "Do that again."

It hurts, but I do it again.

I clench him tight, and Hudson doesn't spare me. He fucks me so hard, it's as if he wants to nail me to the bed.

He shifts, planting both hands on either side of my head. "I want to hear my name when you come."

"Hudson," I say in a near whisper.

He shakes his head. "Not good enough." His words come out hard, like his thrusts.

"Hudson!" I cry out on a ragged breath.

"That's what I'm talking about," he says. "If I don't make you lose your fucking mind, I'm wasting your time and mine. You got that, angel?"

Thrust.

The beginning of an orgasm spirals upward.

"I—"

Thrust.

"I asked you a question."

Thrust.

I can't speak. I can only pant.

"Answer me!"

Thrust.

"Hud—"

Thrust.

"Goddamn, your sweet pussy." He sounds unhinged.

Thrust.

I close my eyes.

I'm right there.

Thrust.

I'm so, so close.

Thrust.

I'm on the brink.

With my eyes closed, I clench hard.

"Jesus Christ almighty!" His voice is unrecognizable.

Hudson angles his body and brushes a finger over my swollen clit.

My body bows, a sharp exhale bursting from my lungs as my orgasm hits me full force.

"Oh, oh, oh." I chant, convulsing underneath him.

Pleasure like I've never experienced in my life zips up my spine.

My heart goes boom, boom, boom in my chest as I tumble over the edge.

"Hudson—"

Bright white light explodes behind my eyelids.

I'm freefalling.

"That's it. Don't you fucking hold back on me."

Coming around Hudson's cock, heightens my orgasm.

I pull him closer. If I don't, I might lose myself to this powerful climax.

Bliss.

Pure bliss.

"Oh fuck." There's urgency in his words. He pumps in and out of me.

Faster.

Deeper.

More urgent.

His cadence is almost violent.

I take it all, my breath heaving, my hips jutting up to meet his body.

"Fuck, angel!"

I can't see his face, but that doesn't stop me from smiling.

The thought of a man like Hudson coming apart between my legs is such a high— Scratch that. The thought of a man like Hudson looking at me like men eat up my twin or wanting me like I'm some sort of sex kitten sends my soul soaring.

Chapter 39

Hudson

I growl as I shoot my load inside Angelica's sweet pussy.

It's been so long since I've had sex with a woman. I swear, I nearly blacked out from how goddamn amazing it felt shooting that first jet of cum into something other than my fist.

And holy Jesus, nothing compares to this woman's pussy.

My heart is jackhammering so hard, stars dance behind my lids, but I can't stop. Unwilling for this to end, I pump my cock in and out of her, milking every last drop of pleasure for a few more strokes.

A part of me desperately tries to take it slow, but the greedy monster inside me won't put the brakes on. There's no stopping the need plowing through my body like a fucking avalanche. Impossible. Once I felt Angelica relaxing underneath me, everything inside me ignited like dynamite.

With my cock still buried deep, I breathe in and out, coaxing my heart to stop beating at a frantic pace.

It seems to take an eternity before I stop coming.

I can still feel the mind-blowing rush through my veins.

Fuck.

When my feet touch the ground, I open my eyes and mesmerizing green eyes stare up at me in amazement.

I press a kiss to her sweat-drenched forehead and brush back the hair that clings to her angelic face.

"You okay?" I ask.

She nods.

I cock an eyebrow.

"Yes, I'm okay."

Since the day bed is too narrow for me to lie beside my girl, I slowly pull out of her before sitting on my haunches.

My eyes sweep along her body.

The blood staining her thighs and my cock confirm that she gave me a gift no other man will ever be able to receive.

She's mine.

Her perfect body.

Her mouth-watering curves.

Her silky, smooth skin.

Her full tits and pert, rosy nipples.

Her sweet, virgin pussy.

Her round, peachy ass.

Mine

All fucking mine.

She looks down at her body before looking at me again.

Shyness pinks her cheeks. "I'm no longer a virgin."

"You were amazing."

She sits up, wrapping her lower body with the towel she was lying on. "You don't have to say that. I'm sure I was awkward, at best."

I frown. "Hey, didn't we already talk about—"

"I'm sure you've had better."

My frown deepens. *"You were fucking amazing."*

"You're not just saying that?"

"No, I'm not. We've talked about this. I don't bullshit, Angelica."

"It wasn't terrible for you?"

My eyes drop to my spent cock. "You felt how hard I was between your legs. I can't fake an orgasm."

Her lips part in a small, shy smile. "You were pretty amazing yourself."

"Is that your way of saying you can't wait to ride my cock again?"

Her expression changes.

The smile slips off her face, replaced by something almost... wistful?!

"What?"

"We're from such different worlds..." She inhales a deep breath. "And we live in a mega city—in different boroughs. On top of that, I mostly work from home. On paper, we should have never met—"

"And that would've been a crying shame."

"I think so."

"You sound uncertain."

"You can have your pick of women."

"What are you saying? I picked the wrong one?"

She sits on her answer for a few beats. "It's almost as if I have to pinch myself."

"Would you settle for me biting your ass instead?"

She explodes in laughter.

"You and your obsession with my ass," she says and swats my chest.

I grab her hand into mine before bringing it to my lips.

"Can you blame me?" I kiss the back of her hand. "Round and plump like a Georgia peach, but bigger, so I can grab it at will."

Her expression is solemn again.

"I'm sure I'm breaking every dating protocol by saying this—"

"I march to the beat of my own drum, so should you. So, fuck dating protocols. Say what you gotta say, woman."

"Okay... You're a lot more than I ever allowed myself to dream of when it comes to a man. And I'm not talking about your money and all your connections. I'm just talking about you, the man."

My chest tightens.

"You make me feel safe... and that's been a foreign feeling for me since my parents died." She shakes her head. "No, that's not what I want to say. You *are* my safe place."

The stupid thump, thump, thump of my heart echoes in my ears.

Chapter 40

Hudson

Damn, Angelica lassoed me real good with her innocence, vulnerability, and overall sweetness. She has me feeling things I can't even comprehend. Three days with her in Bermuda of chilling and fucking, and I just want to chain her to my bed and keep her all to myself.

Adulting isn't always about getting what you want in life.

I have an empire to run. And my girl has a ton of work waiting for her.

The upside about taking a few days of vacation where you cut yourself off from work is getting away from it all. The downside is coming back to the grind. Even with incredible VPs, astute directors, dedicated managers, amazing staff, a kickass executive assistant, and a fantastic executive assistant's assistant, catching up is a bitch.

After we landed early this morning, I insisted on making the trip to Queens to drop off Angelica at her place. Traffic wasn't kind to me on the way back to Manhattan, but it was a small price to pay to spend a little more time with my girl. She joked about me having to buy a helicopter to cut back on the commute. After this morning's hellish gridlock, I might have to consider it.

The rest of the morning was a parade of catch-up meetings with a handful of VPs and directors, tending to a few matters that took priority over everything else, and returning important calls.

After a lunch meeting, I stroll back to my office, a large latte with a double shot of espresso in one hand, a small white bag in the other.

I take a long sip of coffee as I sit down. Satisfied, I drop the cup on my desk.

First things first.

I open a drawer and hide the white bag inside.

Done.

I pull out my phone from my suit jacket and place it next to the cup. Then, I remove my gray pinstripe jacket and drape it over the leather and cashmere valet stand imported from Liguria, Italy. It would be a crime to hang a tailored suit on a hook behind a door. For a kid who never could afford to buy anything more than off the rack in the discount section of big box stores, the idea of importing a fucking standing hanger for your clothing is preposterous. Yet, that's my new reality.

Rolling the sleeves of my white shirt, I'm just about to sit down when my phone rings.

I snatch it off the desk, immediately accepting the call.

"Rory!"

"Hudson, I hope I'm not catching you at a bad time."

"No, not at all." Rory is the only call I would've been willing to take during my time in Bermuda. Everyone else was going to have to wait until I got back into the city. It's ironic he'd call today. "How can I help you?"

"My wife and I have to cut our business trip short." *Shit.* "Our daughter woke up this morning feeling sick. Actually, she was complaining last night, but her grandmother figured some warm milk, cartoons, her favorite blanky, and a little rest would help. It didn't."

"I hope it's nothing serious."

"No, it's just a cold."

"Thank God," I say. "Summer colds are the worst. Although, in LA, it's summer year-round."

"We have a week or two of cooler weather."

Yeah, rub it in.

"Back to our baby girl. She's so young and she's our first born, so, as a result, we're probably blowing this out of proportion. She's with my mother-in-law and father-in-law who love her to pieces and take care of her like the doting grandparents they are. Not to mention, they have a lot of practice with four kids. That still doesn't prevent Mommy from worrying, which means Daddy was also worried."

I chuckle.

"Since it's not a life-or-death situation, we're leaving the day after tomorrow on the first flight out, instead of staying in New York an extra week."

I won't get to meet him before he leaves. I was so close. *Damn.* "I understand."

"I'm in back-to-back meetings all day tomorrow, but if we could have dinner or cocktails, I'd love to meet you before we leave. I know it's last-minute—"

"Absolutely! Just name the time and place."

"Good," Rory says. "Given we're going back to LA earlier than expected, my brother won't fly in. There's no point. It'll just be my wife and me."

"I would've love to meet Roark, but maybe it'll be for another time?"

"My brother and I make all the big decisions together. So,

it's likely you'll meet him." That sounds promising. "You might have to fly to LA, though."

"It won't be a hardship for me to fly to the City of Angels."

"Glad to hear it," Rory says. "Circling back to my better half, Isobel hopes you'll bring Brinley. She had a blast the other night."

"Oh..."

"Maybe you broke things off?"

I debate on what to do, but decide to come clean. I don't want to start a business relationship based on a lie.

"Don't worry about it. Isobel will have to—"

"Brinley's real name is Angelica McQuinley."

"Oh, did I get it wrong?"

"No, you didn't. You're going to get a kick out of this story..."

I end my call with Rory and dial my girl's number.

She picks up on the second ring.

"Hey, angel," I say.

"Are you calling because you miss me?"

"That, and to tell you we have dinner plans for tomorrow night."

"I won't see you tonight?"

I let out a long breath, rubbing a hand over my face. "My executive assistant shifted a lot of meetings and conference calls. I'll be trapped at the office late to accommodate a call with the CEO of a big west coast account who could only talk after office hours and another with a potential big account in Australia."

"I'm crushed, but I get it. You're running an empire."

"We'll video chat."

"It won't be the same, but it's not like I'll refuse."

"Looking forward to it. About tomorrow night..."

"Let me check my schedule. Please hold, Mr. CEO."

"Are you shitting me right now?"

"Are you assuming my schedule is wide open?"

"You told me so this morning."

"Oh."

"So, are you free or not, boss lady?"

"For you, I am."

"That makes me a lucky son of a gun."

"I would have to agree." The amusement in her voice makes me smile. "So, where are you taking me?"

"It's not going to be just the two of us."

"Do you need me to play *Pretty Woman* again?"

"Who?"

"Never mind. You're a guy. You probably have never seen the movie."

"No, I haven't. We're having dinner with Rory and his wife—"

"So, you do need me to play *Pretty Woman*—"

"Who the hell is pretty woman?"

She tells me.

"You don't have to act tomorrow night." I put her mind at ease. "You can be your charming self and use your real name. I told Rory everything—"

"You didn't!"

"I most certainly did."

"Why?"

"Because you're my girlfriend, and it could come out. I want to control the narrative. Not to mention, if I'm going to enter any kind of business relationship with the man, I don't want a detail like that to throw him off and make him think we're liars."

She shrieks. "OhmyGod! What is he going to think of me?"

"Calm down—"

"He's going to think the worst and so will his wife," she says. "We're so knee-deep, my sister had to take a gig as an escort."

"Rory's childhood was no picnic. He knows better than most how to spell the word desperation—"

"But—"

"I explained"—I soldier on—"Arya's gig is temporary. She's arm candy and she doesn't plan on going any further. You told me you gave her an ultimatum, so I assume she won't end up fucking for money."

"That's only true if my train wreck of a sister doesn't renege on our agreement."

"What are you talking about? I thought you went along with the twin swap because she gave you her word, even if that meant landing on Todd's shit list."

She scoffs. "If there's an easy button, Arya will be pressing it like her life depends on it. She's a firm believer in the minimalist philosophy—aka, as little effort as possible." I pinch my lips into a thin line, biting down my annoyance. "Ramsey may be dead, but she still owes Yevsei a lot of money. When she's forced to quit working for Todd and she has to depend on her waitressing wages by working more hours or finding a second waitressing job to erase her debt, who knows if she'll remember our agreement. As she rubs her aching feet at the end of a long shift, it might all go out the window."

What the fuck? "She'd renege on her promise that easily?"

"It wouldn't be the first time. After all, she's the one who was going on and on about paying off her loan shark as quickly as humanly possible, yet, when a stranger invites her to *partay* with him in Miami, she didn't think twice. She was out of here like she was being chased by the bogeyman."

I sit straighter in my chair. "Angelica, Arya needs to grow up—"

"Don't I know it!"

"Pardon my French, but if you know, why aren't you giving her a big fucking kick in the butt? Sometimes, tough love is the only way to get through to certain people."

She lets out a suffering sigh. "It's just the two of us. I let a lot slide"—*far more than you should*—"because Arya is all I have left. My sister is smart. She knows that and she's quick to use that to her advantage—"

"That's just plain wrong—"

"Spoken like an only child."

I don't like her tone. Not one bit.

"If I had a sister or a brother that pulled the kind of shit your sister does, I would've put my foot down." *That, or I would've shaken some goddamn sense into them.*

"You say that because you have no idea what it's like to have a sibling that looks exactly like you and with who you share everything... all the way down to your DNA."

"Are we fighting over your sister?"

"No, we're fighting over the fact you just don't understand where I'm coming from."

~

It's been difficult to shake off the conversation with Angelica.

I tried to bite my tongue, but I just couldn't.

The fact she expects her twin to keep fucking up and picking up after her mess is infuriating. I'm pissed off on her behalf.

It took everything in me to rein it back, even though I was fuming and there's so much more I wanted to say.

I get it. I've been in her life for a New York minute. Her

sister has been in her life since she popped into this world. But I still can't wrap my mind around her unwillingness to put her foot down.

It took me a walk to cool off and another tall latte with a double shot of espresso to have the presence of mind to attend to business. I refuse to let our disagreement about Arya's reckless ways eat up the rest of my day.

A couple hours of focused work later, my phone rings on my desk.

My eyes shift to the screen.

A dry, humorless laugh escapes me.

"Todd," I say, accepting the call.

"Mr. Kincaid," he says. "I hope you are well."

I cut to the chase. "How can I help you?"

"I make it a point to do a postmortem with all new clients and those who need *companionship* for a long stretch of time. It just so happens you fall into both categories." He lets out a theatrical laugh.

"Brinley was fantastic."

"Isn't she?" he says. "I wanted to touch base to see if you might require her *companionship* in the near future, given how happy you are with her?"

"I think I'm good for now."

"Very well," he says. "Brinley still has her training wheels on, but perhaps you're looking to explore *more...?*"

Translation: Would I like to graduate to a paid fuck buddy?

Todd demands a face-to-face with each client. During the meeting, when you least expect it, he'll ask you to smile for the camera before snapping a series of photos. Insurance and protection for his girls. It doesn't take long to discover Todd doesn't fuck around. Pun unintended. Here's the other thing that stands out about him other than the fact he's vertically challenged—he can't be taller than five-feet-one without his high heel booties—regardless if he's speaking to you over the phone or in person, he'll never hint at his profession. The man is a master at saying something without actually saying it.

"Thank you, Todd, but again, I'll have to politely decline."

"Maybe you might require *companionship* for an upcoming business trip? After all, it can't always be all work, no play. At the end of the day, you might need to take the edge off..."

"You're a kickass salesman, Todd—"

"You don't build a premier business that caters to the elite without being one. We operate in different fields, but based on your success, we speak the same language."

"Touché."

"So, Mr. Kincaid, did I tempt you?"

Chapter 41

Angelica

I shove a spoonful of ice cream into my mouth, cursing silently.

The last time I used ice cream as comfort food was a week and a half ago, a day before meeting Hudson Kincaid. Usually, the second the cold and creamy dessert hits my tongue, I'm in heaven.

Right now, I'm in hell.

I dig in for another spoonful.

The moment Hudson ended the call, guilt hit me with the force of a sledgehammer.

In defending my sister, I created a wedge between us.

Le sigh.

I keep stuffing my face.

My phone rings.

I look over my shoulder.

Finally.

I drop what's left of the Häagen-Dazs vanilla ice cream on the countertop and accept the video call. My best friend's face appears on the screen. She's grinning from ear to ear.

"This day is kicking my ass, but I finally got a break."

"Hey, you." I force a smile.

"I was going to say welcome back, *chica*, but remembered, your little getaway wasn't on a Spanish-speaking island. How was Bermuda?" I'm just about to respond, but she jumps in. "By the way, you got a little color. Your green eyes are popping like crazy."

"It was pretty hot down there."

"OhmyGod, the photos of the villa you sent me..."—she places a hand against her chest—"dreamy."

"It was pretty nice."

Sadie frowns. "That's it?"

"I had a pretty good time."

My best friend lifts a hand up like a traffic cop. "Pretty hot? Pretty nice? Pretty good time? You're an editor, for God's sake. What happened to your mastery of the English language? Furthermore, if you had a *pretty good time*," she says, using the fingers of one hand to form air quotes, "why do you sound so unenthusiastic about it?"

"I am enthusiastic about it."

"You could've fooled me."

"It's been a long day, catching up."

She stares at me like I've lost my marbles.

"Your billionaire boyfriend flies you on a private jet to stay at a luxurious villa owned by one of his billionaire friends, complete with majordomo, full staff, pool, and spa. And it's located by the sea and offers a killer view. Yet, you sounded more excited about scoring the last value family pack of toilet paper rolls at Walmart a couple of weeks ago. What happened?"

I avert my gaze.

"Angelica," my best friend presses.

This is going to come back to bite me in the ass. "It's because of Arya."

Sadie's head jerks back. "Your sister was in Bermuda?! How did she know you were in Bermuda? She didn't call me, so it's not like I spilled the beans. Your secret was safe with me. Who's the whistleblower?"

I shake my head. "There are no whistleblowers."

Sadie looks confused. "Huh?"

"She wasn't in Bermuda."

"Explain!"

"Hudson called me not long ago, and we ended the conversation on a sour note."

"Translate that for me."

"He thinks I should let my sister sink when she screws up instead of constantly being her buoy. I think differently. We had an argument."

I tell her everything.

She listens without interrupting.

"Has your sister been in touch since the last time she texted you?"

"No, she hasn't."

"So, she's still enjoying her vaca, drinking, tanning, and partying her head off, while you're fighting about her selfishness with this wonderful man of yours?"

I don't answer.

"You said you were going to put your foot down."

I remain quiet.

She shakes her head. "You're keeping the door open just in case you have to jump into the water and save her misguided ass."

I will admit, my stomach twisted in a knot when I didn't get a text or call from my sister.

"You know how I feel about you constantly being your

sister's life jacket, so I'm not going to harp on about that. I'd just end up sounding like a broken record. What I am going to say is this..."—she lifts a motherly finger, waving at the screen—"it's one thing for Arya to put you in a financial mess—"

"I—"

"Yes, I know." She lifts her hand. "In the end, you went along with it." Her tone is slicing, her expression stern. "Let's be honest, the only reason Ramsey Kenyon III was in your life is because he's another man who wanted to get into Arya's pants by sweet-talking her. He just happens to be a bigger asshole than the ones who came before him."

I bite the inside of my cheek.

"I understand loyalty, but not to the extent of sacrifice. Forget about self-flagellation. What you're doing is the equivalent of climbing the Holy Steps on your knees to seek pardon for sins you didn't even commit. I may not know Hudson, but from everything you've described, he's the gold standard when it comes to boyfriends."

My mouth twists.

Her attention shifts somewhere in the room where she's sitting.

She returns her focus on me. "No matter what I tell you or what Hudson tells you, you have to decide to cut the umbilical cord." She sighs. "You—and only you—have the power to change the imbalance in your relationship with your sister, Ange."

Anguish twists my insides to the point it renders me mute.

By the time Sadie ended the call, my ice cream had turned liquid.

Pissed off, I dump the melted ice cream down the drain.

I even let Arya ruin my ice cream.

Fuck my life.

Luckily, I had too much work to wallow in self-pity.

I dove headfirst into the manuscript I was working on before Hudson called. After an hour and a half of intense work, I lift my arms over my head and stretch like a cat. I'm just about to return to my work when a jarring thought hits me.

I slap my forehead with my palm. "How could I have forgotten?"

I scramble for my phone and shoot Sadie a text.

She calls me back while I'm still holding my phone.

"Hey, I'm having a late lunch, so the timing is perfect," she says when I accept her call. "What did you forget to tell me?"

"Remember the first time I told you about meeting Hudson and how I was gushing over his good looks?"

"Yes."

"And you suggested he might be the one who… punches my V card…?"

Sadie's eyes grow comically wide. "No way?"

"I'm officially no longer a virgin!" I lift a hand over my head and do a happy dance.

"Holy shit!"

"I know, right?"

"You picked the right guy for the job." It had to be him. "How was it? Don't spare any details. I want to hear it all."

I oblige.

By the time I'm done telling her all about my first time, and the times after that, my best friend is fanning her face.

"HAWT!" More frantic fanning. "Not only does this hunk of a man fly you to Bermuda for a little R&R, but you get to lose your V in freaking paradise?"

"You summed it up perfectly."

"Aren't you happy you didn't allow yourself to get pressured?"

"I wholeheartedly agree."

Empathy lines her brown eyes. "Not putting out was the best decision. It would've never been that good with your first boyfriend."

In the end, my boyfriend dumped me because I was unwilling to go all the way. Arya's experience of putting out and then getting ghosted had me holding on to my virginity.

A wicked grin pulls at Sadie's lips.

"What?" I ask.

"Since your sister hasn't been in touch, I gather she doesn't know yet?"

"No, she doesn't."

"Just like your personalities, your first times are like night and day."

I ponder her words. "Until you mentioned it, I didn't even think of it."

She eyes me thoughtfully. "Let's strip away the Caribbean Island and the fact your boyfriend is a billionaire. It could've happened in a shack on a beach, and Hudson still would've treated you with the respect you deserve. It's just the kind of man he is. Arya forfeited respect just to be liked by a popular guy. Look what that got her!"

I wince.

My twin lost her virginity at eighteen in the back of a guy's car who was destined for a pro baseball career. It was humid as the devil's balls on that summer day. The guy, who was her age, used his spit instead of lube because he wasn't about to part with money to buy a bottle. While they were at it, his mom called. He answered, and they started arguing while he was inside of her. When they were done, he drove her home, pissed off at his mom the whole way. When she saw him again, he brushed it off as if nothing had ever happened.

"And it's not like the other guys that came after her first have treated her much better," Sadie is right. "I don't want to bring up our earlier conversation, but I have to." She brings the screen close to her face. "Arya's misguided way to patch up yet another one of her colossal screw ups is what brought Hudson into your life." She narrows her eyes in warning. "Don't let your twin's fuckups—and we both know more are coming—tear you apart."

~

With my phone clenched to my chest like it's a safety blanket, I pace the small kitchen.

It does little to quell the growing feeling of agitation.

I come to an abrupt stop in front of the window by the sink.

Looking up at the sky, I worry the inside of my lip with my teeth.

Decisions. Decisions.

I exhale and resume my pacing.

I can't seem to settle. The conversations with Hudson and Sadie are still looping in my head.

Feeling like a caged animal, I head to the living room.

I pace around some more, then move to Arya's bedroom—our parents' old bedroom. Evidence of her packing in a rush before setting off to Miami are staring at me. You'd think a tornado swept through our apartment. *Typical Arya.*

I need to be a lot more like her—carefree. Being the responsible one, sucks big balls, at times.

As I continue my pacing, I make my way to my own room.

I don't want to be in my freaking bedroom.

I trail back to the living room, push open the balcony doors, and step out. Our balcony is a joke compared to Hudson's sprawling terrace, but it offers a bit of the outdoors. The sun is still high up in the sky. It's hot, but not Bermuda hot.

Sadness engulfs me.

Yesterday, at this time, Hudson and I were cocooned in a blissful bubble.

A day later, that bubble burst.

Fuck.

I turn my face into the breeze and inhale a deep breath.

The wind whips a strand of my hair over my mouth, and I brush it aside. With a sigh, I tilt my head back and stare to where my parents and God reside.

Everywhere I look around the apartment, I see Ashlyn and Chris McQuinley. I still heard Mom's soft voice, feel her warm, vibrant spirit, feel her love. As for Dad, I feel his strength, fearlessness, and his badassness. He always shrugged it off, but few people on the planet would have the *cajones* to become a high-rise window cleaner. I know I wouldn't. When I was dealing with my teen crisis, Mom was always at the ready with milk and homemade peanut butter Oreo chocolate brownies—my favorites. She was an incredible listener. No problem was too big or too small. I could tell her everything. Dad was the quiet type, but when I was troubled, I'd sit next to him. He'd place a hand over mine, dip his head so his would touch mine, and tell me, *"Today may be a shitty day, but tomorrow might be the best day of your life. Hang in there, little one."*

Sigh.

Sadie is an incredible, caring friend, but in times like these, I wish I could talk to my parents.

Mom. Dad. You guys were taken away from us way too soon.

Tears burn behind my eyelids, threatening to fall.

I draw in a deep breath, doing my best to shake off the melancholy.

I close my eyes, hoping that's enough to calm me, but it's in vain. I guess I'll only settle when I face the music.

Summon your lady balls, Angelica!

I sit on one of the two kitchen chairs and stare at my phone as if it has the power to tell me what to do.

Before I talk myself out of it, I call Hudson.

"Hi," I say when he answers.

"I just got off a call. I was just about to touch base." Thank God he hasn't written me off. "I'm sorry—"

"Hey, you stole my line."

He chuckles.

Oh, how I've missed that beautiful laugh.

Regret prompts me to speak. "I mean it, Hudson. I should be the one apologizing. Not you."

"No, angel, I shouldn't have interfered in your relationship with your sister."

"I'm glad you did. But I can get a little testy when it comes to Arya."

"No shit!"

It's my turn to laugh.

"I gather you hated how our conversation ended as much as I did."

"Yes. Also, Sadie, my best friend called, and she ripped me a new one after I told her we had a fight over my sister. She doesn't know you, but already, she's team Hudson."

"You've been talking about me?"

A blush flushes my cheeks. "I might have."

"As long as it's to tell your friend how amazing I am, it's all good."

I told her how much of an incredible lover you are, but no need to inflate your ego. "Cocky much?"

"That, I am." The amusement in his voice doesn't go unnoticed. "It's good to know Sadie is on my team."

"She isn't my sister's biggest fan."

"Glad to hear you have someone in your corner when you need to vent."

"Sadie is the best. I was worried her moving to LA would negatively impact our friendship. Things are different, but we're still really close."

"Good stuff."

"In any case, I didn't call to talk about my best friend. I know you have a busy day and you'll be in the office late, but I was wondering if you might have a few minutes for a break."

"What did you have in mind?"

"I was thinking of dropping by with an afternoon treat."

"As in your fine ass?"

I giggle.

"I was talking about something you can eat that's sweet."

"Ah. You mean your fine ass *and* your sweet pussy?"

"You're impossible."

"You're doing a poor job expressing yourself, darlin'."

"Hey, I take offense to that."

"First, you talk about an afternoon treat. Second, you talk about something I can eat. Third, you talk about something sweet. Of course my mind goes straight into the gutter. After all, yesterday around this time, I *was* enjoying a pretty sinful afternoon treat."

I can't help but sigh.

Sadie is right.

I'd have to be a fool to let Arya stomp all over what I share with this wonderful man.

Chapter 42

Hudson

The call with Angelica, the call I received after hers, and the meeting I just returned from are the equivalent of hitting three back-to-back home runs. I didn't expect to see my girl today. So, her dropping by is a real treat.

"Knock, knock, knock." A voice I've committed to memory singsongs.

My eyes lift to the door I left ajar as an invitation, just as a beautiful brunette pokes her head in.

"It's about time you showed up."

I hired a car for her to drive her to my office. Given the time of the day and traffic due to an evening commute, she might've been better off taking the subway, but no way am I allowing my girl to travel via public transport.

Getting to our office is a whole song and dance due to the high level of security. In order to avoid hiccups, I asked my receptionist to add Angelica's name to the approval list with the security desk downstairs. I also gave my executive assistant and her assistant a heads-up. The latter was in charge of guiding my girl to my office.

"May I come in, Mr. Kincaid?" Angelica asks, hanging from the door.

I cock an eyebrow. "Mr. Kincaid?"

"It sounds more business-like, and it goes with my outfit." She pushes the door open and enters.

I take her in.

I approve.

She looks the part in a black pencil skirt that accentuates her curves and hits her right below the knee, a short-sleeved white blouse with printed black flowers, and high-heel black patent shoes. Even her hair is pulled back. She's only missing glasses to complete the look.

My naughty secretary.

My cock pushes against the zipper of my pants.

I shift in my chair to adjust myself.

Just being in her presence and I'm turned on like a light switch.

"I thought you would," she says with an exaggerated wink. "Thank you for the outfit, by the way."

"I bought that for you?"

"You did."

"Damn, I have impeccable taste."

She laughs. "It was part of the designer items Trenner said *I had to have* since there was still money left on the amount you allowed him to spend for my makeover."

"I'm a damn genius."

"You're cocky, that's what you are."

I wink at her.

She shakes her head.

"Close the door behind you."

"Right."

She does as she's told.

With her hands behind her back, she strides towards me

with an almost timid step, her eyes bouncing all over the place. "Nice digs," she notes. "It's the same clean aesthetic as your home."

"Different designers."

"Of course."

"Did you come here to give me sass?"

"No, I came here to see you. How's your day so far?"

"Better now that you're here."

I'm rewarded with a huge smile.

"Wheeling and dealing?" Her eyes continue to take everything in.

"As a matter of fact, yes. We landed a big contract earlier today."

Right after I ended the call with Angelica, the confirmation came through. Everyone in the office is jacked up about the news, which is why so many employees are still here even though it's seven o'clock.

"Congratulations!" Her wide smile is infectious. "My timing couldn't be more perfect!"

"Come closer." I call her over. "What's the point of coming over for a visit if we're that far apart?" Laughing, she approaches. "What are you hiding behind your back?"

"I got you these." She pulls a hand from behind her back and drops a black bag on my desk. I recognize the shop's logo.

She pulls out a familiar black box from it and places it on my desk.

I stare up at her. "I see you've already adopted Chocolate Chunk."

"It's a bit of a commute for me to get my chocolate fix, but I know you love their treats."

"So, you're not only here to distract me with your body, you're here to tempt me with chocolate. Had we been in my kitchen, I'd combine both."

Her brows draw together.

"I have fantasies of spreading chocolate all over your body and licking it off."

Her cheeks flush a lovely shade of pink.

"You're such a bad influence."

"Yet, here you are."

"I have a good reason to be here. These"—she points to the box—"have nothing to do with temptation and everything to do with redemption."

My arm wraps around her waist, pulling her close. "What are you repentant about?"

"Snapping at you. Being short. Being defensive."

I grab her hand into mine. "You already apologized."

"I know, but I feel bad about it."

"Thank you for the treats and apology."

"Everything is good between us again?!"

"Is that a question or a statement?"

"A bit of both."

I cup the back of her neck and kiss the hell out of her.

Her hands fist my shirt.

I'm hard as wood.

My mouth is greedy on her. Aggressive, even.

A grunt leaves me.

My hands travel down her back until they're filling with her fine ass. I squeeze her cheeks hard. A bolt of electricity travels through me.

She moans against my lips.

Damn, she's killing me.

Suckling her lower lip, I ease the kiss.

She murmurs a sound of disapproval.

I pull away from her.

Her big eyes are filled with lust. There's so much heat in her gaze, no doubt a reflection of my own desire. She swipes a thumb under her lips, but she misses a smidge of lipstick. I help her out, doing my best to wipe it off her skin. Her lips are swollen from the assault.

"Did I answer your question? I ask.

"Okay..."—she licks her lips—"everything is good between us."

"You're certain about that?"

"Very certain."

I chuckle. "What did you get us?" I jerk my chin towards the box.

"Us?" She shakes her head. "These are for you."

"We're sharing." I set her straight.

"If you twist my arm..."

"Damn, you're easy." I wink.

She smiles.

"To answer your question, I got two of your favorites—the others were sold out by the time I got to the bakery." She opens the box. "On top of that, I snagged triple chocolate cookies, gooey double chocolate chip cookies, and peanut butter chocolate chip cookies."

"I approve." I nod. "Anything from Chocolate Chunk carries its weight in gold. Thank you, angel."

"It's my pleasure."

"I also got you a little something."

She stares at me with a confused expression. "You didn't have to."

"I wanted to."

I open a drawer, pull out a white box, and hand it to her.

Her eyes ping pong from my gaze to the box.

"Unless you have X-ray vision, you won't know what's in the box unless you open it."

She hooks a closed fist at her waist. "Are you making fun of me?"

"You should see your face right now."

"You keep spoiling me."

"On your lips, it sounds like I'm committing a crime punishable by death."

"You aren't. It's just that you're so... kind. And generous. And thoughtful. And wonderful."

"That's it?"

She rolls her eyes.

I chuckle.

"Are you going to open the box or not?"

She takes it from me and lifts the lid as if she's expecting to find a bomb.

"Hudson..." Her eyes snap up to meet mine. "Tiffany?!" she says in a soft rush.

The white box was to throw her off. "Since my lunch meeting was at a restaurant located not too far from the office, I walked. On the way back, I passed in front of the window of a shop that sells estate pieces. I thought of you."

"Oh, my God." Her hand runs along the textured surface of the blue box. "You're crazy. Do you know how much things cost at Tiffany?" She lifts a hand up. "That was a silly question. Of course you know."

With trembling hands, she lifts the lid of the second box.

"Mother of God!" She gasps. "Are those diamonds?"

"They better be."

"More diamonds?"

"Is that a complaint again?"

"You've lost your mind." She shakes her head. "I can't believe this."

I reach for the necklace and pluck it out of the box. "Turn around so I can put it on you."

She does.

I clasp the necklace around her neck.

She looks down. "Holy shit!"

"Let me see it on you."

She does a little happy dance as she turns around. "Thank you, thank you, thank you!"

The diamonds wink at me.

I got her a multi-strand platinum chain necklace, suspending six diamond stars—two large ones and four smaller ones.

I trace the chain, stopping at the diamond encrusted piece that holds the falling stars together. "I hope you always remember you shine as bright as a star."

"With this constellation of diamonds hanging from my neck, it's unlikely I'll ever forget."

"Good."

She cups my face. Her touch is warm on my cheek. "Thank you so much." She drops a soft kiss against my lips.

"I'm glad you like it."

Her fingers rake through my hair. "I fucking love it."

"Even better."

Green eyes search my face in wonder.

"I made a deal with my sister, expecting the worst"—she expels a long breath—"and I found you."

"And I ended up with the right twin."

"How can you say that when you haven't even met my sister?"

I take the hand that's cupping my face and thread our fingers. "I just know."

There's a knock at the door.

"Mr. Kincaid!" The timing couldn't be worse.

"Yes!"

"I'm sorry to interrupt, sir, but you aren't answering your landline or phone."

I was hoping for a little alone time with my girlfriend.

Speaking of which, her face is a bright shade of red, and she's staring at me with freaked out eyes.

"There's an important call for you," my executive assistant's assistant says.

Fuck.

The moment is ruined.

Chapter 43

Angelica

We just finished our meal with Rory and his wife.

Rory already told Isobel about the twin swap. Thank God she didn't judge me. Neither did her husband. In fact, Isobel laughed it off, saying that if another human being walking the planet has the exact same face as you, it would be crazy not to take advantage of it. I'm glad she's so easygoing about it. The woman is a delight.

As we were winding down, Isobel started bombarding me with questions. She was intrigued by my connection to Grace.

I was too happy to share my story.

Now, she's staring at me in disbelief.

"I know," I say. "Never in a million years did I expect Grace's book to blow up like it did. Thank God for social media."

"Without you, *The Court Games* would never have seen the light of day," she says, repeating the very words Grace said to me herself.

I blush. "I'm just the editor." I shift in my seat. "Grace is the mastermind behind the epic story."

"True, but without your support and your talent, that manuscript would've either remained on her laptop or it might not have had this level of success had it not been for the editing."

My blush deepens. "I was hooked from the first few chapters, so it was easy work."

She shakes a finger at me in a motherly way. "You're selling yourself short, Angelica."

Hudson wraps me in his arms and pulls me close. "I've been telling her that as well."

I'm officially fifty shades of red.

"Listen to him!" Isobel points to my boyfriend.

My boyfriend.

It's wild to consider him that way.

Tonight is a magical night and another culinary first for me.

Not only is the food at Fogo de Chão lip-smacking delicious, but the experience is out of this world. I had no idea dining at a Brazilian steakhouse includes a continual parade of fire-roasted meats carved tableside by Brazilian trained gaucho chefs. The warm cheese bread was an out-of-body experience. *Good God.*

After a scrumptious meal, and a little too much wine, we're taking a break before ordering dessert. The chocolate molten cake served with a scoop of vanilla ice cream is calling out my name, but I need a breather.

"Have you considered branching out?" Isobel asks me.

I frown. "What do you mean?"

"Grace said her kickass editor literally pulled the best parts of a very messy manuscript that was as thick as an old-fashioned phone book. You pulled out the heart of the story, discarding the fluff and filler. Without you, the book would never have topped the charts or hit the New York Times Bestsellers' list. You have great instinct."

"Thank you." I'm a bit overwhelmed by her praise.

"Which is why I asked if you've ever considered branching out."

"You mean writing a novel instead of being an editor?"

She shakes her head. "I mean, working as a script editor or working as part of a production team? You have everything it takes to become a top-notch screenwriter."

Holy shit.

"My best friend has a one-year contract with Hallmark Channel—"

"Here?" Isobel asks.

I shake my head. "She's a coordinator in their programming team, based in LA. I didn't get selected. She did. I was thrilled for her. She figured she was in. Nope. If she wants to secure a position as a script editor—or any position in the production team—she'd have to apply like everybody else. Those jobs are highly coveted. Unless you're well connected, forget about it."

Isobel brushes her curly brown hair behind her ears.

She's a tall and stunning mixed-race woman with the best TV shampoo commercial hair. I'd kill for those curls.

She leans into the table.

I mirror her move.

We're practically nose to nose, her dark brown eyes fixed on mine.

"You have to keep this a secret."

Isobel Wolfe wants to share a secret with me?

Giddiness bubbles up within me.

I cross my heart. "I will."

My eyes dart to the two men sitting next to us.

I guess they're not sworn to secrecy.

"Don't worry about them. This is just between us girls." She read my mind.

I respond with a nod.

"I know the UTV.com's CEO *very, very* well. And they have production and acquisition teams on both coasts." She straightens. "I'm just putting it out there."

My eyes grow as wide as dinner plates, and then I dissolve in a fit of laughter.

Isobel joins me.

Hudson and Rory get a good laugh at my expense as well.

Tall, dark, and handsome, Rory is more of the brooding type, and I'm surprised to see him laughing so freely.

"Okay, I walked right into that one," I say when I regain my composure.

"Yes, you did," Hudson says.

A presence looming over me forces me to look up.

A man wearing a green checkerboard suit and a white shirt with the top three buttons open is standing at our table.

Do I know him?

He flashes me a tight smile that doesn't reach his eyes.

I greet him with a warm one.

"Brinley," he says.

Brinley?

Oh shit. Brinley!

I'm Brinley. Well, I was.

Did I meet him at Rory and Isobel's event?

But he seems to only have eyes for me.

So, maybe not.

His eyes shift to the man wrapped around me. "Mr. Kincaid."

They know each other?

Hudson's body stiffens. "Todd..."

"Fancy seeing you out tonight." The man's voice drips with sarcasm.

Todd, Todd? As in Arya's pimp?

I feel time slow down as my eyes lift up to the man hovering over me.

"Todd?!" A strangled sound leaves me.

He stares down at me as if I have two heads. "Yes, Todd." My entire world screeches to a halt. "Why do you say that like you don't know who I am?"

Because I've never met you before.

Oh.

My.

Fucking.

God.

I'm so screwed.

I mean, Arya and I are so screwed.

My heart is beating so fast it's as if it's trying its best to pound its way out of my chest.

A trickle of fear runs down my spine as my mind churns at light speed, searching for a way out of this cluster fuck of a mess.

After not giving any signs of life for a few days, Arya texted me this morning to let me know she had spent the last couple of days at Vanna's parents' house lying low. Apparently, there was a lot of drama around DJ Bromley, and they had to get out of Miami undetected. She promised to fill me in. With my twin, anything is possible. Who knows what a lot of drama means? She mentioned she was starting a new arm candy gig tonight. She sent me details about her client and the location of their meeting. My experience with Hudson went as smooth as butter. But you can never be too safe.

I flash Todd an exaggerated smile.

The corner of his eye twitches.

I'm sure I look like an escapee from a mental hospital.

Anything that comes out of my mouth might—no, *will*—incriminate my sister.

When you smile, it lowers people's defenses.

And right now, that's exactly what I need because this man looks like he's about to blow a gasket.

He shoves his hands inside the pockets of his pants. "Can I have a word with you?"

"Well—"

"That wasn't a suggestion!"

"Listen, Todd—"

I place a hand on Hudson's thigh to prevent him from standing up.

A lump the size of a mini watermelon clogs my throat, and my voice comes out meek. "Sure."

I turn to face my boyfriend.

I put on a brave face. "It's okay, Hudson." My voice is light with false bravado. If the earth could open up beneath my feet and swallow me whole, I'd welcome it. "I'll be right back." I swallow hard. "You won't have time to miss me." I flash Isobel and Rory a frozen smile. They both look concerned.

Butterflies flap their wings in my belly in a wild dance as I struggle to my feet.

"Let's go," Todd says, inviting me to step before him. "Straight ahead, past the maître d' desk and make a left," he says from over my shoulder.

I nod and keep walking.

Not long after I make a left, he barks. "Here!"

My feet stop moving.

I don't dare to turn around.

"Brinley," Todd says.

Slowly, ever so slowly, I pivot.

My head jerks back.

When we were in the restaurant, I hadn't noticed how short Todd was. And I hadn't noticed the high heel booties. In my Louboutin shoes, I'm taller than he is.

"What the fuck are you doing here?" It's a rhetorical question since he keeps talking. "You're supposed to be at a charity event with the new client."

I bring my hand to the necklace Hudson gave me yesterday and stroke it, hoping it's enough to calm my nerves.

It's not.

His brown eyes narrow. "You were supposed to wear a choker. Not a pendant."

I let go of my cherished gift.

His eyes travel the length of my body before he continues barraging me. "What the hell are you wearing?"

I look down at myself. "A light-blue dress?!"

It's one of the extra designer outfits I got on Saks Fifth Avenue's personal shopper's insistence, aka Hudson's generosity.

"A light-blue dress?"

"Yes."

"And why are you wearing a light-blue dress?" *Is that a trick question?*

"It's..." My eyes shift left to right, as my mind races.

Todd doesn't give me a chance to come up with an answer. "I thought you understood the client's demand."

Crap.

"For fuck's sake, you were standing in my office and you assured me you had a sexy red dress perfect for tonight."

Shit.

"The client has a fetish for tight red dresses." His eyes drop to my feet. "White shoes?"

"They're designer—"

"I don't give a fuck!"

I jolt.

Okay, that was a faux pas.

"The client wanted black patent leather high heels. You told me you owned a pair."

This is going from bad to worse.

"The same question goes for your lipstick. You're wearing bright pink. The client requested red lips. And you weren't supposed to wear your hair out." He keeps on listing my offenses. "It was supposed to be pulled back in a severe low bun."

My hand goes to my hair. *Fuck.*

"We're in the business of satisfying our clients' demands. If we don't, they go elsewhere." Frustration is rolling off him. "It's as if we didn't have a conversation earlier today." *That's because we didn't.* "If things were unclear, why didn't you text me or call?"

"I... I... I..."

"Since when do you stutter?" His tone drips with disdain. "You... You... You... What?"

I feel so small.

I lick my dry lips.

He shakes his head. "How can you drop the ball after such a stellar first week? Are you suffering from temporary memory loss? Is that why you forgot the client's demands the minute you walked out of my office?"

I'm stumped.

"Answer me!"

I'm so damn nervous, I can hardly keep my hands from shaking. I close them in fists at my side. That does little to stop the trembling.

Say something.

I expel a hard breath. "I'm sorry." That's the best I can come up with.

"You're sorry? You're sorry? You're fucking sorry?" His voice rises in a crescendo. It's as if I had insulted his mother.

"You're sorry means shit," he says. "Your ditziness is costing me money, potentially a client, and the reputation I've carefully built for myself. Three things I take very seriously." He jabs a finger into my face. "If you planned on ignoring everything I told you earlier today, why did you bother showing up at my office in the first place?" *Jab.* "I could've given the client to another girl." *Jab.* "One that wouldn't have wasted my fucking time." *Jab.*

I'm still tongue-tied.

"On top of being hard of hearing"—*Jab*—"you're fucking mute now?"

"Hey, that's enough!"

I turn in the direction of the voice.

Hudson is charging towards us, eyes blazing with fury, an angry finger pointed like a gun at Todd.

I shake my head, hoping it conveys my message. *Stay away or you'll fuck things up for Arya.*

My telepathic skills are shit because Hudson keeps approaching with the determination of a warrior.

He comes to a halt next to me.

Todd takes a step to the side so they're facing each other.

The height difference is comical.

"Dear client, this conversation has nothing to do with you. It's between me and one of *my* girls."

"She's *my* girl," Hudson says.

Todd lets out a humorless laugh. "It happens all the time. Some clients get attached. But I can assure you, she"—Todd points at me—"is one of *my* girls. *Not* yours."

"That's where you're wrong," Hudson says. "She *is* my girl. And you better get your fucking finger out of her face. I don't care who the fuck you are. Don't you dare talk to my girlfriend like that. Unless you want my fist to break your nose, you better watch your goddamn mouth."

"Girlfriend?" Todd blinks several times in quick succession. "Girlfriend?"

"Yes, *girlfriend,*" Hudson says.

This should be a joyous moment, when a man you're crazy about shouts from the rooftops that you're his girlfriend, but right now, it feels like it's the worst possible thing Hudson could've said.

A thousand emotions flicker in Todd's eyes, settling on a cross between disbelief and aggravation.

"She was supposed to be arm candy for a week, not end up as your girlfriend," Todd says. "Let's forget about this crazy revelation for a minute. She isn't supposed to be out with you tonight. Brinley is supposed to be with another client—"

"She isn't Brinley!" Hudson says.

No, no, no.

Todd's eyes shift to mine. "What the fuck are you talking about? This is Brinley!"

I should speak up and put an end to this madness, but I've lost my voice, too shellshocked by the consequences of what my sister and I started a little over a week ago.

Hudson slides his hands in his pockets and shakes his head. "It's not!"

He's so casual about outing me.

Todd's eyes widen in bewilderment. "Then who the fuck is she?"

Chapter 44

Hudson

At Todd's question, my eyes meet Angelica's.

I cock an eyebrow, waiting for her to answer him.

She looks absolutely petrified.

I take her hand in mine and squeeze.

"Is someone going to tell me what the fuck is going on here?" Todd's tone is irate.

"Stop yelling!"

My warning doesn't prevent him from jabbering on.

"This woman looks exactly like Brinley. If she isn't her, then she's her doppelganger."

Angelica's eyelashes are fluttering like crazy.

I coax her to speak. "Tell him."

Todd looks confused as fuck. "Tell me what?"

Isobel and Rory had stared in disbelief as Todd guided Angelica out of the restaurant. So had I.

The only reason I didn't put my foot down is because of my girl's sister.

Even though I could've hired a separate car to drive Angelica to the restaurant, I made the trip from my office to

Queens, and back to Manhattan again, to spend time with her. I asked her about her sister, and she revealed she texted to announce she was back in the city. Given yesterday's fight, I didn't ask too many more questions.

When Todd stopped by our table, I thought it was an ironic coincidence. One look into his angry eyes, and I knew the shit was about to hit the fan. It took me a minute to put the pieces together. When he demanded to speak to *Brinley* in private, two things became crystal clear. One, Todd had no idea Arya had an identical twin sister. Two, the shipwreck twin was supposed to be out with another man. I granted Angelica's wish and let her deal with Todd, but with each passing second, I was growing more and more agitated. Just when I thought I was about to burst, I excused myself from the table.

I expected Todd to be upset. I didn't expect him to be an asshole.

Of all the restaurants in New York City, he had to be here tonight.

Talk about bad luck.

When Angelica still remains quiet, Todd starts losing his shit.

"I have a right to know what's going on here." He stomps his feet strapped in a pair of studded white high heel booties like a pissed off child.

"Simmer down," I say.

I turn my attention to my girlfriend.

Angelica pinches her lips as if she's in pain.

Come on, angel.

Rip the Band-Aid off.

"I'm... I'm... I'm not Brinley's doppelganger—"

"Then who the fuck—"

I lift a hand up and stick it in Todd's face, shutting him up.

"Let. Her. Fucking. Talk." I level him with an icy stare that has him shutting his mouth.

If it was possible for humans to snarl, that's exactly what Todd just did.

Like that's enough to make me shake in my boots.

With a nod, I invite Angelica to continue.

"I'm her identical twin sister."

Todd's head jerks back. "Wh—what?"

"I'm Brinley's identical twin sister."

Todd's wild eyes bounce from mine to Angelica's. "So, you're not one of my girls?"

"No. Not exactly."

"What is that supposed to mean?" Todd's tone is cautious. "Wait! How do you two know each other if you're not Brinley?"

Angelica tells him everything.

For a few long beats, Todd studies her.

I remain silent.

"So, you hired her for the week, not her twin sister?" The question is directed at me.

"Yes, and she's the one I took to Bermuda—"

"Bermuda, as in the island?"

"Yes."

Todd squints his eyes and points lasers at me. "You took one of my girls out of the country without my consent or permission?"

"Technically, she isn't one of your girls. Her sister is."

"Since I didn't know one of my girls and her identical twin were making a mockery out of me, it's a moot point."

"That doesn't change the facts. My girlfriend's sister works for you. Not my girl."

Todd crosses his arms over his chest and places a finger against his lips.

I can only assume he's taking in all the information that was dumped in his lap.

"You're right." Just when I think he's seeing the light, he turns the tables on me. "Given the two of them are in cahoots to dupe me, I plan on suing *both* sisters—"

Angelica gasps. "You can't do that!"

"Watch me!"

"Based on what?" I ask.

"Based on misrepresentation!"

Angelica's shoulders slump.

He jerks his chin in my girl's direction. "This was planned all along."

"No, it wasn't, Todd—"

"No one tricks me without consequences," he says. "You're not getting away with this."

"You're full of shit," I say.

His head whips in my direction. "Excuse me?"

"This isn't the Netherlands. This is the good ol' US of A. It's unlikely you'll be lawyering up anytime soon to go after them, unless you want Uncle Sam to come sniffing around your cash only business."

A look of surprise washes over Todd's face. Then, it's gone, replaced by contempt. "In that case, I'll find another way to send a *strong* message."

"Is that a threat?"

He gets on his toes. "You fuck with me, I fuck right back." Good for him for being smart enough not to wave his finger at me. Had he been stupid enough to do so, I would've broken his whole damn arm.

Angelica lets out a strangled noise.

I stand right in his face. Actually, I have to look down because he's so short. "You better call your dogs off, Todd. You fuck with her, you fuck with me. The same applies to her sister.

You got paid. I sent a generous bonus. No harm, no foul. Back. The fuck. Down." My jaw is clenched so tight, I'm surprised my teeth don't crumble into dust.

We enter a Mexican standoff.

His eyes bulge out of his skull.

His nostrils flare.

His chest heaves.

Is that all you got, little man?

With a huff of annoyance, he straightens his jacket, and squares his shoulders.

"As of right now, Brinley is fired!"

With that, he turns on his high heeled booties and walks away.

He stops long enough to throw over his shoulder, "I don't need *cunts* like that anywhere near my clients."

I'm just about to chase after him to make him eat his words, but Angelica grabs my forearm.

"Please, Hudson, don't."

Chapter 45

Angelica

Last week went by without a hitch. I figured Arya and I were in the clear in regard to Todd. Bumping into her boss wasn't a scenario we planned for. Heck, even if I was wearing a red dress, black patent high heel shoes, painted my lips red, and pulled back my hair in a severe bun, we would've still gotten busted. It's not like I can be in two places at the same time with two different men.

Here I thought we had pulled off the ultimate twin swap, just for everything to explode in my face.

"Arya's days were numbered working for Todd since you gave her an ultimatum—"

"I had it under control," I say, interrupting Hudson.

"He was an aggressive asshole, shouting, and waving a threatening finger in your face. You call that being in control?"

"I told you, I would've handled it. I didn't need you to come to my rescue."

He flinches.

It's as if I had slapped him across the face.

He recovers. "Todd is probably going to rip Arya a new one."

"Fuck," I say. "I need to warn her."

I have to get out of here.

Crap.

I don't have my handbag or my phone with me.

I'm just about to run back into the restaurant, but Hudson grabs my wrist.

"It doesn't matter if you warn her. It's over. Todd fired her—"

"If he plans on going to the restaurant where my sister is having dinner with her client, she should know in advance he'll humiliate her. I would've liked a heads up."

"You aren't joined at the hip, angel. And you're not her parent. Stop taking everything on your shoulders and doing everything in your power to protect her. Your sister isn't pulling her weight. Every time she gets in trouble, you run to her rescue. Can't you see? It's weighing you down."

I narrow my eyes at him. "I'm as responsible as she is for this mess. I agreed to the twin swap—"

"To protect her from a guy you thought was part of the Russian mob—"

"My sister is flawed—"

"We all are." Tension moves over his features. "The definition of adulting is facing the music when you fuck up. You never let your sister take responsibility for her actions—"

"She's the only family I have left."

He lets out a sigh and rakes his fingers through his hair. "I understand that, but—"

"There is no but." My tone is firm.

He stares at me as if he doesn't recognize me.

"I'm coming with you."

"No." I shake my head. "This meeting with Rory is too

important. I don't want to ruin it for you. I've already embarrassed you enough."

He regards me, his jaw working.

"I have to go."

"Let me call the car."

"No need. The restaurant where Arya is meeting her client isn't far. I'll walk." His eyes drop to my heels. I follow his gaze. "Or I'll take a taxi."

"Why not accept the car?"

"There are taxis outside the restaurant. I need to get to Arya as quickly as possible."

"Todd is probably already there."

"If he is, she won't have to face his wrath alone."

"I don't like this."

We stare at each other for a long beat.

I'm an embarrassment to this man. "Hudson, maybe... you and me..."

"You and me, what?"

"We don't make sense."

"What the fuck?"

"My life is a mess—"

"Angelica—"

"Because of me and Arya you ended up in a fight with Todd—"

"Who the fuck cares about Todd?"

A few people walking by stare our way.

"It's not only Todd. It's Ramsey. The Russian loan shark. Apparently, there's some sort of drama surrounding this DJ Arya went to Miami with. And if I know anything about my twin sister, she's going to fuck up again."

He narrows his eyes. "What are you saying?"

"You deserve to be with someone whose life isn't a recurring soap opera. I'll only end up dragging you down." I don't deserve this wonderful man. "Maybe we should cool things off for a bit."

My heart rips in half the second the words leave my lips.

Just kill me now, God.

"Over my dead body."

"Trust me, it's for the best."

"Angelica—"

"I need to go find Arya."

I walk past him.

He reaches out for my arm. "You're giving up on us?"

"I'm protecting you from the shit fest that is my life."

I wriggle out of his hold.

I head inside the restaurant at a quick clip.

Isobel and Rory are still sitting there.

Their eyes are wide with concern as they see me approach.

"Is everything okay?" Isobel asks.

"No, it's not." *Everything has gone to shit. Again.*

With a curt *good night,* I snatch my handbag and my phone from the table.

My lips wobble.

I get the hell out of there before I start to cry.

Chapter 46

Angelica

My text to Arya remains unanswered. I called her and it went straight to voicemail. I'd hate to think Todd is chewing her head off, which is why she isn't responding. Luckily, The Paley Center for Media is a short taxi ride away. I considered walking, to save on the fare, but as pretty as these Louboutins are, I would've ended up killing myself.

What a bizarre twist of fate Arya and I would be this close.

I told my sister I was having dinner with the CEO of UTV.com and his wife, but didn't mention Hudson. Since she's been gallivanting down south and doing a fine job ghosting me, she's unaware things have evolved with Hudson. The plan was to tell her tomorrow face to face. She's sleeping at Vanna's parents' house again tonight because her luggage is still there.

After paying the cabbie, I make my way to the front door to the cultural institution where I hope, and pray, I find my sister before Todd does.

A model-tall and model-pretty blonde with big blue eyes smiles down at me. "Good evening, may I have your invitation, please?"

Crap.

"I don't have one."

"Oh, let me find your name on the list," she says, tapping the screen of the iPad she's holding.

"You won't find my name." She frowns. "My sister is in there with a man. Chances are, he's on your list. It's urgent I speak to her."

Her expression turns to ice. "I'm sorry, but without an invitation, I can't let you in."

"Maybe someone can find my sister?" I point at my face. "We're identical twins."

"There are over two hundred guests attending tonight's fundraiser. That's just not going to be possible."

"I'm desperate. I really, really need to speak to my sister." I'm not above begging.

"Is this a question of life or death?"

I draw the line at lying in someone's face. "No. It's about a sticky situation."

"In that case, the answer remains the same. I'm sorry, miss, I can't let you in."

Fuck.

My shoulders slump.

Then it hits me. If I can't get in without an invitation, Todd might not be in there ripping Arya a new one right about now.

~

I regret not accepting Hudson's car service. A taxi for a few blocks hurt my soul, but it was bearable. Paying for a taxi ride from Manhattan to Queens would strangle me. New York subway can be treacherous at the best of times. Navigating the underbelly of the city in five-inch heels is going to be a bitch. My feet are already aching from the walk from the cultural center to the nearest subway. By the time I make it to Queens, my poor feet will be weeping. But dishing out money I don't have, is out of the question.

Fuck my life.

I'm just about to climb down the stairs when my phone chimes.

It's about fucking time!

Arya: Why are you blowing up my phone?

Angelica: Where are you? I was at The Paley Center for Media, but I couldn't get in because I didn't have an invitation.

Arya: The event was stuffy and boring. The client suggested we skip it and head to a friend's post-crowdfunding-success party, so we hopped in a taxi and we're here now!

Angelica: Why didn't you tell me you changed venue? And why was your phone off?

Arya: My phone was off because it was a requirement at the fundraiser. They brought in this big opera singer from Italy, and they didn't want phones to interrupt her performance since they were recording it. I must've forgotten to turn my phone back on. By the way, opera is a snooze.

Angelica: Did Todd leave you any messages?

Arya: I haven't listened to them yet. I pulled out my personal phone to check my makeup using the photo app, when I realized it was off. I figured I must've forgotten to turn on the work phone as well. I decided to return your call first. What's going on?

Angelica: Todd showed up at the restaurant where I was having dinner.

Arya: How do you know it was him? You've never met him.

Angelica: It's too long to explain via text. Where are you? I'm coming there right now. We need to talk.

I know what I said about spending money on taxi fare, but desperate times call for desperate measures. I didn't expect to set foot in the Pompadour Hotel this soon, but here I am.

After checking with the concierge, I make my way to the room where my sister and her client are. I get out of the elevator and power my way down the corridor.

My feet are killing me.

Ignoring the pain, I make a right. As I march with a determined step, my eyes land on a woman pacing at a distance. She comes to a stop and faces me. She has my height, dress size and foot size, hair, eyes, smile, and face. It's almost like looking into a mirror. Almost. She's dressed appropriately for a party at an adult club, while I'm dressed like I'm about to go for high tea on a sunny Sunday afternoon. Our fashion selections contrast as much as our personalities.

"Hey," I say, approaching her.

She gives me a critical onceover in lieu of a greeting. "You went shopping?" Her eyebrows raise high on her forehead. Her indignant gaze zeroes in on me. "I thought we barely had enough money to afford to eat anything fancier than generic brands of boxed mac n' cheese, but you get a new wardrobe?" The sarcasm is thick.

"That's not important right now."

"So, you *did* go shopping?"

"Arya, I didn't come all the way here to talk about fashion."

Her eyes lower to my chest.

She squints and reaches out a hand. "What's that?"

I place a protective hand over my necklace. "It's nothing."

She shoots me a suspicious side glance.

"Did you listen to Todd's messages?" I veer the conversation away from what I'm wearing.

"I did."

"What did he say?" My tone is cautious.

"He sounded pissed off as hell, but he didn't say much." Thank God he didn't show up here and verbally abuse her like he did me. "He told me to drop by his office first thing tomorrow. In Todd's world, that's eleven o'clock. He's not big on leaving detailed messages. He prefers to communicate face to face. Actual convos equal no trails." *Makes sense.* "Are you going to tell me what's going on? You said you saw Todd, but he didn't mention it. Are you sure it was him?"

"Let's not have this conversation out in the open."

"Why not?"

"Trust me on this." She shoots me a wary stare. "There must be a more private spot where we can talk."

"There's a super glam bathroom, complete with velvet chaise, that way." She points over her shoulder.

"It'll have to do." *Let's just hope no one needs to use it.*

When we reach the bathroom, we find it unoccupied.

Thank God for small favors.

We shuffle inside.

I turn around and watch the door close, hoping there's a lock.

Bingo!

With a twist, I guarantee no one will hear this conversation.

Arya moves to a counter that seems dedicated to primping.

I drop my tiny evening bag and phone on the countertop.

She places her handbag in front of my stuff.

Our eyes meet.

"I'm sure you must've confused Todd for someone else—"

"I didn't. He called me Brinley."

"Shit." Then, realization hits her. "He must've freaked the hell out because I had a strict dress code." She waves a finger up and down the length of my body.

"He did more than freak the hell out. He threatened to sue us for misleading him." Her green eyes widen. "He thinks we plotted this big elaborate scheme against him."

"Oh shit." She worries the inside of her lip. "He knows there's two of us?"

"Hudson made sure he knew."

"Hudson? I thought you were having dinner with UTV.-com's big wig and his wife."

"I met them through Hudson, and he was there."

She scrunches her nose as if she's smelling rancid food. "The contract with him ended days ago. You're still seeing him?"

I huff out my exasperation. "Had you not ignored my calls and texts after skipping town to be with DJ Bromley—"

"Please, don't talk about that asshole." She bats that away with a flick of her wrist. *I swear to all the gods.* "I'm so over him." My ears begin to ring. *Here we fucking go again.* "He first told Vanna and me we didn't have to worry about paying him for the flight, hotel, food, or drinks, then he expected us to have an orgy with his—"

"I don't care about whatever drama unfolded between you and another loser you decided to spread your legs for."

Her head reels back in shock. "Excuse me?"

"Arya, it's like you're a magnet for the worst men in New York."

Her lips purse in a tight line of perfectly applied red

lipstick. "Well, at least I'm not a repressed virgin who's waiting for prince charming to deflower her."

"Maybe you should've waited longer than a New York minute instead of letting a guy who was too distracted to focus on you for your first time."

"That's behind me. I'm twenty-two and I know how to please a man. You're twenty-two and you're clueless." *Bitch.*

"Not that clueless anymore, sis."

"Ah! A new vibrator doesn't count," she says with a laugh.

"My *boyfriend* Hudson punched my V card in Bermuda."

"Wh—what?"

Well, he was my boyfriend when it happened. Now, he's just the wonderful guy I broke things off with and left standing in a restaurant to come to your rescue.

I push the thought aside. "I'm no longer a virgin. And, yes, you heard me correctly, Hudson is my first. He treated me like a queen from beginning to end. Not like a mistake."

"You violated the sister code?!"

"What do you mean?"

"We don't date each other's boyfriends."

"Each other's boyfriends?" I'm incredulous. "Hudson was never your boyfriend. You never even met him."

"But he was *my* client." Her eyes zero in on me. "It's the same thing. That makes him off limits. And I'm pretty sure Todd would have a shit fit if his girls started dating clients."

Her warped logic is laughable. "Let me get this through your head. First off, Hudson was never your boyfriend. Second off, I don't work for Todd, which means, your off-limits comment is ridiculous."

Arya's eyes narrow to slits. "And how dare you keep things from me? You said you weren't going to be available for the next couple of days. You told Sadie you were leaving the country, but you don't tell me, your sister? Not cool—"

"You didn't even have the decency to tell me you were going to Miami!"

"I left you an explicit note. You knew exactly where I was *and* who I was with."

I ball my hands into fists. "You can be so dense sometimes."

"You didn't take time to tell me about Hudson or Bermuda, yet, you wanted to talk about Ramsey?! Give it a rest."

"It was important—"

"Stop obsessing over him. It's not like we have the means to track him down—"

"Don't you dare be blasé about this—"

"I'm being practical. We have to wait for the police to find him—"

"They'll never find him because—"

"Stop being pessimistic—"

"Ramsey is dead!" The surge of anger that punches through me is destabilizing.

"Wh—wh—what?"

I pull in my temper. "Hudson enlisted the help of a friend of his. He's an expert in cyber and white-collar crimes. Anyway, it's a long story. What's important here is what he found out. Ramsey is dead. And our money—along with the money of all the other people he conned—is in a bank account that belongs to the Russian mafia, somewhere in Cyprus. Everything points to the fact Ramsey was in bed with the Bratva."

Arya visibly blanches.

"The Bratva? Russian... mafia? Ramsey... is dead?"

I let out an exasperated sigh. "You missed out on a lot."

"Shit..." She shakes her head. "I can't believe this."

"Once again, I had to hold the fort while you were enjoying life—working on your tan and doing body shots—"

"How was I supposed to know?"

I swear I'm this close from bursting out of my skin.

"You're right, Arya. The stress of dealing with *Vanna* getting dumped was unbearable." I layer on the sarcasm, thick.

"I was being a supportive friend."

"It would be nice if you were a supportive sister once in a while."

"I am."

"Bullshit!"

We stare at each other, both unflinching and equally pissed off.

"We can't all be a high and mighty tight ass like you," she says, breaking the standoff.

I flinch but recover quickly. "If it wasn't for me being a high and mighty tight ass, you'd be fucking homeless!"

"I pull my weight!" She makes a stubborn face. "I have my waitressing job. And I'm sure once I talk to Todd, I'll be able to smooth things over. He's gay, so it's not like I can seduce him, but I'm sure I can charm his pants off."

I shake my head. "Todd fired us."

Her jaw drops.

I soldier on. "One of his girls left the country without his permission."

"But *you're* the one who went to Bermuda and you're not one of his girls." *But a minute ago, you considered I violated the sister code?*

I can't smell alcohol on her, so it's not like I can blame booze for her illogical statements.

"I was still under the *arrangement*," I say with air quotes, "between you and Hudson. We tricked Todd from the get go—"

"This is so unfair." Her hands go flying in the air before resting on her waist. "I'm getting punished for something *you* did?! Fuck that."

My brows lift high. "Are you playing the blame game?"

"That gig was great money. You ruined it for me!"

"You asked me to save your ass because of your vaginal infection, and this is the thanks I get?"

"You didn't save my ass. You got my ass fired!" Her eyes narrow. Something I've never seen before shines bright in them. *Hate?!* "You're always barraging me for not taking responsibility for my actions. For once, I do the right thing, and you fuck it all up. And I know why."

My laugh is short and flat. I even roll my eyes. "You're talking shit."

"You're already doing it—"

"Doing what?" My tone is as sharp as the crack of a whip.

She points an accusatory finger in my face. "Now, you get to stand on your high horse, while looking down at me. You get to throw in my face I'm not doing enough to dig us out of the shithole I put us in. You get to belittle me by telling me I spread my legs for losers." She lets out a sound of disgust. "You fucked this up for me just so you can keep walking around with an air of superiority." She snorts. "And don't kid yourself. Your *relationship* with Hudson won't last." Her tone is mocking.

Bile rises from my gut, filling my mouth.

I hate her so much right now.

"I Googled him. He's so out of your league, it's laughable." My sister eviscerates my self-confidence. "You spend your whole life with your nose between the pages of a book, unless you're editing one, or listening to an audiobook. Whoop-de-do you lost your virginity. He probably took pity on you." My self-esteem plummets even more. "Either that, or he was too eager to pop your cherry for cheap. Todd gets top dollar from clients who prefer virgins. Your hymen could've made us a fortune. You sold yourself short, sis." I'm too stunned by her rant to speak. "Now that Hudson got what he wanted, do you actually think he'll stick around? He's a powerful man with experience.

He can have any woman he wants—women who can get down and dirty."

The smirk on her lips should come as a precursor.

"After all, you're the boring, goody two shoes twin with a stick up her ass. Maybe Hudson should've fucked your ass instead. That would've loosened you up—"

"Shut your ungrateful mouth!" I yell, causing my sister to jump.

My breath heaves as anger consumes every cell in my body, my heart thrumming out of my chest. I stare at her like a wild animal seconds before attacking.

She stares back with horrified wide eyes.

"How dare you?" I say. "I may be the boring, goody two shoes twin, but you're the crap sister."

"I'm—"

I stick a finger in her face. "Shut. Your. Mouth!"

Her jaw drops.

Arya doesn't know what to make of me.

It's called years of me biting my tongue, and taking, and taking, and taking until the dam broke.

I put some starch in my spine. "Why are you like this?" It's a rhetorical question because I keep barraging her. "Since Mom died, you've been a handful. But since Dad died, you've become the absolute worst version of yourself—"

"I was mourning—"

"It's always you, you, you. And fucking you. You're so selfish! You're not the only one who lost her mother and father!" I inhale a fortifying breath and soldier on. "What you just spat in my face was the last straw. Something amazing happens in my life and you shit all over it?! What the fuck? I would've never done that to you."

"You—"

I hold up a hand.

She shuts her mouth.

"You're supposed to be my sister. Not my downfall."

Her eyes narrow.

She's dying to speak, but I must look like I'm unhinged because she holds her tongue.

Smart.

"Here's how it's going to work between us from now on—"

"Who says you can decide on my behalf?" She even lifts a belligerent chin.

She's not as smart as I thought.

"Okay, let me rephrase that. Here's how *I'm* going to operate when it comes to you. The next time you find yourself knee-deep in shit—and we both know you will fuck up again soon, because that's what you do best—you're on your own." I point at her. "*You* clean up your mess. Don't count on me anymore. Heck, I don't even want to hear about it. Talk to your best friend Vanna. As for the apartment, you better start pulling your weight. Allow me to remind you, sis. You're responsible for half the money we need to cover rent, food, utilities, and the internet. No more bullshit excuses. I won't front you the money anymore—which you never pay back, despite your promises. You can shove your puppy dog eyes and crocodile tears up your ass. I'm not falling for it." I run my gaze up and down the length of her body. "I've spent my entire life protecting you. My vow reinforced each time we lost a parent. But it all stops here." I point to the floor. "I'm officially done. I wash my hands of you. You need to grow the fuck up."

Arya is stunned into silence.

Tears blur my vision.

I blink them away.

This feels like a divorce, but I should've put my foot down a long time ago. Maybe she would've shown me a modicum of respect.

Stick to your guns.

I snatch my handbag off the counter and leave my identical twin sister standing there.

She's the last person I ever thought I'd turn my back on.

I struggle with the lock, and finally manage. I open the door with force and bolt out of the bathroom.

By the time I reach the elevator, I'm crying.

To avoid questioning eyes, I make a beeline for the sweeping staircase.

I hurry down the stairs as fast as I can in my high heels.

When I reach the last step, I ready myself to make an exit, but bump into someone.

The impact causes my eyes to close.

Shit.

"I'm so sorry," I say.

Small hands hold me steady. "Angelica?"

My eyes pop open. "Grace?"

"What's going on?" Concern is audible in her voice. "Why are you crying?"

"I—" Tears I'm desperately trying to control, rattle my body. "I—" I'm trembling. "It's—"

Grace rubs her hands up and down my bare arms. "Take your time," she says.

"Everything..."—I inhale a shaky breath—"has gone to shit."

How quickly an evening can turn on its head.

I wasn't sure how Isobel and Rory were going to react after that spectacle. For a half an hour after Angelica left, I tried to pretend my mind wasn't elsewhere. Rory saw right through me. He put me out of my misery when he suggested we continue the conversation when I fly to LA. Thank God I fessed up yesterday. I doubt he would've been as understanding if I hadn't.

I have zero regret chewing Todd's head off for daring to talk the way he did to Angelica. He can shove his fucking attitude up his ass. As for that fight with Angelica, I tried to keep my opinions about her sister to myself, but I just couldn't. Broaching the subject of Arya is like stepping onto a landmine, and unfortunately, it blew up in my face.

"Tread carefully. When broken, some sibling relationships are irreparable."

Bryce's warning is what stopped me from forbidding Angelica from leaving the restaurant, even though every fiber of my being protested letting her walk away from me. I'll give her some breathing room so she can sort things out with her sister, but fuck if she thinks I'm willing to let her go.

After walking Rory and his wife to their chauffeured car and seeing them off, I pull out my phone, hoping Angelica has responded to my last five texts.

Nothing.

What the fuck?

I call her number.

It goes straight to voicemail.

Dammit.

I try again.

Same result.

I compose a quick text.

With my eyes glued to my phone, I will it to show me the three bouncing dots.

The stupid thing won't cooperate.

Since I don't know which venue is hosting the fundraiser Arya is at with her client, there are too many options to even attempt to guess.

I lift my eyes just in time to see my chauffeured Benz come to a stop right in front of the restaurant.

I climb into the backseat.

The chauffeur and I exchange the customary greetings, and he pulls into traffic.

I should go home, enjoy another drink before going to bed while watching a show or a movie to forget all about this drama-filled evening.

There's no way in hell I'll be able to fall asleep until I know Todd didn't go ape shit on her and her sister, and the twins are safe.

Since I have the determination of a Pitbull, I tell the chauffeur, "Change of plan. We're not going to the Upper West Side. We're going to Queens."

I've been sitting in front of Angelica's building for the last two hours.

You'd think I was on a stakeout, waiting for a suspect to come out of his or her hideaway.

There's still no sign of her.

I rang her buzzer so many times, I'm surprised the damn thing didn't break.

If she or her sister were home, someone would've told me to fuck off from the intercom.

Cursing underneath my breath, I compose another text.

Hudson: Where the fuck are you?

Several minutes pass without a response.

I call her phone and get the same result as earlier. It goes straight to voicemail.

I'm tempted to call Todd to get Arya's phone number, but I'm pretty sure I'm on his shit list.

Fuck.

"Do you still want to wait, sir?" the chauffeur asks, his eyes meeting mine in the rearview mirror.

I check the time on my phone.

Midnight.

"I do," I say. "Of course, you'll be compensated accordingly."

The chauffeur nods. "Very well, sir."

I hold his gaze in the mirror. "Make yourself comfortable, it might be a long night."

I let out a suffering sigh before shoving another huge piece of cheesecake into my mouth. If I wasn't this dejected, I'd appreciate the creaminess of Junior's delectable brownie explosion cheesecake. After all, it's not only a Brooklyn institution, it's one of the best cheesecakes in all five boroughs. The last time I tasted one of their cakes, Mom was still alive. It was her favorite dessert place. Dad would buy her favorite flavor and a sampler of the top selling flavors for her birthday each year, without fail. It was a big thing. I've wanted to go back for years, but never did for a couple of reasons. One, we don't own a car. Two, the hour-long commute on public transport to spend fifty dollars for dessert when you're struggling to buy the basics doesn't make sense. On our way to Grace's house, she declared wine and cake were a must, so she made a detour. It just had to happen on one of the worst days of my life.

Isn't it ironic?

"Do you want another glass of wine?" Grace asks.

"Yes, please."

She's still sipping on her first glass. I downed mine.

She pours the remainder of the wine. In my defense, it was a bottle she already had opened.

Once we arrived at her place, Grace bypassed the house tour and beelined straight to her kitchen for sugar and booze.

Exactly what I needed.

"Thank you," I say.

A sad smile curves Grace's lips.

Without her, I would've ended up crying all the way to Queens, eliciting worried glances from subway commuters.

When Grace took stock of my state after I bumped into her at the Pompadour Hotel, she was worried. I was crying and trembling so much, my explanation came out as a blubbering mess. Grace refused to let me go back to my place alone.

Bless her for caring.

I'm just about to take a swig of my drink, but my glass freezes midway.

"Crap!"

Grace's concerned eyes bounce to mine. "What is it?"

"My phone!"

"What about it?"

"I can't remember the last time I had it with me."

"Isn't it in your handbag?"

"No, it's too small. It's one of those designer micro handbags— Shit!" I tilt my head back, my eyes meeting the ceiling. *Argh!* "I must've left it at the Pompadour Hotel."

"Are you sure? Maybe you left it on the countertop at Junior's or it's in my car?"

I meet Grace's gaze. "I doubt it. When I was in the bathroom with my sister, I placed it on the countertop. Now, I remember grabbing my bag, but not my phone." *Fuck.* "Just when I thought my shitty day couldn't get any shittier."

"Wouldn't your sister have retrieved it?"

"Maybe. Maybe not. I bolted out of there after we had a

heated argument, where I yelled at her before ripping her a new one."

"Oh shit!"

"Yeah. Tonight is a night to remember." *Not!*

"We can call the hotel. If your sister left it there, someone else might've found it, unless the cleaning staff got to it first."

"Let's hope so. I can't afford to buy a new phone."

"I'm sure it won't come to that." *Fingers crossed.* "You've been giving me snippets of the evening. What transpired tonight?"

My eyes drop to the empty bottle of wine. "I'm going to need more wine for this conversation."

"It's a good thing we have a wine fridge stocked full with white wine and a nice stock of reds in our wine closet."

My confession comes in an excessive purge of words, spilling out of me with the same force as water jetting from a fireman's hose.

Grace's shocked expression speaks volumes.

She opens her mouth to say something, then closes it.

She does that a few times, and then grabs her glass of wine and gulps down a good swallow of the chardonnay.

"I know, it's a lot," I say. "I'm sure you must think I'm—"

"One, how dare you hide from me the fact you were the one singing my praises to Isobel Wolfe? Two, holy shit, I can't believe how you met sexy Hudson Kincaid. Three, Christ on a cracker, your twin sister is... she's... Jesus..."

"My twin is a train wreck," I say.

"Yes! I wasn't sure if I could say it to your face."

"Everybody else has."

"In that case, allow me to say this. Guilt might be niggling at you for having put your foot down, but you did the right thing. You were carrying way too much on your shoulders. No wonder you cracked."

"Yeah." I nod.

"We're so going to have to tackle Isobel and UTV.com another day, but first things first. Let's talk about your man—"

"I broke things off with Hudson, remember? So, he's no longer my man."

She considers me for a long beat.

I shift in my seat.

"You sacrificed your relationship with a guy who would do just about anything for you for the sake of your sister—your ungrateful sister."

I don't say a thing.

Grace soldiers on. "Arya is jealous. Plain and simple."

I respond with a one-shoulder shrug.

"It's too late now."

"It's not too late."

"I walked away from a guy who was trying to help me. I even told him to butt out. It's the equivalent of slapping him across the face."

"He needs to know what went down between you and your sister."

I let out a humorless laugh. "I don't know his number by heart. Without my phone, I can't get in touch with him."

"But you know where he lives?"

"Err... I do." My brows furrow. "What does that have to do with anything?"

Grace jumps to her feet. "Come on, slip back into your Louboutin shoes. We're going for a ride."

I look up at her. "Where are we going?"

"We're going to pay Mr. Hudson Kincaid a late-night visit."

"That's insane!" I shriek.

She shakes her head. "No, it's not." *Has she lost her marbles?* "Despite everything, Hudson was willing to stand by your side. *You*"—she points at me—"pushed him away. A man doesn't stick around unless he has it bad for a woman."

"I thought all this melodrama would've turned him off."

"Hudson is a powerful man. He didn't need you to push him off the boat. If he wanted no part of the drama, he would've jumped out himself and swam to shore."

It never crossed my mind. "I thought I was an embarrassment to him."

"If he didn't want to be around you, he would've dumped you a long time ago. Either that, or he would've asked Arya's boss for another girl. This is New York, baby. The land of opportunity. A billionaire has his pick... and he picked you."

I hang my head low.

"Chin up, buttercup!"

"You're really going to drive me to the Upper West Side? At this time of the night?"

"Hell yeah!"

I'm incredulous. "What about Kevin? Won't he be home soon?"

"It's boys' night out with his buddies. That's why you bumped into me at the hotel. I was having dinner with a friend from college who lives in Seattle. She's in the city for business." I can't thank my lucky stars enough. Being here with Grace beats being home alone, wallowing in self-pity. Actually, I'd probably be making a trip back to Manhattan to track down my phone. "I'll just text the hubby to let him know I'm a supporting character in your over the top romance. So obviously, I must do everything in my power to reunite the hero and the heroine after their big fight. Dark moment and all..." She says that with such seriousness.

For the first time since I was having dinner earlier this evening, I laugh.

"You're crazy, Grace."

"I'm a fantasy romance author. Sue me."

~

Grace and I waited an hour and a half in front of Hudson's house for his return.

He never showed up.

Eventually, we gave up.

On the way back from Hudson's house, Grace stopped by the Pompadour.

My phone was nowhere to be found.

I'm so over this day.

Since it's a bit late to show up at Vanna's house to see if my sister grabbed my phone, we return to Grace's house.

I really don't want to be alone tonight.

As we drive back to Brooklyn, insecurities niggle at me.

With every mile, I can hear my sister's voice louder and louder.

"Whoop-de-do you lost your virginity. He probably took pity on you. It's not like you can satisfy a powerful man with experience."

Did Hudson hook up with another woman because I chose my sister over him?

The thought makes my very soul ache.

Chapter 49

Hudson

I let out a sigh of frustration.

Pushing back against my desk, I stand up and stroll to the floor-to-ceiling window.

I tuck my hands inside the pockets of my pants to avoid smashing the glass with my fist.

Where the fuck are you, Angelica? And where the fuck is your twin sister?

At about four o'clock this morning, I woke up with a jolt, my neck aching from the weird position I'd fallen asleep in.

It took me a second to figure out why the hell I was still in a suit, sitting in the back of a Benz, with the chauffeur dozing off in the front seat. After attempting to call, text, and ring Angelica's buzzer another dozen times, there was no curtailing the sheer panic creeping inside me. Biting my pride, I called Todd, but it went straight to voicemail. Not willing to take chances, I reported both McQuinley sisters as missing to the police. I even told them about Ramsey and his mob connections.

Then, I contacted Bryce. Even though it was an ungodly time to call anyone, I needed his help. I couldn't shake off the thought that the Bratva had kidnapped my girl and her sister for some bizarre reason. This isn't Bryce's field of expertise, but he knows people who are pros at tracking missing people for a hefty fee.

After returning to my place for a shower and a change of clothes, I had the chauffeur drive me to my office. The only reason I'm here and not at home is because the office is centrally located, making it easy for me to rush back to Bryce's office or go to Queens at a moment's notice.

I look like shit and I feel like shit. I didn't even bother shaving. There's no way I'm going to be able to rest until I hear from Angelica or see her beautiful face.

I need to talk to her. I need... her.

I check my watch.

One p.m.

Goddammit!

I just want to pull my hair out.

My landline rings.

I snatch the phone off its cradle.

"Mr. Kincaid," Tracy, the receptionist says.

"Yes."

"I was coming back from lunch and a woman I thought I recognized was at the security desk. I made my way there, thinking an overzealous security guard was giving your girlfriend a rough time."

My back stiffens. "Angelica is downstairs?"

"No, sir. It turns out I was wrong." I deflate. "I didn't know your girlfriend had an identical twin."

"Arya McQuinley is downstairs?!"

"I cleared her with security. She's standing in front of my desk."

Holy fuck! "I'll be right there."

I hang up and rush to the receptionist's desk.

A woman stands with her back facing me.

"Oh, Arya, here's Mr. Kincaid," Tracy says.

The woman turns around, and my step falters.

Jesus Christ.

I approach Angelica's twin.

"Hi," Arya says with a little hand wave.

I stare at her for a long beat in disbelief.

"Um... I'm sorry to show up like this—"

"You look exactly like her."

"Hence, why we're identical twins," Arya says.

If Tracy had not told me Arya was waiting for me by her desk, I would've made a huge mistake. I would've dragged the woman wearing a yellow dress with big white flowers standing in front of me to my office, thinking she's the woman I'm falling for, to show her how much I missed her. Once behind closed doors, I would've fucked her mouth with my tongue before lifting the dress she's wearing and sinking balls deep inside her sweet, tight pussy. After spilling my seed into her, I would've scolded her for going MIA and skimming a decade off my life. But it's not my girl standing there.

I clear my throat. "I just didn't expect you'd... I've met identical twins, but you can tell which is which. None of them were an exact carbon copy of each other."

"We get that a lot," she says. "It's nearly impossible to differentiate us."

No shit.

I squint.

There's no mistaking Arya's puffy eyes.

I guess I'm not the only one who had a shit night.

My gaze sweeps across the reception area as if I expected to find Angelica. "Where's your sister? I've been trying to track her down since last night."

"That's why I'm here." Her expression is grim. "Can we talk?"

My heart squeezes.

Arya and I are sitting side by side in one of the conference rooms.

"We have a PO Box as an address on our website," I say. "How did you find me?"

"Todd."

"Ah." *I'm surprised.* "He was willing to help you after I chewed his head off last night?"

"When I showed up at his office, he was fuming, but by the time I had fessed up to how everything was my fault, he cut me some slack. Apparently, he grew up poor, and he did a few desperate things back in the day. In any case, he was willing to listen."

I didn't know that about Todd.

"Did he tell you what transpired at the restaurant?"

"He just said because of me, he caused a scene that could've been avoided." Her fingers fidget on her lap. "The only thing I could do was apologize." She looks remorseful, unless it's an act. "Oh, by the way, Todd is no longer mad at you."

My eyebrows rise high. "Just like that?"

"None of this was your fault, Hudson. I started this chain of events, and you got caught up in it."

I consider her for a long beat.

Maybe she's finally seeing the light.

I share everything that transpired last night after Todd spotted Angelica and me at the restaurant. I also share details of last night's stakeout in front of their apartment building, calling the police, Todd, and Bryce. I also tell her about the experts searching for them.

With a quick text, I update Bryce.

Hudson: One twin found. Another one still missing.

Bryce: Copy that. I'll keep the search going until you have an update.

Hudson: Thanks, man.

Arya tells me all about her fight with her sister, not feeling an ounce of remorse for leaving Angelica's phone in the bathroom, to waking up this morning riddled with guilt. After returning to their apartment and not finding her sister, she called Sadie, who chewed her head off. Then, she had Vanna drive her back to Todd's office before swinging by the Pompadour Hotel to find Angelica's phone. No surprise, it was no longer in the bathroom.

"I acted like an ass," Arya says.

"What did you tell your sister for her to storm out of the bathroom like that?"

She averts her gaze.

"Arya."

She comes clean.

My jaw drops.

"I was in shock."

Talk about rude awakening. "I bet."

"I guess I deserved it. I said some really nasty things."

"Why did you do it? I know I'm biased here, but your sister puts your well-being before hers. Why would you turn on her like that?"

Arya twists her lips one way and another.

"Talk to me."

Her green eyes settle on me. And not for the first time, I'm hit with a pang of longing.

"I was jealous," she says.

"Of the fact she had a boyfriend?"

"I've been jealous of her for so long, I can't even remember which incident started it."

I don't get it. "I admire Angelica's tenacity, bravery, her goodness, her fierce protectiveness of you, and the seemingly unconditional love she has for you. On top of that, you have the same face. You're as beautiful as she is. What's there to be jealous about?"

She hesitates. "Angelica has always had her shit together. I was always the scatterbrain twin. After Mom passed away, I became the lost twin, even more so after our father died." Her voice chokes. "I knew no matter what I did, my sister would always be there. I didn't have to grow up. She was adult enough for both of us." She lowers her eyes. "So, I went from *making* mistakes to *becoming* a mistake." She locks her gaze onto me. "The choice of asshole boyfriends was par for the course. Birds of a feather and all..." I listen without interrupting. "I knew which strings to pull with my sister, so it was easy to manipulate her. Angelica McQuinley. Always reliable." She lets out a humorless laugh. "Shy of committing a murder and hiding the body, she would've done anything for me." She waves a finger at me. "You're proof."

"And that's how you repay her?" I couldn't help myself.

Green eyes that don't belong to my girl hold mine for a long beat. "She's only had one boyfriend, but that guy was a *boy*. She's never really been with a man. While I've been on a rampage, beefing up my collection of less than desirable men, she hit the jackpot with you." She lowers her eyes for a beat. "My claws came out."

I shake my head. "That pesky green-eyed monster made you do it."

"Something like that." She lets out a heavy sigh. "I've never seen Angelica as angry as I did last night. She was unrecognizable. She's never lost it before. Not even when our parents died. She cried her eyes out and she was devastated, sure. But it didn't cripple her. She kept moving forward—"

"Probably because she didn't have a choice."

Arya nods. "That too, since I was useless." She doesn't speak for a long beat.

I don't rush her.

"Last night she was... out of control for the first time in her life. This morning it hit me full force. I'd fucked up. Again." She hangs her head low. "I was disrespectful, and I cut her off at the knee. She didn't deserve that."

Damn right she didn't.

After a long beat, I say, "I think your sister needs to hear that."

"I know." A fine sheen forms in Arya's eyes.

I place a comforting hand on her arm and give it a quick squeeze before letting go.

"So, you don't have the faintest idea where Angelica might've gone?"

She shakes her head. "I came here, because I thought maybe she was staying at your place, but now I know you're as clueless as I am about her whereabouts." A tear slides down her cheek. She wipes it away.

"Maybe she's staying at a friend's place?"

"Sadie is her best friend, and she's in LA."

"She must have other friends?"

"She kind of retreated after Dad died, and she's been wearing a lot of hats..."

I sit on that for a second. “Maybe I should get Bryce to get his contact to check hotels.”

“We don’t have the budget for a hotel—”

“I think last night qualifies as extenuating circumstances.”

She shakes her head. “She’d never part with that kind of money. For a hotel room in New York City? No way.”

“Then where the hell is she?” I slam my hand on the conference room table, anger and worry taking the best out of me.

Arya jumps.

“I refuse to believe something bad happened to her—”

“I’m sure she’s somewhere blowing off steam.”

“Where? Think, Arya.” I place a hand on Arya’s arm. “I’m going out of my mind. I regret letting her go last night.”

She bites her lip and glances up at me from under her lashes. “This is all my fault.”

From the corner of my eye, I catch movement in the corridor.

I do a double take.

My gaze clashes with Angelica’s, who’s standing next to a red-faced Tracy.

And if the expression on her face is any indication, Arya’s twin sister is mad as hell...

Chapter 50

Angelica

When I arrived at Hudson's office and Tracy told me my sister was here, I argued she was mistaken.

She assured me she wasn't.

I had to see it with my own two eyes.

The frantic beating of my heart at the idea of seeing Hudson's handsome face again quickly turns to painful thumps as I come to a stop in front of a conference room.

My jaw is practically on my chest.

Thud.

Thud

Thud.

The shock of seeing my sister sitting there with Hudson's hand on her arm destabilizes me.

What in the actual fuck?

How did Arya know where to find Hudson?

Is that why she was trying to convince me I didn't have what it takes to hold on to a man like him?

She wanted him to herself?!

Treacherous bitch.

Yesterday, I tell Hudson we need to cool things off, and now he's hooked up with my sister?

Another reason why I've had only one boyfriend since high school is because when a guy I was interested in met my sister, he always ended up entangled in the *fun* twin. Inevitably, the guy would lose interest in me, hoping he might score with the other twin. Arya wouldn't date them because of the sister code —and citing our taste in men are at opposite ends of the spectrum—but still, it was a slap in the face and a reminder I was the *boring* twin.

Hurt strikes me.

Here we fucking go again.

Last night was enough humiliation to last me a lifetime.

Fuck that.

I force myself to swallow past the bitterness, walk around Tracy, and flee.

"Angelica! Wait!" Hudson's plea comes from over my shoulder, but I ignore him.

You want to be with the fun twin? Knock yourself out, buddy!

These Louboutin heels weren't meant for running, but that's what I do. I run.

As I reach the elevator, I spot the exit sign.

If I wait for a car, he'll catch up to me and feed me some bullshit story.

No thanks.

I push on the door with all my might to open it. I freeze when I reach the first step.

I look down at the million steps that lead down to the lobby and curse under my breath.

I'm trapped in the stairwell.

Great escape plan, Angelica.

My chest rises and falls as I try to catch my breath.

I need a Plan B. Fast.

The door slams against the wall with a deafening bang.

I jump, placing a hand against my thundering heart.

"Where the fuck are you going?"

Hudson's roar has me whirling around.

"It looked like things were cozy-cozy in that conference room. Sorry for interrupting."

His blue eyes narrow to slivers.

If I'm going to get dumped, I'm not going down like a doormat.

Hudson approaches me like a tiger approaches its prey.

There's nothing but a wall of muscles before me and I have to tip my head back to meet his irate gaze.

I glance over my shoulder.

Could I make it down without breaking an ankle?

Um... Maybe not.

"What's so interesting down there?"

I turn my attention on him. His blue eyes darken to the color of a stormy night. "Why don't you go back to your..."—I do a dismissive hand gesture—"*meeting.*"

He narrows his eyes even further, his jaw clenching.

God, I've missed those gorgeous eyes. I've missed every gorgeous part of him.

If I wasn't this pissed off, I'd care that he looks tired.

And what's up with the unshaven look?

I must say, the dark scruff framing his beautiful mouth is—

Focus!

Don't be fooled. He's not who you thought he was.

"I don't like your tone." There's a warning in his voice.

I cross my arms over my chest and lift a stubborn chin. "I don't like being played for a fool."

His eyes flare. "What the fuck are you talking about?"

"You and my sister." Annoyance causes the words to come out in an angry huff.

With a cocked eyebrow that makes him look entirely too damn sexy, his Paul Newman eyes rake over my body.

"Me and your sister?" *Does he have a hearing problem?*

"Yes, you and my sister."

"You're concerned about me and your sister meeting at my office, in plain view, in one of our conference rooms that's as transparent as a fishbowl?" He gives me another onceover. "In the meantime, you're the one wearing the same clothes as last night and you've been MIA for over seventeen fucking hours without an explanation!"

I flinch.

"Do you know how fucking worried I've been?"

I flinch again.

"Cut the bullshit and insinuations about me and your sister."

"I know what I saw—"

"What you witnessed was two people who care deeply about you. We were simply putting our heads together to figure out where the fuck you were. Don't turn it into something it's not."

I'm not convinced. "Oh yeah?" I snort. "My sister has been in Miami all week with DJ, whatever his fucking name is. I never mentioned where you worked because she's been ghosting me. You two have been in contact with each other behind my back. How else would she be here?"

Hudson pinches the bridge of his nose and lets out a long exhale. "*Todd* told Arya how to find me after she fessed up everything to him."

Huh?

"Oh."

"Yes, oh."

"So... you're not interested in the more *fun* twin?"

He stares at me with an expression I can't decipher.

"You *are* more interested in my sister?" My voice cracks.

"Stop it with this nonsense! I just met your sister. She's been sitting in my conference room for twenty minutes. A half an hour, tops. We never exchanged a text or phone call. Not one." He seems to collect himself. "I know I fell for you the second I saw you, and yes, the two of you are so alike, I would've never been able to—"

"Don't tell me Arya tried to pass as me."

He studies me with such intensity. I hold my breath, waiting for the other shoe to drop.

"If I wasn't this relieved to know you were safe and sound, I'd shake some sense into you, woman. Everything that's come out of your mouth in the past few minutes is craziness."

My eyes widen. "Arya isn't here to seduce you?"

Without warning, he grabs me in his arms and brings me to his chest, embracing me in his hold. "No, silly goose. I should take you over my knee for entertaining that line of thought."

I wouldn't be opposed to it.

He drops a soft kiss against my nose. "Arya is genuinely concerned. In fact, she feels guilty about a lot of things."

She does?

"Just so we're crystal clear, I have zero interest in your sister—the fun twin, as you call her. I'm *only* interested in the fucking sexy hellion twin I'm holding in my arms."

I can't help my laugh.

He joins me.

"Now are you gonna tell me where you were all night?" he asks.

"I was at Grace's house in Brooklyn."

He frowns. "Your client? The one I met at the Pompadour Hotel?"

"Yes."

"I didn't realize you had that kind of relationship with her."

"I didn't until last night."

"You lost me."

I share the details of how I bumped into Grace as I was stumbling out of the Pompadour Hotel after a big fight with Arya.

"I had a little wine with dessert when we got to her place, but I deep dived at the bottom of a bottle when we got back from your place—"

"You were at my place? When?"

"I told Grace about putting our relationship on ice because I thought you deserved better—"

"Did you ever hear me say that?" He looks affronted.

I shake my head. "I made the decision for both of us."

"Don't ever do that again. If I didn't want to be with you, I would've dumped your fine ass a long time ago."

"I promise I won't do that ever again." I giggle.

"What's this about you driving to my place last night?"

"Grace was pretty pissed off at me. She took it upon herself to get us to clear the air. She drove me to your place late last night. We stayed in front of your house for a long while, but you never showed up—"

"Because I was doing my own stakeout in front of *your* building."

"Wh—what?"

"When you weren't returning my calls or texts, I had my chauffeur drive me to Queens. I refused to return to my place until I knew you were safe."

I'm speechless.

"I'm not sure when I dozed off, but I woke up at four o'clock this morning. I tried to get in touch again. No answer. I called the police, and Bryce."

"Wh—what?" I really need to start using other words.

He stares at me with a pained expression. "I was worried sick."

I'm shocked. Flabbergasted. Elated.

Since Todd's verbal lynching, I've ridden the tide of more emotions than I've experienced in years. Not since my parents died have I been on this kind of emotional roller coaster.

"You—you did that for me?"

"And I'd do it again like that." He snaps his fingers.

My heart beats a thousand miles an hour at his declaration.

Hot fire burns in his eyes. "Until Arya showed up, I was going out of my mind."

I can't believe he'd go to that length to make sure I was okay.

I place a hand against his chest. "You're such a good man."

He takes my hand and kisses it softly. "You're worth it."

I'm tingling all over.

I'm such an idiot.

"I would've been here sooner," I say, "but like I said, I might've had a few too many to drink last night. Since Grace believes it's impolite to let guests drink alone, she joined me. I don't have any recollection of when we passed out on her couch. Her husband went to work this morning, but didn't wake us up. I can just imagine the sight of us." I shake my head. "In any case, I woke up at twelve, confused. Then everything came back to me. Once again, Grace was a trooper. I got here as soon as I could. I'm so sorry if I made you worry so much."

"That's behind us." He reaches out and brushes a strand of hair before tucking it behind my ear. "I have you back in my arms. Where you belong."

"God, Hudson, when you say things like that..."

"I already told you, angel, I only say what I mean."

With that, he catches my mouth in a fervent, hot, passionate kiss.

He pushes me backwards until my back meets the wall.

I hiss and he slides his tongue between my lips.

Yes.

The press of his muscular body against mine is heaven.

The same goes for his hard cock digging into my tummy as my hand grips the hair at the back of his head, fisting it like if I don't, I'll free fall to the lobby.

Mother of God.

He breaks our kiss with a gasp. "Fuck, I missed your mouth." His mouth dips to my throat, and he peppers hot kisses all over. "I missed every glorious inch of you."

"Last night was a mess."

"Shhh..." His hands tunnel through my hair. With his eyes boring into mine, he strokes my mane. "It's all behind us."

"Okay."

"Enough talking." His teeth find my earlobe, and he bites down. I nearly buckle at the knees. "More kissing and misbehaving."

I'm on the verge of begging him to do it again, but his mouth finds mine.

As he tongue-fucks my mouth, he grabs my ass and lifts me off my feet.

Circling my legs around his slender waist, I wedge him against my aching pussy.

He deepens the kiss, ravishing my mouth, our tongues intertwined in a wild dance.

His hunger for me is brutal.

I tighten my legs around him to pull him closer.

My panties are wetter with each tongue stroke.

Sweet baby Jesus, his tongue is like magic.

I'll never get tired of kissing this man. Never.

When he eases back from the kiss, heaving a curse under his breath, I groan my disapproval.

"This dress is sexy as fuck on you. It was a struggle for me to focus on the conversation last night. All I wanted was to be inside you. I coaxed myself to be patient, as I counted the hours until I had my fill of you. That never happened." *Such a tragedy.* "No wonder I'm as hungry as a wolf." *God, I can't believe how much he wants me.* "If we keep this up, I'll have no other choice but to rip off your panties, unzip my fly, and fuck you senseless against this wall."

Yes, please.

"But you're too loud." *It's as if he could read my thoughts—Wait. What?* "The whole office would hear you scream out my name."

"Hey, I'm offended."

He chuckles. "Own it, angel. You're a screamer when you come."

"It's your fault for being such a great lover."

"Should I lower my standards?"

"No! Don't you dare!"

"My girl loves it when I make her come her head off. Noted."

The predatory way he's looking at me makes me even wetter.

"As much as I want to fuck your sweet pussy—and I'm desperate for you—the last thing I want is for someone to enter the stairwell in an attempt to save whoever is screaming so loud, just to catch me fucking my girlfriend."

I blush.

With care, he lowers me to my feet.

A slow, sweet smile spreads over his face. "To say you're the best thing that has ever happened to me, Angelica, would be a huge understatement."

My smile is wobbly. "You're the best thing to have happened to me, too, Hudson."

"I could've never fathomed falling this fast and hard for a woman I was supposed to hook up with for just one night. A woman who was supposed to be nothing more than arm candy. You're a hell of a lot more." His eyes are piercing mine. "Don't ever doubt how I feel about you. Don't ever doubt us."

My heart gallops.

I place my hands on the hands that are cupping my face. Tears well up in my eyes. "I won't."

"Good."

I'm sobbing now, a complete hot mess.

"Don't cry, angel. Your sister will think I'm the one who upset you."

"They're happy tears."

He chuckles. "Let's go see Arya. You two have a lot to talk about."

As we stroll hand in hand to the conference room, a few of Hudson's employees stare our way.

Crap.

Worried, I glance up at him.

He doesn't seem fazed.

Although, it still bothers me, that brings me some level of comfort. It wasn't my intention to create drama, but it seems I have a knack for doing that a lot lately.

When we reach the conference room, Tracy is comforting Arya.

Hudson clears his throat.

Both Tracy and Arya look our way.

My sister's teary eyes meet mine and she jumps to her feet and runs to me.

I open my arms.

She slams into me and hugs the hell out of me.

"I'm so sorry, Ange, for being an asshole."

"I'm sorry for losing it and yelling at you. It's been eating at me. I didn't mean to do that. I don't know what came—"

"Stop blaming yourself. It's all my fault. Everything that came out of my mouth last night was fueled by jealousy. I— I —" She hiccups. "I was a bitch. You're an incredible sister. Without you, I'd be lost."

I burst into tears.

Chapter 51

Angelica

Two and a half months later

Hudson and I trail behind the maître d'hôtel as we make our way through an animated crowd of Manhattan high rollers. The place is packed. Not surprising on a Friday night at the Panorama Room. The chic, oval-shaped restaurant-slash-bar is located on Roosevelt Island, which sits in the East River, mid-distance between Manhattan and Queens. It just so happens to be one of the best rooftop bars in the city, and one of the few that affords 360-degree unobstructed views of Manhattan. The show-stopping sculptural mirrored DJ booth near the entrance is also a must-see.

Excitement bubbles up when the maître d'hôtel stops in front of a table right in front of the floor-to-ceiling window.

One of the best spots in the house! Yay!

I glance around the room, searching for a familiar face. Disappointment tinges at me as my eyes bounce from one stranger to another.

Bummer.

"Madame." The maître d'hôtel pulls out a chair for me.

"Thank you."

"Your waitress will be with you momentarily," he says, as he helps me to my seat.

Even though the sun has set on this cool October day, the city's lights allow me to see far in the horizon.

It's breathtaking.

I lean into the table. "What a view."

Hudson nods. "Even the second time around, it's something else."

The last time we were here, it was still summer, so even at seven p.m., the sun has not set yet, offering a spectacular view from the 18th floor of this building. We were even able to catch a glimpse of the Bronx.

"Do you know what you want to eat?" Hudson asks.

"I was happy with what we ate last time."

"Same here."

The first time we came, I nearly swallowed my tongue when I opened the menu. Let's just say, this panoramic view comes at a price.

Hudson scolded me when I settled for the cheapest item on the menu and a Perrier with lemon. In the end, we went with the waiter's recommendation. It was food orgasm.

Even though I didn't take a peek at the menu, I'm still fully aware this meal is going to cost a fortune. Hudson and I have been dating for three months, and I'm still not used to his billionaire status. I doubt I ever will be. We keep butting heads every time he wants to spoil me.

A gorgeous woman grinning from ear to ear approaches our table.

My grin matches hers.

I was hoping she'd be our waitress. My wish is granted.

"Good evening. My name is Arya, and I'll be your waitress tonight."

"Good evening, Arya," I say, doing my best to keep a straight face.

"Arya"—Hudson's eyes ping-pong from mine to the waitress—"it's uncanny how much you look like my girlfriend."

"That's one of the blessings of being an identical twin," Arya says.

We smile warmly at each other.

She returns her attention to Hudson. "It seems like you got the better twin, though."

"You mean, I got the *older* twin. I know from personal experience, the other twin is pretty incredible as well."

My sister's cheeks redden. "Thanks for saying that," she says with a touch of shyness.

I reach out and squeeze her hand.

She squeezes back.

My sister was unstoppable when it came to getting herself into reckless situations. But now that her life is more orderly, she's still uncomfortable when Hudson or I praise her.

"What can I get you to start with?" she asks, slipping back into waitress mode.

"*Fleur de Miraval Exclusivement Rosé Champagne*, please," Hudson says.

Ooo la la.

Top scores for that nearly flawless pronunciation.

The combination of Hudson's Matthew McConaughey Texan drawl and the French words is so darn sexy.

Maybe I'll have to ask him to talk dirty to me in French later...

"That's one of our finest labels," Arya says in a professional tone.

"A night of celebration calls for the best champagne in the house," Hudson says.

"How exciting!" Arya says with a grin.

"Very!" Hudson winks at me.

My sister's green eyes shift to mine.

I give her a *I don't know what's going on* shrug.

She returns her attention to my boyfriend. "Would you like appetizers?"

"We'll start with a double order of the shrimp cocktail," Hudson says. "We'll wait a bit before ordering our Tomahawk steaks."

"Very well." Arya grabs the menus. "I'll be right back."

With that, my sister scurries off.

I follow her receding form, proud of the drastic transformation.

We're back to our roots as natural blondes.

But that's just one of the many things that's changed for Arya.

Her classy black blouse and black cigarette pants are a world of difference to the skimpy outfits she used to wear at her previous waitressing job. And they weren't uniforms, they were her selections. Her clothing still flatters her slender curves, but she's no longer desperate to call attention to herself.

"She's doing well," Hudson says.

My eyes shift to his. "It's like night and day."

"The best part is, the decision to change came from her."

I nod. "Yeah."

Miracles do happen.

The fight in the Pompadour Hotel's bathroom was my sister's wake-up call. After our hug fest at Hudson's office, we went back to our apartment and talked all afternoon until it was time to prepare dinner. In the end, I was able to make her understand we come as a package deal, which means her fuckups could shake the foundation of my relationship with Hudson.

She took that to heart.

The next day, Todd called her, ready to give her the *Pretty Woman* position back. To my relief, she turned him down. Instead of relying on the lucrative money she would've made as an escort, Arya picked up as many extra shifts as possible at the SoHo bar she used to work at to pay off her debt to her loan shark.

One positive thing to come out of her Miami trip is this new waitressing gig. Since it's Arya we're talking about, it landed in her lap in the most outrageous way. She overheard DJ Bromley telling someone over the phone Vanna and her would be up for an orgy with a bunch of his buddies. The girls escaped while the DJ was entertaining a crowd at a club. It just so happened they hired a shared ride with a waitress who works at the Panorama Room. Arya and her hit it off, and they kept in touch.

Five weeks after her return, her new friend told her about an opening. She got a job offer after the second interview. Not only has my sister been working here full-time for a month, but the tips at Panorama Room are insane.

"You've been secretive about the reason why we're here tonight," I say to my boyfriend. "Are you going to finally tell me what we're celebrating?"

I only found out during the ride from Queens to the restaurant, Hudson made the reservation earlier this week while he was still in Las Vegas. That's as much as he was willing to divulge.

"I got a call from Rory Wolfe."

I sit a little straighter in my chair.

I'm just about to ask a question, but my sister returns with the appetizers, while another waiter carries the ice bucket, champagne, and flutes.

Arya places our shrimp dishes on the table and the waiter pours the champagne.

With a bow, the waiter disappears.

"Enjoy," Arya says.

"Thank you," Hudson says.

He lifts his champagne flute.

I do the same.

"Here's to Grace Halcyon!"

I wrinkle my nose. "We're celebrating Grace? Why?" Then I quickly add, "She's fabulous and all, but what does she have to do with tonight's celebration?"

"Without *The Court Games*, I'd still be trying to convince Rory to switch payment processor provider."

"You got the contract?! Wait. I thought you were in Vegas. Was Rory in Vegas as well?"

Hudson shakes his head. "Rory called me while I was in Vegas to let me know he and his brother had come to a decision. I had my executive assistant shuffle things around to free up my last day so I could fly to LA. I prefer to close these big deals face to face. After three months of back and forth, Rory and Roark Wolfe signed on the dotted line. It's a huge contract."

"That's awesome! Totally worth celebrating!"

I extend my flute. "To Grace and an amazing deal!"

He clinks it. "Hear! Hear!"

We both take a long sip of the effervescent nectar.

"Wow, this is fabulous!"

"At five hundred dollars a bottle, it better be."

I nearly choke.

I gingerly place my flute on the table, careful not to spill a drop of this very expensive booze.

"Big celebration." Hudson winks.

All righty...

He takes another long sip before dropping his glass on the table. "You know who else we're celebrating tonight?"

"Who?"

"You."

"Me?" I frown my confusion. "We already celebrated last month."

He shakes his head. "We're not celebrating your new position as a junior script editor of UTV.com's New York office. We're celebrating something much more monumental."

We celebrated my new position in Vegas over the Labor Day's long weekend. Hudson flew in Arya and Sadie for the occasion. It was wild.

I was certain the soap opera scene with Todd had left a bad taste in Isobel's mouth. I never found my phone. I refused Hudson at first when he offered to buy me a new one, but in the end, I caved in when he told me he'd give me his old phone and buy a new one for himself. Sneaky bastard. What he didn't tell me was that his phone—the latest iPhone model on the market—was a month old. A couple of days after setting up my phone, I received a surprise text from Isobel. Three rounds of interviews later—two of them in Los Angeles—and I nearly lost my head when I was offered the position. Even though I'm a full-time employee, I kept my favorite clients as side editing gigs. Grace is one of them.

"More monumental than landing a kickass job most editors and script writers would give up a vital organ for?"

"Yes."

I'll humor him. "Let's hear it."

"*The Court Games* was the icebreaker, but your personality won Isobel over. That's why Rory gave me the time of day after so many failed attempts."

"I'm happy I was able to help."

"You did more than help. You kicked the door open for me."

I squirm in my seat. "It's nothing."

"There you go belittling yourself again."

I blush. "Guilty as charged."

"The champagne and fancy meal aren't the only ways I want to show you my appreciation for what you did for me and my business—"

"Hudson, this is more than enough."

"Not as far as I'm concerned." He reaches for the inside of his black suit jacket and pulls out a white envelope. He places it on the table and slides it towards me. My name is scripted in his distinctive handwriting. "Thank you, angel."

My eyes meet his. "What's this?"

"Open it."

"Why don't you tell me?"

"Because it won't be as fun."

"Can't you give me a hint?"

"They're not season tickets to your favorite team sport."

"I don't have a favorite team sport."

"It's a good thing I didn't buy you season tickets, then."

"Joker."

"If you think I'm going to make it easy on you, I won't. If you're too afraid of finding out what's in that envelope, fine by me. I'll simply say, if you don't open it, you're missing out big time."

He's piqued my curiosity.

I grab the envelope and carefully open it.

I peek inside before meeting Hudson's gaze.

His passive face doesn't give a hint.

Hmm...

I summon my lady balls and pull out a sheet of paper.

When I unfold it, my jaw drops to the table.

What in the actual fuck?

I squint, hoping that's enough to make the gargantuan amount that's staring back at me a lot smaller.

Nope.

The enormous number is still staring at me.

I'm hyperventilating.

Dear God and all the saints above.

I tear my eyes from the check with an eye-popping number and stare up at Hudson in shock.

I'm speechless.

A cocky grin splits his gorgeous lips.

I find my voice. "Are you insane?"

"That's not quite the response I was expecting."

"I can't accept this. I mean... this is a lot of money." *A lot of freaking money.*

"I know it's a lot of money, and yes, you can accept it."

I shake my head vehemently. "No, I can't. I didn't do enough to deserve this."

"I disagree," he says. "The contract with UTV.com is extremely lucrative. Not even my top salespeople were able to make headway with the Wolfe brothers. Those LA moguls are tough nuts to crack... but you did." He points to the check I'm still clenching in my trembling hands. "That's the kind of bonus I would've given to anyone in my company who would've been able to close that deal."

"Oh." I can't think of anything more to say.

"Remember what I've been telling you since the beginning?"

"This goes beyond buying me a new designer wardrobe at Saks and expensive jewelry."

"You're right. But back then, you were just a woman I had the hots for." His gaze shifts to my mouth before locking onto my eyes. "If I can't take care of the woman I love, what kind of man does that make me?"

The world stops spinning.

"Wh—what?" I croak. "You—you love me?"

He stands up, rounds the table, and lowers himself to the floor next to me.

He grabs my hand and kisses each of my fingertips, one by one. "Yes, angel. I fucking love you."

I'm surprised I could hear that past the thumping in my ears.

Every day, I've fallen in love a little more with Hudson Kincaid, but I was too afraid to let him know how I felt.

"I love you so much, Hudson." My voice cracks. "I thought... maybe it was one-sided."

"You know it wasn't."

Elation and relief thrum through my veins and my heart blooms.

He loves me.

"Okay, maybe I knew you liked me a little."

"You're so full of it."

I laugh. "I didn't want to assume."

"Good thing I told you how I feel about you." His eyes bore into mine. "I want more of you, angel. Every damn day."

I swear, this must be a dream. And if it is, God, don't you dare wake me up.

"Me too."

His boyish smile is endearing. "Are you going to let me take care of you?"

I respond with a one-shoulder shrug. "Yes."

What's the point of fighting him? He always gets his way.

My gaze lowers to the check.

This money represents the financial freedom I never thought Arya and I could ever hope for.

Bye-bye crushing student loan.

Hello worry-free living.

Anemic savings account, you're getting beefed up.

Here's looking at you, saving for a down payment on a house.

Old TV, you're out. We're getting a brand-new flat screen!

Trusted old MAC, you're getting a baby sister.

Sexy gray dream-couch featured on my vision Pinterest board, you're so mine!

Yevsei Dzhikiya, consider Arya's debt paid. Sayonara, Mr. Loan Shark!

For the first time in forever, we're ahead of the game.

"Is that a *hell yes* or just a *meek yes*?" Hudson asks.

I shake my head. "It's a hell yes, you crazy man."

"It's about fucking time," he says. "I love you. So damn much, angel."

"God, Hudson—"

He grabs me by the back of the neck and crushes my lips in a passionate kiss.

I drown in this wonderful man.

A few people around us clap and whistle.

"We're drawing a little too much attention to ourselves," he says, breaking the kiss. "We'll pick up where we left off when we get to my place later."

The naughty promise sends a flurry of excitement between my thighs. "I'll hold you to it."

"Dirty girl." He maps my neck with his mouth.

I giggle.

He stands to his full height and returns to his seat.

He takes a long sip of champagne.

I grab the check made out to my name, tuck it back in the envelope, fold it, and hide it in the safety of my handbag.

Holy shit.

I just can't believe this.

"Thank you, Hudson, from the bottom of my heart. This money will go a long way. Finally, I'll be in the black." Within a few days I can be debt-free. Unbelievable.

"You earned it." He holds my gaze. "Now that you've accepted the money, I can tell you about the catch."

My eyes widen.

And... the other shoe drops.

"What catch?" My tone is cautious.

"That amount isn't a onetime thing."

"Huh?"

"That money is a bonus for helping me land the most coveted account. Every month, my company will be collecting a percentage of the transaction fees from UTV.com, which will be colossal. On top of that, Rory and Roark are opening a lot of doors for me, which means even more business—"

"It's all good, right?"

"Yes."

"So... what's the catch?"

"The check was for effect. From now on, for the duration of the contract, a percentage of the transaction fees my company collects from the Wolfe brothers will be deposited straight into your bank account. Every. Single. Year. And since we're taking over their account next month, you'll get another nice check for this year."

I'm dead.

Epilogue

Hudson

Nine months later

The waiter stacks our empty plates. "How was the food?"

"Outstanding," Angelica says at the same time as I say, "You live up to your reputation."

The waiter smiles wide. "We like happy diners."

"We're coming back for sure," Angelica says.

"Absolutely," I say.

Latte di Rosa is a high-end Italian seafood and homemade pasta restaurant in Brooklyn. Other than the exquisite Barolo Riserva imported from Italy that will set you back by two-hundred-sixty-dollars *per glass*, the backyard patio is another distinctive aspect to the restaurant. Scaffolding has been decorated with five thousand large silk flowers resembling hydrangeas and jasmine, transforming the backyard of this Michelin-starred eatery into the perfect setting for a night out with my girl on a perfect July evening.

"Would you like to see the dessert menu?" the waiter asks.

I look at my girlfriend. "I'm going to have dessert, but I'll need a minute... or ten."

"The lady has spoken," I say.

"Would you like more wine or coffee maybe?" the waiter asks.

"I'm good for now," she says.

"Same here," I say.

"Let me know when you're ready for dessert," the waiter says before scurrying off.

I run a languorous finger along her arm. "I missed you."

"You already told me that."

"You have a problem with me telling you again?"

"Nope!" She grins from ear to ear.

I was in Australia for the past two weeks with a few of my VPs, meeting with a handful of big accounts we recently acquired. The face-to-face paid off in securing new business. The trip Down Under was a great investment of time. But it meant being away from my girl.

I came back yesterday morning. The jetlag is a bitch, but no way was I going to postpone tonight. I missed my girl something fierce.

As much as I would've loved to take Angelica with me to Australia, it wasn't possible. Last month, UTV.com secured the rights to Grace's novel with plans to turn it into a multi-season series. While I was away, my girl was in LA for a week-long brainstorming session between the West Coast and East Coast screen writers who are part of *The Court Games* production team. Yeah, my girlfriend is kicking ass and taking no prisoners at her new position.

Speaking of UTV.com, Sadie joined the New York office a couple of weeks ago. She's part of the acquisition team that scouts through lists of great books to pinpoint the gems that would make riveting TV series or movies.

"I love the dress on you."

"I was planning on wearing something else, but *someone* had fashion demands for tonight." She makes a show of rolling her eyes dramatically.

I cock a brow. "Are you saying I'm a tyrant?"

"That's exactly what I'm saying."

"Haven't we already established you always benefit from me being a tyrant?"

"You're mistaken, Mr. Kincaid. We haven't established anything. *You're* the one who determined that on your own without requiring my input."

I tsk. "Such sass."

"I'm telling it like it is."

Damn right I had requirements about her fashion selection for tonight.

She's wearing a red dress with frilly short sleeves and a plunging V-neck that shows off her spectacular tits. The bottom part of the dress flares out in a seductive way. Since I know shit about women's fashion, Trenner, Saks Fifth Avenue's personal shopper, helped me pick out the dress and new designer shoes Angelica is wearing to celebrate her new promotion. The man knows his stuff. He's been my ally over the past year every time I wanted to surprise the gorgeous woman who stole my lonely heart.

She's still smiling wide at me.

I saw that beautiful smile every day on our video chats, but nothing compares to experiencing the full voltage of that beaming smile when she's sitting right next to me.

She brushes a strand of hair behind her ear.

I'd still love her if she were bald, but I prefer her as a blonde than a brunette.

The contrast between the vibrant color of the dress and my girl's golden hair is arresting.

She could stop traffic.

My eyes dip to her neckline where a constellation of diamonds nestles between her breasts.

Even though I've bought her two other necklaces, her favorite one remains the one with the dangling stars. My chest swells with pride every time I see it on her.

"The cat got your tongue?" she asks.

Everything about her expression suggests she thinks she has a leg up on me.

Such innocence.

"I can disprove your statement like that." I snap my fingers.

"You want to prove that by you being a tyrant, we both benefit? Ha! Bring. It. On."

I lean into the table. "What color are your panties?"

She jolts but recovers quickly.

Her eyes shift left to right.

She's assessing how closely the other patrons are sitting to our table. I'd bet my fortune on it.

We're not the only ones out here, but each table is isolated thanks to all the natural and artificial shrubbery. The music playing from the speakers helps to keep conversations private.

"Why do you want to know?"

"Don't answer a question with a question."

She pulls her lower lip between her teeth. "They're white."

"What kind?"

She cups her hands around her mouth so only I can hear. "I'm wearing a thong."

"In other words, you're wearing a scrap of fabric."

"A *sexy* scrap of fabric," she says, lifting her pointy little chin in a hoity toity way.

You have no idea where I'm going with this. "So, it's easy to maneuver."

She frowns. "You mean shift? Move around? Remove?"

"All the above."

"Well, yes. It's not like they're glued to my behind."

"Sounds like you're wearing a perfect item to..."—I look over his shoulder before returning my attention to her—"touch yourself."

Her eyes take over her face. "Wh—what?"

"I don't believe I stuttered."

She surveys our surroundings before returning her attention to me. "You can't be serious."

"I'm as serious as my hard-on."

Angelica stares at me like I have two heads.

Technically, I do. And the one between my legs is eager to break free from my pants.

Epilogue

Angelica

Holy shit.

Even if I thought Hudson was pulling my leg, the way he's staring at me from under his heavy-lidded eyes, suggests he means business.

"You're insane," I say.

He holds my gaze.

I can't believe he's suggesting something this bawdy. In the mind-blowing year we've been dating, he's tempted me into doing filthy things outdoors. So far, it's been on his terrace—*his private* terrace—where it's just the two of us. I was freaked out the first time, but it didn't take me long to become a convert. It's not hardcore exhibitionism, but it's still plenty naughty. The thrill of potentially being caught or the exhilaration I have at the thought a neighbor could hear my moans as I succumb to Hudson's wicked ways has always been an aphrodisiac.

But this is different.

First, this isn't out of sight. Second, we're not alone. Third, forget about people potentially hearing me. They would *definitely* hear me.

"We don't have all night, angel. Eventually, the waiter will come back to our table." His tone drips with cocksureness. "Best to get on it." *Bastard.*

There's a steady buzz of activity surrounding us—diners ending a meal or starting one, wait staff bringing food and drink, the clatter of cutlery, the clinking of glasses, music playing, and the general hustle and bustle of a restaurant. True, the setting offers some privacy and the other patrons are too busy enjoying their meal to pay us any mind.

Still...

Why am I considering obeying him?

I blame the tingling between my legs on the fact I haven't seen him in two long weeks.

"You're thinking about it..."

My cheeks blush hot.

Damn him.

"Busted, dirty girl!" The predatory look in his eyes is my undoing.

I'm not one to back down from a challenge, but this one is pretty out there. He's made it his mission to push me outside of my comfort zone, but this is wild, even for him.

"With the white linen tablecloth draping to the ground, covering your lap, no one will know. The noise of your fingers playing with your slickness will be muffled by the music. Your heady scent will drift away. No one will know. It'll be our"—he waves a finger between us—"little secret."

My pussy clenches.

Good God.

I'm sitting on the banquette against an ivy-covered brick wall, strung with tiny lights.

From his vantage point, Hudson is the one who's exposed to the courtyard.

A rush of dampness wets my thong.

Hudson flashes me a smoldering grin. "Live on the wild side... just do it."

"And you're just going to watch?"

"As much as I'd love to join you, in my case, it might be too obvious. I'll derive pleasure from watching you come your brains out in the middle of an unsuspecting audience."

I bite my lower lip, a nervous thrill coursing through me.

I can be meek, or I can be badass.

I grab the napkin that's on my lap and place it on the table.

Holy shit, I'm doing this.

"You're a daring little one." Hudson's expression is unreadable. "Pull your—" He stops mid-sentence.

"What—"

He lifts a finger, silencing me.

He snatches his phone from the table.

What the hell?

"Where's your phone?" he asks.

"Err... inside my handbag." My voice is hoarse.

"Grab it."

I'm confused as fuck, but pull out my phone.

"Power it up!"

I do as I'm told and place the device on the table.

I'm still not sure what's happening.

Hudson's fingers fly on his screen.

His gaze meets mine.

"What are you doing?" I ask in a little voice.

He points at my phone just as a message flashes on my screen.

Hudson: This is a lot more private.

I lift my gaze. "You're the devil incarnate."

Hudson: Not long ago I was a tyrant. Did you just give me a promotion?

I narrow my eyes at him.
He winks.
His attention moves to his phone.

Hudson: You can thank me later for helping you cross another item off your bucket list.

"Who said it ever was?" I ask.

Hudson: We both know it was.

I roll my eyes.

Hudson: Think about it. You get all the perks of being an exhibitionist without having to perform for anyone other than me.

Okay, that's a definite selling point.

Hudson: Pull your dress up. I want your hand underneath your dress.

I tug my dress up until my fingers touch my bare thigh.

Hudson: A little higher. We don't want a wet spot.

Panic hits me hard.

Hudson: Do you as you're told and it will be okay.

I nod.
I bunch my dress around my waist.
There.

"Good," he says.

Crisis averted.

Hudson: I bet you're already wet for me. Nod once if I'm right.

I know no one can hear a text message, but that doesn't prevent me from scouring the terrace for confirmation.

The coast is clear.

I trail a finger over my damp panties.

I answer him with a jerky nod.

Hudson: I didn't even need you to answer. It's written all over your face.

Bastard.

Hudson: Slide your fingers between your dripping pussy.

I do as I'm told.

Hudson: Nod every time you've completed a command.

I nod.

Hudson: You might need to hold on to your phone or else it'll go into sleep mode.

Good idea.

Hudson: Now you're ready to play.

Honestly, it's as if I left all good sense at the door.

Hudson: Slide your fingers against your clit.

I let out a low moan.

Hudson: I'll take that as a nod.

Hudson: I want your fingers plunged deep into your juicy pussy.

I close my eyes and slide two fingers inside my wetness.

Fuck.

"Eyes on me," Hudson says.

My eyes fly open.

"Better." He holds my gaze for a few breaths. "Let's keep going."

His eyes lower to his phone.

My eyes lower to mine.

Hudson: Fuck yourself.

Mother of God.

I slide my fingers in and out of my greedy pussy.

Hudson: How does it feel?

How the hell am I supposed to answer that question?

I settle for, "Really good."

Hudson: I wish it were my fingers, my tongue, or my cock bringing you pleasure.

Hudson: We'll just have to wait until later.

I nod.

Hudson: Which option can't you wait to ride first?

He's playing dirty.

"All of the above." It's a struggle to speak as my fingers slide in and out of my pussy.

Hudson: My little slut is horny.

"It's your fault." My tone is accusatory.

His grin is lethal.

Hudson: We started the evening with me being a tyrant, but now I'm the devil incarnate. I have a reputation to live up to.

I should've kept my mouth shut.

Hudson: When I finger-fuck you, I always make sure to give your clit plenty of attention.

Hudson: Make sure not to neglect it.

I hate how he knows my body better than I do.

I curse under my breath when I pull my fingers out of my pussy.

Hudson: I can't tell from the expression on your face if that was pleasure or pain.

I glower at him.

Hudson: Pleasure. Definitely pleasure.

If my clit wasn't in so much need of attention, I'd give him a piece of my mind.

My fingertips skate around my clit. The sublime sensation sends a shiver through me.

This is so wrong.

No one can hear us, but I'm certain my desire is written all over my face. Anyone looking at me would instantly know I'm up to no good.

You'd think that would be enough to stop me, but it doesn't.

Hudson: Stroke that clit good.

I don't need any convincing.

I stroke over and over again.

This feels so fucking good.

I bite my lower lip to keep from moaning too loudly.

Hudson: That good?

Overwhelmed by the lust taking over my body, I'm too far gone to speak.

I nod.

Hudson is staring at me.

The desire I read in his blue eyes ratchets my own.

Hudson: Your greedy little clit must be so hard.

That would be a yes.

I nod when I remember he can't read my thoughts.

Hudson licks his lips, his hungry eyes locked onto mine.

Holy Jesus.

I'm so freaking turned on.

My nipples strain against the fabric of my strapless bra. I curse the fact both hands are busy. I need to squeeze my breasts, it's almost agonizing.

My breath quickens as I pick up the pace, stroking my clit faster and faster.

Hudson: Good girl. Keep stroking.

I don't disappoint him.

Hudson: Fuck. My fingers are so jealous.

I should be conflicted right now.

The angel sitting on my right shoulder is telling me this is wrong. The devil sitting on my left shoulder is telling me this is so damn good.

I'm too far gone to listen to the angel.

The devil made me do it...

Hudson: Same for my tongue.

Hudson: It pisses me off to no end to know your sweet juices will go to waste because I won't be able to lap up every last drop.

The man is killing me.

Hudson: I want you to apply more pressure on that little clit.

Pleasure races through my bloodstream, heat engulfing my whole body.

My fingers work my clit faster and faster.

Hudson: Look at my dirty little slut getting herself off.

Hudson: Even if someone were to approach our table and catch you in this compromising situation, you wouldn't be able to stop.

Hudson: You need to come as much as you need your next breath.

"God, yes."

Hudson: It's a shame I won't be able to hear my name on your lips.

God, I can't scream. I just can't—

A man approaching, cuts through my naughty train of thought.

The movement of my hands between my dripping pussy comes to a screeching halt.

Fuck, fuckity, fuck, fuck!

"Are we still doing okay here?" the waiter asks.

My breath stops.

I'm surprised I can hear the question over the hammering of my heart.

Hudson flashes me an innocent smile before shifting his attention to the waiter. "Yes, we are." He returns his focus to me. "Isn't that right, sweetheart?"

What the fuck is he doing?

I'm in no position to hold a conversation.

I shoot daggers at him.

His choir boy smile widens.

Bastard.

"Uhhhh," That's all I can manage.

I clench my phone, as if that's enough to stop my body from trembling.

"Was that a yes?" the waiter asks me.

My breathing is labored. "Uh-huh."

The waiter squints.

It's with herculean effort I manage to freeze a tight smile on my face, praying that guilt isn't written all over it.

"Do you need more water?"

I'm sure my cheeks match the color of my dress.

Thank God, he doesn't suspect what I'm doing underneath the tablecloth.

"Uh-uh," I say with a jerky head shake.

"Might I suggest the sorbet or gelato dessert? Both options are very refreshing and great precursors to a more elaborate one." The man is persistent. I must look like I'm about to combust.

Luckily, we're sitting outside. I'm pretty sure I reek of sex. If we were sitting inside, the waiter would have sniffed me like a dog hunting for truffles.

"It's a warm night," Hudson says, shifting the waiter's attention away from me.

"We deserve it after the winter we had," the waiter says.

"It was brutal," Hudson says before sending a cocky look in my direction.

Damn you.

"If I wanted frigidly cold winters, I'd be living in Alaska," the waiter says. "Don't even get me started on spring. It rained more here than it did in London."

"Thank God for a hot summer in the Big Apple," Hudson says.

This isn't the time to talk about the weather, guys.

"I'm sure it shouldn't be long before we're ready for dessert." With that, Hudson puts an end to this wasteful chitchat.

Finally, he dismisses the waiter.

There are more important things here. Like my pending orgasm.

"Excellent." The waiter seems pleased. "We have a dessert menu, but if you'd like, I can go down the list of daily specials."

No, no, no. Go away.

"That will give you time to think about it."

Hudson makes a show of thinking, tapping his chin with his finger.

He better not agree to this.

"Sometimes too much time to think things over only muddles the brain," Hudson says. "Sometimes you just have to be spontaneous about it—jump in with both feet. Especially when it comes to *sweets*."

"Great attitude!" the waiter says. "Flag me down when you're ready."

"We will," Hudson says.

With that, the waiter is off.

Thank you, God.

My boyfriend turns his attention to me. The lust I read in his eyes earlier is back in full force.

"You didn't participate much in the conversation. I gather you were... a bit tongue-tied." If both hands weren't occupied, I'd flip him the bird. "Let's pick up where we left off."

The man is unwavering on the best of days, but today, he's unleashed.

He points at my phone.

Hudson: Finish yourself off.

I nod.

Hudson: I don't want you to stop.

Hudson: Not until your hot and dripping pussy is clenching around your fingers...

Hudson: And you have to bite your tongue to keep quiet so no one knows you're being a bad, bad girl.

Hudson: I can't wait to see how that plays out since we both know you can't come without screaming your pretty head off.

Hudson holds a PhD in dirty talking. He's also a master at sexting. This is a whole other level of wantonness.

I meet his gaze and give him a look that says, *challenge accepted.*

"This is going to be fun," he says.

"I'm going to make you eat your words."

> Hudson: I'd rather eat you, but I'll have to wait.

> Hudson: Enough sparring. Start moving your fingers. I'm ready for dessert.

Operation Depraved Angelica resumes.

My hand slips between my pussy lips.

In no time, I pick up the pace.

"*I'm so wet,*" I mouth.

He levels me with a feral stare that makes my clit sizzle.

"*I'm so hard,*" he mouths back.

Dammit.

This is fifty shades of hotter than hell.

> Hudson: Rub your clit harder. I know you like it rough.

Damn him for knowing me so well.

Our eyes lock onto each other as I rub myself off in the outdoor patio of a chic New York restaurant.

A year ago, if someone had told me I would consider doing something this scandalous, I would've accused the person of being high *and* drunk.

Yet here I am.

I blame the handsome man sitting across from me for corrupting me in the best possible way.

My breathing quickens.

My face is so flushed, I'm sure I'm glowing in the dark.

The beginning of an orgasm tingles at my core.

Yes.

I let out a low moan.

Hudson: I just want to shove the plates to the floor and bury my hard cock in that gaping mouth and fuck your gorgeous face.

Jesus Christ.

Hudson: You're close. I can feel it all the way down to my balls.

My hand moves faster between my legs.

If I don't come, I'm going to die.

Hudson: You have no idea how beautiful you are when you come.

Those words are my undoing.

I drop the phone on the table, grab the napkin, and shove it into my mouth to curtail the cry of pleasure that threatens to escape from my lips.

Hudson's face becomes blurry as my climax hits me with a delicious shudder that has my whole body trembling. It's so intense, I jerk against the table, causing the glasses of water to wobble, liquid spilling on the tablecloth.

Shit.

"Look at that, you proved me wrong." Hudson's eyes glint. "Not even the tiniest of cries." He leans into the table, "From now on, I'll have to stuff your wet panties into your mouth..."

God Almighty.

I swear, I come a second time.

It takes me several long seconds to recover.

Hudson doesn't rush me.

When my eyes are able to focus on the dirty devil sitting across from me, there's no missing the wicked grin stretching his lips.

Just when I think he can't up the ante, he shocks me.

"Give me your hand." Hudson's voice is a whiskey drawl.

I obey, sliding my hand out from under the table.

My fingers are glistening, slick with my juices.

This is so embarrassing.

Hudson clamps a firm hand around my wrist and brings my wet fingers to his mouth.

"It's about fucking time I had my dessert."

The next thing I know, he sticks my dripping fingers into his mouth and licks them clean.

I'm too shocked to even speak.

Oh.

My.

Fucking.

God.

Epilogue
Hudson

As the chauffeured car nears Angelica's street, I send a quick text.

The countdown begins.

Satisfied, I tuck my phone inside the pocket of my jacket and glance at my girl's profile.

Her eyes are lost on the horizon, admiring a still animated Queens.

I didn't think she'd go for it.

The shy woman I met a year ago at the Bymark Hotel's Crawford Lounge would never have had the courage to be that bold.

My girl has come a long way.

As I watched her come so beautifully, my hard-on threatened to poke a hole in my boxer briefs and rip my pants. I was white-knuckling my phone in the hopes of containing the monster lengthening between my legs. It was in vain. Angelica looked so ready to be fucked. It took everything in me not to give into my bestial urges and sink into her balls deep right there on the table without a care if we had an audience or not.

My cock swells, imagining her sweet pussy desperate for every thick inch of me.

Damn.

I'm in fucking agony right now, still stiff as a board, but my need for her will have to wait.

The car pulls up in front of her building.

"Do you want to stay the night? Arya is at her boyfriend's place for the weekend. If you're too jetlagged—"

"We have to finish what we started at the restaurant."

She lowers her eyes and says from underneath her long lashes, "It's only fair we even out the score for the evening."

"Glad we're on the same page."

She laughs.

I get out of the car and round it to her side to help her out of the vehicle.

We walk hand in hand to her building.

An elevator ride later and we arrive on the fourth floor.

Angelica pulls her key out of her handbag and freezes just before sliding it into the lock.

She presses her ear to the door.

"What's going on?" I ask.

She looks over her shoulder. "It sounds like there's music coming from our apartment. Arya must've forgotten to stash away her laptop."

"Maybe she got distracted by Todd."

Angelica laughs. "I'm sure you're right. Those two are so in love, it's ridiculous."

In an ironic twist of fate, her sister has been dating a guy who has the same first name as her former handler. Todd Hamilton looks nothing like the other Todd. Arya met the twenty-eight-year-old medical software developer eight months ago at the Panorama Room, where she still works.

Fun fact: The other Todd's real name is Lionel Wooster.

The things you learn when you go out with a guy for a drink when you're no longer on his list of clients.

In any case, things are serious between Todd and Arya. According to my girl, it's her twin's first real relationship. Todd is good for Arya.

Angelica returns her attention to the door.

She unlocks it and steps inside.

I follow right behind her.

She halts.

"What's going on?" She turns around in a circle before looking up at me. "Hudson? What happened?"

"What does it look like?"

"Where did all these rose petals come from?" Her eyes dart around the living room, carpeted in petals. "And the candles?" Her gaze drops to the coffee table. "Oh my God, a tower of chocolate truffles? And one of profiteroles?" Her gaze keeps ping-ponging all over the place. "And the vases of... more red roses? And white ones?"

There were too many reasons not to move the trip to Australia. Still, no way was I going to allow that to stop me from making this evening happen. Luckily, I didn't have to do it alone.

She fixes her attention on me. "What did you do, you crazy man?"

"This is all for you, angel." I bring my hands to her shoulders. "We met one year ago today. You were wearing a red dress—a different one—"

"It was my first time wearing a red dress."

"And I'm the lucky bastard who was on the receiving end of that dress. The moment I saw you standing there, looking so fucking beautiful, I was a goner."

She brings her hand to her mouth. "Hudson." My name comes out muffled.

I drop to one knee.

Angelica's eyes widen in shock.

I grab her hand.

"Dear God." She fans her face with her free hand.

"There are so many spots I could've asked for your hand in marriage—the Crawford Lounge, the forty-first floor of the Bymark Hotel, The Fifth rooftop bar on 5th Avenue, Bermuda, the Panorama Room, or even my brownstone. But in the end, I could only think of one place—the apartment you've been living in since you were five years old."

She dances from one foot to the other. "You're going to make me cry."

"Angel, you're already crying."

She cries harder.

I reach up and wipe away her tears.

It doesn't make a lick of a difference.

I soldier on. "I know this is going to sound old-fashioned, but you have to remember I'm just a southern boy, living in the big city. If your dad were still alive, I would've put on my Sunday best to come over and ask for your hand in marriage. Then, I'd ask your mom, hoping they both agreed I was good enough for you."

She laughs through her tears.

"Since your parents are sitting at God's table with my parents—" My voice catches.

Along with Yonas, two of my other favorite people are in heaven.

My heart twists.

Angelica squeezes my hand.

I squeeze back.

I shake out of my melancholy and focus my attention on the woman I love beyond words.

"I love everything about you. I love your lightheartedness,

kindness, strength, protectiveness, fierceness, and most of all, I love the fact you picked me."

"How could I not pick you?" Her voice trembles. "On top of being the most handsome man in the world—"

"That's a tall statement, angel."

She giggles. "You're my rock."

We exchange a warm smile.

"I couldn't possibly see myself with anyone else but you," she says.

"You're the only woman in the world for me, Angelica." I reach between two vases of white roses set on the coffee table as my decoys, and find a jewelry box I knew would be hiding there.

I lift it, open it, and present her with the ring.

Angelica's jaw drops.

Her hands fly up to her face. "That is so beautiful."

"I want to live the rest of my life with you, angel. Angelica Eden McQuinley, will you do me the honor of becoming my wife?"

"Yes, yes, yes!" She does a little happy dance. "A thousand times, yes."

"You have no idea what it means to me that you'd be willing to take that leap of faith with me."

"It's not a leap of faith when you're embarking on a lifelong journey with the person you were meant to be with."

"Damn right we were meant to be together."

I take her hand into mine and slip the ring on her finger.

"Mother of God!" Her breath hitches as she stares at the ring. "It looks even better on my finger than it did in the box."

My gaze rises to her. And then I smile.

I got my girl a custom ring made with two pear-shaped diamonds—one pale canary yellow and the other clear, set on a platinum band encrusted with tiny round brilliant diamonds.

I stand up. "I agree."

I cup her gorgeous face in my hands and take her lips with my own. I taste the sweetness of the tiramisu she had for dessert as my tongue slides into her hot, waiting mouth.

Fuck, I need this woman's mouth every damn day.

I press my hand to the small of her back, fusing our bodies together as I deepen the kiss, our tongues tangling in a passionate dance.

She moans, and I feel it all the way down to my balls.

If this kiss goes any further, I'll have no other choice but to carry her to her bedroom and show her how much I've missed her.

Patience, Kincaid.

I pull away from her.

I have a few more surprises for her before fucking her brains out for the rest of the weekend.

She admires her ring, her eyes twinkling. "It's perfect."

"You're sure?"

"Absolutely. It's as if you found my secret Pinterest *My Big Day* board."

"Nah, I had a much more reliable way of figuring it out that didn't require me stalking your social media accounts."

She flashes me a complicit smile. "I have a sneaky feeling I know your source," she says with an exaggerated wink. "Speaking of the devil, my sister is going to freak out when she finds out you popped the question and I said yes. She's probably going to need sunglasses when she lays her eyes on my ring."

"Why wait?"

"You're right. Let's do a selfie!"

"I have a better idea." I don't give her time to process my words. "Come on out!" I yell. "She said yes to becoming Mrs. Kincaid!"

"Who are you talking to?"

An explosion of claps, cheers, and hollers erupt in the apartment, drowning the music playing in the background.

Arya, Todd, Sadie, Grace, and Kevin rush into the living room.

Angelica's hands cover her mouth. Her green eyes are enormous.

Arya runs to her sister.

The twins hug the hell out of each other.

Then, my girl does the rounds.

She's in tears by the time she's done hugging everybody.

"Oh my God!" Angelica says. "We weren't alone!"

I shake my head. "No, angel. I wanted to share this moment with your favorite people. I also made sure to capture the proposal on video."

Her brows touch.

I point around the room. "Hidden cameras captured every second since we stepped inside your apartment."

"You're crazy."

I pull her into my arms and kiss the top of her head. "You know damn well I'm crazy about you and I always will be."

"I'm the luckiest girl in the world."

"Well, *the luckiest girl in the world*," I say, and she giggles, "there's something I've been wanting to ask you."

"I'm afraid to ask."

"But you know I'm still gonna ask it?"

"Nothing stops you, Kincaid."

"You're right about that."

"All right, let's hear it," she says with a bring it on hand gesture.

"Move in with me."

She flinches.

When she recovers, she pulls her lower lip between her teeth.

Her mind is racing.

I know what's going through that pretty little head of yours.

Her gaze shifts from mine and she looks over her shoulder at the six-foot-one-inch brown-haired man who has a possessive arm draped over Arya's shoulder.

Todd grabs Arya's left hand and lifts it.

Angelica's twin wiggles her fingers, flashing a dazzling diamond ring that's a near carbon copy of the one I got her sister. Arya's ring is a combination of a pink sapphire pear-shaped diamond and a clear one.

"Oh my God, you got engaged?!"

"Yes!" Arya says.

She runs to her sister.

With their hands interlaced, the twins jump up and down like schoolgirls, squealing.

"When did this happen?" Angelica asks her sister when they stop bouncing like jumping beans.

Arya's eyes move from mine to Todd's before fixing her gaze onto her sister's. "Todd and Hudson coordinated everything behind my back."

Angelica turns to look at me. "Seriously?"

I nod.

Arya keeps talking. "While I was helping your boyfriend plan this"—she twirls two fingers over her head—"my boyfriend was planning his own proposal with the help of my best friend and his sisters. I was a little thrown off by the early dinner reservation at Michelin-starred Le Bernardin in Midtown Manhattan. Now, I know why."

"We planned a back-to-back McQuinley twins' proposal," I say.

Angelica shakes her head at me.

Todd kisses Arya's cheek. "Anything else would've been wrong."

"What he said." I agree with my partner in crime.

"This is unbelievably romantic," Grace says, tearing up. Kevin embraces her in his arms, and kisses her on the forehead.

"I couldn't have said it better." Sadie fans her face.

I wink at her.

She's also been instrumental in making tonight happen without a hitch. Same for Grace. Neither Sadie, Grace, Vanna, or Todd's sisters knew we were planning the double proposal.

That was our secret.

Todd and I have been talking about it since I confessed I might need his help with my original proposal idea. That's when he admitted he was also planning to pop the question. So, we decided to double the surprise factor.

"Ange," Arya says, forcing my fiancée's attention onto her. "Todd asked me to move in with him." She looks at her fiancé for a beat and returns her focus to her sister. "I said yes because I knew you would say yes to your man." Arya wipes away tears rolling down my fiancée's cheek. "I know you, sis. You would've sacrificed your happiness not to leave me behind."

Angelica's mouth twists.

Everyone on the planet knows she's a loving nurturer who takes care of everyone else.

Now, it's my turn to take care of her.

"There's no reason why you can't move in with Hudson." Arya smiles wide. "We *both* get to live our happy ever after with the man of our dreams."

"This is amazing," Angelica says. "Our fiancés are amazing."

"We both snatched keepers," Arya says.

Angelica runs to me. "Yes, Hudson, I'll move in with you. I want to wake up nestled in your arms every single morning."

"Angel, you've made me the happiest man in the world. We're going to have a wonderful life together."

Her words act like a defibrillator on my racing heart.

"The best."

I find her lips and kiss her until we both run out of air, to a soundtrack of whistling, clapping, and cheering.

Bonus Scene

Hudson

After giving my name to a hotel employee posted at the greeting desk, I enter the Seymour Lounge.

My buddies and fellow VIP Den members, Logan Ellison and his brother Walker, stand up to greet me.

After a few back slaps and handshakes, we take a seat on the modern wingback navy-blue armchairs.

A waiter rushes our way.

"What do you want to drink, Kincaid?" Logan asks.

I look up at the waiter. "An espresso martini—" I shake my head. "Nah, that's not gonna do it. I'll have a vodka Red Bull, please."

With a bow, the waiter rushes off.

"Hard day?" Walker asks.

I meet his gaze. "Hard week."

The waiter is back with my drink.

Two other waiters trail behind him, carrying trays of appetizers.

My nostrils tingle, the aroma awakening my appetite.

I'm already salivating.

The staff displays everything with a flourish.

We thank them, and the trio disappear as quickly as they appeared.

My gaze drops to the lip-smacking Mediterranean and grilled meat platters.

Damn.

"This looks delicious. Especially considering I didn't have time for lunch today."

"Same," Logan says.

"I barely managed to stuff a blueberry muffin down my throat at eleven this morning." Walker checks his statement gold watch. "It's eight p.m. now, which means I've been running on air and adrenaline all day."

"I've been on the same diet," I say.

Logan points to the feast. "Dig in."

He doesn't have to tell me twice.

"Don't mind if I do."

Logan and Walker pile a generous amount of appetizers on their plates.

The medley of flavors explodes in my mouth, and I have to suppress a moan.

For a few beats, we enjoy our food in silence.

The Ellisons have the Midas touch when it comes to hiring the best chefs in the city.

I wipe my mouth with a white cloth napkin before placing it on my empty plate. "Thank you. That hit the spot nicely."

Walker nods. "It did."

"The joy of carrying the world on your shoulders," I say. "Your days are so jampacked, you can't even manage to squeeze in the time for a meal. Today was a carbon copy of yesterday. Busy, busy, busy."

"I hear you," Logan says. "Thank God not every day is as

frantic as today's breakneck pace, or else I'd have to hang up my CEO hat."

"If you decided to take a step back, you'd still have your three siblings to hold the fort." *Not in my case. One of the downfalls of being an only child.*

"Have you considered..."—Walker levels me with a serious stare—"finding a new business partner?"

"No." I shake my head. "Never."

He holds up his hands in truce. "It was just a suggestion."

"I appreciate your concern, but I have trust issues. Been burned a few times."

"In that case, I understand your reticence," he says.

"I just have to make peace with the fact I'm the only captain. Thank God for my incredible crew."

"The payment processing industry you dominate is a world apart from the hospitality industry," Logan says. "Still, I'm in awe of you. I'm the CEO of this massive conglomerate of hotels, corporate rentals for professionals and executives, restaurants, lounges, and bars, but my siblings are my allies when it comes to big decisions. I have Walker"—he jerks his chin in his brother's direction—"Kayla, and Tristan to bounce ideas off. When things are murky, they help me see through the fog. And when the shit hits the fan, they're there to help me weather the storm. Same for my cousins spearheading operations in the different states and countries we have flagships in. You're steering your vessel alone."

I loosen my tie. "So often, I fear I'll suffer the same fate as the Titanic."

"I was paying you a compliment, Kincaid. You're taking it like an insult."

"I'm not."

"Sounds like it to me." Logan shifts his attention to his brother. "Am I wrong?"

"You're selling yourself short, Hudson," Walker says. "Your company is thriving. You're kicking ass and taking no prisoners."

"Ever since..." I expel a heavy breath. "Every day, I feel like it was a lucky day—a fluke—and the next day, I'll wake up, and the other shoe will drop." A lump forms in my throat, forcing me to loosen my tie even more.

"I understand where you're coming from," Logan says.

My eyebrows hit my forehead.

Logan narrows his eyes at me. "Don't look so surprise, Kincaid."

"It's not something I ever expected you to say. From the outside looking in, you're juggling all your balls with ease, whereas I'm juggling glass balls, praying they don't drop and shatter."

"Just because I'm not steering this vessel alone, doesn't mean the pressure isn't on. It's on. Every. Single. Day. Long-standing companies go belly up all the time. I thrive for success. Not to become a statistic—"

"Because when you become a statistic, hard-working people end up without a job," I say.

He nods.

"I'm known for being an uncompromising boss—"

"He is," Walker says.

"At least I'm not known for being a grumpy boss."

"Asshole!"

The Ellisons enter a Mexican standoff for a few long beats.

I clear my throat.

Logan swings his gaze my way. "I have zero tolerance for underperformers and even less for slackers. Don't get me started on this new epidemic mentality of quiet quitting. You want to do the bare minimum? No problem, but don't expect me to pay you. I have no problem telling them, *'You're fired!'*.

But letting good people go because of downsizing due to the fact we're not crushing it, that's unacceptable to me. True, there are circumstances you don't see coming, and therefore, you can't plan for. Albeit a natural catastrophe or for an unfathomable reason, the world would come to a standstill, my mission is to avoid having to downsize at any cost. That's what gets me up in the morning, fired up, and ready to go. Some might say I'm hardcore..." He shrugs. "Whatever. And yes, that responsibility can be overwhelming at times. Hitting—or surpassing—your goals year after year demands dedication, which would explain why I don't have a life outside of the family business."

"And it's not only the CEO who feels the heat," Walker says. "As the second in command, I feel the pressure as much as my big brother does."

I never thought they could relate. After all they have each other to lean on.

"My anxiety over making sure I don't fail the hundreds of employees depending on the money my company wires to their account every other week isn't stealing my breath like it used to when I was saddled with the crushing and heart-wrenching reality that I was going to have to manage the company on my own, but it's always at the back of my mind." *Niggling at me. Making me doubt I'm fit for the job.*

I never expected to be doing this by myself.

It wasn't supposed to be like this.

But then again, losing people I love is the story of my life.

Time to change the subject.

I scour the empty space. "You guys keep buying up hotels and renovating the ones you've acquired. This is an impressive renovation."

"The Seymour Lounge is our most ambitious renovation at the Bymark Hotel," Logan says.

"Only to be surpassed by the nearly completed renovated Banks Lounge," Walker says.

"Which 90s supermodels are associated with your latest renovations?"

"This lounge is named after Stephanie Seymour," Walker says, "and the other lounge is named after Tyra Banks."

"I'll have to Google them," I say. "I enjoyed being educated on the supermodels associated with the other lounges in the hotel."

"You're welcome," Logan says.

"Fucker."

He ignores my jab. "Our visions often clash when it comes to creative decisions, but when our sister wanted to leverage her adoration of 80s and 90s supermodels, we were on board after googling those beauties," Logan says.

"I bet."

"In my humble opinion, the models of our generation don't measure up," Walker says. "For the few who are gorgeous, they're replaceable. The 90s supermodels are irreplaceable. That breed of superhumans were the epitome of beauty, they all had a memorable personality that shone on photos and on the catwalk, and they weren't size double zero."

"You sound like you're their freaking casting agent," I say.

"Guilty as charged. I've spent too much time googling them, but can you blame me?"

"I was content gorging on slim beauties until a couple weeks ago."

"Who is the mythical creature who has the superpowers to make a pigheaded man like yourself change his tune?"

"You're lucky I consider you as a friend, or else I'd kick you out of my hotel, Kincaid."

"Avoiding the question, Ellison?"

"We hired a new station chef in one of the restaurants at

the hotel. She's smoking hot." He does a chef's kiss. "She's a brunette, so, not my usual MO. But damn, I'd break all my rules for her."

Walker's head whips in his brother's direction.

A blast of icy cold air, that has nothing to do with the A/C, engulfs the lounge.

"What?" Logan asks.

Walker's nostrils flare.

"Why are you looking at me like you want to gouge my eyes out, or worse, plunge a dagger into my chest?"

Walker's jaw ticks.

"Jesus, Walker, you look like you're about to blow a gasket. What the fuck is your problem?"

Slowly, the younger Ellison pulls his gaze away from his brother and settles his furious eyes on me.

Whatever is going on between you and your brother, don't take it out on me, buddy.

"As someone born and raised in Texas, I'm all for curves," I say. Give me a drop-dead gorgeous woman with slender tempting curves anytime of the day... or night.

Logan lifts his martini glass. "I'll drink to that!"

I do the same.

Logan and I take a swig of our drinks.

Walker remains mute behind a wall of silence.

Logan's eyes meet my own. "You're coming to the official opening of the Seymour Lounge next week?"

"Wouldn't miss it."

"Is your director of French communications going to be your plus one?"

"It will only be lil' ol' me."

"How come?" Logan asks. "I thought she was your wingman at events."

"She'll be in Paris, meeting new prospects," I say. "You guys will be here, your brother and your sister, the Kellers will be here as well. Bryce Van Der Linden and his brother-in-law Nikolaj will also be here. There are fewer chances I'll open my mouth and say something to someone who gets easily offended and ruffle their overly sensitive feathers." The Ellisons chuckle. "So, I'm coming alone like a big boy."

"I was looking forward to seeing your director of French communications again," Logan says. "Speaking of drop-dead gorgeous women, that beauty is all that and more. I fail to understand how you're able to work with her and not want to flip her over your desk and fuck her senseless every day. Unless you have her on one of your conference room tables, drilling into her as strings of sexy French words spill from her pouty lips."

Tell me how you really feel about her. "There are labor laws."

He gives me a non-committal shrug.

"I make it a point not to agree with my brother as often as I can, but Logan is right. That woman is sex on legs," Walker says. "But I understand your dilemma. Office romances are..."

"Ill-advised," I say.

"I was going to say tricky, requiring finesse, and paperwork spelling out it's consensual," Walker says.

"Have you ever been in that position?" I ask him.

"Nah. I'm the master of my balls. R words—romance and relationship—open the door to more drama than I have the capacity to handle."

"Love is a disease, and I'm as allergic to relationships as my brother is, but if it weren't for our friendship, I'd ask your director of French communications out."

I hold Logan's gaze. "She'd turn you down."

The corner of his lip curves up. "I'm very convincing when I put my mind to it."

"Trust me, she'd turn you down."

"You'll never be on the receiving end of—"

"She's a lesbian."

Logan's head jerks back.

That shut him up.

Walker's eyes widen. "No shit."

I nod. "She's always preferred women."

"I'm heartbroken," Logan says.

Did he just pout? "Do you even have a heart?"

"Don't quit your day job, Kincaid."

Walker points a finger at me. "Good one."

Logan pulls at the sleeve of his shirt peeking from underneath his navy blue checkered jacket. "It doesn't matter if I'd rock her world in bed—or against a wall, or on my desk, or in the back of a car, or on the terrace of one of the suites in the hotel, or somewhere we might get caught—I don't have the right equipment."

My eyebrows arch high.

No, he hasn't been obsessing over her. "Boasting your own praise again, Logan?"

"I'm not tooting my own horn. It's an irrefutable fact. All my past lovers will attest."

I shake my head.

Logan crosses a leg over the other. "If she won't be accompanying you, that opens the doors to possibilities for the evening. There will be a lot of gorgeous women present."

"This is the perfect moment for me to fess up for why I suggested we meet—"

"So, this wasn't about us spending quality time together?" The sarcasm is thick in Walker's voice.

"No, we won't be braiding each other's hair tonight or painting each other's nail in bubblegum pink."

"I'm crushed, Hudson." He's full of shit.

"You'll survive, Walker."

"Okay, so you didn't want to connect for a touchy-feely, bonding evening. What's on your mind?" Logan asks me.

"At the charity event we attended a couple weeks ago, you two—along with your brother—educated me on the art of executive dating." I pause, my eyes shifting from one brother to the other. "I'd like to know more."

Walker slides his attention to Logan. "Sounds like our friend is looking to hire an escort."

Logan nods before his eyes lock onto mine. "It's been a long time. You're finally ready to get your dick wet." He rubs his stubbled chin. "Which kinks are you looking to play out, Kincaid?"

"You can take the boy out of Texas, but you can't take the Southern out of the boy."

Logan tilts his head to the side. "Care to translate?"

"I don't kiss and tell."

"Even when you're paying for it?" Walker asks.

"Even when I'm paying for it."

No way am I revealing all the filthy things I intend to do to the woman I'll be matched with...

Bonus Secret Chapter

For a bonus secret chapter about Hudson and Angelica (we meet up with these two love birds three years later while they're doing a little roleplaying at one of the lounges at the Bymark Hotel), subscribe to my newsletter!

www.MyRomanceAddiction.com

Who's The Next Filthy Rich Book Boyfriend?

The next spin off features the owners of the Bymark Hotel.

As I write the Ellison brothers' books (Logan, Walker, and Tristan), I invite you to keep binge-reading books set in the same world. The Very New York Billionaires series kicks off with Xavier Keller, aka Max Keller's cousin. Max is part of the Billionaire Factor series.

Brooding billionaire Bryce is the first book boyfriend I ever wrote. This *Pretty Woman* retelling comes with a warning...

"Panty-melting hotness!" —Amie

"Exceptionally provocative and hot!" —Purple Jewels

"From the first moments, I am completely and thoroughly entranced." —Blueocean*

"Kept me reading late into the night!" —mflora

"Hooked from the beginning!" —Atlanta Whitlock

"From NY, to Paris, to Vegas, this one is fantastic all the way!

Scarlett Avery writes a hot romance that you will feel deep down." —Camilla Rogers

Binge-read it now: Billionaire Factor—Bryce

Psst... you can read a sneak peek of Billionaire Factor—Bryce at the end of this book.

Reviews are like a cherry on a sundae—they make all the difference.

It only takes a few minutes to leave a review, which makes a huge difference for an indie author like myself.

Here's the link to leave a review for: A Very Wicked Arrangement

Scarlett's Book Banter!

Dear Sexy Reader,

I want me a Texan billionaire like Hudson. Raise your hand if you loved, loved, loved Hudson.

Angelica is so sweet. She was carrying so much on her shoulders until she met the perfect man who wanted nothing more than to take care of her.

I've always wondered what it would be like to be an identical twin. I thought my first identical twin romance would've been two brothers, but this was too good of an opportunity to pass up. Two women who have the same face agree to do the ultimate twin swap. The drama that could result from such a reckless decision is the perfect set up for this romance.

My initial goal in writing Hudson's story was to link back to Bryce, aka the first romance book I ever wrote and the first book boyfriend I ever fell in love with. I wanted a 2.0 version to the *Pretty Woman* retelling theme. Before even writing the book, I knew Bryce would have a cameo appearance. I didn't expect he'd have this much involvement in the story. Authors know this. Sometimes characters take the reins and change the course of the story. This is one of the cases. I'm quite happy Bryce insisted on more "page time".

One of the things I love is to bring back troublemakers or colorful characters from other books. After racking my brain to find the catalyst to the dark moment, I decided to leverage Todd. He played his role to a T.

About Bryce

Bryce is a brooding and cynical three-times divorced tech tycoon. His *Pretty Woman* retelling is super spicy and it has all the feels. Let me tell you, that salacious scene in Vegas will leave you hot and bothered. And the romance between Bryce and the woman who brings him down to his knees will make you swoon.

Jamie Betts loves Bryce's story so much, she read it *nine* times before she ever became one of my proofreaders. As it stands, she's read it *thirteen* times and counting.

Bryce Van Der Linden holds a PhD in dirty talking and he's dominant AF. The man is alpha billionaire deliciousness.

Binge-read it now: Billionaire Factor—Bryce

About Rory and Isobel Wolfe

This couple was first featured in Billionaire Hotshot—Roderick.

Rod Wolfe is Rory's youngest brother. Rod is a former all-star drummer of one of the most chart-topping rock bands. As a second career, he co-owns of a video production company. Like Hudson, the Wolfe brothers had it rough growing up. Like Hudson, their success has allowed them to land in a much better place in life—something that was unfathomable while they were struggling as kids and teenagers. Rod meets the woman who brings him down to his knees in different circumstances from Hudson, but both overprotective alphas would do whatever it takes to keep their girl out of harm's way. Both Rod and Hudson are intense and both are broken inside... until they find their perfect match.

Billionaire Hotshot—Roderick is a breathtaking friends to lovers romance so deep, so gripping, so engulfing, you'll need days to recover.

★★★★★ "I think my boss was probably wondering what was so interesting on my phone and why I had a huge goofy smile on my face whole day today. Absolutely amazing and fantastic book, and highly, highly recommended." —Snookumz

★★★★★ "I love this story. It's passionate and protectiveness wrote to perfection." —Marsha Gail

★★★★★ "Hot, steamy scenes with a lot of emotions come into play. The HEA is sooo awesome." —Anne Young-Cronister

Binge-read Rod's story to your heart's content!

P.S. Who loves reviews? I do! I do! Thanks a *billion* in advance!

P.P.S. I keep writing because of your hunger for my stories. Thank you for your fervor, love, and loyalty. I'm humbled and incredibly grateful. Without you, there's very little reason to keep coming up with new stories.

P.P.P.S. For access to an EXCLUSIVE Secret Chapter, go to the next page!

Get the Secret Chapter for A Very Wicked Arrangement!

Thank you for purchasing this romance!

I have an EXCLUSIVE Secret Chapter to share with you!

For the Secret Chapter, we meet up with Hudson and Angelica three years later while they're doing a little roleplaying at one of the lounges at the Bymark Hotel.

Trust me, you're going to love the extra tidbits.

When you sign up on my list, you'll receive an email with further instructions!

Sign up TODAY!

www.MyRomanceAddiction.com

***If you've already signed up to my list from previous books, you can visit the same page to download the Secret Chapters and/or Storyboard for this romance. ***

Sneak Peek of Billionaire Factor—Bryce

Chapter 1

I*'m not nervous.*

No, I'm not.

I exhale a shaky breath.

Fuck, I'm nervous.

I check the time on the phone I'm clenching.

Five minutes to six.

The Midtown lights sparkle all around like the finest jewelry, reflecting off every surface, including the impressive glass entrance door behind me. This is a beautiful and luxurious part of New York City.

The familiarity of the neighborhood is the only thing bringing me comfort.

A *Pretty Woman* gig at twenty-eight wasn't on my dream board... but here I am.

Nothing like overachieving your life goals. Not!

As I count down the minutes until my *date*—aka, my first client—texts me with further instructions as to where to meet him, a car drives by with windows down, blaring out a Latin song. It's a tune from my childhood. My heart breaks.

My parents would die if they knew what I'm about to do.

My sister would murder me.

The ghost of my beloved abuelita will haunt me tonight.

I've failed my family.

I shake off the paralyzing thoughts.

You have to do this.

You need the money.

You're past due on the electricity bill and if you don't make a payment in the next couple of days, you'll be living in the Stone Age.

I sigh.

If I knew how to hack into my neighbor's Wi-Fi without getting caught, the thought of not having electricity wouldn't frighten me so much. I can live off rice and beans. I can even live without coffee—*God, that would be torture*—but I can't live without the internet.

I'm already neck deep in shit, no need to suffocate in it.

I trusted Lucifer and now I'm paying the price.

What about me makes me so damn gullible?

With shaky hands, I smooth down my dress.

I hope I look the part.

Todd—my booking agent—said the client wants upscale and sophisticated.

Fingers crossed this meets his standards.

I extend a foot.

Since skyscraper heels are a staple in a high-priced escort's wardrobe, thank God I didn't sell these secondhand-shop-find Christian Louboutin shoes in my quest to keep afloat.

My eyes move from my shoes to my phone at precisely a quarter past six. My escort-gig-only phone flashes a text message from my first client.

> Bryce: Amanda, when you arrive, please make your way to the Trouble's Trust bar area. I'll be sitting at a table and I'll have an unlit cigar in an empty cognac glass. I'll see you soon.

Amanda.

Right.

Must remember I'm Amanda Hardy. Not Sofia Herrera.

Show time!

I stride towards the doors of the hotel I've been standing in front of for twenty, nail-biting minutes. The automatic doors open, and I head for the bar area. I know Bryce is paying for my services for the night and since I get an outrageous hourly rate, I shouldn't be too picky, but still, I hope he looks... decent.

The Towers at the New York Palace Hotel on Madison Avenue is one of the city's top-rated luxury hotels. It's the hangout spot for the elite, wealthy, and influential. The Trouble's Trust exclusive cocktail bar is renowned for its ambiance and the ultra-rich clientele who choose to relax in this premier location. I've heard of this place and I've read about it on so many blogs, but I've never been inside until tonight.

All of New York is here.

You can smell the money in the room.

As I walk by a tall blond guy who gazes at me with a flirtatious smile, I can't help but blush. He's probably in his early forties, and dressed in one of the finest suits I've ever seen on a man. For a second, I wonder if it's my first client.

No.

This guy is standing.

Bryce was clear about the fact he'd be sitting at a table.

I flash him a shy smile in return, secretly proud of the fact I look good enough to elicit this kind of reaction from a stranger.

I scour the room for Bryce. Even with my five-inch heels,

I'm still short and it's difficult to make my way through the crowded bar and nearly impossible to locate my date.

An older gentleman approaches me. "You look lost, my dear."

"Yes, I'm trying to find a friend."

"I wish you were looking for me." There's a sparkle in his brown eyes. "The beautiful ones are always taken," he says with a touch of disappointment.

I don't know what to say.

He points to the corner of the room.

I get on my toes, but a wall of people blocks my view.

The older gentleman gently pushes aside a few of the dressed to kill New York socialites to allow me to see the man waiting at a table. "The lucky fellow over there might be the one you're looking for."

"Thank you. I'll see if it's him," I say before walking towards the man sitting alone.

As I approach him, my eyes drop to the cigar in the cognac glass.

My client.

My heart skips a beat when the man turns to look at me.

Holy smokes!

Todd (without a last name) suggested I Google Bryce to avoid the newbie mistake of asking too many basic—code word for *dumbass*—questions.

There was a lot of information on Bryce's success, but very few photos of him. It's surprising a tycoon has been able to keep such a low profile in the media. In this age of viral gossip, overnight stardom, and airing one's laundry on the internet, I don't know how he's managed to remain invisible to prying eyes.

Forty-four-year-old Bryce Van Der Linden is the workaholic CEO and founder of Linden Corporation—an empire that generates several billion dollars every year. He's a college dropout. After many failed attempts at success, he got into the internet security business and built the most important company in the industry. Many international governments depend on him to keep their sensitive data safe.

Although a native New Yorker, the mogul currently lives in Silicon Valley.

Lucky me. My first client is smoking hot.

Don't forget the cardinal rules.

I replay Todd's 101 crash course in my head.

"One, this is a business transaction, not a dating service. Two, get the money before giving him a blowjob or allowing him to fuck you. Three, don't go over time or else he's getting your sweet ass for free. Four, don't fall in lust or love with your client. Five, don't share your personal drama. They don't care—they're buying a fantasy. Keep these five rules in mind and you'll be a success in this profession. Your ultimate goal is for him to require your services again, and again, and again."

I don't intend on making any of those mistakes. This is a temporary gig until I get back on my feet, and I'm determined to make this last a lot longer than my failed stint as a waitress.

"Bryce?" His blue eyes meet my dark brown ones. "I'm Amanda," I say, offering my hand.

"Amanda. It's a pleasure to meet you," he says, getting up to greet me.

God, he's tall.

I'm only five feet two, and nothing turns me on more than height on a man.

He's dashing in his tailored black suit that fits his athletic body like a second skin. His white shirt is crisp and offsets his black tie. His silver cufflinks add flair to an already impeccable outfit. I can't resist a furtive glance down at his stylish black shoes.

Nice.

He wears success well.

Conscious I might be ogling his shoes with too much attention, I lift my gaze.

His blue eyes glide over me, taking in every inch of my purple dress and black Louboutin heels. He lingers a little too long on the décolletage of my dress, where I squeezed in my breasts and arranged them so they look tastefully revealing.

What I lack in height, I make up for with boobs.

He gallantly pulls out a chair for me. "Please, sit down."

I barely have time to drop my clutch on the table when a waiter appears.

"Would you like a drink, Amanda?" Bryce asks.

"Please. A drink would be perfect," I say, grateful for the opportunity to calm my nerves.

"What can I bring you, ma'am?" the waiter asks.

"I'll have a gin and tonic, please, with lime. No cucumber."

"And for the gentleman?"

"I'll have an Old Fashioned, please."

Bryce thanks our waiter, and he disappears.

"The service is impeccable here," Bryce says, as he closes the cocktail menu. "That's why I always stay at this hotel when I do business in the city."

"It really is an incredible location, and it's my first time here."

God, I'm so worried I'll say the wrong things.

I'm really not sure what kind of conversation to make when a man pays for you to be at his beck and call.

"Let me go over how the evening is going to unfold," he says, holding my gaze.

All right. No chitchat. Straight to business.

"I'm all ears."

He cocks a brow.

Even his eyebrows are sexy.

How can that be?

I scan his gorgeous face, overwhelmed by the intensity of his eyes. Don't get me started about the few sexy strands of gray hair that caress his temples.

Tall, brown-haired men with blue eyes usually leave me weak in the knees, and Bryce Van Der Linden is no exception.

Silver fox in the making.

I approve.

He clears his throat.

Crap. I'm ogling.

I sit straighter in my chair.

Hit me with your best shot. "I'm listening."

"The event starts at seven-thirty. The car will pick us up at ten past, and we'll arrive in good time since the venue where the Camus Cognac Cuvee foundation dinner will take place is located near this hotel."

"I see."

"You'll stay by my side during the evening and act like my charming date." *Copy that.* "I've secured your services from six-thirty to one in the morning, but I don't expect we'll stay until the end. The driver will drop us off here, I'll pay you, and the driver will take you home."

Wait. Aren't I supposed to get paid first? I guess we're going to a gala, and that's not something Todd mentioned in his list of rules.

Shit.

Bryce continues talking. "There will be a lot of international businesspeople with deep pockets, and if you can help smooth the interactions by throwing in a few sentences in their native tongue, I'm sure it will help me close more deals in the coming weeks."

"I should be able to manage easily."

"Todd told me you have a translation degree, and you speak Spanish, French, and Italian."

"Yes, and yes."

"Since I can barely say hello in any of those languages, I'll count on you to break the ice. Are we clear?"

I nod. "You want me to smile, be charming, and when the opportunity arises, flirt with potential clients in their native tongue."

"Yes, but don't flirt your way into another man's bed when I'm footing the bill," he warns.

I didn't expect that answer.

My inexperience as an escort shines bright.

Embarrassment colors my cheeks.

His face softens. "From what Todd tells me, you're smart and you pick up on things quickly."

"I am and I do." I smile despite my discomfort.

The waiter returns with our drinks and some tempting appetizers. A few sips of my gin and tonic gives me the courage to ask a question I've had on my mind since Todd told me that the uber-successful and very eligible Bryce Van Der Linden was the first client of many to get in touch with him to secure 'Amanda's' services.

"Bryce, may I ask a question?"

"Of course."

"What should I say if someone asks about our relationship? How should I refer to you?"

"Good question. There's a strategic reason behind hiring a gorgeous and sexy woman who speaks multiple languages. People will spend more time admiring your beauty and being impressed by your language skills than figuring out our relationship, but if someone were to ask, simply tell them you're my director of international business. It's a quick and simple way to put an end to any further questions they might have about us."

"Got it. My language skills were the determining factor in selecting me over the other women at the agency?" *Did I just ask that?* "I'm sorry, Bryce. That came out the wrong way. I'm not questioning your decision," I say, fumbling over my words.

He leans in dangerously close, his cologne—which I'm sure cost an arm and a leg—tickles my nostrils.

Holding my brown eyes with his dreamy blue ones, he places a hand on top of mine, and says in a suggestive voice, "Your language skills are a bonus. I selected you because you're beautiful and you have an incredibly curvaceous body."

His silky words make my nipples stand to attention and send tingles cartwheeling to my pussy.

Good Lord.

~

Although the evening is a glamorous gala where some of the richest and most successful businesspeople in New York City rub shoulders, it's tiresome. I spend the evening glued to Bryce's side, shaking hands, smiling, making small talk in four languages, and faking interest in what's being shared with me.

You'd think, with that much money, they'd know how to have more fun.

Bryce is all business during the gala. Other than a few conspiring looks we exchange during the evening, we don't have much time to interact with each other because there are too many important people to meet.

"I'm going to freshen up. I'll be back in a few minutes," I say before leaving his side.

I reapply my makeup and lipstick with meticulous attention, in the hopes of buying myself some time away from this boring evening. I assess the final result, and head out of the bathroom.

I set off in the direction of the bar, determined to find a way of making this evening more bearable, but a voice stops me.

"That was a long bathroom break, Amanda."

I turn around, startled.

I recover. "You know us women, we take much longer than men." I feel like he's caught me doing something wrong. "I was going to get a drink. Want one?"

"No, thanks. As for your drink, you'll have to take it to go." I flinch. "I can't shake another hand or make any more small talk." *You and me both.* "I called the chauffeur. The car is outside."

"I'll nix the drink idea."

"Let's go." He places a hand on the small of my back and I bask for a moment in the shiver that runs up my spine.

As we drive back to his hotel, I stare out the window, a bit nervous about what Bryce expects of me now that the gala is over.

"Amanda?"

Slowly, I turn my head to meet his eyes.

"You were really great tonight and I can't believe you survived the last three hours like a real champ," he says.

"It was a fun evening."

"You're a bad liar. You were trying to escape at the end of the evening by pretending to go to the bathroom."

Busted!

I'm unsure if he's amused or offended by my attempt to escape.

"I can't blame you," he goes on, "The only fun thing about this evening was watching you move in that form-fitting dress that hugs every single one of your curves to perfection. I couldn't take my eyes off of you the entire night."

I don't have time to respond to Bryce's boldness. He places a finger at the base of my throat, and draws a sensual vertical line downwards, navigating between my breasts. His finger finds its way to my nipple, stroking it through the fabric, and I can tell from his hungry eyes that we're both taking pleasure from his salacious act.

"It should be illegal to have such a hot little body as yours," he whispers in my ear.

God.

He pinches my nipple, eliciting a gasp from me. The chauffeured car stops and he pulls away from me. "I'll come around."

My heart is pounding. "Okay."

He gets out, circles the car, and helps me out, takes me by the hand, and leads me to the front door of the hotel.

"I have your money upstairs. Follow me," he commands.

We grab an elevator, and when the doors close behind us, Bryce corners me. Without saying a word, he holds my gaze while running one of his hands under my dress, as he cups my breast with his other hand.

When he squeezes my breast and an ass cheek at the same time, I can't help but let out a carnal muffled sound. The elevator bell and the opening doors separate our embrace. Bryce drags me with a sense of urgency to his room.

He pushes the door closed and slams me against it.

I gasp, excitement fluttering through me.

He slides a hand under my dress and up my thigh, until his fingers reach the crotch of my thong, grazing my pussy through the lace.

"Hot," he says, "and wet." He tugs my panties down, leaving me panting, my own wetness trailing down my trembling legs.

I don't need telling to step out of them.

He picks them up and tosses them over his shoulder.

"I want you facing that wall," he orders.

On a shaky exhale, I do as I'm told.

He unzips my dress. It pools at my feet.

"Step out of it."

"Okay."

A swishing sound lets me know he tossed my dress over his shoulder, too.

I'm about to remove my heels, but he stops me with his husky voice. "The heels stay on. You look sexy in them."

"Okay." I'm down to one word in the English language.

I'm so out of my depth.

He unhooks my bra, releasing my engorged breasts and hard nipples.

I exhale with pleasure when he cups my breasts with both hands.

"Fuck!" He growls in my ear, squeezing my breasts and thumbing my nipples. "I love your big tits." His voice is filled with desire.

The intensity of the fire burning inside me is all-consuming. I'm so turned on, I could melt.

He presses his body against my back and his hardness rubs against my ass before he slides one hand between my legs. I can barely breathe by the time his fingers slide inside me.

"You're bare. Just how I fucking like it."

I reach behind to grab his cock, but he puts an end to my eagerness with two words. "Not yet." I relax against him, opening my thighs as he slides two fingers in and out. "I've wanted to hold your big tits in my hands since you walked into the bar, Amanda." He kisses the back of my neck. "I knew the moment Todd showed me your photo, I just had to have you." He grabs my hair and pulls my head back. His lips flirt with mine. His thumb nudges my clit.

Kiss me... Devour my mouth.

Please...

He doesn't.

His wicked fingers are doing things to my pussy that are threatening to make me lose it.

Jesus.

I'm delirious as he slides his fingers out of me and traps my clit between them.

My forehead is firmly pressed against the wall as I curve my back to lift my ass higher to give Bryce all the room he needs to work on my clit. I can't help but grind against his touch as he presses his naked chest against me.

Wait.

When did he have time to remove his jacket and shirt?

He massages my clit, drops a kiss on my ear.

I whimper.

Mother of God.

"Your clit is so fucking hard. I want to make you come."

His words are intoxicating.

My heart nearly stops when he pinches my nipple. "Fuck!"

"That's it. That's what I like to hear. Are you going to come for me, Amanda?"

"Yes. Yes please."

Soft kisses down my neck, a hard twist of my nipple, and a masterful flick of my clit, and I'm done.

And then he stops.

"Don't stop!"

"No?"

I'm shaking, trembling. "Please."

His fingers slide back to my clit, his lips to my neck, his hand to my breasts, cupping, squeezing.

"Fuck," I say again and his hard cock jabs at my back. He squeezes my tit and pinches my nipple and flicks at my clit so fast, I hear myself moaning loudly and my orgasm hits me hard.

This has to be a record.

Bryce Van Der Linden is truly gifted.

I almost fall down on my knees because my legs are so limp, but Bryce catches me and lifts me in his arms.

He walks me to the bed, and then grabs up my lacy panties off the floor.

He lifts them to his nose. "I could get drunk on your heady scent."

He drops to his knees to help me back into my panties.

As he pulls them up my legs, I stop him.

"They're a bit wet," I say, embarrassed by how quickly he brought me to climax.

"In that case, why don't I hold onto them until I see you again." He doesn't wait for my consent, just tugs them right back off and shoves them in his pocket. "Let me grab your money."

What? That's it?

I'm a bit confused and disappointed, but when I see the huge pile of money in Bryce's hands, I remember Todd's advice, and snap out of my fantasy world and back to reality.

"We've been together for about four and a half hours. Right?"

"I think so," I say.

"Do you want to get dressed while I count your cash?"

Since I've never done this before, I'm not sure if this is normal or if I did something to turn Bryce off. I thought I'd have to pleasure him, but he's sending me home.

"I've hired the driver for another few hours. You can either go home with him, or grab one of the taxis in front of the hotel and I'll give you extra money for the fare."

I try to get up and move, but my legs are still shaking.

I've never been touched like that before.

I've been single for a few years now, and I've had to learn how to take care of business, since my ex-boyfriends were incapable.

Bryce succeeded where others failed.

Unbelievable.

Speaking of the sexy as fuck billionaire...

He's staring at me as I try to compose myself.

Did I screw up somewhere, and have I blown my first job as an escort?

God, can I not even get this right?

Bryce hands me a bulging, black, zipped-up pouch containing my fee. "Have you decided?"

"Decided?"

"About your ride back home?"

Oh. "I'll grab a taxi."

"Right. I'll cancel the car."

As he stands there with his phone to his ear, I look him up and down, my eyes stopping at his crotch.

I'm more than confused.

His bulging erection could be seen from the Moon, and threatens to break through his pants, yet here I am putting my clothes back on.

He catches my questioning gaze.

I want to get down on my knees, unzip his pants, and take him into my mouth, but his body language says otherwise.

"Ah," he takes his wallet from his back pocket, pulls out a hundred-dollar bill, "for the taxi."

He really is sending me home.

I screwed up. Big time.

Sneak Peek of Billionaire Factor—Bryce

Chapter 2

My phone ringing wakes me up.

I'm way too tired to bother looking to see who's calling so early, so I just answer it.

"Hello." My voice is groggy.

"How did it go last night with your first client?" Cassie asks.

I'm silent for a moment because I don't know how to start explaining what happened.

Cassandra Fitz-James, my former part-time employee at my short-lived business, introduced me to Elite Encounters Escorts. I lost my last job waitressing at a local lounge two weeks ago after a jackass grabbed my ass with both hands. I jabbed him with my elbow. When he folded over, I slammed the tray I was still holding over his head.

His explanation? *"I wanted to know what your round ass felt like in my hands."*

Asshole.

Don't fucking mess with a financially ruined woman if you know what's good for you.

Cassie and I have grown closer during my financial meltdown. Over drinks where I poured my heart out, she shared a life-changing secret.

"Sofia, I make more money in one month as a high end escort than most people make in a year."

That revelation was like the light bulb went on.

Desperation will make you do the unthinkable.

"Sofia, say something. You're making me nervous." The worry in Cassie's voice brings me back to the moment.

"I'm here."

"Talk."

What time is it?

I check my clock.

Eight a.m.? It's way too early.

"Hello, I'm waiting."

"Okay, okay," I say. "You wouldn't believe last night if I told you."

"Try me."

"This stays between us."

"I promise."

"Not a word to Todd."

"Not a word."

I sit up in my bed. "I spent the night with a heavy hitter who—"

"I want a name."

"Bryce Van Der Linden."

"You were so secretive about the identity of your client," Cassie says. "I didn't want to push since it was your first. Girl, Bryce Van Der Linden is not only hotter than hot, but contrary to a lot of the clients you'll have, he's eligible."

"When I first saw how handsome he was, my jaw dropped and I had to force myself to keep my cool."

"How did the evening unfold?"

"I screwed up, and Todd is going to be so pissed off at me."

"What do you mean you screwed up? Give me the scene-by-scene."

"After a formal briefing over drinks, Bryce took me to a stuffy and boring gala with a lot of extremely rich people where I had to flirt in different languages. When we were on our way back to his hotel, he groped my breasts in the back of his chauffeured car. When we got to his hotel, he dragged me to his suite, where he gave me the most intense orgasm of my life. And then, he unceremoniously sent me home with a pouch full of money and no explanation as to why we didn't have sex, or why he didn't want me to return the favor."

"What? What do you mean?"

"Which part didn't you get?"

"I got it all. I can't believe Bryce would do that to you. You seduced him."

"Did you hear the part about him sending me packing?"

"A lot of girls have spent the evening with Bryce, including myself. He comes across as all business, distant, and intimidating. What you've described—that carnal and sexy side of Bryce—isn't the man I know. Sure, he's fucked a few of the girls because he's paying for you to do whatever he wants to do with you, but he never reciprocates. You are hired to give him pleasure, not the other way around. I've been out with him a few times, but we've always parted ways right after the event."

"Not sure how this helps me."

"The Bryce Van Der Linden I know, the one a lot of girls have talked about, would never give a woman he hires so much pleasure unless you've seduced him and he's into you."

"Then why push me away?"

"Remember, this is business. He might have gotten caught up in the moment and he took a step back, trying to save face."

"It doesn't make sense to me."

"Men hire us to be seen with the hottest women in New York to make other men jealous and have them think they have a bigger dick than they do. They don't pay several thousands of dollars per night to give us pleasure. What Bryce did, suggests you got him."

"I got him?"

"Bryce will book you again within the next day or so. I'm certain of it."

"How do you know?"

"If he made you come in the way you've described, he'll be back for more. Besides, Todd told me Bryce took one look at your photo, and he was sold."

"You're just trying to make me feel better—"

My doorbell rings.

"Are you expecting company this early?" she says, suggestively.

"No. Wait a second. I'm going to see who's at the door." I put on a robe to cover myself and run to the door. It's not my baby sister Ciara because she always announces her arrival with her sultry voice while she knocks my door down.

"Who is it?" I ask.

"Your fairy godmother. Joking. It's Todd. Your booking manager." *A fancy title to hide the true nature of your job.* "Open up. We need to talk."

Shit, shit, shit.

I'm in trouble for last night.

"Todd? What's wrong?"

"Nothing is wrong. I have something for you."

After unlocking my multiple locks—safety first—I open the door.

Todd is standing there with his arms wide open as if he's on Broadway ending a performance with a grand ta-da!

He brings his hands together, and tucks them under his chin, cocks his head to the side, sighs and just stares at me.

"Why are you looking at me like that?"

"You scored!"

"Scored what?"

"Darling, you mean whom, not what."

"I'm confused. Is this about Bryce?"

"Why else do you think I'd be standing at your door at eight fifteen on a Friday morning? It has to be critical for me to get up this early."

"I'm listening—Wait! Cassie is on the phone."

"Tell her you'll call her back," he shouts as I run back to my room to grab my phone.

"Cassie, Todd told me to tell you I'll call you back," I say, running back downstairs.

"Sofia, call me the second that princess leaves!" she says.

"I will."

"What did she say?"

"She called you princess."

"And you know it!" he says, snapping his fingers at me. "Back to business. You made quite the impression on Mr. Van Der Linden last night."

Since I'm still unsure why Todd is here, I tread carefully. "He liked how I was able to interact with the crowd in multiple languages."

"Sofia, quit the bullshit! You're working for an escort service, not a diplomatic agency."

"Sorry."

"Bryce woke me up very early this morning. I made the mistake of leaving my work phone on, and he called me at seven-thirty a.m. to tell me that he *needs* to get in touch with you. Since he's aware of the privacy rules of the agency when it comes to contacting the girls directly at their home, he asked me to track you down."

"Why did he call so early? What's so urgent?"

"He wanted to have flowers delivered to our agency, so I could deliver them to you."

I'm stunned by Bryce's sweet touch. Here I was thinking I had screwed up. "Where are the flowers?"

"They're in the taxi. The meter's running."

"In the taxi? You didn't want to grab the bouquet before ringing my bell?"

"Before I grab them, you do realize there are no florists open this early in the morning?"

"You're right." *Wait.* "What do you mean by *them*?"

"You have to see it to believe it. Bryce said you were such exceptional company, he hired a hotel staff member to run to a wholesaler and pay whatever it took to get flowers to you before nine a.m.!"

"What?"

"Darling, I don't know what you did to the man, but he's been hiring girls for years and I've never, ever, ever, *ever* heard back from him the next morning, unless it was to complain."

"Wow! I'm speechless."

"If you're speechless now, you won't be able to find your words when you see how many bouquets he sent you. But before you step outside, you need to get rid of that robe." Todd waves a finger at me.

"Let me run upstairs and put some clothes on. I can't stand the suspense any longer," I say, as I climb the stairs two by two to jump into my jeans and a t-shirt.

Todd takes me to the taxi, and when he opens the door to the back seat, all I can see is a magnificent wall of flowers.

"They are so beautiful! Are they all for me? Are you sure, Todd?"

"Yes, all of these are yours, courtesy of a very happy client."

It takes Todd and me at least twenty minutes to bring in all the flowers.

"He also wants you to have this." Todd hands me a big box. "You better make yourself hotter than yesterday, because he's booked you again—only a few hours after your first date. This is not the norm for most of our clients."

"Are you joking me?"

"I never joke about my girls, money, or clients."

"I can't believe this. I was a bit nervous last night and I wasn't sure how he felt about the evening."

"I'll say it again. You scored! I've got to run. Do me proud tonight and text me on your work phone to let me know everything is okay."

"I'll text you. I promise. Thanks for coming over so early and delivering these."

"I don't know what you did to Bryce, but girl, keep up the good work."

When Todd leaves, I open the big box. There's a smaller box that reads *Open Me First*. When I open the smaller box, there's a little folded note.

'You were delicious last night. I want a second serving of you. I'm hard thinking of your perfect breasts and hard nipples. Meet me at the hotel at the same bar at six-thirty tonight.'

Not bad for my first gig.

I unfold the tissue paper and gasp.

Agent Provocateur underwear?!

Holy shit!

Guessing my size was easy, since he kidnapped my lace

panties, but how in the world was he able to guess my bra size so precisely?

The set Bryce selected for me is a revealing nude lace, scattered with glittering Swarovski crystals, which includes the bra, panties, and garter belt. The bra criss-crosses at the front around the neck and the panties have the most unusual cut I've ever seen—they are a set of high-waist briefs and the back has a cutaway that reveals the upper part of my butt cheeks.

Bryce knows what he wants and he has the money to buy it.

Considering basic bras at Agent Provocateur start at three hundred dollars, this set must have cost thousands.

I know he bought this to satisfy his own fantasies, but I'm giddy.

I spend the day running errands.

I stop at the bank to put the money Bryce gave me into my account. It's an insane amount for the effort I put in, considering he did all the work, but I won't complain. I used some of my earnings to buy a dress for tonight. A rich woman dropped off her freshly-dry-cleaned items for sale as I was wandering around the shop. The second the sales assistant placed the dress on the rack, I snagged it.

By four o'clock, I make my way back home to get ready for my second date with Mr. Van Der Linden.

I kiss my fingers and touch the wooden frame before stepping into the house.

It's a ritual.

Thank God, I still have a roof over my head.

After my financial debacle, it's the last thing of value I've still managed to hold on to. I guess I should say, the second thing of value—my body is the other. Since the house is under my baby sister's name, my creditors can't come after it.

This is humiliating.

But the money keeps me going.

I'm determined to dig myself out of this hell hole on my own.

In his note, Bryce was vague about the type of event we're attending tonight, so I decide to play it safe and dress the part of the escort to the fullest.

Before leaving, I check myself one last time in the mirror.

Not bad.

I'm quite pleased.

The straightened blonde hair and perfect makeup add more drama to the white dress I'm wearing. I took some of the money Bryce gave me to buy a pair of shoes. at the same where I bought the dress.

I shake my head.

Some women are so rich, they can drop off brand new shoes at a secondhand shop because they're last season.

I sigh.

To have that kind of life...

I stand taller thanks to these white leather heels adorned with a lace-like pattern that ties with a leather strap around my ankles.

They're super sexy!

When I arrive at Trouble's Trust bar, I expect to see Bryce, but he's nowhere to be seen.

Have I made a mistake on the meeting location?

As I scour the room one more time, my phone chimes.

Bryce: You look hot. It's nice of you to have made the effort, but your white dress won't stay on too long. My cock is already hard, and I'm waiting for you in my room.

He was here, watching me?!
Why is that such a turn on?

The door is ajar when I arrive at Bryce's room. Although I'm unsure what's about to happen, I push open the door and step inside. Bryce is sitting in the dark and the city lights are the only source of light allowing me to make out his features.

"Close the door and come closer," he commands.

I do as I'm told.

His gaze takes in every inch of me.

"Did you use the money I gave you yesterday to buy those shoes?" I don't have time to answer. "They are so very sexy. I hope you'll keep them on when you show me how perfect the underwear I got you looks on your curvy body. Before I forget, your money is on the table in the black pouch."

"Thanks."

"Do you like the underwear? I hope it fits?"

"I do and it does."

"Show me."

"In the dark?"

"Remove the dress. I'll see what I need to see." His tone is abrupt.

I drop the handbag I'm still clinging to on the table near the black pouch containing my money for the night and walk back to where I was standing.

"I already have a hard-on, don't make me wait any longer," he says in a raspy voice.

I'm nervous and my hands are shaking. I'm about to remove my dress as if I'm at home alone, but then I remember why Bryce is paying me.

He wants sexy, not ordinary.

As I get ready to turn up the sizzle factor, I unleash my inner bad girl.

"Make me want to beg for it, Amanda."

Message received.

The deep sound of his voice makes me wet. I remove the dress slow and sexy, with my back facing him, so he can enjoy the cutoff lace briefs he bought for me.

"So damn hot," he says, as I reveal the underwear.

When I turn around to face him, he's towering over me, barefoot.

Did he leap from the chair he was sitting on to where I'm standing?

His fingers trail down the side of my face and along my jawline before encountering my lips. When he pushes a finger inside my mouth, I shiver as my nipples harden beneath the lace bra. He pulls me closer, and his hands slide over my shoulders and down the front of my chest until he reaches my breasts.

"You should never wear a bra. Your tits are too perfect," he says as he unhooks my bra, releasing my breasts. "Put your hands up above your head."

It's as if his words cast a spell over me, and I follow his command without resistance.

He leans down to whisper in my ear, "I want more of you. I didn't get enough last night, but I was afraid if I tasted more of you in one shot, I wouldn't be able to recover."

He pulls a silk tie from his pocket and tightly wraps it around my wrists.

Panic rises.

This has never happened to me before with any of the men I've been with in the past.

His warm voice calms my fears. "I don't want to hurt you. I

want you to surrender to me, so I can bring you more pleasure than you've ever had."

His free hand slides under my lace bikini briefs and travels slowly down to my hungry pussy until he reaches my clit. I moan, remembering how well my body responded to his sensual touch less than twenty-four hours ago.

His mouth covers mine, his tongue pushing through to meet mine before he pushes his fingers inside my yearning pussy. His digits slide in and out of me with ease, intensifying my wetness.

Bryce glides his fingers over my hard clit and circles it until I have no choice but bite my lip as an outlet to the intense pleasure.

His mouth moves back to my ear and he whispers, "I want to make you come again."

His words send a wave of heat right through me.

"I want to make you come as well," I manage to whisper.

"Plenty of time for that," he says, "it's all about you for now."

Everything happens in a blink of an eye.

He undoes the tie around my wrists, wraps it around his neck, lifts me in his muscular arms, carries me to the bed, and throws me down on the mattress.

I yelp.

He stares at me with lust dripping from his eyes as he tears off his shirt and removes his pants. His boxer briefs are next.

Holy fucking shit!

This is the first time I've seen his chiseled body, and I can't help but admire his perfectly formed pecs and the tightness of his six-pack. His magnificent cock is long, thick, and cut.

The man is packing.

"Turn on to your stomach, I want to see your gorgeous ass."

I roll over.

"Damn. Your ass looks dangerous in those panties."

I beam at the compliment.

"Oh, you find that funny?"

"No, I'm flattered."

Lowering his body, he kisses my ass with the perfect balance of gentleness and forcefulness. He finds my clit and rubs it.

For a few long minutes he gives me more pleasure than any other man has ever given me before. I sink into it, loving every caress, every kiss, every nibble at my skin.

All movement stops.

I groan my discontentment.

"I'm not going to make you come with my fingers tonight. I have other plans for you."

"Oh."

"Let me suit up."

I peer over my shoulder as he wraps his long, hard cock in a condom before walking back towards me.

Thank you, God. Tonight won't be a repeat of last night.

He's going to fuck me!

"I've wanted nothing more than to be inside you since you left me last night, Amanda."

Why send me away, then?

Any confusion vanishes because he leans down, grabs the side of my panties with his teeth, and yanks them down my legs.

Dear God.

"Sit up."

I do as I'm told.

"Hands in front of you."

I obey.

He pulls the tie from around his neck and wraps my wrists.

He's good at this.

"On your knees."

He takes my tied hands and helps me assume the position.

We're both kneeling, facing each other.

I'm intimidated by the massive erection pressing against my stomach when he leans in to sink his teeth into my shoulder.

Ahhhh!

He caresses my breasts and squeezes my nipples before sucking them into his mouth. The sweet sensation of the warmth of his tongue over my erect nipples sends crazy shivers of desire dancing down my back.

More please!

His hands move from my breasts to my lower back until he's gripping my ass cheeks. He lifts me up, sits back onto the mattress, and then sits me on his lap. I wrap my legs around his waist.

"Your ass is fucking amazing," he whispers in my ear. "I can't wait to fuck it."

I tense.

My hands are still tied, my arms wrapped around his neck.

He has all the power over me.

"Not tonight, but soon," he says.

I should object. Tell him I don't roll that way, but I don't.

What's wrong with me?

This guy has me all tangled up—

No, no, no.

'Rule number four. Don't fall in lust or love with your client.'

Bryce lifts me up, putting an end to my delusion.

Focus.

He lowers me an inch at a time onto his cock.

Hell, that feels so good.

His massive erection would make a porn star jealous.

His blue eyes are so intense, they search my soul as we stare at each other.

"You okay?" he asks.

"You're..."

"Huge?"

"Just a bit."

"When I'm around you, I'm so fucking hard. It's like my cock turns to steel."

He shouldn't say things like this because it fucks with my head.

'Rule number one. This is a business transaction, not a dating service.'

Bryce holds me tight as he gives a final thrust and I feel him, deep inside.

"Goddamn," he says, fucking me. "Your pussy is as sweet as I expected."

He picks up the pace and I clench around his assault.

The sustained friction of his pelvis against my clit is sublime.

The climactic buildup causes me to throb in staccato pulses.

I can't believe this.

What is it with this guy?

Magic fingers and a magic cock?

He leans into me, causing even more pressure in the pit of me.

The shift is my undoing.

"Bryce! I'm—" I throw my head back to contain the pleasure. It's in vain. I come all over his cock.

He grabs my hair and pulls hard.

The hot sting of pain intensifies my climax.

My body convulses as I groan like a slut.

"Jesus!" I sink against his hard body.

I'm limp from ecstasy.

For a few long beats, I remain slumped against him.

"I'm not done with you," he says.

I don't know if I can take any more, but I keep that to myself.

He lifts me off his lap and sets me on the bed.

Straddling my body and unties my wrists, freeing my hands.

His eyes are burning with passion as he yanks off the condom, tossing it on the floor.

"I want to come between your luscious breasts," he says, his beautiful cock bobbing before my eyes.

Hell yes!

He dips his cock between my breasts, and I squeeze them together. Bryce thrusts his hips back and forth. He reaches down and slides two fingers inside me to gather my wetness before licking it off his fingers and smacking his lips.

"Delicious," he says.

The head of his cock is an inch away from my mouth as he thrusts faster.

I can't help myself, let go of my breasts, and grab his cock.

"You want me to fuck your face?"

I nod.

"Then beg."

"I want you in my mouth."

"Tsk. I said, *beg*."

I frown.

He cocks a brow.

It hits me.

"I want you to fuck my face."

He rolls his eyes. "Like you really want it, Amanda."

Oh, I want it.

"Please, Bryce. Please fuck my face."

He offers a wolfish grin. "With pleasure." *I hope I'm not biting off more than I can chew, so to speak.* "Open wide." He sighs as his cock stretches my mouth.

I moan around it.

"You're going to swallow my cum?"

I read the anticipation in his eyes. I nod and close my eyes to enjoy his sweet cock.

Having him inside my mouth, with his hips thrusting back and forth, is more than my body can take. I reach down to relieve my aching clit.

"Dirty girl."

I caress my clit, as he thrusts nice and slow inside my mouth.

Fuck.

I squeeze his butt cheek hard as the buildup between my legs becomes unbearable.

He hits the back of my throat, and that triggers him.

"Christ!" he roars.

I'm done.

We both come at the same time.

His cock slides out of my mouth, and he collapses spent next to me on the bed.

"You're fucking amazing," he says, still breathing heavy from the climax.

His praise gives me wings.

He's paying to have sex with me. He doesn't have to butter me up.

"I'm not just paying you lip service." It's as if he's reading my mind. "I really mean it. You're fucking amazing."

"Thank you. You're pretty amazing yourself."

He winks.

The one time I meet an incredible man, he's off limits.

Fuck my life.

We both lie in a comfortable silence, him stroking my back. Me, caressing his chest.

It hits me.

Oh, shit. How could I forget?

"Bryce?"

"Yes?"

"The flowers you sent this morning are breathtaking. Thank you so much. It was so sweet of you."

"I wanted to find flowers that matched your beauty. The hotel staff who went on a goose chase for me, sent me photos of what was available at the flower market. Since I couldn't decide, I told him to buy a large variety."

"You don't do things in half measures?"

"It's not in my DNA."

"Noted."

I roll onto my side, and glance at Bryce's handsome face. "I'm ready for another round, if you are."

He looks down at his cock.

Oh... I'm not the only one who's ready for more.

His blue eyes meet mine. "Not before we get some food."

"You mean room service?" I ask, stroking his hardening erection.

"No. I mean, you showing off your sexy dress and those shoes. We're going out," he says. "Once I have some food in my system, I'll ride you again. I promise."

"So, I have to wait? Is that what you're saying?"

Holy shit? When did I become a sex maniac?

He pulls me close. "Only for a few hours. I've been smarter this time around. I booked you until three a.m.," he says.

"Food, then more fucking? Can I convince you to reconsider?"

"You—" He lets out a soft moan when my tongue explores the interior of his ear.

"Are you sure you want to go for a bite to eat?"

I've never been this bold in my life.

"It's going to be uncomfortable for me to walk around with an erection. We might as well put it to good use."

That's all it takes to change Bryce's mind.

"I couldn't agree with you more," I say with an angelic smile.

"Don't act so innocent. It's your fault I'm in this state," he says. "You're lucky I have a box of condoms waiting to be used."

"Very strategic thinking on your part, Mr. Van Der Linden." I climb on top of him. "I'll do all the work."

I love being on top because it gives me an intense climax I can't get in any other position—

Slap.

I yelp.

"I control this ride." He cups my breasts with his big hands, groping them. "But the idea of having my eyes on your tits as you bounce off my cock is too tempting."

Imagine that. I have the upper hand.

Binge-read now: Billionaire Factor—Bryce

Very New York Billionaires

A Very Bossy Billionaire (Xavier)

A Very Fake Boyfriend (Zane)

A Very Wicked Arrangement (Hudson)

Xavier and Zane Keller are **Max Keller**'s cousins, and they kick off this smoking hot spin-off.

Max is part of the **Billionaire Factor** series. The Very New York Billionaires and the Billionaire Factor series are in the same world.

Billionaire Factor—Bryce

Billionaire Factor—Nikolaj

Billionaire Wedding Factor—Nikolaj

Billionaire Factor—Max

Billionaire Factor—Easton

You'll find **all my books** and **reading order** on my site:
www.ScarlettAvery.com

I hope you enjoyed ***A Very Wicked Arrangement***! Can't get enough of Hudson and Angelica? Subscribe to my mailing list and you'll get instant access to an exclusive ***A Very Wicked Arrangement*** secret chapter and/or storyboard. Just use the QR code below.

Already subscribed? You would've received the link in the first email I sent you. If you can't find it, you can email us. If you've changed your email address, simply resubscribe.

About the Author

USA TODAY Bestselling Author Scarlett Avery unapologetically pens all-consuming love stories featuring sexy as sin billionaires who have the determination of a thousand warriors. These filthy rich heroes bow to no one. Only the women who steal their hearts can bring them down to their knees.

Scarlett's stories are intense and passionate, emotional and steamy, and leave you begging for more. In other words, they're the perfect blend of swoony and sinful. Once you start reading Scarlett's novels, there's no going back!

Fair warning...

You should always expect edge-of-your-seat twists.

Printed in Great Britain
by Amazon

26792850R00315